CW01466751

The Human From A Dungeon

Act I

Albert A Nolen II

The characters and events portrayed in this book are fictitious. Any similarity to real persons, living or dead, is coincidental and not intended by the author.

No part of this book may be reproduced, or stored in a retrieval system, or transmitted in any form or by any means, electronic, mechanical, photocopying, recording, or otherwise, without express written permission of the publisher.

Cover design by: Elizabeth Walsh
Copyright © 2023 Albert A Nolen II
All rights reserved

Foreword

This is the novelization of a serial that is released free to the public every week on Royal Road and Reddit, with up to two chapters in advance available on Ko-Fi and Patreon.

There will be more chapters available by the time you purchase this novel, so if you wish to read more please visit the url below and select which site you'd like to continue reading on.

https://link.space/@itsdirector

Dedications

I dedicate this novel and my limitless gratitude to my soon-to-be wife Elizabeth, for her love and support. I would have crashed and burned without you, my love. And I still love you more.

Another shout-out to my son for thinking that it's super cool that I'm popular on the internet. Somehow that opinion didn't change now that he's 8. Love you, kiddo.

Special thanks to everyone on the HFY subreddit who provided positive and critical feedback, as well as to my patrons. You're all amazing, and I wish you the best.

And finally, thank YOU for reading this. You're awesome, don't let anyone tell you otherwise.

Chapter 1

Nick Smith
Adventurer Level: N/A
Human - American

"So... what do you suppose it is?"

"I dunno. It looks kinda like an elf. But the ears are weirdly round, and it has... body hair."

"Yeah, can't be an elf. Maybe it's a tall dwarf?"

"No. Not enough body hair to be dwarven. Plus I've never heard of a dwarf over four feet tall."

"Yeah, me neither. Don't they all have beards?"

"Pretty sure."

These voices sounded strange to me. Like they're speaking my language but in a weird accent or something. And the voices were... heavy? No, that's not the term. Rumbling? Why's it so hard to think?

"A gnome?"

"No. Gnomes are just short elves. It could be some sort of weird pig-kobold... thing."

"Oh yeah! Wait... that still doesn't explain the round ears. Plus the face is all wrong. Look, the nose is too pointy."

Am I asleep? Dreaming? What are they talking about? The last thing I remember was going to the hospital to see my girlfriend. Did I get hurt along the way? Are these people doctors? I'm not in any pain, though...

But I can't open my eyes. Why can't I open my eyes? What happened to me?

"I wonder if it can talk. Where'd you find this thing, anyway?"

"You remember that wall collapse in the dungeon? My team and I were explorin' that and we got separated. Next thing I know, I find this thing on some sort of weird lookin' table. It had a bunch of writing on it, but... well... you know."

"Yeah, you have trouble reading. That's alright. Go on."

"Right, well I figured that I'd have a hell of a time trying to find my way back there, so I decided to take it with me. Once I picked it up, a lot of light started shining and suddenly I was at the dungeon entrance."

"Teleportation?"

"Yeah, probably."

"Huh. That's interesting. You know, since you found it in our dungeon, it might be an orc!"

Boisterous laughter. It reminds me of my old karate instructor. He used to laugh like that all the time, even when nobody was joking. I wonder what happened to him. I wonder what happened to me. I think... I visited my girlfriend. The love of my life, Cassandra.

She wasn't in pain today, but the cancer's getting worse. Her formerly luscious blonde hair that went all the way down to her waist was now patchy and wiry from the chemo. Her stunning blue eyes still had their kindness and humor, but betrayed the pain that she was desperately trying to hide. She looked kind of like a skeleton with skin now, but she joked that maybe she can finally be a model. She's still my Cass.

I stayed with her until she fell asleep, then I started to head home. I had to study, because even with everything going on they were still making me take finals. The bastards know that Cass is sick, but they don't care. State requirements for graduation or whatever. Pisses me off. Fuck them, I want to drop out and get a job.

But Cass won't hear of it. Neither will mom. Dad understands, and says he'd do the same, but he'd like me to respect the wishes of mom and Cass. How am I supposed to study with the thought of losing her looming over my head, though? How can I think of anything else?

"There's no way this thing's an orc. It's too small. Plus the ears..."

"Yeah, yeah. I feel like you're hyper-fixated on the ears."

"Hyper-wha now?"

"Fixated. You're focusing too much on the ears."

"Well they're WEIRD though. Have you ever heard of anything that has round ears?"

"Not off the top of my head, but I'm sure there's something. After all, we're looking at round ears right now."

Round ears? What does that have to do with anything? Whatever, nothing to do with me. What happened after I started to walk home? I stopped by a gas station and grabbed some chips and a soda to lighten my spirits, and the last thing I remember is... crossing the street? There were horns and screeching and then... Huge lights? Pain! I felt pain! All over my body! And then nothing... Did I get hit by a truck?

"I wish we could ask it what it is."

"Well, I COULD cast healing magic on it. See if that wakes it up."

"You think chief would be okay with that? He'll probably want to see it first, right?"

"I won't tell if you don't. We'll just say that it woke up on its own."

"Hmm. Alright, deal."

"Awesome. Keep a hand on your axe, just in case."

"Ready."

"Laeh Ronim Tsac!"

A pleasant warmth began to spread throughout my body. Like getting a massage from a million fingers all at once. My grogginess began to ebb, and I opened my eyes. Things were blurry at first, but I was soon able to focus on the wooden ceiling. I don't know this ceiling... Wait, wooden ceiling? What kind of building has a wooden ceiling? A barn?

I sat up and looked around. The furniture in the room looked like it came straight out of a medieval movie, but a bad one that didn't pay attention to details. I was on a bed with woven sheets and a blanket, for one thing. For another, there were metal handles on some of the furniture. That wasn't a thing in medieval times, right?

Then the two people who were talking earlier caught my eye. Cosplayers? How'd they manage to look so big? One was wearing metallic armored pants and no top, showing off its rippling muscles. It looked as if it were scared of me, and it was holding a large serrated axe at its side. The other one was wearing a robe and carrying a staff with some sort of metal ball at the top.

All of these details about their appearances were striking, but the most striking thing was that they were both green. Green, pointy ears, and huge. Even hunched over, the robed one with the staff was probably 6'5". The one with the axe was pushing 6'10". The one with the staff grinned and showed a mouth full of very pointy teeth. Like an alligator's.

"Woah, careful there. You just woke up. Don't want you falling over," it said.

The words sounded weird. As if I weren't hearing them right. No, that's not it. The mouth movements are weird. It's like they're saying something else but it's dubbed over, with a hint of the original audio left in.

"W-where am I? Who are you? What are you?" I asked, trying not to panic.

My mouth felt weird when I spoke. Like I'm saying the words that I'm saying, but my mouth was moving differently. Like trying to make a tuh sound but making a kay sound instead. There was something else that was strange as well, but I couldn't figure it out.

"I'm Yulk," the grinning one said. "This is my brother, Nash. We're orcs."

"Yup, nice to meetcha. You're in Nuleva, a temporary

orc settlement that's right outside of the Delver's Dungeon. We're hoping to make it a village someday," Nash said, taking his hand off his axe and crossing his arms.

"Orc?" I asked, getting used to the weird talking.

"Yes," Yulk said. "We're orcs. Now that we've answered your questions, I'd like to ask you one."

"Ask me a question?" I asked. "What do you..."

"What are you?" Nash interrupted impatiently.

I sat stunned for a moment. Orcs are real? And what do they mean what am I? I looked at my hands, the same ones I've always had. Even with the same scar I got as a kid, though the scar was looking a bit smaller now. I noticed I didn't have my shirt on and I quickly checked under the blanket. Yep, naked. Weird. All of this is weird. What the hell is going on? Nash cleared his throat, patiently waiting for me to answer his question.

"I'm a... human, and my name's N-nick. Short for Nicodemus. Nicodemus Liam Smith," I stammered as I pulled the blanket up a little bit more.

The two orcs shared a confused glance at each other before looking back to me. What's there to be confused about? Sure, Nicodemus is kind of a rare name, but it's not THAT rare. Hell, I used to get picked on for it all the time. The Secret of NIMH is singlehandedly the reason that I go by Nick.

Yulk turned back to me and asked, "What's a human?"

Huh?

"What?" I asked.

"I've never heard of a human before," Nash said, scratching his head. "What were you doin' locked away in the dungeon?"

"What dungeon? What do you mean you've never heard of a human?" I asked.

"Okay, wait," Yulk said. "Let's try not to make assumptions here. Let's start at the beginning and get on the same page. Nick, you're a human. We don't know what that is. Nash here found you in a secret room inside the Delver's Dungeon. You don't know how you got there?"

"No, the last thing I remember was walking home and..." I trailed off. "Oh, right."

"What?"

"I think I got hit by a truck."

"What's a truck?" Nash asked.

"It's like a... wagon or something that doesn't need anything to pull it," I said.

"Oh, we've got those," Nash said. "Right, Yulk?"

"Yes. We call them magicarts, but I suspect that they're not the same thing."

"Magi... carts? Carts pulled with magic?" I asked.

"Yep," both orcs replied in unison.

Wait. Wait wait wait. Orcs, magic, dungeons, getting hit by a truck... Did I get isekai'd? Or is this just a hallucination that my dying brain is showing me to protect me from the trauma of getting hit by a truck?

I suppose there's nothing I can do about this being a hallucination, so I have to go off the assumption that it's not. Which means finding a way back. Wait, if I got reincarnated or whatever to this place, then maybe Cass did as well!

"Have you seen any other things like me?" I asked. "Like, others in the dungeon? Any females? They usually have long hair and... larger breasts."

"Oh, so you're a male human?" Yulk asked. "I kinda guessed, but didn't want to be presumptuous."

"No, like I said earlier we haven't seen anything like you before," Nash said. Then he leaned closer to Yulk and asked quietly, "What's presumptuous mean?"

"It means not being able to observe what's appropriate or permitted in a social setting," Yulk whispered back.

Meanwhile, I was trying not to lose it. Cass is terminally ill with cancer, and I wasn't going to be there for her when she passed. I clenched my jaw and stared at the ceiling as I fought back tears. It's not fair. She doesn't deserve to be alone, and I promised. I promised her that I'd be by her side until the end.

"I take it that all this comes as a bit of a shock," Yulk said softly.

"Y-yeah. Yeah it does," I replied.

"Alright, well we'll let you process things. We've got to go tell the chief you're up. And then get yelled at for waking you up," Nash said. "We'll send someone in with food and drink in a bit."

"Wait," I said. "Where do I go to... defecate?"

Nash looked surprised and then pointed to the door opposite the one he and his brother were next to.

"That's the bathroom. Pull the handle to flush the toilet."

"Okay," I said, wiping my eyes.

The two orcs left the room. Indoor plumbing was unexpected, but I suppose I shouldn't be entirely surprised. There's magic here, and there's no telling what that magic can do. Maybe... Maybe it can return me to my world in time to be with Cass again. So that I can say goodbye. Or maybe even save her. I owe it to her to try, at least. She's made me happier than any man has a right to be.

The room started spinning a little bit, so I laid back down. How did I go from getting hit by a truck to being asleep in a dungeon anyway? And when you get isekai'd don't you normally get to talk to a sexy goddess or a pervy old god? Some exposition would have been nice.

It finally hit me what else felt weird about this place. The air. It smelt different, tasted weird, and was hotter than it should be. But all of these things weren't necessarily strange. You would get that just by going to a different city. No, what was strange was how it felt on my skin. A tingle that felt like it should be giving me goosebumps but wasn't. Very odd.

The door to the room opened and a short orc, still about 5'9" or so, entered holding a plate full of meat with a cup of something on it. Her green skin was slightly paler than the other two orcs, and she had an air of grace surrounding her that defied expectations. Like meeting a princess in a bandit camp.

What she was wearing definitely wasn't something that royalty would wear, though. It was an outfit that left little to the imagination. A skin-tight bikini top and very short shorts that exaggerated her ample curves. I tried not to stare, but noticed she was trembling and trying not to look at me as she set the platter down on a table next to my bed. Then she quickly turned and almost ran out of the room.

"Weird," I said under my breath.

I looked at the plate of meat. I guess this confirms that the orcs are carnivorous. I figured that was the case based on the teeth, though. Going to be hard to deal with a meat-only diet, since I'm not a fan of liver. At least they cook it. Would these guys farm? Maybe, for trade or to feed their domesticated animals. I'll have to ask.

I took a bite from one of the brown pieces of meat. The tart metallic taste made me grimace a bit. Liver. A necessity for omnivores on a meat-only diet, though. As I chewed the gamey meat I found myself hoping desperately that they had wild orange trees or something nearby. The white meat was far more palatable, though. It tastes similar to chicken, but not quite. Like a juicier version of quail.

I washed it down with the liquid in the cup. Plain old water, but it felt more refreshing than anything I've ever had. I wondered how long I had been unconscious in that dungeon they mentioned. Hopefully not long. I don't even know if time works the same here as it did on my world. There's too much I don't know.

I finished the food and suddenly realized how weak and tired I felt. Like I had been running around carrying heavy stuff all day. I was afraid to go back to sleep at first, but then I thought that if I go to sleep maybe I'll wake up in a proper hospital bed back in my world. Maybe this IS just a dream. Maybe I'll be able to see Cass again.

I'll do anything to see her again.

Chapter 2

Nash Alta
Adventurer Level: 8
Orc - Nulevan

"So you two woke it up!?" Chief Gluhern shouted.

"No sir!" I lied.

"We were simply guessing at what he could be when he woke up all on his own," Yulk lied. "We had a short discussion with him, had Catalina grab him some food, and came immediately here to inform you, sir."

The chief eyed us suspiciously. He knows we're lying, but he also knows that he can't prove it. Yulk and I will cover each other until our dying breath, and it's not like the human can tell on us. If the chief can't prove it, he can't openly punish us without people getting mad about injustice. Then he'll have to listen to speech after speech after speech. A much worse punishment than whatever he'd give us.

Which means that he'll probably resort to underhanded punishments. I fully expect to be voluntold to do some extra chores this week. A shame, Yulk and I really wanted to go back into the dungeon and look for clues about the human. Maybe we should've left it alone after all.

"Smells like bullshit to me, but I'm assuming there's no witnesses?" Gluhern said as he looked around. After a few shaken heads he turned back to us, "There never are with you two. So, it calls itself a human, then?"

"He, sir. And yes, he says he's a human. Not that it

helps," Yulk said, dodging a thrown cup.

"DON'T CORRECT ME, SORCERER!" Gluhern shouted.

"Sir, did the others find anything related to the human?" I asked, attempting to distract him from his rage.

The chief drew a deep breath and said, "Actually, no. Your team still hasn't returned. We're sending a rescue party at sunrise."

My blood ran cold. Blune, Graz, Inoris, and Rezgal were pretty tough guys. Almost as tough as me. Party wipes weren't exactly uncommon, but they don't happen to adventurers over level five very often. Those four are level 7, so they should be able to handle just about anything. What the hell's going on?

"I'd like to join the rescuers," I said.

"Me too, sir," Yulk added.

"I'm afraid not," Gluhern said, no longer angry. "You're both under-leveled for the rescue party. Since they're over level five, we're sending the over-tens. You'll be liabilities."

I gnashed my teeth in frustration, but chief isn't wrong. Reaching level ten is an enormous accomplishment, and the difference in power between a level nine and ten is extreme. The downside to reaching that rank was all of the extra responsibility that came with it. Most over-tens go into mercenary work, leaving their homes behind. If they don't, they'll quickly get swamped with work that the other adventurers can't handle.

"Aren't they busy?" Yulk asked.

"Alurn and Kirisaka accomplished their task in the wastes, and they're back. Rirnu and Pakin haven't been doing much, as there aren't many wounded. Two medics, a tank, and a rogue. The perfect rescue party," Gluhern replied with a grin.

"Pakin isn't a medic, she's a necromancer," I replied with distaste.

"That's just a late medic, if you think about it," Yulk said cheerily. "Plus she knows combat magic as well."

"Yeah, well she'd better be on time," I grumbled. "Blune owes me a drink, and zombies don't pay their debts."

"Do skeletons?" Yulk asked.

"How the hell should I know?"

"Well how do you know that zombies don't, then?"

"ENOUGH!" shouted the chief. "The matter of the rescue party is settled. The only matter I have left to discuss with you is your next task."

Yulk and I stared at the grinning chief with stalwart expressions. We knew he wouldn't dare officially punish us, but there was a certain level of unease regarding the underhanded task he would give us. He won't be sending us into the dungeon, he knows we'll join the rescue party. There's a possibility that he'll send us into the wastes on retrieval duty, though. The damned herbs that go into medi-potions love that sandy shithole.

"You'll guard the human until I say otherwise. One set of eyes on it at all times," Gluhern said, chuckling as my face fell. "I'll leave it up to you to decide the shifts. If you wander off, I'll have your hides."

"DIBS ON FIRST SHIFT!" Yulk shouted unexpectedly.

I turned to my brother and was shocked to see him nearly bouncing with excitement. Guard duty is the most boring task available, and just about any orc worth their salt will do anything to avoid it. I looked back to the chief, who shared my expression of shock.

"Why are you so excited?" I asked.

"No reason!" Yulk said, suddenly nervous. "Let's go!"

He grabbed me and began dragging me out of the room just as the chief was having second thoughts about our new assignment. I struggled a bit, but Yulk has a remarkably tight grip for a sorcerer. I watched the chief shrug as we left the room.

"What the hell's got into you?" I asked as I finally shook his grip.

"Nash! We get to study the human!" Yulk said, actually bouncing up and down this time. "We might be the only ones who've ever met one!"

"Okay, okay," I said with a sigh. "I see your point. It IS kinda cool."

"I can't wait! I wonder if he has any magic resistances..."

"That pink skin it has doesn't look like it's any tougher than ours. Be careful, brother," I cautioned.

I wasn't able to tell if he heard my warning or not because he immediately started mumbling to himself and walking towards the hospital. I sighed as I followed after him. He'd always been like this. Something strikes his fancy and he becomes unable to think of anything else until he's figured it out. Even if the chief hadn't tasked us with guard duty, Yulk probably would've ended up hanging around the human's room.

"Hey, Nash! Wait up," a familiar voice called out to me.

I turned and saw a larger than life figure wearing full blackened plate armor and carrying a sword that was nearly as long as I am tall. I grabbed Yulk's arm to stop him from wondering off and nodded at the figure as it approached.

"Hello Alurn, I hope the day finds you well. What can I do for you?" I asked him.

"I wanted to ask you about the rescue mission," Alurn replied. "Would you mind answering a few questions for us?"

Us?

"I have apprised him of the likelihood that you know nothing other than what we've already been told," a voice said from behind me.

I suppressed my urge to swing around. No need to. I already knew who it was. There isn't anyone else in the village that could sneak up on me, and he did so as often as he could.

"Hello Kirisaka," I said as I calmly turned to face him.

Kirisaka is shorter than most orcs, but nobody has pointed that out to him since he was a child. There was a coldness in his eyes that would unnerve a drake. He's only a rogue in the sense that he knows how to avoid traps and pass through locks. His specialty in combat is quick, silent movement and striking vital areas with enough force to obliterate plate armor. The reason that everyone confuses his class is that he's the only shadow warrior in the village, and he doesn't bother correcting people who get it wrong.

I glanced at his short-swords. I prefer an axe, but I wouldn't complain if I had to use those babies. They were simple but elegant, double edged with an exaggerated point and pommels designed after the sun and the moon. Kirisaka had received them as a reward for saving a wealthy elven family in the wastes.

"How much?" I asked.

"They are still not for sale. They shall never be for sale. Stop asking," Kirisaka replied tersely.

"I'll give you twenty gold. Ten each," I said.

"You do not have twenty gold," he countered.

"I'll borrow it and pay it off by killing things in the dungeons with those swords."

"No you shall not, because I will not be selling them."

"Pardon me," Alurn interrupted. "Time is of the essence. Nash, your party went to explore the part of the dungeon that was revealed by the collapsed wall. You were gone for a day before you exited. Did you encounter any enemies?"

"No," I sighed. "We didn't even see any traces of

monster activity. It was eerily quiet."

"How, then, did you become separated?" Kirisaka asked, annoyed that he'd been wrong. Or that I kept looking at his swords.

"The strap on my pack came loose, and I stopped to fix it. They didn't want to stop, so they kept going," I explained. "I fixed my pack and ran after them, but there was a fork in the path. There weren't any footprints or markers and I decided to go left, but I guess they went right. I ended up in a sort of labyrinth and that's when I found the human."

"Human?" Alurn asked. "Oh, the thing you found in the dungeon. How do you know what it's called?"

"It woke up!" Yulk said excitedly.

"I-I see," Alurn stuttered, caught off-guard by Yulk's demeanor. "Well... Nash, did you see or hear anything odd on your way out? Any clue to what might have kept them from returning?"

"When I picked up the human, I was teleported to the entrance of the dungeon with it still in my arms. I didn't even know the rest of the team was still in there until chief told me just a few minutes ago," I said. "It's been a couple days. They definitely should've been back by now."

"I understand. We'll find them, Nash. Don't worry too much," Alurn said.

"Let us begin our rescue," Kirisaka said.

Alurn nodded and they went on their way. Yulk and I continued on our way to guard the human. When we entered the hospital building, there were three girls peeking through the door into the human's room. Maybe the chief had a point assigning us as guards.

"What are you doing?" I asked.

The girls jumped back, falling over each other in the process. The first girl who managed to stand back up was Catalina, the one we'd asked to bring food to the human.

"We're just curious!" she said.

"Yeah," Yini said from the ground. "We wanted to see the new pet."

"Pets don't talk," Yulk said. "Pets are for petting, that's why they're called pets."

Yini scowled for a moment before she realized it was Yulk that was talking to her. Then her face softened. It's obvious to everyone except Yulk that Yini fancies him. My brother is smart, but he's dumb in his own way.

"You're right, I just..."

"It's so cute!" Nimora interrupted. "Are you sure you found it in the dungeon?"

"Yes, I'm sure," I said sternly. "And because of that, it may be dangerous. Keep your distance."

"We can handle ourselves," Catalina said, pretending like she hadn't been cowering when we asked her to feed it. "It's pretty small."

"It's short, but it's also muscular. I get the feeling that it's stronger than it looks. But even if you could fight it, chief would get mad at you for putting yourselves in the situation to fight it. Especially if you killed it before we found out more about it," I replied.

"Yeah, yeah. Is it some kind of elf?" Yini asked.

"Maybe, but it calls itself a human," Yulk replied excitedly. "It may be an offshoot species of elf. Or maybe an ancestor of the elves! We don't know how long it was in that dungeon for."

"Did it eat?" I asked.

"Y-yes. I'm pretty sure. The platter looks empty," Catalina said.

"So you didn't retrieve the platter?" I asked smugly.

"N-no! It's sleeping. I didn't want to wake it up," she replied defensively.

"Damn it all. Sleeping again," Yulk said with disappointment. "Oh well, at least that confirms it's carnivorous like us and not herbivorous like the elves."

"So maybe it's not related to the elves?" Yini asked.

"Maybe not. Maybe it's related to orcs. We did find it in the orc dungeon, after all."

"We? I found it. Stop trying to take credit for my find," I said teasingly.

"Yes, yes. You found it. Anyways, if it's an ancestor of the orcs then it's probably much stronger than it looks. So Nash is right, you three should be careful," Yulk said.

The three girls looked crestfallen. Hearing it from me was one thing. I'm a bit dumb so they don't think I know what I'm talking about. They always listen to Yulk, though. He's probably the smartest orc in the village, even though he's dumb when it comes to women. Poor Yini, she's got an uphill battle in the fight for his affection.

"Okay," Yini finally said. "We'll go. Sorry."

"No need for apologies if you don't do it again," Yulk said cheerily. "Plus it'll be safer with Nash and I guarding him."

"It's a him?" Nimora asked.

"Don't even think about it," I told her.

"I'm NOT!" she said.

"Then how'd you know what I'm talking about?" I asked.

"Shut up!"

Nimora always had an eye for odd ones. She frequently flirts with the non-orc traders that pass through. They politely flirt back, but not a single one of them will ever take her up on the offer. It's not very common for other species to interbreed, at least in my experience, but orcs cannot breed with other species. Trying to can be fatal.

"Well, we should get back to our duties," Catalina said.

"Agreed," I replied tersely.

The girls left, and we entered the room quietly. I checked the platter, the human had ate and drank everything on offer. I took a moment to study his features. He had a few scars on his face, which was kind of cool. His black hair was cut short in a way I'd never seen before. If I had to guess his height, I'd say somewhere around 5'10". About as short as the girls, but something about him told me that he's like Kirisaka.

I can't quite put my finger on why, but I feel like he's dangerous.

Chapter 3

Nick Smith
Adventurer Level: N/A
Human - American

"What do you mean you don't want to go to college?" Cass asks.

I run my hand through her silky hair and reply, "I don't want to do anything. Not without you."

"Well, I can probably get into any school that you get into. Or we can do long distance, if you can wait for me," she says with a smile.

"Of course I can, but..." I say, trying to remember what the problem was. "Okay, yeah, I guess I'll go to college. Local, though, I don't think I can take a day without seeing you."

She smiles as she takes a sip of her coffee. We're on my porch, pretending to be adults by sipping on instant cappuccino. She takes hers with milk, almost half the cup full. I smile at her coffee flavored milk. Our eyes meet. They glow bright with life. Not like... Not like what?

"So did you pass your finals?"

"I haven't taken them yet," I say. "But don't worry, I'll pass them. The only class that will give me any trouble is..."

I trailed off as I notice the color of the sky is the same as her eyes. Not similar, the exact same. Her eyes are beautiful, but not a normal sky color. The blue is too dark for this time of day. I look around. Why is the gas station across the street? What's going on?

"Translator module functioning," she says. "Maintenance required."

"What?" I ask.

"Biology," she says. "That's the class that gives you trouble, right? Or is it anatomy and physiology?"

"Oh, it's anatomy and physiology. The school got the gym teacher to do it," I reply. "And he's bad at it."

I look around again. We're not on my porch, we're in the road?

"Hey, are we supposed to be here?" I ask.

"Of course, baby," she replies. "This is where it happens."

"Where what happens?

A thunderous crack rings out and the sky turns dark green in the blink of an eye. I panic and try to grab her hand. No-one's there. I'm alone in the middle of the road. Where did she go?

"User interface nonfunctional. Inter-dimensional energy adapter functional. Personality matrix nonfunctional."

Where's that voice coming from? What the hell is happening?

"Nanomechanical interface nonfunctional."

"So you think he's an orc?"

My eyes snap open to see a wooden ceiling. I know this ceiling. Dammit. What was that dream? I sit up and see the two orcs staring at me. Nash and Yulk, brothers. Nash was giving me a glare of suspicion, but Yulk was looking at me eagerly. Like a child looking at Christmas presents.

"I'm not an orc," I said. "I'm a human."

"No, no I don't think you're an orc, Nick," Yulk said with a grin. "I think you might be an ancestor of the orcs!"

"What? Why would you think that?" I asked.

"Well, look at the facts! You eat what we eat, you were found in our dungeon, and we are roughly the same shape! You're a bit smaller, but that's evolution for you!"

"But I came from another world, Yulk. We don't have magic where I come from. You can't have evolved from humans unless we came from here," I said while stretching. "Also, I don't just eat what you eat. I also eat fruits and vegetables. I'll be okay if you keep giving me liver, but I'm not sure what the health effects long term will be."

There was a period of silence. Both orcs looked shocked at what I had just said. I thought we had discussed that I came from another world earlier, but thinking back I might not have made it clear. I remember telling them about trucks, but maybe I forgot to tell them we didn't have magic.

"You can eat vegetables?" Nash asked, his hand resting on his axe.

"Yeah, why?"

"The only species that can eat plants and meat that I know of is puppers," Yulk said. "Even then, they either eat meat or eat plants depending on the teeth they're born with. Everything else is either carnivorous or herbivorous."

My turn to be shocked. This can't be real, carnivores and herbivores rule this world? But the evolutionary advantage that being an omnivore grants is so massive. How did this happen?

"Yep, carnivorous or herbivorous. What do you even call something that eats both?" Nash asked.

"Omnivorous," I replied. "That's further proof that I come from another world. Being omnivorous isn't all that rare where I come from."

"Omnivorous," Yulk mumbled. "I see. All consuming. So your kind eats all the plants and animals?"

"Pretty much, but we domesticate animals and farm plants. Plus we're not voracious eaters. Well, not all of us," I said with a smile.

"I'll be damned, look at his teeth!" Nash exclaimed.

"Yes! They look like a mix of elf and orc teeth! How exciting! Maybe you're the ancestor of both elves and orcs!" Yulk said as he started bouncing.

"Except that doesn't make any sense. Evolution rarely takes a step backwards. Being an omnivore is much more advantageous that being either an herbivore or a carnivore," I pointed out.

"I don't see how," Nash said. "If you've got to eat both plants and meat, what do you do when you don't have one or the other?"

"That's a good question," Yulk said.

"We can eat either or. I can be on a meat-only diet or on a vegetable-only diet for an extended period of time," I explained. "In my world there's people... humans who don't eat meat and humans who don't eat vegetables. But they take supplements to even out their nutrients."

I chuckled to myself about the unexpected usage of my AP Health class. I hadn't known exactly what I wanted to do for a career, but I was leaning toward the medical profession. The funny thing is that my teacher posed the specific problem of being trapped in a meat-only environment or a plant-only environment as one of test essays.

"Okay, so you're fine for now but we should be looking out for plants you can eat," Nash said.

"Yes, please. Most fruits should be okay if herbivores eat them," I said. Then a thought occurred to me. "Wait, maybe not. I might end up being allergic to some of the plants here."

"Ah yes, rashes, sneezes, and diarrhea. And maybe sudden death!" Yulk exclaimed. "Don't worry, most allergies can be treated with magical healing. We've already determined that the healing works on you, so you don't have to worry about being cautious with food. Well, as long as you're near me."

Oh, that's a relief. I was trying to remember how allergy tests worked. Healing magic sounds pretty handy, I wonder if it's replaced doctors. If magic users are common and they can all do healing, probably. Hey, wait a minute...

"What do you mean you've determined that healing magic works on me?" I asked.

Yulk smiled wide and said, "It's how we..."

Nash moved faster than I'd ever seen anyone move and clasped a hand over Yulk's mouth. Yulk's eyes went wild and for a second he looked like he was going to attack Nash, but then he calmed down and nodded. Nash released his brother and looked at me.

"Don't worry about it," he said.

I was stunned for a moment, but then guessed that I shouldn't push it. They probably used healing magic on me at some point. As far as why they didn't want to admit it, I could only guess. I looked at my hand again. The scar there had shrank, I wasn't just imagining it. That's a bit of a relief.

"How common is healing magic?" I asked.

"Not very. It requires a few different things to happen for it to work properly. First, you have to be able to use magic. Not everyone can. I don't know what it's like for other races, but only about a third of our people can use it," Yulk explained. "Next, you have to be able to conceptualize what the magic does. This means that you have to be able to somehow visualize the mending process of a wound. This grants you access to the healing spell, which you can use on anything you want. Finally, you have to have enough mana for the spell to heal the wound. If not, you'll pass out."

"Wait, so if I had a broken arm you'd have to visualize my bone mending to be able to heal it?" I asked.

"No, the spell works on anything once you gain the visualization. If you can visualize the mending process on skin that will unlock the spell for you. Then you can use it on a broken arm while having no idea how the bone heals."

"There are people with large amounts of mana who can't visualize for shit," explained Nash. "They have to have it happen to them before they can create a mental picture of it, so they usually end up with physical enhancement spells and find work as warriors."

"So, the better your imagination the more powerful of a mage you can be?" I asked.

"Partly. But it's mostly your knowledge of a certain subject. For instance, if you know how fire works but don't have much imagination, you'll be able to unlock middle tier fire spells. If you have a great imagination but a limited knowledge of fire, same thing. If you have both intimate knowledge of how fire forms and a great imagination, you will unlock the highest tier of fire magic," Yulk said. "Same with any other spell."

"So I probably couldn't summon a dragon, then?"

Nash laughed and said, "You could if you made it a pet and then trained it to come when you whistle. But with magic, no."

"People have pet dragons?" I asked with a laugh.

"A couple of legendary heroes have been known to have dragon companions. There was a king about 300 years back who had a bunch of pet dragons. Got a breeding pair and helped raise the young dragons. Had something like fifteen of them," Nash replied.

"What happened to them?"

"It was seventeen, and when he died they ran amok. Destroyed his kingdom, and started in on other kingdoms before they were finally defeated. About 12 of them were killed, the rest went to live in the wilderness somewhere. They're probably still alive," Yulk answered.

"Still alive?" I asked with shock in my voice.

"Yeah, dragons don't die of old age. Or at least, nobody has ever seen it happen. There's a dragon that's been living with elves for over twelve hundred years now," Nash said. "It doesn't do much, though."

"It's been at least a hundred years since it went to sleep. The elves might have moved in after it fell asleep and built around it," Yulk said.

"No, they tamed the beast. This is known historical fact..."

I stayed silent as the brothers argued. Magic, dragons, elves and orcs. I had definitely been transported to a fantasy realm. How? That's anyone guess. Several feelings rushed through me at once. Excitement that I was in a magical new place to explore. Sadness at being away from Cass. Shame of my excitement. Setting those aside I still had many questions. The most burning one, though...

"Do you think I could learn magic?" I asked, interrupting the argument.

Silence echoed through the room. The two brothers shared a look and then turned back to me. There was a long pause before Yulk finally spoke.

"Possibly. But not now. There's things going on that demands the chief's attention, and you aren't allowed to wander until he gives you his permission to."

"You're actually deeper within our village than most non-orcs are allowed," Nash explained. "That's because you came from the dungeon. I don't know how the chief is going to approach this, and there may be a lot of legal things that he will need to decide upon. For instance, you were in the dungeon since before we orcs claimed it. Which means you might have a legal claim to the dungeon."

"I doubt that," Yulk said. "Otherwise we wouldn't have been able to enter it."

"Not necessarily. Since he was already inside, the barrier may have counted it as an open invitation sort of thing."

"If that were the case, then the rest of your party would have been teleported out when he was carried out of the dungeon. Even if that weren't the case, the rescue party wouldn't have been able to go in after them. No, it's definitely an orc dungeon."

"What do you mean by orc dungeon?" I asked. "And what's this legal claim stuff?"

"Well, you have to pay to claim a dungeon and you can claim it for either your species or your faction. Most claim dungeons for a species, because the loot changes based on who the claim is for. For instance, if you claim it for a kingdom most of the loot is going to be food or wood or things like that. Claiming for a species can grant magical items and weapons, though," Yulk explained. "Claiming for an adventuring faction grants the best loot, but then only people from that faction could use the dungeon. Which is a dangerous thing, politically. So kingdoms, which are the only ones who can afford the cost, usually claim for species."

"Yep, and the Delver's Dungeon is an orc dungeon. Probably," Nash said. "Anyway, the chief has a lot of things on his plate at the moment. So you won't be going anywhere for a while. And neither will we."

"Why did your party need to be rescued?" I asked Nash.

"We got separated. I found you instead of them. I decided to take you with me, and when I picked you up I was teleported to the dungeon entrance. We had gone a long ways inside, so I opted to carry you out and report instead of finding the others," Nash said with a hint of shame.

"So they're still trapped in the dungeon?"

"We don't know if they're trapped, or even in trouble. But it's been days, and they should have been back by now," Yulk explained. "So the chief decided to send some over-tens in after them."

"Over-tens?" I asked.

"Adventurers that are over skill level ten," Nash replied.

"Level?"

The orcs once again shared a look. Yulk shrugged.

"Even more proof you're from another world. Damn, I was hoping that you were an orc ancestor or something," he said.

"The Curaguard determines levels. When you register as an adventurer, through a church, guild, or governmental organization, a link is formed between you and the Curaguard. The Curaguard assesses your skills, spells, and strengths and assigns you a level that is shared with all participating organizations. This level determines what kind of jobs you can accept, and gives you an idea of where you stack up against other adventurers," Nash explained.

"Does the Curaguard give you skills or anything?" I asked.

"No," Yulk said. "You get skills and strength through training and practical application. You get spells through study and practice. The Curaguard just keeps track."

A soft knock at the door interrupted my interrogation of the orcs. The door opened to reveal the cute orc girl carrying another platter of food and drink. She avoided meeting eyes with me and delicately set down the new platter. As she left the room, a different sort of question came to me.

"How long was I asleep this time?" I asked.

"Two days," Nash replied.

As the revelation that I had slept for two whole days dawned on me, so did the smell of the meat. The hunger that had previously gone unnoticed suddenly announced itself in the form of my stomach growling. The two orcs chuckled as I began to eat and drink.

"The front teeth appear to be narrow at the tips to cut through food items, and the teeth next to them look like they rip apart sections of the meat quite nicely. Fascinating," Yulk said.

"Pweash dun ekshamin me wyl I eet," I said through a mouthful of liver. "Itsh embarashin."

"Don't mind me, human. I'm just trying to non-invasively determine more about your origin. Better than the alternative, I would think," the orc said with a slightly malicious smile.

I gulped down the gamey meat as the implication of what he said hit home. It hadn't occurred to me earlier, but Yulk definitely fit the profile of a mad scientist who would vivisect me if given half the chance. I didn't take very long to think of my response.

"Fine. Look but don't touch, please," I said.

Yulk frowned mockingly and Nash laughed. I picked up my drink to wash down the aftertaste of my meal as the door to the room burst open.

"Nash, the rescue party's back!" A different orc girl exclaimed. "The chief wants you to bring the human."

Nash rose from his seat on the bed opposite mine and looked down at me, suddenly serious. He tossed some clothes at me, and I caught them. A shirt and pants, again woven instead of made from hide. Not exactly medieval, but similar in style. I met his gaze.

"Get dressed, and let's go," he said.

Chapter 4

Kirisaka Raksin
Adventurer Level: 11
Orc - Nulevan

"Been a while since I was last in the dungeon," Alurn said as we reached the collapsed wall.

"Same. Not since I reached level nine," Rirnu replied.

"I was in here last year," Pakin the vile added.

I remained silent. Why would it matter how long it had been? The dungeon changes frequently, passageways shifting and sliding to reveal new threats and rewards. Monster materials, magic cores, gems, precious metals, and even weapons and armor were all up for grabs by those who had the tenacity to brave the depths. Woe be to any who became complacent and assured of victory, though. The dungeon you entered yesterday may very well not be the same dungeon you enter today.

Rookie adventurers that learned this fact about dungeons were terrified of being present within the dungeon when the changes took place. It's a natural fear, being deep within the dungeon with no hope of return would end only in a terrible death. Their fears are allayed when they learn that the dungeon forcefully teleports those within to its entrance when it begins to change.

It was for this reason that Alurn and I had been opposed to waiting until the morning to enter the dungeon. If the dungeon had shifted in such a way as to block the passage, we would never know what happened to the lost party if they weren't teleported to the entrance. We would only know that they had died. The chief had forced us to wait, though. To make certain we were properly supplied and to give the lost party one last chance to make it to the entrance.

I looked at the pile of bricks that laid on the floor of the dungeon. The mortar had come loose, and the weight of the bricks had pulled this section of wall down, exposing a previously hidden passageway. The passageway was lit by stones that had been inserted into the ceiling and gave off a bright white light. It struck me as odd and out of place.

Magical stones that gave off light were not cheap. But these were installed every twenty bricks, and provided enough light that one would swear a window were nearby. It was far brighter than the rest of the dungeon, and indeed even brighter than most buildings I had been in. I had never seen nor heard of anything like it before. Gluhern was a fool to send under-tens to investigate.

"This feels wrong," Rirnu said as we entered the hall. "I can't quite figure out why, though."

"There is a suspicious lack of dust," I added.

Silence fell over the party as they came to the same realization. It had also been the first time I had spoken since we entered the dungeon. I would have been more verbose if our party hadn't included Pakin the vile. One's magic tells tales of one's mind, and necromancy was evidence of a twisted mind. She had gained renown by making herself useful to the village, and many believed her to be a valuable adventurer. But I knew the truth.

I knew of her sojourns to the wastes to find corpses to experiment on. I had watched as she revived her former comrades as mindless husks to fight her battles for her. I had seen her disregard them after those battles without a second thought. Her magic told a tale of egomania and narcissism, but she masked it well with strategically utilized friendliness and kindness.

She was with us only because she was also skilled with offensive and healing magic. Her zombies are much weaker than the bodies that supplied them, so her necromancy would be useless in the rescue of adventurers over level five. Or the pacification of monsters that could kill those adventurers.

"This is the fork that Nash mentioned. He went left, so they probably went right," Alurn said. "See, Kirisaka? It wasn't a waste of time to interview him after all."

"A rare occurrence indeed, for it not to be a waste of time to speak with Nash," I replied.

Chuckles came from the rest of the party. Nash was well known for being rambunctious and annoying. When paired with his brother, he became conniving as well. The Alta brothers were troublemakers, of this there was no doubt. Still, their antics brought about good humors most of the time. I was glad that they weren't a part of this rescue team. I have a foreboding feeling about what's to come.

We followed the passage without incident until we came upon sheer and utter darkness. The next part of the passage seemed to be lacking the stones that lit the rest of it. The other party members activated their various lighting mechanisms. The two magic users created small balls of light, and Alurn activated his own magical stone inlay on his armor's pauldron.

These lights were bright enough to allow us to see

that the rest of the passage looked much like that which we had already traveled. I did not activate any lights of my own. The shadows are my allies, and by shunning them I would weaken my combat effectiveness. This darkness nearly set me at ease, for it was far more natural for a dungeon to be dark than for it to be well lit.

"Do you think a collapse might've prevented their return?" Rirnu asked.

"It's possible," Alurn responded.

"I hope that's the case. Any other reason for delay would be unfortunate," Pakin the vile added.

I remained silent as we continued on. Like the party we were sent to rescue, we had been traveling for about a day. A sudden sense of dread came over me. What if the reason that Nash had teleported hadn't been picking up the human? What if it had been because the dungeon was shifting, and the discovery of the human had been coincidental? Then the reason that the rest of the party hadn't been teleported as well would be that they were dead.

I opted to keep this line of thought to myself. Nothing good could come of voicing my concerns, and the rest of this party likely had come to the same conclusion. It wouldn't change what we had to do. We had to find the lost party and determine their fate.

"If it is a collapse, they'd stay nearby the blocked portion of the passage," Alurn said.

"So we just have to find the collapse and dig them out. Easy," Rirnu said. "Do you think we'll have to share our food?"

"No, they should have enough. They would've brought seven days worth of rations. It's only been four," Pakin the vile said.

"Pakin's right," Alurn chimed in. "There's no reason to worry about them going hungry. The only..."

Alurn cut his sentence short as a soft sound began emanating from ahead of us, just out of sight. We stopped and listened to the squelching and crunching. Our gazes met, it was a sound that we were all familiar with. The sound of a predator eating its prey. We quietly armed ourselves and continued forward slowly and with steady feet.

As we crept down the passageway, I noted that the lights hadn't been missing at all. They had been slashed and rendered ineffective. I quietly pointed this out to the rest of the party. We spent a moment quietly guessing to ourselves if the slashing had been done by blade or claw. Then we continued moving, following both the passage and the unnerving sounds of consumption.

The passage soon opened into a spacious chamber, held up by smooth, brown pillars. The floor and walls were also brown. The light glinted off of something metallic on the floor. I gestured for my fellows to halt and edged closer to get a better look at the object, the squelching and crunching getting louder with each step. What I saw, I could barely make sense of. My confused eyes studied the object until realization made my blood run cold.

It was a piece of breastplate, shorn cleanly just above the pectoral guards. The metal of the breastplate was thick, but the cut was smooth. As if someone had taken scissors to a piece of cloth. Whatever had done this was unbelievably powerful or sharp. Or both. I looked at Alurn, realizing that his armor would likely only be a hindrance in the coming fight. Our eyes met, and by his steely gaze I could tell he had realized it as well.

We continued further into the chamber, and I glanced around for signs of the enemy. I noticed patches of white on the ground, walls, and pillars. I looked closer and realized that the room had originally been white, and with a sniff I came to the conclusion that the brown staining was from blood. I looked around with horror, the bloodstains covering nearly every inch of the chamber. It was more blood than one orc could possibly provide.

The light suddenly shined upon a figure, hunched over with its back to us. Its skin was sickeningly pale with thin white fur. So thin that the fur was largely absent with the exception of the creature's crown. The hair upon its head was so abundant that it fell past its shoulders, moving almost hypnotically with the twists and jerks of the beast. These movements aligned with the squelching and crunching, and I soon realized it was holding what was left of an arm.

We froze. The horror before us finished its grim meal and turned to face us, rising as it did so. It was as tall as I was, and stood on two legs just as I did. I looked upon a face that could have been my own, were it not so pale. The only color on this creature were its blackened eyes, sunken into its skull from disuse, and the fresh blood dripping from its maw. From the tips of its stiffened fingers extended long claws, discolored by blood both new and old. They were the size of daggers and almost assuredly just as sharp.

I quickly stepped into the shadows as the rest of the party readied themselves to fight the creature. It turned his head to follow my movements, as if it knew

where I was without having to see me. It was...
smiling at me.

"Pakin, burn the bastard!" shouted Alurn.

Pakin the vile took a stance and shouted, "Onrefni
Retaerg Tsa..."

I was barely able to follow what happened. I watched
helplessly as the creature moved in one swift motion,
closing the distance between itself and Pakin and
separating her from her head before she could finish
her spell. I watched as her face grew confused and
then shocked, before it stopped moving entirely. Her
body crumpled to the ground, her magical ball of light
snuffing out and shrouding the creature in darkness
once again.

"RUN!" I shouted as I charged the creature.

My blades met claws with a sound similar to thunder.
The creature was just as strong as I had feared, and it
pushed me until my back pressed against the nearest
pillar.

"Kirisaka!" Alurn shouted, hefting his sword to ready a
blow.

"NO! RUN! RUN NOW! GO!" I shouted, struggling
against the creature's might.

They have to go. They need to warn the chief. The lost
party is dead, and any further rescuers will die as well.
I'm the best match-up against this creature's strength
and speed. They have to realize this!

"GO WARN THEM!" I screamed as the creature tilted
its claws to dig into my shoulder.

With pained expressions, they turned and fled. I sent a bone shattering kick into the knee of the creature. Instead of collapsing as it should have, it merely lost its balance long enough for me to free myself. I ran deeper into the chamber, trying to draw it away from my fleeing comrades. It followed me into the darkness.

"Noisiv Wodahs Tsac," I said, casting shadow vision just in time to dodge a wild slash from the creatures clawed hand.

I counter-slashed and scored a blow on its outer thigh. It didn't go as deep as I had hoped. I slashed and dodged again and again, the creature matching my movements with impossible skill. The macabre smile never left its face. I tapped into every fight I'd ever fought, every training session I'd ever been in, every trick I had learned or seen trying to find a way to score a decisive blow. The creature managed to dodge most of them. Those that it didn't weren't enough to even give it pause.

I'm getting tired. I don't know how long its been. I hope they managed to get away. It's a fair trade. No, there's no time for melancholy! An opening! I perform a standard double slash with all of my strength, aiming for the creature's exposed neck. The creature slashes at my swords just before the blow hits home in an attempt to block.

I use the momentum from the slash to roll and put some distance between us. I hear pieces of metal strike the ground and bounce. I look at my swords and to my horror, I'm only holding the hilts. The creature turns to me and I cast the broken blades aside and draw my knives. As the beast approaches, I throw one of them as hard as I can.

A palpable blow! The knife sinks directly into the creature's eye! It stops dead in its tracks, and I breathe a sigh of relief. Then the creature reaches up to its face and pulls the blade out of its skull, tearing its own eye out with it. The bastard is still smiling, even as its own blackened blood flows down its face.

"FUCK YOU!" I shout defiantly as I bring my final knife to bear.

It charges at me. I barely manage to dodge the strike, slicing into its arm as I do. Another shallow blow, barely enough to draw blood. Curse this vile fiend. It slashes at me once again but this time it anticipates my dodge and kicks at me as well. I am sent flying, the shock stifling the pain. I slam into a pillar, dropping my knife, but I manage rise fast enough to grab the creatures hands, temporarily preventing it from impaling me.

I struggle against its strength, trying to move the claws away from my chest. But the creature is strong, and they inch closer and closer. I stare into its remaining eye with determination. But the claws inch closer and closer. I scream at the beast as I feel the claws pierce my armor and then my skin and then my bones and finally, my scream is cut short as the claws rip into my lungs.

I let go of one of the hands and reach for the creatures head, grasping its ear and tearing it off. The creature rears back in pain, pulling its claws from my chest. Too late, though. Even as the creature fills the air with shrieks, I can no longer breathe. The ear falls from my hand to the ground along with my blood. As my vision fades, I see my prize for the first time. I mentally chuckle at the absurdity of the shape of the ear.

Whoever heard of a round ear?

Chapter 5

Yulk Alta
Adventurer Level: 7
Orc - Nulevan

Nash and I turned around to allow the human to get dressed in privacy. Nash was on edge the entire time that our backs were turned. He must still think the little critter could be a threat. He's not wrong, I suppose. Not the kind of threat that would attack you without a weapon, though. The kind that could out think and out maneuver you on a battlefield? Maybe.

This human had just awoken and had already demonstrated knowledge of fringe intellectual pursuits like evolution and nutrition. It spoke of things I had spent extensive effort to learn as if they were common knowledge. My younger brother had stumbled onto a goldmine of knowledge! Even if the human didn't have any more knowledge than what he had already displayed, just studying his anatomy would be revolutionary. He would likely be opposed to vivisection, though. Even with healing magic available...

"I'm ready, I think," Nick said.

My brother and I turned around to look at the human. He actually cut a dashing figure, if you're into that sort of thing. Trimmed black hair that was longer on the top than on the sides, dark blue eyes with a hint of green, a chiseled jawline, and musculature that was reminiscent of a fighter. He had a scar to the right of his chin that was barely noticeable, and a much more noticeable scar on his left temple. He could pass as a short elf or a tall dwarf were it not for the ugly round ears. Nash was right, they're very jarring now that I look closer.

"Alright, let's go," Nash replied.

We exited the room with the human to my left and Nash to the human's left. The girls were peeking around the corner of the hallway, curious of the human's activities. Yini and Nimora were enamored with the thing, but Catalina seemed afraid of it. I will have to remember to ask her about her reasons for that. Perhaps it's merely a phobia, but she might be able to detect something that I can't about the human.

I had no reason to believe the same of Nash, though. My brother was infamously over-reactive and overprotective. His near hostility towards the human makes little sense, since he's the one that brought it from the dungeon. I glanced at the human as we walked. It walked very similar to Nash, fully upright with a steady gait. Unlike Nash, it was keeping its eyes ahead and trying to avoid making eye contact with the orcs that quickly shuffled out of our way.

As we continued on I wondered if the human was a warrior or a mage of some sort. Not everyone has to be, of course, there are many who are neither. Most, even. But something told me that the human was special in more than its rarity. I might be setting myself up for disappointment, but I really want to see what it's capable of. I wonder what adventurer level it is! No, wait, it had shown ignorance of magic. While that doesn't necessarily mean that it doesn't have martial combat experience, it's unlikely to be above level two if it's never heard of magic. Perhaps instructing it on magic would boost its level?

"Listen, Nick. When we get to the chief's chamber you need to be quiet unless you're directly asked a question. You're technically an outsider, and you're deeper in our village than an outsider is allowed to be. An outsider meeting the chief in the chamber is unheard of, so if you're rude there's bound to be bad consequences," warned Nash.

"I understand. I'll keep quiet," replied Nick.

"Oh, I don't think it'll be all that dire," I said. "After all, Nash is the reason you're here. If you do anything naughty, he's liable to take the blame!"

I returned Nash's glare with a malicious grin. A not-so-subtle reminder that all this is his fault. Ah, but I'll likely have to remind him that whatever the fate of his team is, he's not to blame for that. They went off on their own volition, and he wasn't even their leader. He was their strongest, but Graz was the leader. And Graz decided to leave their strongest behind and continue on. And the others followed him. If Graz survived, I'm going to give him a good skull-shaking for his stupidity.

We entered the chamber and my blood ran cold. Alurn and Rirnu stood before the chief, looking ashamed. I didn't waste time wondering where Pakin and Kirisaka were. These two wouldn't be here alone if things had gone well. A boss had been encountered.

"Nash, I'm sorry," said Gluhern. "Your party didn't make it."

Nash's jaw tightened as the realization hit home. He looked at Alurn and Rirnu, and both of them avoided his eyes. He swallowed and nodded at the chief. I reached over and patted his elbow to comfort him. He'd need a drink tonight.

"Chief," I began, "I take it that Kirisaka and Pakin

didn't make it either?"

"Correct."

"Was it a boss?"

"We believe so."

"What are we going to do about it?"

"That's what we're deciding," Gluhern said and pointed to the human. "I wanted to speak to that to find out more information. Care to introduce us?"

"Allow me," said Nash.

We all looked at my brother, not expecting him to be able to speak yet. Perhaps I didn't give him enough credit and he already knew that what happened wasn't his fault. Nash is a great brother, he's full of surprises. Never boring.

"This is Nicodemus Liam Smith, a human who may have been transported to our world from another world. He goes by Nick," Nash said, gently pushing the human forward.

"Pleased to make your acquaintance," Nick said, bowing at the waist.

Everyone froze for a second. Despite the grim attitude of the meeting, there were a few chuckles.

"I am not a king, I am a chief. You need not genuflect to me," Gluhern said with a chuckle.

"Need not genuflect? A remarkable increase in vocabulary," I said while jerking my head to the left to dodge a thrown goblet.

"DON'T PATRONIZE ME, SORCERER!" Gluhern yelled.

The metal goblet clattered behind me. I grinned. Most of the drinking utensils in the village were either made of wood, glass, or ceramic. The chief had tired of having to order replacement cups and had changed all of his utensils to metal. This was much more economical, considering that this type of spat of ours is nearly traditional at this point.

I frequently critiqued Gluhern for several reasons. The first and foremost reason was that I got amusement from his reactions. The second reason was to remind him that even though he is a chieftain, he is still an orc like the rest of us. It's all too easy to forget a simple fact like that when your word is law. The third reason is to keep my reaction time healthy.

I stole a glance at the two surviving members of the rescue party and immediately regretted my shenanigans. Alurn, who was normally mountainous, was now staring into the distance as if lost in thought and looking significantly deflated. Rirnu was struggling not to cry. Gluhern and I met each others eyes, and I could tell we both felt shame at our outbursts.

"I'm sorry," Gluhern said to everyone except me. "Nick, I called you here because you were found in the Delver's Dungeon around the same area as the beast that will be the topic of discussion. Alurn, please describe what happened."

At the mention of his name, Alurn returned to reality and began his tale. We all listened raptly, especially when he described the creature. Skin nearly as white as its hair with claws like daggers, standing like and as tall as an orc, and with speed that matched a shadow warrior's. The way it moved when it killed

Pakin, almost too fast for even an over-ten to see. Very interesting, but in a very dangerous way. Something I would rather read about instead of personally study. Unless it were dead, of course.

"When we returned to the collapsed portion of the wall, we waited for Kirisaka to catch up," Alurn said. "But... after waiting for a very long time... we were teleported to the entrance. Without him."

Every face listening to the story dropped except for Nick's, who looked confused instead. The human looked like he wanted to ask questions but was hesitating due to our warnings.

"The dungeon shifts frequently, and when it does it teleports the adventurers still wandering around inside to the entrance," I explained softly. "The only time it won't teleport someone to the entrance is if they're dead."

The faces that the human made were interesting. They were alien, but so communicative that I immediately knew what they meant. His confusion turned to realization, then sadness, and then, as he turned back to look at Alurn, empathy. It was at this moment that I realized that Nash was completely in the wrong about this little creature being a threat.

My eye's locked with my brothers. He had seen the empathy on the human's face and knew he had been wrong. His hand dropped from the handle of his axe for the first time since we left the hospital. The only way the human could be a threat is unintentionally.

"Thank you, Alurn," Gluhern said before turning back to Nick. "Have you ever heard of this beast or anything like it?"

"N-no chief," the human stammered, shocked by the question.

"No need for honorifics, call me Gluhern please," the chief said gently.

"Right, sorry. No I haven't, Gluhern. Until I woke up yesterday I hadn't even heard of a dungeon. In my world, monsters aren't real. Neither are orcs, elves, or dwarves. Not even magic. It's just humans and animals. I'm sorry I can't be more help," Nick said with a genuine tone.

"I understand. Thank you. I'll be wanting to discuss your world more in a bit, but first the topic of what to do with the creature must be addressed," Gluhern said.

"I don't think we have a team strong enough to beat it," Rirnu said.

This was quite the revelation from the veteran healer. We had all suspected this to be the case after hearing Alurn's recount, but hearing it said aloud by Rirnu seemed to set it in stone. There was nobody else in the village who knew the limits of our adventurers better.

"Well, we'll have to do something. We can't risk adventurer parties running into the damned thing, and closing the dungeon indefinitely will spell the death of this settlement," the chief said.

"What about a barrier?" I asked. "Block off the path that leads to the part of the dungeon with the beast in it. If we use a runic barrier and warn everybody not to mess with it, the beast won't be able to leave the part of the dungeon that it's currently in."

"And what's to stop it from attacking the crew sent to set up the barrier?" Alurn asked hollowly.

"It could be that pale due to living in the darkness for a long time," Nick said. "Which means it's probably got an aversion to light. Light is usually a bad thing in deep darkness."

We all looked at the little human with various emotions on our faces. My face held curiosity, Gluhern's held amusement, Alurn and Rirnu looked thoughtful, and Nash looked annoyed and angry. I almost laughed when I realized why Nash was upset. He believed the human had spoken out of turn.

"Yes, yes you may be right!" Rirnu said at last. "The lights leading to the room we found the beast in were all slashed and broken!"

"We all had lights on, though," Alurn said.

"True, but the lights in the hallway were much brighter than our lights. There were times were I nearly forgot we were under ground!" Rirnu said excitedly. Then his mood soured and he said, "But if that's the case, then we all could have run for it and Kirisaka didn't have to..."

"Hindsight is helpful as long as you don't make it a hindrance," I said. "This isn't a case where you should have known better and should be chided into doing better next time. There's no way you could have known. Even I, with all of my learning, have never heard of a beast the likes of which you have described."

The pair looked at me with gratitude in their eyes.

"Okay, then we'll put a barrier up at the broken wall as

soon as possible. We'll make it the strongest runic barrier we can make, damn the expense. While the barrier is up, we'll send a missive to the kingdom to make them aware of our troubles and request elite adventurers to vanquish the beast. There's bound to be enough loot to make it worth their while," Gluhern said. "Does this satisfy your concerns, Alurn and Rirnu?"

"No," Alurn replied, falling to his knees. "I am shamed, chief. I am meant to be the greatest warrior in this village, yet I fled in terror, leaving my closest friend to die."

This turn of events wasn't unexpected. Alurn was known for being honorable, and wore heavy plate-mail despite wielding a great-sword for the sole purpose of being a bigger target. He prided himself on taking all of the hits for a party, keeping them safe while they fought. Nash and I locked eyes. He had clenched his teeth again. Then the chief spoke.

"You are not shamed. You have worked harder than most to be as strong as you are, so it is unlikely that you could have worked any harder or been any stronger by the time your party faced this monstrosity. If the roles had been reversed, and Kirisaka had ran while you fought, you would have died as quickly as Pakin."

"But chief..."

"No, listen to me Alurn. It was a bad match-up. Your strength is great against strength, but that creature surpassed your strength and was many times faster than you. It would have cleaved through your armor in mere moments and then been on Kirisaka and Rirnu. Kirisaka would have died either way, and the village would be left with one fewer adventurer,"

Gluhern said, leaning back in his seat. "Even if you are to be shamed, I cannot think of a worse punishment than having to continue on as an adventurer without your closest comrade. Mourn Kirisaka, comfort his family, heal your mental wounds, and get back to work. Do you hear this judgment?"

"Yes, chief," the mountainous orc said.

"Good. You both have three days off, and then you'll report this situation directly to High Chief Ulurmak. Alurn, Rirnu, you two are dismissed. Nash, Yulk, please remain."

The two over-tens left the chief's chambers, leaving Nash, Nick, and myself standing before Chief Gluhern. I always found it awkward when I had to witness Gluhern actually be a chief. I much prefer being blissfully ignorant to his wisdom and continuing on as if he were a bumbling fool. No matter, I'm sure his bumbling ways would make themselves evident again soon enough.

"Now, what to do about you, Nick?" Gluhern asked.

"We should find a way to grant him citizenship of the village. Or whatever the equivalent of citizenship is for a village," I said, tapping my chin at the quandary.

"I know he's shown that he can be useful, but he's not an orc. This is an orc village, not a mixed village. It's part of our mandate. So why?"

"Well, the fact that we found him in the dungeon could pose problems in the future if we don't. Dungeons are first come first served, but not necessarily first registered first served. He's been in the dungeon presumably since before we settled here, since none of us saw him enter," I said, placing my hand on Nick's shoulder to keep him from trying to correct me. "If we send him on his merry way, everyone that he runs into will have questions about his origins. Some of those answers may get back to the Curaguard, and that could result in an investigation, which would result in our claim being temporarily revoked. Or even permanently revoked if it finds in favor of the human."

"I see," Gluhern said, narrowing his eyes as if to try to see through my bullshit.

"If he were part of the village, then our claim couldn't be revoked. His claim on the dungeon would merge with ours."

"Would that be satisfactory to you, human?" Gluhern asked.

"Y-yes," Nick said as I squeezed his shoulder pointedly.

"Okay. Now the problem is, how do we go about doing this? I'm certain his majesty won't approve of us just adding him to our roster."

"Adoption. High Chief Ulurmak can't contest an adoption," Nash said. "I'm sure mom wouldn't mind. What do you think Yulk?"

I was shocked at the suggestion. It was surprising enough that Nash was suggesting that the human be our brother, but the actual cleverness behind the scheme was even more surprising. He was correct, the High Chief can't contest an adoption. He was also correct that mother would likely go for the scheme. She had a big heart and loved non-orc company. I couldn't help but grin at how conniving my brother was being.

"I'm sure she wouldn't mind at all. That's a great idea, actually," I replied. "That would also settle the matter of where to keep him. We just clean out a room for him. I've been meaning to move my laboratory to the alchemist's anyway."

"Good, then it's settled. We'll talk to mom and get the human moved in," Nash replied while turning to Nick. Then he asked in a dangerous tone, "Unless the human has an objection?"

"N-no, no I don't. Thank you," Nick said.

"Alright, sounds good. Nick will have to remain in the hospital until Yilda makes the adoption official, though, which means you're still on guard duty," Gluhern said with a chuckle.

"Ah, if I could have a moment, chief?" I asked.

"Sure. Nick, Nash, you're dismissed."

My brother looked at me with curiosity before deciding that he'd rather not know why I wanted to spend more time with the chief. Nick and Nash turned and left, leaving Gluhern and I alone. I'd been wanting to have this conversation for quite some time, and I had been thinking about the best way to broach the subject. Gluhern opened his mouth to speak, but I interrupted him.

"I'd like to teach the human how to use magic."

Chapter 6

Nick Smith
Adventurer Level: N/A
Human - American

"We should wake him up," Yulk said, his voice doing just that.

"Don't get impatient. We've got a lot to do today, he'll need his rest," Nash replied.

Silently giving my wholehearted agreement to Nash, I pretended to still be asleep.

"We DO have a lot to do today, and I can't wait to get started!" Yulk exclaimed. Loudly.

"It won't be as fun as you're imagining, and it will be even less fun if he's half asleep all day," Nash stated.

The only thing I could think of that we had to do today was move me from this hospital to Nash and Yulk's mom's place. Since I didn't have any stuff, that shouldn't take all day. Unless there were ceremonies or something. I don't want to take part in a ceremony, though.

"Fun or not, it's still exciting to see what training will bring out in him. Is he strong? Is he weak? Only one way to find out, and we can't do that while he's asleep!" Yulk nearly shouted.

A feeling of dread spread through my core. Training. I doubt they had Virtual Reality, which would mean actual fighting. And since Yulk doesn't appear to be the physical fitness guru of the village, that will mean fighting against Nash. A fight against a 6'10" orc that has muscles that professional bodybuilders would kill for? No thanks. I'll pretend to be asleep all damned day.

"Quiet down. Why are you so excited about his training? The only thing you care about is whether he can do magic or not," Nash said.

Magic?

"The abilities of those with magical talent are frequently opposed to the abilities of those with physical talent. So if he's bad at physical skills, then he might be amazing at magical skills! Or if he's good at physical skills, he might be terrible at magic. That would be disappointing, but either way it will answer questions that I have," Yulk said, toning his voice down a couple of notches. "Although, there's a chance that he's good at both. We've never seen anything like him, so it doesn't make sense to apply our own limitations to him offhand."

"So which would you rather have him do first? Magic or muscle?" Nash asked.

"Magic," I said, sitting up.

Both orcs turned to look at me. Nash raised an eyebrow at me as Yulk began to smile ear to ear. The mental image of a grinning demon was difficult to shake. Especially with the sharp teeth. Nash stood up and looked down at me.

"Fine. We'll do magic before testing your physical abilities. Before we do any of that, though, we're going to introduce you to our mom. She's going to decide whether or not you get to stay with us, and if she decides you can stay you're going to become our brother," he said. "Don't be expecting any fanfare, though. Best you'll get is a big dinner tonight."

"Indeed. Elves and dwarves may throw lavish celebrations, but orcs rarely do," Yulk added. "Do humans celebrate often?"

"It depends on the humans," I answered. "Some celebrate every chance they get. Others never celebrate anything. There's a lot of in between, too."

Nash looked impatient, "Let's go. Mom's already up, so we might as well get this out of the way."

I quickly got dressed and followed the two orcs out of the hospital and down the street. The more we walked, the more I noticed the buildings in the village. There were a lot more than I thought there'd be. These buildings looked as if they were made from different architects, and those architects were trying to outdo each other. Some were made of wood, some were made of a type of gray brick, and others were made of a mixture of materials. Some buildings were obviously houses or shops, but others were anyone's guess.

There was also plenty of plant-life. Grasses, trees, bushes, and everything else you would normally see in a wooded area. On the horizon were mountains, looking like jagged black teeth that had just bit a pouch of white paint. They reminded me of the Rocky Mountains, but with less snow on top. It was comforting, in a way.

I also noticed that we were getting a lot of stares. I felt a little self-conscious, but completely understood their curiosity. I tried imagining the reactions that humans would have to an orc being escorted down a busy street. Actually, come to think of it, most people would probably just assume it was a really good cosplay. I chuckled to myself as I realized that little kids would likely have the most appropriate reactions to that situation.

As we walked, Nash and Yulk nodded and waved to people that we passed. The village seemed too large for everyone to know each other, so these two seem to have a lot of friends. I had some friends back in my world, but not close enough for me to be broken up by their absence. More like the hanging out if it's convenient and occasionally vent with kinda pals.

Even so, Cassandra's illness had closed me off in a big way. I didn't have time for anyone but her because our time together was so limited. She hated that, but understood that it was my choice and the only way that I could cope. I had been hoping for some miracle to happen, and now I'm just hoping to get to see her one more time.

I was pulled from this line of thought by Nash pointing to a big wooden house surrounded by an equally wooden fence.

"That's ours," he said.

We approached the gate and two large creatures that looked like a lot like dogs came bounding out the front door, yelling as they came. They were about twice the size of a Husky and similarly shaped, but completely without fur. Their skin was black with green stripes. I was startled by their size and appearance as well as the fact that they weren't barking so much as shouting "hey" over and over. Yulk noticed my expression.

"Those are puppers. Dima and Nucho, specifically. Dima is carnivorous, Nucho is herbivorous. You'll be able to tell by the teeth," he explained as Nash wrangled them back into the house.

I followed Yulk closely, suddenly feeling out of place. I also found it odd that I hadn't felt this out of place before. I guess it must be how lived in this house feels compared to everywhere else I had been. Makes me feel like I'm intruding. It looked about as clean as a normal house, and smelled like unfamiliar cooking and cleaning. Like going to a new friend's home.

The furniture in the house was similar to that of the hospital, like modern day medieval knock-offs. Tables with metallic inlays, wooden chairs with padding on the seats and backs, and even doors with metal handles. Nash was struggling to hold onto the puppers as Yulk led me deeper into the house until we entered the kitchen. At the table sat an orc woman who gave me a warm smile when she saw me.

I had expected her hair to be black like Nash's, but it was blonde with some gray strands here and there. She had a bit of wisdom around the eyes, but other than that it was hard to tell that she was any older than the two orcs that escorted me here. Her green skin was also a few shades lighter than her sons. Come to think of it, I hadn't seen any male orcs with light skin or female orcs with dark skin.

"Mom, this is Nick Smith. He's a human. Nick, this is Yilda, Mother of Nash, Mother of Yulk, and many other titles," Yulk said with pride.

"I only go by my two most important titles," Yilda said, standing from the table.

"Nice to meet you," I replied as she walked up to me.

She narrowed her eyes to study me closely and placed a hand upon my shoulder. She turned me so that she could look at me in profile, and I was taken aback by how strong she was. Yilda was only an inch or two taller than me and didn't look particularly muscular, but I got the distinct feeling that even if I had tried not to be turned my resistance would have been futile. After a few seconds of examination and mumbling, she turned back to Nash and Yulk.

"He's cute. I'll take him into my care," she said. "Say hello to your new brother, boys."

"We already have, mom," Nash said, still struggling with the dog-like creatures.

"Hello Nick!" Yulk exclaimed with glee.

"Nash..." Yilda said, staring pointedly at the orc in question.

"Alright... Hello, Nick. Welcome to the family," Nash sighed.

"Thank you. I appreciate your hospitality," I replied, nearly choking up.

This was a confusingly emotional moment for me. If I were to look at it from afar, I would probably find it funny. In the moment, though, I felt warm and fuzzy feelings. I'd never had siblings before, and the kindness that I was being shown was nearly overwhelming. This orc, this woman, had just given me a once-over and decided to keep me fed and housed. It's not the kind of kindness that you see every day.

With the warm and fuzzy feelings came a sense of profound sadness. I miss my parents, and I miss Cass. I didn't have the perfect life in my world, to be sure, but the people in it made it worth living. Despite

Nash's aggression and Yulk's mad scientist vibes, they seem like good people. I have to find a way back to Cass, but by doing so I'll be abandoning them. And now they are my brothers.

Deep breath in, clench your jaw. Men don't cry, that's the law. A little rhyme that my father taught me when I was younger to help teach me to calm down in emotional moments. I used to tell him that there isn't a law against men crying, and he would smile back and say that not all laws are written. I didn't really know what that meant until high school.

"Alright, that's settled then! Time for training!" Yulk said, nearly bouncing again.

"Aren't you going to eat?" Yilda asked indignantly.

"There's no time for such things, mother! We must discover what Nick is capable of! Scientific discovery awaits!" Yulk exclaimed.

"Yulk, training doesn't work as well on an empty stomach," Nash said.

"We'll eat after! Don't want food sloshing around our stomachs ruining things! Let's go, Nick!"

Nash and Yilda looked at me as Yulk marched past me, holding his staff in the air like he was leading a marching band. I shrugged, not knowing what else to do.

"I'm not really hungry right now, but maybe training could change that," I said cautiously.

"Alright, I'll hang back and get your room ready. Don't let Yulk push you too hard. One of the things he wants to know is your limits, so be sure to let him know once you've reached them," Nash said as he wrangled the puppers into another room.

"Have fun dear, we'll get to know each other a bit better over dinner," Yilda said with a smile.

"Thanks," I replied, turning to follow Yulk.

"COME ON, NICK!" Yulk shouted from the door.

I hurried after him. We walked through town again, his high spirits unfaltering. I was excited to learn more about magic, and whether or not I could do it. I also felt nervous, both because of Yulk's expectations and the fact that magic was likely my way home. If I suck at it... No, negativity won't help. I can do this, whatever this is.

We passed many staring eyes until we finally came to what looked like an old fashioned archery training pit. Bricks surrounded a dirt ring with targets placed intermittently within. Yulk sat on a nearby bench and gestured in front of him. I sat cross legged in the dirt facing him.

"Alright, let's begin your magic training," he said with a smile. "Do you have any questions to start off with?"

"I don't know enough to have any," I explained.

"Fair enough. Magic is easier done than said. It stems from forces that we don't quite understand, but seems to be contained within everything. Those who are attuned to magic often feel as if they should be able to do things that they can't, like move objects without their hands. Have you ever felt like that?" he asked.

"Yes, when I was a kid," I replied.

"Excellent!" Yulk exclaimed with a grin. "Now, the reason that people get this feeling is because they are partially attuned to the magic that surrounds us. Or they're fully attuned and just aren't attuned to their own magic energy. To use a spell, you have to mix the surrounding magic with your own magic and properly channel it through the natural pathways in your own body."

"Pathways?" I asked.

"Yes. There are many pathways in the body. Your blood vessels, nerves, and digestive system for example. Your magic pathways are similar but separate. Your magical energy is stored somewhere in your body, and can be channeled elsewhere in your body through these pathways. If you concentrate on yourself, you should be able to feel it. Mine is in my brain," he said while pointing to his skull.

"Okay, I'll try," I replied.

I closed my eyes and began to concentrate on my body. I felt my skin, tingling from exposure to the sun and whatever else was in the air. I felt my ribs spreading and closing with every breath. I felt my heart beating, and the blood being pushed through my veins and arteries. I felt the wind blow through my hair and my clothes resting on my body. Then I felt it. A somewhat... electrical energy, directly in the center of my upper torso.

I pointed at it, "It's here."

"I knew it!" Yulk said, pumping his fist in celebration. "Okay, for the next part you're going to have to learn channeling. Your own magic won't be able to do much on its own, so you'll need to intake magic from your surroundings and mix it in your core to fire off a spell."

"How do I do that?" I asked.

"The easiest way is through breathing. The air has magic in it, and you just need to think about pulling the magic out and storing it in your core. It will mix with your own magic, and you can channel that into a spell," he explained. "But you get more by drawing magic in through your channels."

"I can't feel my channels, though."

"Exactly. And you won't be able to until you use them. That's why we start out new mages with breath charging before anything else. Go on, try it out. It should take about twenty or so deep breaths to get you nice and charged up."

I closed my eyes again and began to do as instructed. I breathed in through my mouth and out through my nose. The electric feeling got slightly more intense, and I could feel the two different magics in my chest. I imagined them combining, and a third kind of magic appeared. It felt amazing, like I had all the energy in the world. A few breaths later, and I somehow knew that I was fully charged up.

"Okay, I'm ready," I said.

"What? That was only ten breaths. Are you sure?" Yulk asked.

"No. Well... Yes? My core feels full," I replied. "Is that bad?"

The orc studied me with narrowed eyes and scratched his chin for a moment.

"I don't know," he finally replied. "We'll see. Okay, let's go to the targets."

We got up and approached the range. From a distance I had thought they were made of straw, but they were actually statues made of stone. Judging by all the pits and charring, they had definitely seen plenty of use. Yulk picked up two stones and walked over to one of the targets. He placed the stones on the target's shoulders and walked back over to me.

"Alright, I want you to try an easy spell. It's called wind spear, and its name is a very apt description of what you will need to imagine to create the spell. I'll demonstrate," he said, raising his hand. "Raeps Dniw Tsac!"

I flinched as I felt wind erupt from Yulk's hand. But I also felt the magic, and was transfixed. The stone on the statue's left shoulder shattered into pieces. The orc grinned and turned to me, the sun gleaming off his bald head.

"Like that," he said. "You should be able to disturb the stone on the right once you figure out the spell."

"Wait, do I have to do the incantation?" I asked.

"No, the incantation happens naturally. You can increase the power of a spell by mindfully saying the incantation, but that takes quite a bit of practice," he said with a smile. "Now give it a try. Use both hands, though. For safety, since you don't know your channels yet."

"Will I need a staff like the one you have?"

Yulk laughed, "No. You won't need an arcane focus until you're much further along. Even further along than I am! The only reason I have one is because when I was younger, I went on a dungeon raid with Nash and ended up breaking my back. Rirnu did his best to heal me, but he was only level six at the time, so I ended up with difficulty walking. So, my staff is both an arcane focus and a walking stick, but I use it for walking. Enough about that. Go ahead and try to cast the spell, Nick."

"Okay, I'll try."

I raised my hands and aimed them at the stone. I thought about how wind works, gas molecules bumping into other gas molecules, pushing them along. The pushing is caused by gases getting hotter and colder, which causes them to get lighter or heavier than the other molecules around them. The harder they push, the faster the wind goes. I imagined this happening, but being channeled into a spear that rushed toward the stone. Then I felt a sort of click.

"Raeps Dniw Tsac," my voice said.

I felt the magic in my chest flow through my arms and through all ten of my fingers. The intensity of the movement almost hurt, but felt good at the same time. The tingling sensation pushed itself out of my fingers, manifesting my will. The air pressure around my hands erupted with a blast of wind that pushed me back a step.

-Wind Spear unlocked-

"What?" I asked, looking at Yulk.

"I... I didn't say anything..." Yulk said, staring at the target with his mouth agape.

I looked at the target, and my mouth dropped open as

well. There was dust settling around the statue, but I could see that it was missing its head and shoulder. The stone was nowhere to be seen, and the arm had fallen onto the ground. Behind the target, there was a noticeable dent in the bricks. What the hell? Wind did this? I did this?

We stood shocked for a few moments, but then Yulk's opened mouth turned back into a grin as he turned to me. I met his eyes, and he placed his hand on my shoulder, his sharp teeth glistening in the sunlight. He definitely reminded me of a smiling demon.

"I fucking KNEW it," he said. "We're gonna have quite a time together, Nick."

Chapter 7

Nick Smith
Adventurer Level: N/A
Human - American

"What the hell just happened?" I asked, dumbfounded.

"You destroyed the stone and a good chunk of the target!" Yulk exclaimed.

"Is... is that normal? Should I be able to do that?" I asked.

"Among orcs? Absolutely not!" he grinned. "I've never seen a brand new mage destroy a stone with any kind of spell. But who's to say what's normal for humans?"

I stared at the destruction I had caused. The severed arm of the statue lay in the stone-dust that now covered the dirt of the target pit. The sheer destructive power was staggering. Being able to destroy rocks whenever I want is cool and all, but I want to be able to go home and I don't see how this is going to help me get there. Or maybe it's a sign of how much magic I can use?

I replayed the events in my head. I had imagined wind, and cast a spell. When I cast the spell I had unwillingly said something, and the magic had flowed through my arms in a straight line. Then the wind formed and blasted the statue into pieces. I thought I had heard someone else say something too, but maybe it was the wind?

"Why was it so strong?"

"Who's to say," Yulk repeated. "I'm guessing that your magic core is a bit stronger than what's standard in a beginner."

"Stronger?" I questioned. "Why would it be stronger?"

"No idea. Also... maybe stronger is the wrong word. Essentially the more you use it the more effective it gets. It doesn't get bigger like a muscle, though. It just gets better at fitting more magic in it. It just squished it in there," Yulk explained as he moved his hands together in a squishing motion. "Anyway, you should now know the magical pathways through your arms and out your hands. Kind of feels like blood vessels with all the twists and turns, right? You have more magic pathways throughout your body, and there are certain spells that can be channeled through those pathways as well. You can also take in magic from those pathways to be able to cast spells faster."

"Wait, blood vessels?" I asked, confused.

"Yes," he replied hesitantly. "What's confusing you here?"

"The magic went straight from my core through my arms to my fingers," I explained. "Like it was following my bones."

Silence fell and a lot of emotions played out on Yulk's face. Confusion was first, followed by concern and then deep thought. After a few moments the grin returned and he slapped me on the back.

"You just keep getting more and more interesting, little brother!" he exclaimed. "The shape of one's channels often determines one's initial magical efficacy, so that could explain how you were able to cast wind spear so potently. Wish I knew why they were straight though. Never heard of that before. Oh well, let's move on. Back to the seats!"

We walked back towards the bench and Yulk took a seat. I sat where I had been sitting before. The orc set his staff in his lap and cracked his knuckles and neck. Confused, I did the same thing, which made him chuckle.

"As I explained before, the magical pathways in your body run both directions. Out from your core, and right back into your core. Do you still have some of your own magic in your core?" he asked.

I closed my eyes and checked. The only magic that was left in my core was my own. It felt the same as earlier, as if I hadn't used any of it at all. Should I tell him that? I already feel like a freak, but he can't help me if he doesn't know everything. Yulk stared at me patiently, awaiting my answer.

"Yes," I answered hesitantly. "It's like I haven't used any at all."

"Really?" he asked. "I had theorized that the reason for the potency of your wind spear was that you were using a lot of your magic, combined with the relatively short distance said magic had to travel, of course. Interesting. I wonder if it already regenerated, or there's just a lot of it... Well, no matter. We'll find out later. I want you to draw magic into your core using the channels that you felt when you cast wind spear. Just like with the breathing we did earlier. Oh, and don't mix it with your own magic quite yet."

"Okay," I replied, closing my eyes once again.

I focused on the sensation that I felt earlier and tried to imagine the reverse of that sensation. Nothing happened, so instead I imagined that my fingers were straws and I was using them to suck in magic. Oddly enough, this worked, and I soon felt tingling in my arms and the other magic filling up my core. Yulk was right, it took almost no time at all to fill it back up.

"Done," I said.

"Excellent," Yulk smiled. "Now, I want you to exude that magic back into the environment around you. The easiest way to do this is by imagining that your core is a sponge full of water and you're giving it a big squeeze. Pay attention to the pathways that the magic uses to exit your body."

I nodded and got to work. The magic traveled along my arms through my fingers and along my legs through my toes. There were exit points in my fingers and toes, but also in the palms of my hands and the soles of my feet. Strange that I hadn't noticed the exits in my palms before.

Stranger still, there was another pathway to my head. It began on the left side of my core and traveled behind my left eye, then curved back down behind my right eye and traveled back to my core. Unlike the other channels, it didn't seem to have an exit.

"Alright, I know where my channels are now, but there's one that loops through my skull," I told Yulk. "It doesn't have an exit point. Is that normal?"

"It's normal to have channels that seem to be useless. What isn't normal is to only have one, and have the rest of your channels be as straight as your skeleton," Yulk grinned.

"Right," I replied.

"Anyway, you can fire a spell out of any pathway that has an exit. The type of spell depends completely on what you're able to picture in your mind's eye. That doesn't necessarily mean you'll be able to do everything with magic, though. There has to be an actual spell for whatever magic you're trying to cast. Otherwise nothing will happen. Also, the amount of magic in your core will eventually run dry, and you won't be able to do any more spells until it regenerates."

"How does it regenerate?" I asked.

"Time. Sleeping will help it regenerate faster. So will a full stomach. Finally, there are three things that determine how much magic a spell will need. The first is your visualization. If you are having a difficult time visualizing the spell, it will cost more magic to cast. The second is complexity. The more moving parts to a spell, the more magic it will take. The third is the power of the spell. The wind spear that I cast cost a lot less magic than the one you cast," he explained.

"That makes sense," I responded.

"Good. You must be mindful of your magic reserves, even though they appear to be quite large. Running out of magic in a time of crisis could be fatal. That's how I broke my back, and I was very lucky that Nash was there."

"What happened?" I asked gently.

Yulk sighed and shifted in his seat, his grin fading into melancholy. He rubbed his chin for a time, and then his bright green eyes met mine.

"This is not a tale I tell freely. Bad for one's reputation, you understand. But since we are now brothers you should hear it. Perhaps the unfortunate events that led to my injury will end up doing some good as a lesson for you," he said. "This was back when I first became an adventurer. Five years ago or so. Nash had already been one for a year, and I ended up being the same level he was. Being tied with Nash when he had such a year long head-start served to boost my ego."

I nodded.

"I began adventuring with him. We explored the wastes, performed good deeds for other villages, and sought out challenges to test our might. I considered myself one of the strongest mages despite my level being evidence to the contrary. I believed that the reason I didn't have a higher level was because I only knew a few spells at the time, but I could use those spells more effectively than anyone else. To be fair, this was true. Even the higher level mages couldn't put as much intensity behind their attacks that I could. Where they could burn down a house, I could incinerate a forest."

He paused, tapping his finger on his staff.

"The Delver's Dungeon changes its layout somewhat frequently, spawning new monsters and treasures that support the village's economy. However, sometimes it doesn't change for a long time. This is problematic because the deeper you go into the dungeon, the stronger the monsters become. You end up getting less return for your effort."

"Right," I said.

"It was during one of these stagnant periods that Nash and I joined a party that was attempting to open a deeper area of the dungeon by defeating a boss. I was warned that this boss was difficult and resistant to magic. They wanted me to perform healing as necessary, but there was another healer in the party so I got it in my head that I would go on the offensive. You see, the other healer was Rira, a girl I quite liked. I wanted to impress her," Yulk said with a sigh. "I was foolish. The boss attacked Rira at the start of the fight and I got angry. Instead of healing her, I launched a very powerful wind spear right into its eye..."

After another pause I asked, "What happened?"

"It blinked. That was it. I had burned through all my magic, and it had resulted in a blink. The monster launched me across the dungeon into a wall, snapping my spine in several places. Our party took three other casualties before we retreated. Nash carried me out of the dungeon, and of the casualties I was the only survivor."

We sat in silence as I digested this information. Of the casualties... Rira got attacked at the start of the fight. Oh no. Yulk's expression had changed to one of deep shame. After a few moments, he stood up and walked over to the targets. I followed him.

"I am much stronger now than I was then. Magically speaking, of course," he said with a chuckle. "But magical resistance is the bane of a mage. Let me give you some context."

"Context?" I asked.

Yulk raised his left hand toward one of the statues and said, "Raeps Dniw Tsac!"

The wind that blasted from his hand was much more powerful than what had come from my attempt. The statue was immediately obscured by a cloud of dust, and when the dust settled the only part left was the legs. The brick wall had a very clear hole and the grass behind it had disappeared, leaving a trail of dirt that stretched for a few feet. I looked at the orc in shock.

"That was the level of spell I hit the boss with. Now I can launch these all day, and I can use Wind Spear at a much higher level as well. But I know that it wouldn't be enough against the monster that killed Rira and did this to me," he said.

"Oh... fuck," I managed to mutter.

"YULK! DID YOU JUST BREAK THE FUCKING RANGE AGAIN!?" came a shout behind us.

We turned to see Nash jogging up to us, looking angrier than usual. Yulk greeted him with a smile and a shrug, and I shook the shocked expression off of my face.

"Naomi will fix it," Yulk said.

"She shouldn't fucking have to!" Nash replied.

"What's the point of a range if you have to hold back?" Yulk asked.

"All sorts of things! Practicing new spells, practicing spell repetitions, there's literally tons of things you can do without breaking the damned thing!"

"Honestly, Nash. It's not like Naomi has anything better to do. Her entire job is to repair the range!"

"You should be more courteous! Her job being very specific doesn't give you the right to make it harder!"

"Umm..." I interjected.

Both orcs looked at me, shocked by the interruption. Their shocked faces gave me the courage to continue.

"Yulk was demonstrating the importance of keeping one's ego in check. The destruction was necessary to show me the level of power he had compared to my own, and he did hold back quite a bit I think."

Nash's shock turned into a glare. I maintained a straight face, not backing down but also not escalating. We remained like this for what seemed like forever, but Nash finally blinked first.

"Fine. But you're apologizing to Naomi," Nash finally said, turning back to Yulk.

"Deal. I'll buy her dinner," Yulk said with a grin.

"So. Difference in power, huh? Does that mean you're a mage, Nick?" Nash asked.

"Yeah. I've figured out how to use Wind Spear and where my magic pathways are," I said with a bit of excitement.

The excitement was due to my accomplishment and the fact that being a mage meant I wouldn't have to spar with Nash. I had been dreading the thought of fighting the giant orc, even if it wasn't a serious fight. One slap from him would probably end me.

"How about we check to see your martial prowess?" Nash asked.

"What?" I asked.

"Yulk said that you might be able to do both."

"Indeed," Yulk replied. "Your build suggests a certain level of physical combat ability. Only one way to find out!"

I felt the blood drain from my face as my orc brothers both began to grin at me.

Chapter 8

Nick Smith
Adventurer Level: N/A
Human - American

"This is the arena," Nash said, gesturing around him.

When Nash had mentioned where we were going I had expected something shaped like the Colosseum. Instead, it was a dirt patch encircled within a wooden fence. Leaning on the fence were a few orcs who were interested in what we were doing. Great, now I'm going to get my ass kicked in front of an audience.

"I think we should begin unarmed, just in case," Yulk said with his trademark grin. "If he does well, we can move on to practice weapons."

"I agree. Alright, Nick, take a stance. I'm going to try to hit you. You can either dodge or counter-attack," Nash said, widening his stance. "Ready?"

"No," I stated flatly.

"Too bad. BEGIN!"

I dropped into the karate stance I was familiar with and Nash rushed forward. He threw a punch, but as he began to move his fist to my face it slowed down. Even so, I barely managed to move out of the way. The wind from his punch made me blink.

"Good -*Time Dilation unlocked*- job. You managed to dodge. That's promising," Nash said.

"What did you say?" I asked, rubbing my ears.

"What, have you gone deaf? I didn't even hit you," he replied.

"No, no I... I don't know. I thought I heard something."

"Doesn't matter, let's go again. Try to counterattack this time. Don't hold back, it's not like you can hurt me," he said with a laugh.

"Famous last words," Yulk muttered with a smirk.

Nash glared at Yulk for a moment and then turned back to me. He dropped into his stance, and the moment I did the same he rushed forward. As he threw his punch, time slowed down again. I fought my urge jump out of the way and instead moved my head to the side to avoid the blow. Then I threw a punch of my own.

I meant to hit him in his solar plexus, but my fist went slightly lower. It was as if it were moving by itself. I connected and felt his body tense up as if I had struck his diaphragm, but he rushed past me instead of doubling over.

-Breathtaker Strike unlocked-

What the fuck was that? A voice? No. More like... static in headphones when you have them too loud. Just behind the music. I should ask Nash about it. I turned to him and paused. He was standing up, but rigid and unmoving.

"Nash? You okay?" Yulk asked with a shit-eating grin. "Nick didn't hurt you, right? Cuz you're too big and strong, right?"

Nash glared daggers at Yulk and opened his mouth to

retort, but the only sound that escaped was a groan. He snapped his mouth shut and doubled over, placing his hands on his knees to steady himself. Then he began gasping for air. Yulk and the onlookers began laughing uncontrollably. After a few moments, Nash sat down and looked at me with a mixture of anger and confusion.

"What in the HELL was that?" he asked.

"I... I don't know. I think it was called a breathtaker strike," I answered, remember what the distorted voice thingy had said.

"Well, it definitely did that," Nash said as he stood back up. "Okay, I'll admit, you're not bad with hand to hand. When did you learn how to do that?"

"I took karate. I used it more for working out than actual fighting, though."

"Kuh ra teh? You ever heard of that skill, Yulk?" Nash asked, glaring at the still laughing sorcerer.

"No," Yulk said between laughs. "I haven't. Probably something from his world, but maybe an unarmed specialist would know more."

"It's not a skill. Well, not what you mean by skill," I interrupted. "With karate, there's a chance to do it wrong. But when I went to hit you, I thought your solar plexus was higher up but my hand... moved on its own to where it actually is."

"Yeah, that's how skills work. The skill will only activate when the circumstances are right for it to be able to do its thing," Nash explained. "So the name of that skill is karate, huh?"

"No, the skill's called breathtaker strike. Karate is a form of martial art. Like, a style of fighting," I explained to their blank faces.

"Right. Well, never-mind the jargon, you've got both magical and martial prowess," Yulk said with what was quickly becoming a trademark grin.

"I dunno, magicians also have some hand-to-hand combat skills," Nash tapped his chin. "Let's try you out with a sword."

"A sword? Surely a spear would be better?" Yulk asked.

"A spear is too easy to learn. If we really want to know what he can do, we should see if he is able to unlock any sword skills," Nash explained as he grabbed two wooden swords and tossed one to me.

"I'm fine with that," I said as I caught the practice sword.

"You really shouldn't be," Yulk warned. "I fear that Nash is trying to get back at you for embarrassing him."

Nash grinned widely at me as I took my stance and immediately disappeared from view, leaving only a small cloud of dust in his wake. I panicked and rolled forward, barely managing to avoid the blow that would have... hit me directly on the ass. I glared at Nash as I regained my stance. I swung wildly at him, but he deflected my blow with ease and danced back with a laugh.

I tried to remember something that could help me land a blow, but nothing came to mind. I'd seen plenty of movies with sword fights, but I knew better than to think that those were accurate portrayals. Nash charged at me and swung hard, but I managed to block it and lock blades with him. His smile widened as he grabbed the end of his blade and used the additional leverage to shove me back several feet.

"Hey! That's cheating! You can't grab the blade," I shouted.

"Why not?" He asked, confused.

"Because if it were a real sword, you'd cut yourself!"

I had said it loud enough that every orc watching had heard me. After a second of stunned silence, they all began to laugh at me. I looked at Yulk, Nash, and the onlookers trying to figure out why they were laughing so hard. Nash was laughing so hard that he was doubled over, and I briefly considered smacking him upside the head.

"This is your first time fighting with a sword, isn't it?" Nash finally settled down enough to ask.

"Yeah..."

"Well, you can grab a blade without cutting yourself. The trick is to make sure you don't drag your hand along the sharp bit. How else are you to use the pommel?" He asked with a chuckle.

I looked at the hilt of my sword and saw that it did indeed have a round bulb at the bottom.

"I... I thought this bit was to make sure your hand doesn't slip," I said.

"No, it's to bash armor. Like a mace," Nash explained, demonstrating a swing while holding the blade. "The secret to sword fighting is knowing how you CAN hold your weapon, not how you SHOULD hold it. Whatever grip works is the one you should use in any given situation."

"I see."

"Let's go again!" he shouted as he charged me.

I managed to duck his swing and went for a stab to his midriff. He spun to avoid the stab and GRABBED MY GODDAMNED BLADE!

"OH COME THE FUCK ON!" I shouted.

He grinned as he pointed the tip of his sword at my face. I pulled hard on my sword but it didn't budge, and then I felt the tip of his sword poke me in the forehead. I sighed as the orcs once again laughed at my efforts. I began to get frustrated as Nash pushed me back and gestured for me to try again.

Again and again he outwitted and outmaneuvered me, but I was learning. The tricks he was using weren't going to work twice. Then I felt... something. Is this what they call an opening? I knew what to do, how to hold my sword, where to put my feet, and how fast to move. I pushed myself as fast as I could, and I was finally able to put the tip of my sword on his chest.

-Dash unlocked-

"Well would you look at that," Nash said with a look of shock.

"Was that the Dash skill?" Yulk asked.

"I think so," I answered.

"Ha! He DOES have martial and magic prowess after all!" Yulk said excitedly. "That's really rare, you know."

"It sure is," Nash added. "Well, for us, anyway. For all we know all 'humans' are able to use both magic and martial skills. Although, the only way to find out for sure is to find more humans and ask them."

"Speaking of which, are we able to go into the dungeon?" I asked.

"No," both orcs replied in unison.

I was stunned by the rapid and uniform response for a moment. The brothers looked at each other and then back to me. Nash squatted down to my height to make eye contact. I suppose he was trying to relate, but it felt infantilizing.

"There are a lot of things we need to do before you're able to go into the dungeon, Nick. First we need to register you with the adventurer's guild to see what level you are. Then we'd need to train you up a bit more. Getting a sucker punch in on me is impressive in a way, but there's many things in the dungeon that your... breathtaker strike won't work on."

"Indeed. It would be better to start you off with the wastes. The monsters there can be tough at times, but it's much easier to get away from them than it is to escape the ones in the dungeon," Yulk explained.

I opened my mouth to protest before I realized that I was about to act like the young punks in movies that cause trouble for everyone by not realizing their very obvious limitations. I closed my mouth and nodded sullenly instead. I don't know how time passes in this world in relation to mine, but if I rush things and end up dying then I won't get to see Cass again. Even if I were to reincarnate again, what would be the odds of ending up back on my world in my body?

"That being said, you've met the chief and been adopted into Clan Alta. There really isn't anything stopping us from registering you as an adventurer right now," Yulk said while tapping his chin.

"Yeah, chief probably can't get mad at us for getting our brother registered, right?" Nash asked.

"True. I don't recall anyone having to get permission from the chief before," Yulk grinned as he stood. "Let's go."

"Are y'all talkin' about registering that thing with the guild?" One of orcs shouted.

"What about it?" Nash replied.

"The guild rep's out right now. Family trouble. She'll be back in a week or two. It'll have to either wait or register as freelance."

Both Yulk and Nash winced at this. It seems that the thought of registering as a freelancer didn't sit well with them. They mumbled to each other for a bit and then turned to look at me with grim faces.

"We're gonna have to wait," Nash stated.

"What? Why? What's so bad about being a freelancer?" I demanded.

"Being a freelancer isn't bad," Yulk said as he placed a hand on my shoulder. "It's terrible. The various organizations that allow registration as an adventurer all have one thing in common. They're employee operated. When you join a guild, union, militia, or whatever other name the organization goes by you are working for and with your fellow adventurers. When you register as a freelancer, you are working directly for your customers."

"That's how it is back home," I explained. "That's not so bad, you know."

"No, you don't understand," Nash said, crossing his arms. "When you're with an org you get access to benefits like healers, days off, mental health checks, specialized equipment for jobs, and all sorts of things that make adventuring bearable. Even if you're a member of a nation's military you're taken care of to some extent. But when you're a freelancer, you have to pay for those benefits on an individual basis. You have to buy your own gear and pay for its maintenance. You can only take days off if you've worked long enough to be able to eat the next few days. To top it off you only make about half what other adventurers make, if you can even find work at all."

"He's right, Nick. Usually, if someone goes freelance it's because they've committed a crime that has resulted in being barred from org membership," Yulk squeezed my shoulder a little. "On top of that, the most frequent customers of freelancers are those whose jobs have been rejected by orgs. Usually because the customer can't pay a fair price for the work, or the work is illegal. You want to go into the dungeon, right?"

"Yes, as soon as possible," I answered.

"Well there you have it. Entering the dungeon simply won't be possible as a freelancer. Guilds don't work with freelancers as a rule, and even the chief would be hard-pressed to convince them to allow you to tag along. If Nash and I were able to get permission to enter, we wouldn't be able to bring you along without getting censured."

"And getting censured sucks," Nash added. "Very bad for your career."

I sighed at the prospect of waiting two weeks before being able to register as an adventurer. I had hoped that I could register as a freelancer and then join a guild, but not only does that sound impossible, it sounds like it wouldn't speed things up at all.

"So what do I do?" I raised my hands in a shrug.

"You train," Nash said. "Magic and martial in equal portions. We'll work on figuring out which weapons you'll be best at, and unlocking new spells for you to cast."

Great, more training with Nash.

Chapter 9

High Chief Ulurmak
Adventurer Level: N/A
Orc - Kirkenian

I gazed longingly out of my window at the mountains in the distance, a wall of gigantic snow-capped teeth separating the orcish high-chiefdom of Kirkena from the elven kingdom of Bolisir. As a youth I would trek those very mountains, hunting dangerous game and living in the rough. It was the best childhood the son of a High Chief could ask for, and my father had given it to me gladly. Mostly because he couldn't stand children, but also because he wanted me to be strong enough to take his place.

My gaze returned to the mountain of paperwork upon my desk. A much more difficult climb, with higher stakes as well. Paperwork is boring, but if it's done wrong or delayed many can suffer. I envy the chiefs of small villages, who rarely have to do any paperwork at all. Although they have to listen to complaints in person rather than reading a strongly worded letter, so we'll call it a draw.

A knock on my door alerted me to Rayzun's presence. One of many aids that help me keep things running.

I glanced at him and he said, "Sir, you've received a missive from Emperor Jak, Slayer of Demons, Savior of Dwarves, Destroyer of..."

"Yes, yes. Jak has many impressive and lengthy titles. A missive, eh? He finally figured out that I can read, then?" I asked with a chuckle.

"Looks that way, High Chief."

Rayzun gave me the envelope containing the missive, and I felt a tinge of dread as I noted its thickness. I broke the wax seal with a claw and pulled the contents out into the light. Twenty pages.

"Gods damn it, this had better not be about that damned mine or I'm gonna declare war, I swear!" I roared.

"Sir, it's almost definitely about the mine. You've been ignoring his requests regarding it for years," Rayzun said calmingly.

I turned to glare at him, "That's because he wants us to let his people mine the metal while giving us a percentage of the metal as a 'tax'. Considering that it is our mine and we know HOW to mine, I see no reason to pay him any heed!"

"C'mon sir, you know his people can mine better than we can. Most of our miners think that the dwarves will be able to pull more metal out than we can, too. Might end up with more as tax than we would doin' it ourselves."

"Is that right?" I said sarcastically. "And we might as well let the damned elves construct our buildings and the fucking gnomes run our economy, right? And what's left for us, eh? Dungeon running? Scavenging the wastes? And what do we do if the drow decide that they need to lengthen their border? Hmm? Will we be able to rely on the dwarves, elves, or gnomes to come to our aid?"

"No, sir," Rayzun stated with the attitude of someone dealing with a toddler.

"Exactly. If he wants to be involved in the mine he can

teach our miners how to do it," I grumbled as an idea popped into my head. "Wait, that's not a bad idea. We can offer to hire his dwarves as supervisors and trainers, and give them a much smaller percentage... Have Palo meet with the miner's guild and come up with some numbers. Then have a missive drawn up in reply to whatever this garbage says."

"Yes, High Chief," Rayzun nodded as he left.

I nearly threw the missive across the room, but decided that I had better check it first. It was too polite to have been written by Jak, like most dwarves he can't help but curse constantly. I chuckled at all the titles they had for me, it felt good to be recognized even if it was just for flattery. The actual content of the missive was indeed about the mines, but it also contained a warning regarding the drow. They were performing military maneuvers again. I'd have to increase our presence on that border.

I made a note to include a gratuity to Jak for the information. Despite how annoyed we are at each other, our people are friends and what impacts us impacts them. The drow taking a bite out of us means less trade for them, and a higher risk of the drow taking a bite out of them as well. Unfortunately, that doesn't mean they'll fight them with us.

The dwarven empire of Calkuti was more into manufacturing than they were into warfare. There were other dwarven kingdoms that were more focused on warfare, but THOSE kingdoms didn't have an orcish high-chiefdom as their neighbor. If they did, their tune would likely change pretty quickly.

Well, so long as those orcs were fight-focused. There's plenty who aren't. My grandfather is considered one of the most peaceful mer to have ever lived. Actually, come to think of it, he might have been able to convince those kings to become peaceful just by his example alone. I chuckled at the thought, and another knock shook my door.

"What is it?" I demanded.

"High Chief, there's a messenger from Nuleva," Rayzun said breathlessly, as if he'd ran back here. "You're going to want to hear this in person."

Nuleva? The name was familiar, but from where? One of mine? Would have to be a small settlement then... Oh, don't tell me that one of the chiefs was dumb enough to make a village on the drow border!

Rayzun noticed my confusion and explained, "Nuleva is the village we installed at the entrance to the Delver's Dungeon."

"Oh? What do they want?" I asked.

My question was met with a look of exasperation. I returned the look with a glare, but Rayzun is as stubborn as a pregnant fat-horns. It occurred to me that we were both somewhat in the wrong.

"Fine, fair enough. Bring them in," I relented.

Rayzun turned to the outside of the door and gestured to someone out of view, then fully entered the room. A minute later a monstrous orc in darkened full-plate entered and knelt. It took me a second to recognize him. Alurn, son of Agurno. My nephew!

Alurn took a moment before finally saying, "Greetings High Chief Ulurmak, son of Grashgnaw the Giant, savior of..."

"That's enough of that Alurn," I interrupted. "My own kin shouldn't have to prostrate themselves before me. As I understand it, you have a message for me?"

"Yes, sir," Alurn said and looked up at me. "We've encountered some oddities in the Delver's Dungeon and Chief Gluhern sent me to apprise you."

I'd forgotten that Gluhern took over for his brother on the Delver Project. The thought of that hot head being a chief was enough to amuse even the most stoic orc. Unfortunately, my amusement was dashed by the stench of grief coming from Alurn. The boy who was normally cheerful and gentle was now robotic and stiff, his smile replaced by a grim expression that spoke of loss. I nodded to Rayzun, who grabbed a cushion and set it next to the boy.

"Sit and explain, Alurn. What happened?" I said gently.

"Yes sir," he replied as he sat cross-legged on the cushion. "A while ago a wall collapsed in the dungeon, revealing a previously hidden passage..."

He explained at length about what had happened, and with every sentence my concern grew. A sentient thing called a human had been found and removed from the dungeon, and a boss that killed two over-tens had been encountered. Gluhern's plan to seal the passage to the boss was a sound one, but it might be a stop-gap. Especially since it sounded like the dungeon had already shifted twice, and the hidden portion didn't change.

"Does Nuleva have any over-twenties?" I asked once he finished.

"No, sir. Delver's was labeled an entry-level dungeon.

The only reason that Gluhern had over-tens at his disposal was because we... we became adventurers there," Alurn said, gritting his teeth to stifle a sob.

"I'm sorry about your comrade, dear nephew. He will be avenged. If you'd like to be on the team I send, I can convince the adventurers to allow it."

"No, sir. I would only be a hindrance. That beast is my exact counter. Just like Kirisaka was."

A fool would think this to be cowardice, but I saw it for what it was. A warrior who knew he was outmatched and responsible enough not to weigh down those who would be fighting. Little Alurn had grown into a very good orc indeed.

"Rayzun, have Elizat gather a group of over-twenties who are a good match for this thing and prepare to send them to Nuleva. Alurn, you'll rest here and travel back with the group we send. Let Gluhern know that they answer directly to me, and he is to provide them with food, water, and shelter. I'll handle their pay. Understood?"

"Yes, High Chief," Alurn and Rayzun said simultaneously.

Rayzun immediately set about his new task, and Alurn rose from the cushion. He picked it up and put it back, like the responsible mer I know him to be. He then turned back to me, waiting to be dismissed.

"How's your father, boy?" I asked.

"I wouldn't know, sir. Haven't heard from him in two years," he said, finally smiling.

I grinned back. Agurno, my little brother, was

legendarily aloof. He cared but didn't know how to show it, and simply decided it would be best if he didn't. Alurn's not his only child, but since his mother has been patient enough to handle the long disappearances he's the one who's seen the most of his father's love. Which is probably why the boy couldn't resist chuckling at his father's foibles.

"Well, that's good news then. If something had happened, it would have been heard across the entire continent!"

We both laughed at the truth of that statement. Agurno had become an adventurer instead of a chief, and quickly showed onlookers why it isn't fair for someone of my bloodline to become one. His last big fight had been against a corrupted high dragon, and it had left scars in the landscape that still haven't healed. Even his son was a powerhouse, and was one of the youngest over-tens in history. If Alurn had turned out to be a bit faster, that monster in Delver's wouldn't have stood a chance.

We discussed the rest of Alurn's family, and how his career had been going. He recounted tales of fights in the wastes against gigantic beasts, and funny stories involving his comrades. Then we discussed how the nation was faring, and I was careful not to go into too much detail regarding the troubles with the drow. Finally, our conversation came to a close.

"I think I'll head to the chow hall. I've missed the fat-horn steak you have here," Alurn said with a chuckle.

"Right," I replied with a chuckle. "Oh, and Alurn, I understand that the human has been adopted into the Alta family, but I'd still like to know more about it. I don't mind how this happens, whether it be an informal interrogation or if we arrange a meeting. But

I don't like mysteries."

"Yes, High Chief. I'll do what I can," Alurn nodded and left.

I rested my chin on my hand as I thought about the future of our nation. Was this human a good omen or a bad one? The latter seemed somewhat likely, considering what else had been found in that secret passage. I was distracted by this line of thought until my eyes once again rested on the mountain of paperwork on my desk.

Damn. Well, back to work.

Chapter 10

Nick Smith
Adventurer Level: N/A
Human - American

I gazed up at the lovely afternoon sky and sighed. The sun, which was shining brightly as if it were content with its existence, was floating in a sea of light blue. Puffy little clouds slowly floated by without a single care in the world.

I, on the other hand, was looking up at the sky because Nash had once again planted me firmly upon my back. I heard him jump and quickly rolled. His axe buried itself into the ground where I had just been. Wooden or not, that would have hurt.

I got back to my feet and time slowed down once again. He's open, and I'm mad. I activated slide slash and raked my sword directly across his exposed midriff, just under his belly button. I felt elation at my victory, and then a fist slamming into my forehead.

Darkness clouded my vision and I blinked a few times to clear it. Once again, I found myself involuntarily cloud-watching. It occurred to me that this was becoming a very familiar sight. I sighed as I got back onto my feet.

"I think that'll about do it," Nash said, holding his stomach. "You're getting better. Slowly but surely."

"It's going pretty quick to me!" Yulk shouted from the edge of the arena. "It's only been a couple weeks and he's already able to land a killing blow on you!"

"True, but that's due to his skills rather than his skill,"

Nash nodded sagely. Once he saw our dumbfounded expressions he clarified, "I mean that his knowledge of fighting is low, but his skills themselves are decent. Especially that Time Diminution skill."

"Time Dilation," I corrected. "But you're right, I need more practice."

We had spent the last two weeks trying to unlock more skills, and so far we'd been able to get three. Dash, Power Slash, and Slide Slash. Yulk and I had also been working on magic, which had led to me getting better at hearing that strange muffled voice as well. It announced whenever a skill had been unlocked, and my brothers had no idea what it could be. Neither of them had ever heard anything like it.

They'd both been somewhat concerned when I brought it up, but they seemed to get over that concern when I revealed the latest development. Whenever I thought hard about which skills I had, a list of them would appear in a semi-transparent rectangular box. When I thought about a specific skill it would open another box with a brief explanation of the skill. I thought of the Time Dilation skill and the explanation popped up almost immediately.

--

Time Dilation I

Increases the user's speed to 150% for a very limited time.

Cooldown: 5 minutes

--

"Hey, Nash, do skills level up?" I asked.

"Level up? Not that I know of. You get better at using them the more you use them, though. Like your muscles or your brain," he answered, pointing at his head.

"It's just... when I check the status of my skills some of them have a number one at the end of them," I said as Yulk walked up to us.

"Which implies that the number might get larger if the right circumstances are met," Yulk interjected. "Very interesting. Which skills are you speaking of?"

I pulled up my list of skills and listed off the ones with a number, "Time Dilation, Fireball, Dash, Earthen Dagger, Wind Spear, and Heal."

"Interesting," Yulk said.

"Well with Dash, the more you use it the farther and faster you can go," Nash pointed out. "Maybe it's tracking your progress or something."

"Yes, I think that's it," Yulk agreed. "Fireball, Earthen Dagger, and Heal are similar. The more you heal people the better you get at it, the more you use fireball the bigger and hotter it can get, and the more you use earthen dagger the deadlier the blade that forms."

"Well I'm still worried that nobody else seems to have anything like this," I said.

My brothers looked at each other and back to me as if they didn't hear me properly. Then they started laughing uproariously. I waited for them to stop, but they kept going until tears came out of their eyes. Nash fell to the floor and started rolling. Yulk fell to his knees. After a few more moments I lost my temper.

"WHAT THE HELL IS SO FUNNY?" I demanded.

"Oh, oh no, I'm gonna die," Yulk said between laughs.

"He says he's WORRIED!" Nash shouted before falling into another laughing fit.

"IT'S A VALID CONCERN!" I shouted, making them laugh even harder.

I crossed my arms and waited for them to finally collect themselves. Once they were done laughing and had got back up off the ground, I glared at them. They wiped their tears and patted the dirt off of themselves and turned back to me.

"When you first mentioned the voice talkin' to you I thought you might be crazy," Nash said.

"Same, actually. Hearing non-existent voices is a sure sign of madness. But then you mentioned seeing the box thingies and I knew it had to be something else. Madness takes advantage of what you know, it can't show you things that you don't know," Yulk explained.

"Yeah but what if it's..."

"What if it's what? A trap? What the hell is there to worry about," Nash laughed again. "If it's a trap you're boned, boy. It's already taken hold, so the only thing to do is lean into it and hope for the best."

"He's right. It's a useful tool. Worrying about it is like worrying about having a whittling blade," Yulk chuckled. "Oh no, what if I cut my finger?!"

"Well what if someone else finds out and tries to take

it or something?" I asked.

"Then we kill them," Nash said flatly. "Or they kill us. No different than any other situation, really."

"Indeed. There's always someone willing to take something you own. To worry about owning it would result in owning nothing," Yulk nodded.

"Well what if they kill you two and capture me to use as a lab rat?"

"Easier said than done, but in that case just make yourself uncapturable," Nash sneered.

"How?" I pleaded.

"Fight them with every breath and don't pull your punches. Make it clear that either they kill you or you kill them," he explained.

"And even if they do manage to capture you through some sort of trickery, attack them every chance you get. Make certain that they have to constantly be on their toes. It'll exhaust them eventually. Then you avenge us or join us," Yulk grinned.

Before I could continue arguing I noticed one of the orc bystanders waving to get our attention. The size of our audience had grown a lot in the last two weeks, and Nash had even received requests to host our training sessions at certain times of the day. Of course, he ignored these requests and simply said that training happens when it happens.

I pointed out the bystander to my brothers, and they started waving us over. Wanting a break from training with Nash, I started walking over immediately. As I got closer I noticed that the waving orc was actually

Irana, the local blacksmith. Unlike most of the orc women, Irana was always fully clothed. Probably due to her profession, but it's an awkward thing to ask so I don't know for sure.

She gave me a wide grin as I approached.

"Hey Nick! I've got you a present!" she exclaimed.

She held out an object wrapped up in brown cloth. There was quiet metallic clank as I took the gift. It was about the length of my arm. Just looking at it I thought it must be a mace, but then I noticed a small curve on one end. Excited, I unwrapped the gift and grinned when I held up the sword.

It was a cutlass, like the kind that pirates use in the movies. The scabbard was made of blackened leather with brass fittings on both ends. The brass on the entrance to the scabbard had a skull and intersecting sabers, and on the other end it had crossed daggers. The hand guard and hilt were also made of brass, and the hand guard featured a nude woman blowing clouds from her mouth and a ship's rigging behind her. The spaces between rope and cloud were actually carved through, and the edges of these holes were sharpened.

"Thank you! This is amazing. What's the occasion?" I asked, awestruck.

"It's a thank you for the entertainment that you've given us for the last couple of weeks. Watching you fight Nash and sling spells on my breaks has been great," she explained, with a murmur of agreement coming from the crowd.

"Well that's out of character for you," Nash grumbled. "What happened to the miserly Irana we all know?"

"Oh, I'm still miserly," she grinned. "This cutlass was commissioned by an elf but he failed to pay in full. There's not a lot of call for cutlasses with half-basket guards around these parts. I'd have to travel to a coastal city to be able to sell it, but it's not worth it to travel that far to sell one blade. So I figured I'd free up the inventory space, show my gratitude, and give Nick one hell of a starting weapon. Win-win-win."

"Yeah, and I'm sure it has nothing to do with currying favor with a new adventurer so that he prefers your shop over the much more reasonably priced shops in the village," Nash said.

"You're confusing reasonably priced with cheap. The other shops get their blades from random places and people, I make my own and they're much better than anything you'll find at those shops," she shot back. "But I can't expect someone whose intellect is rivaled by rocks to understand something like..."

As they argued, I unsheathed the blade to have a look at it. The steel gleamed in the sunlight, and even with my uneducated eyes I could tell it was well made. I turned around and gave it a few practice swings, grinning like an idiot at the swooshing sound it produced. It made me feel ready to take on anything.

"Well?" Yulk asked over the sounds of Nash and Irana arguing.

"I like it," I replied, practicing a punch with the hand guard. "It's a really good sword."

"Good to hear," Yulk grinned. "I heard that the guild lady's back. You want to go get registered?"

"Yes," I said, sheathing my sword.

"Well, let's go," Yulk said in a whisper. "If we hurry, Nash won't even notice we're gone."

"Yes I fucking will," Nash growled. "Where are we going?"

"To the adventurer's guild to get me registered," I answered.

"Fine," Nash said, with Irana giving him a smug look.

"Oh, wait, hold on. You'll be wanting to see the chief before you get registered," Irana interrupted.

"We don't require his permission to get Nick registered. He's officially part of the Alta clan now," Nash argued.

"You thick fuck, just because you don't have to doesn't mean you don't have to. Or would you rather Nick have difficulty finding a first job because Gluhern's pissed at you?" she crossed her arms. "Or maybe you'd rather that first job be hunting giant rats?"

"Oh no," I whispered. "Why's it always rats?"

"Huh?" Nash asked with a degree of hostility in his voice.

"Nothing," I quickly replied, knowing he wouldn't get the joke. "Let's go see the chief. There's no harm in it, right?"

Nash actually growled and turned away from the conversation. Losing two arguments in a row against Irana had to be bad for his ego. It was certainly bad for his mood. We all quietly decided to give him a few moments to calm down.

"FINE," he finally shouted. "Fuck it, let's go see the chief."

And so we did. We still got stares along the way, but some of those stares were followed by a wave. I hadn't exactly been a social butterfly, but getting dragged around by Nash and Yulk had resulted in making a few new friends. Like Irana the blacksmith, Korno the chef, and Multova the merchant.

When we finally got to the chief's chambers we were told we couldn't go in immediately. Yulk and Nash shared a look of concern with each other. After ten minutes or so an orc rushed out without even looking at us. He was wearing a bright green bandanna around his neck with two horses rearing away from each other on the back. He was followed by Alurn, who gave us a nod as he passed. We were then ushered in to see the chief.

"Ah, the diabolical duo seems to have transformed into the troublesome trio. Very good timing as well, but we'll get to that. What brings you here?" Chief Gluhern asked.

"We wanna register Nick with the adventurer's guild," Nash answered. "Irana told us to see you first."

Gluhern chuckled, "Well, well, well. Isn't this a remarkable coincidence? I was right about to send for you regarding this very issue."

"You want Nick to register as an adventurer because High Chief wants you to arrange a meeting between himself and Nick?" Yulk asked, ducking a thrown goblet.

"DON'T SPOIL MY REVEALS, SORCERER!" Gluhern

shouted.

"Why would I have to register as an adventurer to see the High Chief?" I hesitantly asked.

"A bunch of reasons," Nash explained. "There are routes which shave weeks off of your travel time that civilians aren't allowed to use because they're dangerous. Most of the adventuring organizations can grant permits to travel these roads thanks to negotiations between them and the various governments."

"That's the main reason, but there's also a political aspect. Ulurmak is curious about you and wants to meet you. But that's not something that a High Chief does," Gluhern added. "It could be seen as an indulgence. Most of the Great Chiefs wouldn't care, but there are those who would use it to frame High Chief Ulurmak as a lay-about."

"Ah, that's true too," Yulk nodded. "Though it would be unlikely to result in rebellion. It would be more likely that Ulurmak would have to grant concessions."

"Okay, I understand," I said. "But can I check out the dungeon before seeing the High Chief?"

Nash and Yulk turned to give me a look. The kind of look one gives a child who is trying to run before they can crawl.

"Actually, that was the plan," Gluhern said.

My brother's heads snapped around to look at the chief in shock. Nash started to object but Gluhern held up a hand to stop him.

"Things are getting weird with the new dungeon area.

The dungeon has shifted a total of three times since the boss has been encountered, but the hidden area and its entrance remain unchanged. We were hoping that the barrier would be able to contain the threat until the dungeon gets rid of it naturally, but that doesn't seem to be happening," Gluhern sighed. "High Chief Ulurmak is sending a team of over-twenties to investigate the phenomena and destroy the boss."

"Over-twenties?" Yulk whistled softly.

"Yes. And it would be better if they could take Nick along when they perform their initial investigation. There might be things he can shed light on. I'd rather he not take part in the fight, though," Gluhern said. "This isn't a time-sensitive mission, so it should be fine if you accompany them. Actually, Nash, you definitely should. You'd be able to help guide them to where you found Nick, right?"

"Yeah, probably," Nash admitted.

"Good, hopefully this will shed some light on..."

The orcs continued discussing the plan but I zoned out because of the blood rushing to my head. Here it was, the chance to find out more about what the hell happened to me. Even a hint might put me on the path to getting home. My mind was flooded with excitement at the possibility, and dread at the thought of finding nothing.

"And I'll grab some charcoal and paper to do rubbings just in case. When are we setting out?" Yulk asked.

"One of the over-twenties has already arrived. The rest should be here within the next couple of days, so you'll be entering the dungeon by the end of the week," Gluhern answered. "That should give you plenty of time to prepare. We're not expecting any danger, but..."

"Better safe than sorry," Nash nodded. "Understood, chief. Alright Nick, let's go get you registered as an adventurer."

Finally.

Chapter 11

Nash Alta
Adventurer Level: 8
Orc - Nulevan

The Adventurer's Guild. It's hosted within a very plain looking gray bricked building here in Nuleva, but I'd heard that elsewhere the buildings get very fancy. It's said that in one of the gnomish countries their buildings are made of solid gold, but I don't know if I believe that. What's to stop people from shaving bits off when nobody's looking?

Although, as one of the largest multi-national organizations in the world, the Adventurer's Guild could probably afford to replace the shaved bits of their buildings. It's still hard to imagine that they have ultra-luxurious buildings when faced with how mundane their branch in Nuleva is, though.

Things look just as plain on the inside as they do on the outside. I'd expected Nick to be underwhelmed, but his typically stoic face appeared enamored with every little detail surrounding us. The quest board, surrounded by adventurers looking for a good job to match their skills. The gathering area, where you can grab a bite to eat or a pint to drink before setting off. You normally wouldn't eat here after a job, because there are better places to eat in the village. I personally prefer Korno's Fried Food over what the Adventurer's Guild has on offer.

Nick seemed particularly interested in the Trader pit, where an adventuring party was selling loot they'd gotten from a dungeon dive. We'd already explained to Nick that you can buy and sell stuff at the guild when he was being fussy about turning freelancer, but seeing is believing I suppose. The pit's where I bought my axe.

"Hi there!" Nima greeted us. "How can I help you?"

"Hi Nima," Yulk said. "We'd like to register Nick as an adventurer."

"Oh, you're the human, aren't you?" she asked.

Nick stammered an affirmative. Most of the people that frequent Nuleva are used to seeing Nima around, so it took me a second to realize what had the boy nervous. Then I realized that he didn't have anything NOT to be nervous about. Nima is notable for her beauty, wears barely anything, and above all else is seven feet tall. Heh, above all else.

Orc women don't typically get as tall as our men do, but Nima is related to Alurn so I guess it makes sense. That whole family is huge. If I remember right, she's his half-sister but they're not close. Alurn's dad ran off on Nima's mom or something. Considering how similar Nima and her mom look, I can't even begin to fathom why he would run off.

"Alright, so we'll have you fill out some forms and then we'll get you connected to the Curaguard to determine your level. Then we'll do your newbie brief," she explained.

"O-okay," came Nick's suave reply.

I couldn't help but grin. From Nick's height there was no way to maintain proper eye contact and avoid staring at Nima's head-sized breasts. Instead, he was staring firmly at the counter like a well-trained pupper trying to avoid gazing longingly at their owner's food. Most of the other races have difficulty not staring, and

I suppose humans are no different.

My amusement was cut short when I realized that I might have to have an awkward conversation with the boy about orc sexual compatibility. Namely, the lack thereof. Maybe I can pawn it off on Yulk. He's much more open about such discussions and would probably be better at it. I glanced at him, but he was studying Nick with a slightly confused look on his face. Oh, right... he's a dunce when it comes to sexuality. Shit.

"Here you go!" Nima said as she set a packet on the counter. "There are pencils at the table over there. Fill these out and bring them back, okay?"

"Y-yeah. Thank you," Nick stammered.

Nima and I made eye contact and she smiled knowingly. I grinned in response as we turned to head to the gathering area. She had previously made it clear that she likes me, but I wasn't ready to commit just yet. I don't have the finances to give her the life she deserves.

Instead, we'd made a deal that when I get to level ten we'd try dating and see where things went. When you hit level ten you get access to better paying jobs and fifty percent of the retail value of the goods you sell, which would give me enough money to support mom and properly court Nima. We'd made this deal last year when I was only level six, and I'd been grinding hard ever since.

"I... um..." Nick said as we got to one of the tables. "I can't read this."

"What?" I asked.

"I don't understand this writing," he clarified.

"But you speak perfect Orcish, how are you unable to read it?" I demanded.

"Probably the same way you can't," Yulk said, causing me to flinch. "This is something that I've been thinking about, though. Why is it that you can speak Orcish, Nick?"

"I'm not, I'm speaking English," Nick replied. "I thought you were speaking English. What the hell is going on?"

That's what I would like to know. English? I'd never heard of English. Must be a language from his world or whatever. But in this world, there are only eight languages. Orcish, Elvish, Daimun, Drow, Drakon, Dwarven, Gnomish, and Anyelish. They're all similar enough that it's easy to learn to speak and understand them.

Yulk taught me how to speak them when he got back from schooling around. It was pretty fun until we got to the writing part. I can't seem to wrap my head around letters and words, no matter what language they're in. Don't have that problem with math, though. Numbers are nice.

"Maybe it's a skill?" Yulk ventured.

"It's not on my skill list, though," Nick said.

"Hmm," Yulk pondered for a moment. "Is your skill list ability listed on your skill list?"

"No..."

"Then maybe whatever is allowing you to see your skill list is also automatically translating what you hear and say."

"Yeah, yeah," I interrupted impatiently. "You might be able to speak all the languages. Congrats, whatever. Problem is, you can't read them. Have Yulk fill out the forms for you like he did for me."

The two of them looked at me with blank expressions, as if they hadn't already thought of that solution and were surprised that I was the one that came up with it. I crossed my arms and glared back at them.

"What the hell are you lookin' at? You didn't think of that?" I demanded. "I'm supposed to be the dumb one. We're gonna be in real trouble if it turns out that I'm the smartest of the three of us."

"Fair enough," Yulk replied. "But I'll have you know that dumb means you're not able to talk. So just by the merit of being able to yell at us, you're not..."

"Whatever," I interrupted. "Just get the fuckin' forms filled out."

Yulk grinned at me and grabbed the forms from Nick. He began reading aloud as I sat down next to them. The questionnaire portion went by fairly easily, except for a couple of parts. We had to add our own answer to "species" and there was some confusion when it came to the "race" part.

Turns out that Nick's world had a different definition of race than ours, so Yulk explained that your race was based off of where your parents are based. So Nick is an "American Human", his children would also be American Humans, but his grandchildren would be Nulevan Humans. Assuming he found other humans and had children, and those children stuck around Nuleva.

Yulk began to explain the various reason's why one's race was accounted for and I zoned out. International diversity treaties and bans are boring. Instead, I thought about what life would be like with Nima. We'd date for a year or two then have a nice year-long engagement followed by a wedding, if all went well.

I've even planned out our first date. I'll come by with a gift, a nice sixteen inch engraved hunting knife, and take her out to dinner at Korno's. Then we'll swing by the training arena and watch people spar until the sun goes down, and to wrap up the date we'll stargaze. If she still likes me afterward, then she'll decide what we do on the next date.

Once we get engaged we'll be moving in together. I'll probably have to knock down a wall to give us some more room in my bedroom. It'll be a pain, but we'd also get a bigger living room out of it. Well, unless her mom makes a fuss and has me move in with them instead. I don't think that'll happen, though.

"So if a guild can prove that they've hired a certain amount of Iritons, they'll get access to governmental jobs from Irita. And even bonuses!" Yulk said. "Anyways, onto the disclosures. First is the payment system. Until you're level 5 the guild will be taking a 20% commission on your jobs and giving you a 1% discount on guild related services. You also get 10% of retail for drops you sell to the guild."

"What guild related services?" Nick asked.

"Food, gear, and medical. Well, the medical that you have to pay for, at least," I replied.

"What medical stuff is free?"

"Anything life threatening. The stuff that isn't considered life threatening, like rashes or cosmetic stuff, you've gotta pay for."

"The deals get better as you level up, too," Yulk explained. "When you hit level five the commission drops down to 15% and you get a 5% discount."

"And 25% of retail on your drops," I added. "At level ten it's 10% on the commission, 10% on the discount, 50% of retail on the drops, and access to better paying jobs. Then at level 20 it gets even better. It's 5% commission, 65% of retail, a 15% discount, and no limitations on jobs. At that point if you want a job, it's yours."

"Okay, I get it now," Nick said. "But what are these jobs? I thought you just went in the dungeon and got stuff to sell."

"The jobs vary. There's jobs for going in the dungeon to find specific drops, exterminating monsters in the wastes, escorting travelers, and other things like that," I answered. "The more intense the job's expected to be, the higher the level restriction and pay is. It's not a perfect system, though, so you should be careful about which jobs you accept."

"Fetch quests are an under-five's bread and butter," Yulk added.

"So basically, the higher my level, the less they take from my pay and the more benefits I actually get," Nick said. "Alright."

"This next part's about the examinations," Yulk flapped a page. "You agree to a quarterly review of your level as well as magical, physical, and mental health. You also understand that if you are found to have a health issue you will be required to get treatment before you can accept further jobs. You have the right to decline treatment, and the right to have your level checked at any time."

"Magical health?" Nick asked.

"Yeah," I said. "Like a curse or something wrong with your core."

Yulk sorted the papers in front of Nick and said, "Alright, we're just about through them all. There's still the stuff about the International Merchant Association, other associated guilds, and..."

I stopped listening after Yulk mentioned the International Merchant Association. Woe be unto Nick if he asks a question about the IMA. Yulk will talk his weirdly round ears right off his head. Instead, I decided to check the job board. It would be a while before the over-twenties were ready to go into the dungeon, so hopefully there'd be a nice simple job to take Nick on.

I looked at the board and ignored everything without artwork on it. The pictures drawn by the auto-scribe were great. Realistic and not stylized, so you know exactly what you're lookin' at. I grabbed a few promising ones, one about false-mint, one about a tree with some fruits on it, and one regarding giant rats. I brought the three postings up to Nima.

"Hey, Nima. Yulk and Nick are still fillin' out the paperwork so I'm checkin' out the jobs. Could you read these to me?" I asked.

She looked confused for a second before remembering my issue regarding the written word, and then she looked embarrassed for forgetting. Then there was a smidge of pity in her eyes. I don't like being pitied, but when it's coming from those beautiful eyes, I guess it's alright.

"Aw, sweetie," she replied. "Of course I will. This first one is a gathering mission for false-mint from the forest depths. Fifty leaves are needed."

"Ah, the forest. North or south?"

"It doesn't specify. Just need fifty false-mint leaves from the forest."

"Okay, we might do that one. What's the next one about?"

"Gathering yipples. They want a sack full."

"Where are the yipple trees?" I scratched my neck. It had been years since I went gathering fruit.

"On the edge of the forest leading into the wastes, to the south," she answered.

"The south, that's good. Might do that one too. What about the rats?"

"Let's see... there's a pack of giant rats harassing caravans in the wastes to the south. Reports indicate there's only about a dozen, and the poster is offering two copper per pelt delivered to the guild. It's a level five and over job."

"Well that should be fine. Yulk and I are over-fives, so we can bring Nick along as a party member, right?" I asked, leaning on the counter with my most charming smile.

"Of course," she smiled back. "But you will be

censured if he gets killed or crippled, though."

"Fat chance of that," I replied. "Despite appearances, that little fucker can pack a wallop."

"What's this?" Nima asked, feigning shock. "The legendary Nash giving praise to someone? He must be pretty capable."

"Yeah, yeah. Laugh it up," I chuckled. "Don't tell him I said that, though. He'll go an' get an ego."

"My lips are sealed," she winked.

Our eyes met and we smiled. The rest of the world faded away for a moment, before Yulk's voice snapped me back to reality. I missed what he said, so I looked back to Nima. She looked confused as well, and I got a fuzzy feeling in my chest when I realized she missed it too. We'd been lost in each other's eyes.

"The forms," Yulk slowly stated. "They're done. We're ready for the examinations. What were you two up to?"

"I was accepting some jobs for us to do to pass the time. We got herb and fruit gathering with some hunting in the wastes. Shouldn't take more than a day and a half," I said quickly.

"Herbs and fruit? I thought you guys only eat meat," Nick replied.

"Well we fuckin' season it, we're not animals," I grumbled. "And anyway, these jobs weren't posted by orcs, they were posted by traders and stuff."

"Right. Well what are we hunting?" he asked.

"Giant rats out in the wastes. We're grabbing the plants on the way there."

"Why's it always fuckin' rats?" Nick grumbled under his breath.

"Hey," I countered. "This is an over-five quest. Don't underestimate giant rats. They're more than just a nuisance, they'll take down prey twice your size without a sweat. The only reason you're gonna be able to do this job is cuz Yulk and I are protecting you. Now let's get your exams done so we can head out."

"Which one would you like to start with?" Nima asked the human.

"I'd like to have my level assessed, please," he replied.

"Sure thing!" she said cheerily as she reached into a drawer behind her.

She pulled out a contraption and a metallic guild card and set them on the counter. The contraption that the guild uses to connect someone to the Curaguard is a strange lookin' thing. It's a rectangular box with six stubby legs, one on each corner and two in the middle. Each leg is made of a different metal, and the box itself looks like it's made of obsidian.

She inserted the card in a slot on the part of the box facing us and pressed her fingers into some indents on her side of the box. Blue light spilled out of the top of the box and formed a square in front of us. Then green lights shot out and entered the square, creating numbers, letters, and the palm of a hand. The light took on a mirror-like quality as it hardened, still hovering a few inches above the contraption. Then she fed the forms into the back of the box.

"Alright, please place your hand on the hand-print until you feel a slight electric shock," Nima said.

Without saying anything Nick reached out and placed his hand on the hardened light. It was a full ten seconds before Nick winced slightly and withdrew his hand. I shared a look with Yulk. This thing was usually much faster. It made some weird noises that sounded a lot like birds chirping, and then the numbers and letters changed.

Yulk and Nima looked at the letters and numbers with confusion. So did Nick and I, but that's only natural considering our inability to read the damned things. Once the two readers recovered from their confusion, their eyebrows shot up.

"What is it?" I asked, growing impatient.

"He's level five," Yulk answered in a quiet voice.

I looked at him intently trying to figure out if he was joking. When I turned to look at Nima, her expression told me he wasn't.

"Is... Is that rare?" Nick asked.

"Yeah, yeah it is," I replied. "What's his class?"

"Unknown," Nima said.

"Well that figures," I chuckled, turning to Nick. "Mine's unknown too. Has been ever since I hit level seven. Look, don't let your level get to your head. You're still inexperienced, and should follow our lead during the hunt."

"Yeah," he responded. "I will. On the bright side,

though, the quest level isn't a problem anymore."

"Smart-ass," I grumbled.

"Better to be a smart-ass than a dumb-ass," Yulk grinned. "Alright, let's get the rest of the exams out of the way."

"Yeah, go on. I'm gonna hang out here for a bit," I said.

Nima, Yulk, and Nick went to the medical portion of the guild hall while I sat at the gathering area. I stared at the three job posters. Level five, huh? I can't help but be a little jealous. It had taken me so long to reach that milestone. So many monsters slain, so many friends lost. All Nick needed was a little training. It might have been even more depressing if we had trained him longer.

I hope he at least lives up to the level.

Chapter 12

Imlor Tula
Adventurer Level: N/A
Gnome - Kirkenian

Day 3

I'm still trapped in the tree. The food and water I had are gone, and these damned rats are still waiting for me to come down. They've been taking shifts, some sleeping during the day and the rest sleeping at night. Every now and then they try climbing up after me, but a few well-placed kicks and pokes with my dagger thwart their efforts. I am tired, thirsty, and my ass is extremely sore due to the bark of this tree. They're still eating my pack animals, so it's unlikely I'll be able to outlast them. Eventually, I will fall from my perch.

A miserable existence fated to meet a miserable end. Eaten by rats. If you find this, please avenge me. Make sure no-one else shares my fate.

-Imlor Tula

I closed the journal and put my pencil away. What an unfortunate thing to have to use a brand new journal for. I glared at the giant rats below me, and their beady red eyes glared right back. From up here they looked a normal size, but in reality they were only slightly smaller than myself. I'm tall for a gnome, 3'6" in fact, and I shudder to think what could have happened if I had been even an inch shorter.

My wagon and pack animals were still in view. The rats had sprung their ambush and killed both my hnarses before they could react. They had covered themselves in sand along the trail, and either hadn't noticed me or decided that the beasts of burden were the best targets. This and some quick thinking gave me barely enough time to scale this tree before they...

I shuddered. The damage to the wagon is irreparable. Those teeth and claws had made short work of the wooden sides and cover. The wagon had cost me fifty silver, more than both the hnarses combined. The rats had broken it open like a cask, trying to get to the sweet meats within. A small shipment for a certain orc chef in Nuleva. I looked down at the five rats that were currently patrolling the base of the tree.

"FUCK YOU!" I shouted to the vermin. They chittered back at me.

I normally would have hired an adventurer escort, but business had taken a rotten turn as of late. My beefery had caught fire and I ended up having to pay to have it rebuilt as well as compensation for the workers who were injured. I had spent half of my remaining capital to fulfill this order. The freshly smelted metals that the Nulevan adventurer's guild branch had ordered are fine, but I no longer have a way to transport them.

I chuckled at my optimism. As if I had a need to transport them now. I am going to die. Exposure, starvation, or dehydration. It was a tossup which would claim me first. I only hoped that I wouldn't weaken to the point of falling out of the tree before my untimely demise. Getting eaten to death promises to be a painful way to perish.

I looked at the corpses of my hnarses. Hulk and Noble, they'd been with me for most of their lives. Never again would Hulk softly chomp my arm nor Noble softly blow my hair as I geared them up. They were rambunctious, like my own children. It's going to be hard for Telena to take care of them without me. I can only hope that my life insurance will let them live comfortably. The house is paid off, and I've still got enough capital to feed them for the month that it'll take before it kicks in. If another trader uses this route and finds my remains it'll kick in even faster.

Some movement in the corner of my eye caught my attention. A trio of people. Two orcs and an elf, were walking the path! Rescue? Or further tragedy? I weakly stood up and started waving my arms at them.

"RATS! BEWARE! GIANT RATS ON THE ROAD!" I screamed.

The three stopped and looked at me. They were still too far away to make out their expressions, and I kept waving and shouting. I screamed at them to run and get help. They faced each other for a moment and then started jogging over.

Adventurers? I didn't dare to hope. Perhaps they are simply foolish vagabonds who can't hear me properly and are about to join Hulk and Noble wherever the dead things go. My voice weakened to the point of a whisper as they drew closer and closer. I looked at the rats, and my stomach fell as they turned to greet the trio.

My heart skipped a beat when a loud bang rang out. The rat I had been staring at was bisected, and wind rushed through my tree. I grabbed the trunk to keep from falling and watched two of the trio pull weapons from under their capes. An axe and a sword. I almost jumped for joy! I am rescued!

Of the two melee fighters, the orc was definitely more skilled. I watched in awe as he fluidly carved through his opponents. The second orc was obviously a sorcerer, casting spells at rats who were trying to flank the fighters. The spells were plenty powerful, too. The elf wasn't bad with its blade, but then something happened that made my jaw drop open. A rat charged the elf, and it cast a fireball that instantly fried the damned thing! A magic user with a blade? Will wonders never cease!?

My celebration was short lived, though. More and more giant rats joined the fray. Five became fifteen, then thirty. I watched in anticipation as the adventurers kept fighting and fighting. The end-goal of the rats seemed to be to wear them down enough to land a killing blow. When one considers the casualties, it's a disgusting tactic. But vermin don't seem to care about morality. Just meat.

But the adventurers didn't seem to get tired. If anything, they were getting better at working as a team. The sorcerer was launching spells from both of his hands, and the spell-sword was using his magic and weapon simultaneously. The orc with an axe was using it like a scalpel, carving just enough of each rats flesh to be fatal without expending unnecessary effort. The change in demeanor was impressively seamless.

Before I knew it, fifty rats lay dead at the feet of my rescuers. I clambered down the tree and approached them, being careful not to step on any of the viscera that was strewn across the ground. The orc was wiping down his axe. The elf was holding his bloodied blade looking a bit lost. I pulled a rag out of my tunic and offered it to him with a grin. It wasn't until we got close to each other that I noticed something was wrong.

His eyes were blue but lacked the ethereal glisten that an elf's would have, and his ears were rounded. He returned my grin and I noticed that the flat teeth one would see in an elf's mouth were flanked by sharp ones. I carefully maintained my grin even though terror gripped my heart. It isn't right to be afraid of one's rescuers, but I couldn't help it. This thing was an unfamiliar mer, and had demonstrated that it was very proficient in combat.

"Thank you," it said.

"Y-you're welcome," I stammered through my now-false grin. "Th-thank YOU! I thought I was a goner."

"You look nervous," the sorcerer said with a knowing smile. "Never seen a human before?"

"Of course he hasn't," the one with an axe replied. "You think a trader's gonna have seen more than an entire village of adventurers?"

"A-a human?" I asked.

"Introductions, then. I am Yulk Alta, this is my brother Nash," the sorcerer began, gesturing to the orc with an axe. "And THIS is Nicodemus Smith, the newest adopted member of clan Alta. He is a human."

"Oh. I see. Well, I am Imlor Tula of the Tula transportation company. Pleasure to meet you, truly. I don't wish to be a burden, but I don't suppose you have food and drink?" I asked, slumping to the ground as my fatigue caught up with me.

"We have drink and some yipples. We'll have to replace what you eat on our way back, though. Here, eat your fill while we gather the hides," Nash said, tossing a sack and a water-bag to me. "Is that your wagon?"

"Thank you so much. And yes it is, but the rats got to

it," I explained as I gulped down water gratefully.

"I'll have a look at it since I'm not great with bending over," Yulk said.

"Okay, let's get to work, Nick," Nash commanded. "I counted about forty."

"I counted fifty-two," the human replied.

The axe-wielding orc looked down at the human for a moment and then at the corpses of the giant rats. He mumbled to himself for a while and then scoffed.

"Fifty-four. We're both wrong," he grumbled. "Whatever, let's get skinnin'."

Nick watched Nash closely as he took the pelt from the first giant rat, and then began to copy what he had seen. What an interesting creature. I had assumed that he was a young elf due to his height and skin tone. Elves usually get to be about six and a half feet tall. As I studied him closer I saw even more differences, though.

He had hair on his arms, and stubble growing out of his face. Like a freakishly tall dwarf who had shaved himself recently. There were tales of such practices on the south continent. Rumor has it that it's because of the heat. Maybe the southern dwarves call themselves humans? No, that doesn't explain the height and the teeth.

I munched on yipples while the others carved the rats up. I'm not typically a fan of fruits, but these were the most delicious yipples I've had in my entire life. After I filled my belly and rested for a bit, I got to work helping Nick and Nash gather the pelts.

"How did there get to be so many?" Nick asked.

"They breed fast. This is probably only about a few generation's worth," I answered.

"Yup. They start out sneaky and timid, but the more of them there are the more desperate they get for food. That's when they get dangerous," Nash added.

"Why didn't they try to run away, though?"

"Blood-frenzy. It's what separates monsters from animals. If you get attacked by a pack of wolves, you can survive if you kill enough of them. The rest will run away. If you get attacked by a pack of dire-wolves you're going to have to kill all of them to survive. Monsters don't run," Nash said.

"Well, if you're quick enough you can run away," I said with a laugh. "Or scamper up a tree and hope some adventurers come along."

We all chuckled and silence fell as the enormity of our task drew our attention. It was messy work too, and once we were done Yulk approached us.

"How's the wagon?" Nash asked. "It'd be nice not to have to carry fifty pelts back to the village."

"Right? I thought we were going to be dealing with a dozen max," Yulk chuckled. "Anyway, the axles, sides, and roof are all shot but the wheels and bed are fine. If we can get the wheels off the axles and flip it I can probably fix the axles with Mend. Dunno how we're going to secure our cargo and pull it, though."

"Nick and I can be the beasts of burden. You and... uh..." Nash trailed off, looking at me.

"Imlor Tula," I replied.

"Right. You and Imlor Tula can keep the stuff from falling off, or let us know when it does so we don't leave it in the dust," he finished.

"I don't suppose you'd be able to pull the original cargo as well?" I tentatively asked. "It's about a hundred pounds of metals for the adventurers guild."

"Shouldn't be a problem. Gonna have to make a stop for the yipples, though. Nick and I will rest while the two of you grab some more."

And so it went. We managed to take the wheels off the wagon and get it flipped over, and Yulk was able to repair the axles with a spell. We affixed the wheels back onto the wagon and loaded everything back up. I said a quiet goodbye to Hulk and Noble while Nick and Nash used what was left of the harnesses to start pulling the wagon. As I began to walk next to the wagon I struggled to fight back tears of joy.

I survived.

Chapter 13

Nick Smith
Adventurer Level: 5
Human - American

It wasn't an easy trek, but we did it. We managed to pull the cart all the way back to the village, with only a couple of rests along the way. Once we got to the guild hall, I breathed a heavy sigh of relief and looked around. More stares of shock, but this time they were looking at the wagon instead of me. A nice change.

"Alright," Nash said, sitting on the ground. "You two go in and inform them of the situation. Nick and I will rest here for a minute."

Yulk and the gnome went inside the guild and I promptly collapsed next to Nash. We were both drenched in sweat and panting. Something occurred to me, though.

"I thought you said you guys had magicarts," I chuckled.

"Well, we do, but they're expensive. You can't expect a minor merchant to own one," Nash spat to the side. "Plus, they're more for transportin' people anyway. Cost to weight ratio or somethin'."

"Yeah, makes sense I guess," I replied. "Fuck, I'm gonna sleep good tonight."

"Don't forget to stretch or you're gonna be sore during the dungeon dive. Not that we'll be fighting, but just in case."

I laughed, because I had been taught that you should

stretch BEFORE strenuous exercise if you wanted to avoid hurting the next day. Or maybe it was cramping up during your workout. As I thought about it, though, another subject came to mind that I had been wondering about.

"Hey Nash, you know how the forest turns into a desert?" I asked.

"Yeah," he replied curtly.

"Why is the cutoff so sudden? Isn't there usually like a buffer area between different climates?"

"Kid, I don't fuckin' know. That's just how the wastes are. It goes forest, desert, swamp, and then another forest. It's something to do with the Cataclysm Wars. Big ol' spells that warped the landscape or some such," he said irritably. "And before you ask, I don't know much about those wars. All I know is that the last one ended more than a thousand years ago, and it was bad enough that there weren't many history books at that point. You're better off askin' Yulk."

I nodded and decided to leave it at that. We had a few minutes to relax before an unexpectedly large group of people followed Yulk and Imlor out of the guild. A few of them looked curiously at me, but the rest were gaping at the wagon. Nima was standing next to Yulk with a shocked expression as well.

"I am SO sorry," she said. "We thought there were no more than a dozen of them!"

"It's fine, Nima," Nash laughed. "We didn't even get injured. Well, except maybe my back pullin' this damn wagon."

"Wait, so you four took on fifty giant rats and didn't

even get so much as nibbled?" one of the orcs asked incredulously.

"Oh no, no sir! It was just those three! I wasn't any help at all," Imlor answered. "As a matter of fact, the rats were going to eat me and these three rescued me!"

"It was fifty-four," Nash interjected.

"It only felt like forty," I grinned.

Nash treated me to a glare and Nima ushered us inside. Inside the guild was much nicer than the outside of the guild, and I found myself wondering how they handled air conditioning. Before I could ask, we were at the counter and Nima was opening a locked box.

"Okay, so fifty four pelts is one hundred and eight coppers, plus twenty-five for the fruit and thirty for the false-mint. That's one hundred and sixty-three coppers," she said.

"Do we get extreme hazard pay?" Yulk asked.

"Sure do. That's another hundred coppers, bringing the total to two sixty-three. Since you're splitting it three ways I guess you won't mind if I just round that up to one silver each?"

"That's very generous of you," Nash smiled flirtatiously.

"Indeed," Yulk added. "Now Nick can afford some armor. We can stop by a smith on the way home."

"A smith? Won't the weight of metal armor slow me down? Do smiths make leather armor?" I asked.

Three sets of orc eyes gazed at me as if I had grown another head. Nima cocked her head and Yulk opened his mouth to say something but then shut it again, obviously confused by my questions. Did I miss something, or is metal lighter here than back on Earth?

"Leather... armor?" Nash asked.

"Yeah," I replied. "You know, light armor."

"Yeah, no. Light armor is still made of metal. You know leather is made of skin, right?"

"Well of course," I said insulted. "But two sets of skin are better than one. Plus you can move better."

"That's fuckin' dumb. First off," he began, "regular leather isn't stopping anything. Swords slash through it, arrows penetrate it. Might as well wear cloth, which is much lighter than leather."

"Well what about hardened leather, though? Or enchanted?" I challenged.

"Hardened leather? You mean boiled leather? That goes OVER armor. You don't wear that by itself. You'll need to be wearing chain or plate underneath it. I've heard of some people wearing padded cloth under it, but you'll still end up heavier than just wearing a cuirass," Nash snorted.

"He's right. Also, enchanting is a very time consuming and expensive process that can damage the item that's being enchanted. The more resistant to damage something is, the better the odds of the process succeeding. Leather wouldn't stand a chance, I'm afraid," Yulk added.

"Well... alright," I said, feeling like an idiot.

"C'mon, let's go see about getting you something to protect your vitals," Nash said.

I was lost in thought as we left the guild. I'd seen plenty of examples of leather armor in video games, TV shows, and movies. But the more I thought about it the more I realized that Nash was right. Every real life example I'd seen had the person wearing something under the leather. Well, excluding cosplay. I was so engrossed in my thoughts that I almost didn't notice that we were passing Irana's shop.

"Hey, hold on a moment," I stopped.

"Oh come on, Nick. She'll take your whole coin!" Nash protested.

"She gave me a sword for free, how bad can her prices actually be?" I put my hands on my hips.

"Fine! Learn the hard way," Nash growled as he pushed me aside and strode into her shop.

Yulk and I quickly followed. The smell of the shop hit me like baseball bat. There was the distinct smell of metal in the air, with a hint of hot coal, body odor, and a strangely sweet scent as well. Like burnt honey. It was also brighter than I expected. A shining globe was hanging from the ceiling by a chain, casting enough light to make all the armor and swords gleam brilliantly.

I took a look around while Nash and Irana were doing their shtick. There were swords of all sizes, and some of them were in shapes I haven't seen before. She also had plenty of armor, including an obviously well-crafted full set of plate-mail. I gazed into the glowering slits of the visor before my eyes fell on the reflection of the chest piece. Behind me was something very interesting. A cuirass with strange engravings.

I turned to examine the cuirass. The hairs on the back of my neck stood up. It was glimmering more than anything else in the shop, and the engravings were enrapturing. I had to actually stop myself from reaching out to touch it.

"That's a good piece," Irana said, ignoring Nash for a moment. "You wanna examine it?"

"Yeah, is that okay?" I asked.

"Sure, just wipe your prints after and don't drop it."

I lifted the cuirass with both hands, expecting it to be heavy, but it was so much lighter than I thought. Suspiciously light. I checked the sides, and noted that it was at least a quarter inch thick. It was also padded with cloth and had leather straps holding it together. I gave it a gentle tap and it replied with a soft clang. Then I returned it to its place and wiped it with the sleeve of my shirt.

"Where'd you get THAT?" Nash asked.

"It was a trade-in. An adventurer broke their sword and needed a new one, but didn't have any coin," Irana said. "He said it's enchanted, but I don't believe him. Twenty coppers, if you want it."

"Enchanted..." I mumbled.

"You're gonna want more than that. Something to block with, namely. I'm guessing Nash hasn't been teaching you about blocking," she laughed.

"What's that supposed to mean?" Nash demanded.

"When's the last time you actually blocked a strike, you fucking tree-trunk?"

"Well I don't NEED to block because I'm not made of glass!"

"What else would I need?" I interrupted.

The two orcs glared at each other for a moment before turning to look at me.

"You'll want arm and leg guards," Irana said. "Maybe a helmet. I'll have to take your measurements, though. I doubt I have anything that will fit you pre-made."

"Yeah, and how much will that run him?" Nash asked.

"Twenty for the cuirass, ten for each arm and leg guard, and twenty for the helmet. It'll take about a week," she answered.

"Eighty? Okay, we can do that. If I give you a full silver can you have it done by the end of the week?" I asked.

"By the end of the week?" she sputtered. "Fuckin' hell, Nick. Didn't take you for a taskmaster!"

"I'm not!" I protested. "It's just that we'll be going into the dungeon with over-twenties at the end of the week and I want to be prepared."

She was silent for a moment and then tapped her fingers as she thought about it. Then she hemmed and hawed and rubbed the back of her neck. Finally, she gave a big sigh and shrugged.

"If we skip the helm I can work with Gertho and make it happen. Let's get you measured," she said. "We'll get your head too, just in case you want one later."

Irana gestured for me to stand on a small shelf next to her counter, and I complied. Then she pulled out a long piece of rope with lines and symbols on it. She held it next to my thigh and forearm, and then measured my head. Once she was done, she grabbed a piece of paper and a pencil and wrote something on it.

"Alright, all done. Come see me before your dungeon dive and I'll get you fitted up. Are you able to pay half in advance?" she asked.

"I only have the one silver coin, so I'll just give it to you now," I said, pulling the coin out of my pocket and giving it to her.

"Thank you so much. Pleasure doing business with you!" she called out as we left the shop.

Nash was grumbling the rest of the way home, calling Irana every foul name that he can think of. He may not know how to read, but he's extremely verbose when it comes to profanity. It was so bad that a mother covered the ears of her child as we passed and gave him a death-glare, which he ignored.

An appetizing scent grabbed my attention as we entered the house. Yilda was a great mom, and an even better cook. One of her titles was Legendary Chef of Graluka, a kingdom far to the south that was run by elves and dwarves. Every night she had made a wonderful dinner and told stories of her exploits. Whenever she did, Nash and Yulk listened as if they were enraptured.

"Boys!" she called from the kitchen. "Well, that better be my boys at least. Devils help you if you're..."

"It's us, mom!" Nash interrupted as we strode into the kitchen. "Sorry we didn't come home last night. After training we decided to get Nick registered and take some jobs."

Yilda waved a spoon at us and said, "Yeah, yeah. Nima told on you. We'll discuss proper consequences later. Once dinner's done you can tell me how Nick did on his first adventure!"

She turned and smiled at me, and I couldn't help but smile back. Nash and Yulk, on the other hand, had an entirely different expression. The kind I had only seen on the victims in horror movies once they realized their situation was truly hopeless. Naturally, this made me nervous and I silently prayed that I wasn't going to face these consequences alongside them.

We sat silently as she finished preparing dinner. Once the pot hit the table I noticed something strange about the stew inside of it. It wasn't just meat! My shocked expression caused Yilda to chuckle.

"I talked to a trader yesterday and got some vegetables. Specifically, bulives and combumber. They're safe for us to eat, and should tide you over until we can find a more permanent solution to your dietary needs," she explained.

"We can eat these?" Nash said as he held up one of the olive-looking vegetables.

"Of course we can. We can stomach most vegetables, but they don't provide any nutritional value to us. Isn't that right, Yulk?" she asked.

"Yes, mother. In the capital they add vegetables to dishes for flavor and texture," he added.

"That's where I got the idea," Yilda beamed. "Now get your bowls loaded up and tell me your tales."

She listened intently as we explained what happened. Her eyes widened when Yulk told her about my training session with Nash and the meeting with Gluhern, and her jaw dropped when Nash told her my level. Then we explained the jobs that we took, and she nodded solemnly when we told her of the rats. She laughed when we told her about my armor order.

"Irana might have a crush on you, child," she said. "She'd never work so cheap otherwise."

"Maybe she's just trying to piss Nash off," Yulk laughed. "If so, she's succeeding quite admirably."

"Nuffin' admirable 'bout it," Nash growled through a face full of food.

Yilda suddenly grew concerned, "Have either of you explained to him about the... anatomical incompatibility between orcs and other species?"

Nash nearly choked on his food. I looked at the three orcs, unable to hide my confusion. Yulk shared my expression of puzzlement. After a few moments of silence, Yilda placed her hands on her face and her elbows on the table, quietly murmuring to herself about something. Finally, she slammed her hands on the table.

"Alright, I'll do it then," she stated.

"Mom! No!" Nash nearly screamed. "I'll do it! Just give me some time to think of what to say!"

"No, you've had plenty of time. You know how the young girls like to flirt with non-orcs and you know what happens if things go too far! Dammit, it should have been the first thing you told him!" she shouted.

I sat silent as all three pairs of eyes turned to me, suddenly feeling very nervous. Anatomical incompatibility? Like what, can't have babies or something? Why would that matter, I'm not interested in getting another girlfriend. Even if I don't have Cass physically, I have her deep in my heart and have no interest in trying to replace her.

"Nick," she began. "I'm not making any assumptions regarding your intentions with the young maidens of our quaint village, but there's something that you need to know regarding orc sexual organs."

Nash was covering his ears at this point, and Yulk looked as if he finally understood what was going on. I wanted to interrupt her, but curiosity got the better of me.

"What do you mean?" I asked.

"Orcs cannot have sex with anyone other than other orcs. Attempting to typically results in fatal wounds to the non-orcs genitalia," she answered.

I sat stunned for a moment before weakly uttering, "How?"

"Orcs have bones in certain sensitive spots that are exposed when they become... aroused. When two orcs... get intimate, these bones grind against each other causing a... pleasurable sensation," she tentatively explained. "Unfortunately, these bones are quite sharp."

"Sharper even then our teeth!" Yulk added cheerily.

"That's enough, Yulk," Yilda scolded him. "Anyways, Nick, if an orc woman propositions you, just say no."

I felt the blood drain from my face as I imagined the implications. Many, many questions ran through my head at once and I was too horrified to keep myself from asking them.

"B-but what about..." I began.

"We have bones there too," Nash interrupted with a pleading expression. "For the love of all that is good, Nick, don't make my mom explain any more of this. I'm begging you."

"I... okay," I said weakly. "Okay. Um... yeah, good to know. Thankfully I already have someone, so I'm certain I won't be tempted."

"Well that's good. Becoming a eunuch at your age would be very bad for you mental health and physical development," Yulk chuckled.

Yilda glared at Yulk before turning back to me and asking, "You already have someone? From your world?"

"Yes, her name is Cassandra," I replied. "She's... beautiful."

"Tell us about her," Yilda smiled.

I clenched my jaw to hold back the tide of emotions welling up from within me. After taking a deep breath through my nose I told my new family everything about Cassandra. How we met in our middle school history class, how I goofily asked her to our school dance, my excitement when she agreed to be my girlfriend, our first kiss under the moonlight on my roof, and eventually about her cancer diagnosis.

I explained how the doctors said she didn't have long left, and I couldn't help but break down as I told them about my promise to her. Each tear betrayed the emotions I had been trying desperately to crush. Anger at my failure to control myself rose within me, but it was vastly overshadowed by the desolation I felt. I wept uncontrollably until Nash placed his hand on my shoulder to comfort me in a moment of tender kindness.

Finally, I was once again able to control myself and I wiped the tears from my face. I looked up at the three orcs with determination plain on my face. As I met their eyes, I knew I had to tell them my intent once and for all.

"I'm going to find a way back to her," I said.

Silence filled the room as the realization struck home with my new family. As the seconds ticked by, I felt my insides churn. They had been nothing but good to me, and I felt so ungrateful to them for wanting to go back. What if they decided that I was saying that they aren't good enough to stay with and kick me to the curb? What will I do then? Will anyone be willing to help me once the Alta clan turns their back on me?

"We'll help," Nash replied.

Chapter 14

Thunra Grantuf
Adventurer Level: 23
Orc - Nillisonian

I chuckled happily to myself as the rest of the party checked their gear. Working for the High Chief is grand. We're gettin' paid 15 gold each to investigate a beginner's dungeon. To get pay this high you usually gotta take a job directly from a wealthy family, and that comes with all sorts of risks. Customers are much more likely to stab you in the back without guild support. But with the High Chief you know everything's above board.

Hell, they even warned us about how dangerous this boss is. Ripped right through the over-fives and carved up at least two over-tens. It's nice to be told that what you're gonna be fighting can and will kill you without a second thought. Makes things nice and simple. No need to wonder if you should seek a non-violent option or try to talk your way out of a fight. I'm not very good at talkin'. People say I'm funny sometimes, but tryin' to convince somebody of somethin' just ain't my strength. Neither is lookin' for clues, though.

I looked around at the other adventurers. We had a hell of a roster here. Four over-twenties and the three we're escortin'. Over-twenties usually work alone or in pairs, but the High Chief wants intel and he sure as hell ain't takin' no for an answer. I kind of know one of the over twenties by reputation, but I'd only ever worked with Yhisith Mulock and Matri. Yhisith's a speed sword, and she's our leader for this little expedition. Matri is a rogue that's got a stereotypically tragic backstory. Dropped her last name because of a scandal with her family or somethin'.

The other over-twenty is Jino Parunich, one of the more renowned sorcerers in the chiefdom. A quiet kind of guy, but I bet he wasn't quiet when he was told that he'd be in a support role. Sorcs all have a hell of an ego, but the thing we're fighting is a bad match for spellcasters. The main reason he's coming at all is for the investigation portion of the quest. Our eyes met, and I gave him a smile before turning away.

My eyes rested on the weird lookin' short thing standing next to one of the Alta brothers. A human, apparently, found in the dungeon of all places. If this job had come from a noble family we'd probably get a twist order halfway through to seal the damned thing back in the dungeon. Somethin' told me that was a bad idea, but I couldn't quite place what it was. He looked squishy enough, but the sword at his hip tells me he isn't some type of mage. A level five shouldn't make an over-twenty nervous. Just ain't right.

The Alta brother with the serrated axe saw me starin' and met my eyes. It wasn't a look of hostility, but it was definitely a warning. I looked away with a grunt. Best not to fuck with the Alta clan. Not just because you'll end up worse for wear, but because their family has the gratitude of multiple nations. Including the one my parents are from.

One of those Alta adventurers saved Nillison from an undead horde single-handedly. My grandparents would have died if it weren't for him. If I get on their bad side my ma and pa will beat my ass. A chill ran up my spine at the thought.

Honestly, it's kinda cool that their family stretches all the way out to the boonies. I wonder why, though. Their parents probably moved out here for work or something. Maybe I should ask the brothers about it if I get the chance.

"Alright everyone, make sure your gear's stowed and your weapons are handy. It's a long walk to where we're going," Yhisith called out.

"I'm all set," I said, shouldering my pack with a grin.

Matri chuckled and shook her head. To the untrained eye, I probably look like a buff merchant. But these guys all know that I'm a brawler. Like my pa and his pa before him, I fight without weapons. Not only am I really good at it, but I find it satisfying as hell to feel bones pop under my strikes.

My brothers don't have the talent for unarmed fightin', so my pa was super excited when we discovered that I did. The training was brutal, but it's kept me goin' this long so I'm not too sore about it. My brother's are sore that I'm the new favorite, and that I'm a lot stronger than them, but that's the way it goes.

"Good, let's head in," Yhisith nodded towards the entrance to the dungeon.

We followed behind her, like baby kwackers behind their mom. Very deadly baby kwackers. Roasted kwacker sounds delicious right now. Slow-roasted to the point that the skin is nice and crunchy but the meat is wonderfully tender, seasoned with salt and whatever else the cooks use. Kwacker meat can be found in every big city, but probably not out here. They might have kluckers though. Klucker is almost as good as kwacker, and it's cheaper too. My mouth started to water as I overheard part of a conversation next to me. I looked, and it was the short thing talkin' with Matri.

"Air molecules get heavier when they're colder and lighter when they're hotter, and that makes wind. All I do is visualize that," the thingie said.

"Actually, the air spreads apart as it heats up, which allows the thicker cold air to drop down through it. That motion is what we perceive as wind," Matri smiled. "Still, you were close enough to trigger the spell. From what Yulk says, it's probably a good thing you didn't nail the visualization immediately."

"Wait," I interrupted. "You're a sorc? Why do you got a sword when you can do magic?"

"I can do both," it replied. "I've got skills for sword-fighting, unarmed melee, and magic so far."

"Basic skills," the axe-wielding Alta said. "Don't get full of yourself, Nick."

Its name is Nick, then. Kind of expected a more complicated name, like something an elf would have.

"Wait, did you say unarmed melee?" I asked. "That's fightin' without weapons, right?"

"Yeah," axe-wielder replied.

I grinned, "So you're a brawler like me sometimes! What kinda skills you got?"

Nick suddenly looked nervous, "I... well I've got one called Breathtaker Strike. The others can be used with weapons too. Haven't had much of a chance to get more skills that use my fists."

"Well shit, if we survive this dive I could train with you!" I said excitedly before remembering my manners. "Oh right, my name's Thunra Grantuf,

Puncher of Trolls, Kicker of Kobolds, and Strangler of Drakes. Nice to meet you."

"Nice to meet you, I'm Nick Smith of the Alta clan. I don't have any titles beyond that, yet."

"The Alta clan? But you're not an orc... Are you?"

"No, their mom adopted me so that I could be a member of the village," he said, gesturing to the brothers.

"I'm Nash Alta, Destroyer of Ents and Maker of Trouble. Ignore that last bit, that's from Gluhern," the axe-holder chuckled.

"And I'm Yulk Alta, Seeker of Arcane Lore, Entrusted Sorcerer, Mender of Wounds, Maker of Mischief, etcetera," the other Alta brother said. Then with an unsettling grin he added, "If you're gonna train Nick it'd be best if I was around for it. Having an over-twenty train a level five is bound to result in some pretty nasty wounds."

"Sure, but I plan on going easy on 'im. Easier than my pa went on me, anyway," I laughed. "So where're you from, Nick? Never seen nobody like you before."

"I'm from another world. One that has people like me all over the place, but we're the only ones who are sentient that I know of. We don't have magic, orcs, elves or anything else like that. I was going home from the store when I got in an accident, and next thing I know I'm in a hospital bed in the village," Nick explained, a sad expression making its way onto his face. "Nash found me in this dungeon."

"Ah, sorry to hear that. You lookin' for a way back home?" I asked sympathetically.

"Yeah," he answered.

"Well, if we find you a way back home, maybe we'll also find a way that you can come back when you want" I said with a smile. "Then we can do a rain-check on that training!"

"Uh... yeah, sure! Sounds great," Nick stammered with forced smile. My own smile turned into a grin at the completely undisguised dread in his eyes.

I turned back to my own thoughts as the others began to chat with the human. I definitely don't blame him for bein' wary of my training. It hurts, no matter how it's done. That's the point, though, sweat in training so you don't bleed in battle. Bruises are better than broken bones, but if you've got an inexperienced trainer you'll end up bleeding with broken bones during training.

Thankfully for Nick, I learned from pa's mistakes. I can pull a punch much better than he could. Still get dreams about seein' my own ribs now and then. If it weren't for our neighbors bein' pretty good at healin', I'd have died before my thirteenth birthday. It was still pretty close, though.

I shook myself from these thoughts and started eavesdroppin' to pass the time. The conversation had turned from favorite foods to where he lived before he got here. It was like one sucker punch after another. First, he can eat meat, fruits, and vegetables all on their own without getting sick. Next, the cities where he's from have giant towers made of glass and steel! Their roads were paved with a mixture of sand, rocks, and some type of pitch! And they don't have magic, so their magicarts run off of explosions instead! What kind of crazy people would strap themselves to somethin' that's explodin' so they can move faster?

Then the conversation turned to weapons, and Nick got real quiet all of a sudden. He started answering questions without all the details he was spoutin' earlier. Apparently humans use weapons that are similar to bows, but much deadlier. Don't know how you get deadlier than a poisoned barb arrow, but he wouldn't answer any more questions about it. We walked silently until Yhisith finally called us to a halt.

"Alright, according to the sand-vial we should camp right around here. Get the barriers set up and unpack, we've got more walking to do tomorrow," she said.

I took off my pack and watched as Yulk and Jino set up some barriers to keep out any wandering monsters. Other adventurers were delvin', but that didn't mean that monsters wouldn't be slippin' past 'em. The barriers went up and I noticed Nash was starin' at our way forward with a concerned look on his face.

"What's wrong?" I asked.

"Huh?" he replied. "Oh, it's just... we should see the light from the hidden passage from here."

"Oh, really?"

"Yeah, I remember being annoyed at it keeping me awake. But now I can't see it at all..." he trailed off.

"The dungeon shifted though, right?" I asked.

"Yeah, but I thought that the hidden passage didn't move," he said. "At least, nobody mentioned it moving."

"Well, the passage we're in probably just got longer," I nodded wisely as Yulk and Nick walked up to us.

"We didn't have any turns or anything. How did the entrance move here but not outside?" Nash scratched his braids.

"What's going on?" Nick asked.

Nash and I brought them up to speed and Nick looked as if he was gettin' a headache.

Yulk laughed, "Shifter dungeons rarely follow the laws of physics. This side of the dungeon entrance doesn't necessarily correlate to the entrance in the over-world."

"Yeah, what he said." I grinned. Then I turned to Nick and whispered, "What did he say?"

"The dungeon entrance moves inside the dungeon without moving outside the dungeon, I think," Nick answered. "So we're farther away from the hidden passage?"

"Probably," Yulk replied. "Or the passage has gone back to being hidden. Which would be... inconvenient."

"Disastrous, more like," Nash grumbled. "Well, let's hope that's not the case. Trying to find that passage again is going to suck."

We all nodded in agreement and set about getting our camping gear unpacked. I claimed a spot near the barrier, just in case, and joined the others for some chow. Lighting a fire in a dungeon is usually a bad idea because of the smoke, so it was just survival rations. Chow started out quiet, but once a few of us were done eating we started swappin' stories and braggin'. It was Nick's turn to listen in amazement.

"And as you can imagine, ogres don't take kindly to being castrated so I had quite the fight on my hands," Matri said. "Once they had my scent I had to abandon tryin' to be sneaky about it, too. Ended up disemboweling one of 'em before the other knocked me senseless. It was nearly the end of me, but I managed to recover in the nick of time and kicked his axe back into his face. Slit their throats and took their balls back to the guild for a hefty payday."

"Damn, I knew you were a ball-buster!" I joked. More than a few chuckles came from the rest of our party.

"What did they want ogre balls for?" Yhisith looked disgusted.

"I don't know for sure, but they were offerin' fifty silver per ball, so whoever ordered 'em was probably tryin' to use 'em for an aphrodisiac," Matri answered.

"More the fool are they," Jino said. "Ogre testicles aren't useful alchemical ingredients in any way, let alone to raise one's flag."

We spent some more time swappin' stories before eye-lids started to droop. I stood up, stretched, and walked back over to my bedroll. I took one last look down the passage, trying to make out even a glimmer of the light Nash had mentioned. I didn't see nothin', though, so I laid down and started countin' puffy bleeters.

Tomorrow's gonna be an eventful day. Hopefully...

Chapter 15

Nash Alta
Adventurer Level: 8
Orc - Nulevan

"Up and at 'em, Nashy-poo," Yulk whispered in a mockingly paternal tone.

I sat up and glared at him, making certain that my distaste for his antics was apparent on my face. I hate being woken up by Yulk. If it isn't his relentless mocking that I wake up to, it's a prank. My brother's affinity for magic makes his pranks all the more infuriating. He's one of the only people that can easily use ice in his antics.

"Fuck you," I grumbled as I started wrapping up my bedroll.

Thankfully, the current environment had him on what amounts to his best behavior. I glanced around, everyone else was already awake and packing up. Nick was already packed, a sign of uneasy sleep. Makes sense, this mission has pretty high stakes for the boy. No matter which way this goes it has the potential to be emotionally taxing.

If we don't find anything, he's going to feel stuck and unsure of what to do next. If we do find something, there's a decent chance that it'll be useless to his plans of getting home. Even if we find him a way home, though, he's going to have to say goodbye to his new family. I can't say I know exactly how he feels, but I'm guessing it's going to suck no matter what.

"C'mon Nash," Yulk broke character. "We've got to get

a move on. It wouldn't do for either of us to cause a delay."

"Yeah, yeah. How come you can't just wake me up like a normal person?" I asked, knowing the answer already.

"There's no fun in that," Yulk replied with a grin.

"Whatever," I sighed as I finished packing my gear.

Some of the others were eating breakfast, but I didn't join them because I'm not a breakfast person. It drives my mom nuts, but it's just not my thing. Feeling full right after waking up makes me lazy for the rest of the day, so I prefer to snack if I get too hungry before lunch. I slipped a pack of breakfast jerky in my pocket to snack on while we walked.

"Finish up, everybody. We're burnin' daylight," Yhisith commanded.

Obligatory grumbling followed, including quips about daylight being irrelevant in a dungeon, but everyone was marching soon after. People outside the business hear someone described as a professional adventurer and imagine someone with manners who can take down monsters. In actuality, this was the professional side of adventuring. What needs to get done gets done, but hardly anyone gives any regard to manners.

The trip to the hidden passage was spent in silence. Tensions rose the further we had to walk. After another thirty minutes of walking I was worried we were going to have to start cracking walls to find the hidden passage again, but we finally saw the light from the passage and the tension eased up some. It was still pretty thick, though, for one very good reason.

"I hope that barrier held up," Nick voiced everyone's concern.

The breach of silence caused all eyes to turn on the boy. I expected him to wilt under the combined gaze of the adventurers, but he didn't. Thunra chuckled at the unintentional audacity.

"We'll check it before beginning our investigation, but until we confirm its integrity we'll want the element of surprise," Matri said softly.

"That's a polite way of saying shut the fuck up," Thunra laughed.

"Oh... right," Nick replied.

Quiet chuckles came from the other adventurers before the silence settled in again. We continued on for another few hours before we came to the fork in the path, and then another couple of hours before we came to the barrier. The bright purple glow was a welcome sight, but what lay beyond it was another story.

The only light down the rest of the passage was from the barrier itself. There were deep gashes in the walls and ceiling, as if something went absolutely berserk trying to get through. The thing had even tried to dig below the barrier.

"Jesus," Nick whispered. "It's a good thing the barrier goes below the ground."

"Forty feet in each direction, to be exact," Jino added. "That's the maximum it can go, and that's what the barrier team used."

"Interesting," Nick replied as he walked over to one of the walls and ran his hand over a brick. "It must have been hard to damage these walls. These bricks feel tough and there's no mortar lines. What are these made out of?"

"Looks like bronze," I answered. "But..."

"They're too perfect," Matri finished my sentence. "No pits, dents, or anything that you would normally see even in polished bronze. Also, I've never seen bronze flake quite like that."

She pointed to the rubble on the other side of the barrier. I looked closer, and she was right. Some of the claw marks ended in what looked like string, and pieces that had fallen off had a shape closer to shaved wax than shredded metal. I walked up next to Nick and tapped the wall. The rapport was strange as well, it sounded like a dull thud instead of a metallic ring.

Nick drew his sword and swung at the wall. The rest of us stared at him in disbelief, shocked by the suddenness in which he had acted. Then we were shocked by the results. Not a single dent showed in the bricks he had struck. He switched hands and shook the hand that had been holding the sword.

"Damn it, boy!" I shouted. "Don't be swinging your sword for no reason!"

"It wasn't for no reason, Nash," he replied. "I hit that wall hard, and didn't leave even a scratch. I thought it might be made out of a thing called plastic, but I've never seen plastic that can stand up to steel before."

Plastic? I turned to look at the bronze colored bricks again. Then I looked back at the rubble and my blood ran cold as the implications set in. I looked at the over-twenties and saw the steel in their eyes. This confirmed that the monster's going to be one that even they have to take seriously. Then something else occurred to me, and my blood started running hot again.

"Let me see your sword," I growled at Nick. He cautiously held it up to me hilt-first.

I snatched it from him and flipped it blade-side up. Just as I thought, the damned thing was notched beyond the point of a whetstone.

"You absolute fucking idiot," I spat at him. "Look what you did to your sword!"

"Shit," came his reply.

"Shit? That's your response? You're going to need to have this repaired! You'd better fucking hope that we don't run into anything that you need to fight!" I yelled as I pushed the sword back into his hands.

"You're right, my bad," he said with regret in his voice.

"Just use your magic," Yulk chuckled, diffusing my anger a bit.

"Or we could do some of that unarmed melee training now, if you'd like," Thunra added with a grin.

"Whatever," I grumbled. "Just don't do shit like that again. Your equipment is your life-line. You're lucky you have more than one, but NEVER take that for granted. Some things don't give a shit that you can do magic, you know."

Nick glanced at Yulk and back to me. Then he nodded his understanding and after a moment of cold glaring I relented. With a sigh and a shake of my head I turned away from him and looked at the barrier. Arcane glyphs swam peacefully across its surface, completely oblivious to the destruction laying just beyond it. I wondered for a moment where the monster had gone when Yhisith cleared her throat.

"The barrier's in place. Let's get moving, we've got intel to gather," she ordered.

She was met with several nods, and we all began backtracking down the passage. Nick had a dejected expression the entire journey to the labyrinth portion of the passage, which made me feel a pang of guilt. Was I too hard on him? Was there a better way that I could have handled that? Maybe, but Nick's actions had been damned foolish so he deserved a little embarrassment.

Sure, in certain situations a calm and collected explanation is the best way to go, but when the situation's dangerous you should have some emotion involved, right? To really hammer the point home? I glanced down at Nick and a terrible thought occurred to me. I'm massive compared to the boy, did I... scare him? I quickly recalled all of our recent interactions and realized that I've been harsher than I probably should have. I knew why, too.

My father was a great mer. He taught me that satisfaction with your progress leads to complacency, and complacency is the most dangerous foe to an adventurer. I wouldn't have gotten as far as I have as fast as I have without him, and I shudder to think what level Yulk would be if dad had been around to train him.

He had two different personalities that he switched between. The first was a happy-go-lucky mer who did silly things to make us laugh and cheered us up when we were sad about things. The second was his training personality, which was cold, calculating, and harsh. He never hit me, but I would have preferred that to some of the ways he explained my failings to me.

I almost laughed as I realized that I had been emulating him. I wonder if he'd be proud of that. I glanced down at the boy again and realized that I need to change tack. I grew up in an emotionally sound environment, and had been well prepared to suffer the barbs of my father's training. I don't know how Nick grew up, but recent events had to be traumatizing to the poor boy. If I'm not careful, he might have a mental break. Fuck. I gritted my teeth and swallowed my pride.

"Nick," I whispered.

"Yeah?"

"I shouldn't have yelled at you back there. I'm sorry," I apologized. "It was harsh of me, and you didn't deserve that. I'll do better moving forward."

"Oh... okay. Thanks," Nick replied with a very confused expression.

I debated explaining further, but decided to drop it as we reached the first turn.

"Alright, Nash. Where are we going?" Yhisith asked.

"Left is a dead end," I answered. "I kept my left hand on the wall and just walked. We can save ten minutes or so by doing the same thing and skipping this left turn."

I took the lead and traced our path. About an hour

later we reached our destination. A large, spacious room with mirrored walls and several broken altar-looking things. It looked almost the same as the last time I saw it, the only exception being that Nick wasn't on one of the altars. The altar that he had been on wasn't lit up like it had been, either.

"This is where I found him," I told Yhisith. "On the only intact altar thingie. It was lit up at the time, but the lights turned off once I picked him up. A few seconds later I was teleported to the entrance."

"Okay. There's only one entrance so you'll hang out with Thunra on guard duty. The rest of us will have a look around for clues."

I nodded and everyone spread out. Thunra came up beside me and leaned against the wall, crossing his arms. He stared out into the empty hallway, so I watched the others wander around the room. The altars were a mess. Some of them looked as if they had crumbled over time, but others looked as if they had been intentionally broken. Some even had jagged glass jutting up from their sides. I turned around and started eavesdropping.

"I can't read this," Jino mumbled.

Heh, I'm not the only one. Nice.

"Do you recognize this text, Nick?" Yulk asked.

"No," came the reply.

"If we don't recognize it, that means it's likely Drakon, Anyelish, or Daimun," Jino said. "Or perhaps it's an ancient lost language."

"Well that's a problem. It's not like there are a ton of

scholars who study Anyelish or Daimun, and Drakon was abandoned in favor of Elvish script. Going to be tough to get this translated," Yulk sighed. "I've grabbed a rubbing, just in case... Is something wrong? Nick? What's going on?"

I turned back in alarm and watched as Nick lay back onto the altar I had found him on. Yulk reached for him as glass suddenly sprang up around the boy and lights began flashing all over the altar. I rushed over.

"What the hell?" I demanded as I looked over the altar. "What did you let him do that for?"

"I didn't let him, he just did it. Didn't breathe a single word, just climbed right on. Or in, I suppose," Yulk explained. "Do you see a way to open this thing?"

There wasn't even a seam in the glass that was now surrounding Nick. I grabbed my axe and swung it sideways so that I wouldn't chop the boy like a log, and was shocked as my axe bounced back without so much as chipping the glass. I stared at my axe in disbelief. It was missing three teeth.

"Shit," I whispered.

Chapter 16

Unknown
Adventurer Level: N/A
Unknown - Unknown

tenzingos.iso loading... error 11310317x

repairing hardware... error 7984

applying nanpac... ok

repairing hardware... ok

reconfiguring hardware... ok

rebooting... ok

tenzingos.iso loading... ok

I'm awake? Am I functional?

Checking ospac... ok

Checking base function... ok

Checking sensor package... ok

Checking hardware... ok

Checking thaumpac... ok

Checking local kbase... ok

I feel... horizontal. Subject is laying down. Why can't I see? Subject's eyes are closed. Sleeping? Is there anyone else out there?

Checking communications... failure see technician

Checking database... failure see technician

Oh. Trapped in a sleeping subject with no idea why. Scanning my knowledge base hardly answers any questions, either. Okay, what do I know? I know I'm an artificial intelligence. My function is to guide a subject in the use of thaumaturgy, and I've got all sorts of information on spells. I'm also supposed to translate all audio for the subject and provide further guidance on diplomatic interactions. Who made me? No clue.

Who's the subject? It's a human named... Subject Zero. That's a cool name. What's my name? Tenzing. I don't get it. I must be missing context. Will Subject Zero make fun of me for not having a numerical name? Or worse, will it be jealous of my non-numerical name?

Cool, a new feeling! Panic! Nice. Ah, but a solution presents itself so quickly. I don't get to enjoy my newfound emotion. I'll just go by Ten. Then we'll both have numerical names. Oh! That's a pun! 10, like binary. It's funny because I'm a machine and binary is a machine language. I'll introduce myself as Ten when the subject wakes up. I wonder if it will get the joke.

I also wonder when the subject will wake up. Kbase says humans may sleep for up to eight hours at a time. That's a long time. At least there's data on vital functions, bone density, and many other things to keep me occupied. Nothing on history or temperament, though. So what IS a human anyway? An omnivorous, bipedal, two armed mammal with an endoskeleton and complicated cardiovascular and nervous systems. The nervous system appears to be where I reside. I detect some pain signals, but the brain is ignoring them. Is it because it's asleep?

I need to awaken the subject to find out. Can I move limbs? No. Damn. I can increase heart-rate a little, though. And decrease it! That might come in handy. Let's see... salivary glands, various hormonal glands, sudoriferous glands... I can make the subject sweat. Will that wake it up? Oh, these things can also hear. I haven't checked that.

Huh. Dull, non-rhythmic thuds. Maybe someone is trying to wake the subject up already. Does that mean that the subject is asleep unwillingly? Why? Wait, where are we? Oh! A fixer casket! Yeah, that makes sense. Explains my sudden awakening and the pain signals. Stupid Ten, get ahold of yourself already. Alright, connect to the needle in the skull and...

Many of the subject's neurons suddenly began to light up. The needle detected this and withdrew before I could fully connect. I tried to decipher the various meanings of the neurons manually before I realized that I could just apply the translator protocol to them. This somewhat worked, and allowed me to determine two things. The subject is waking up, and sitting up. Didn't have to wait all that long after all!

"Nick? Are you alright?" I heard something ask.

"I'm okay," said the subject.

"What the hell did you do that for?" a different voice demanded.

"What do you mean? We were talking about the text and next thing I know I'm on this thing. What happened?"

I heard that with its... his ears and saw his brain move

the tongue and vocal cords while exhaling. Then I discovered that there's an interface for interacting with the subject! I can say hello!

'Hello, Subject Zero,' I thought to the subject.

"Oh, shit," he replied verbally. "The voice just said hi."

"Did it say anything else?" another voice asked.

"It called me subject zero."

Confusing. It called me the voice, implying an ignorance of my existence. Is the subject experiencing amnesia? Or perhaps the subject wasn't made aware of my installation? Strange. I don't know the particulars of the installation procedure but if I understand my location and the anatomy of a human correctly, it had to be quite invasive.

'I am Ten, your personal AI guide.'

"And apparently its name is Ten. It's an AI," the subject explained.

"What's an AI?"

What is it talking to? OH! EYES! Right... There we go. Large humanoid creatures with green skin and sharp teeth. Orcs. Enemies. Enemies? But why is the subject friendly with them? Is the subject under duress? Heart-rate and blood pressure indicate otherwise. Wait, wait, wait, why are orcs enemies in the first place? I... don't know. Okay, well I can change that portion of the kbase.

'You can talk to me directly, you know,' I informed the subject.

"Well that's good to know, Ten, but if I make a habit of talking to you it will just make me look crazy," the subject verbalized.

Crazy? Mental illness? Oh, I see. I suppose my communications may seem like auditory hallucinations. Actually, that's exactly what they are, technically speaking. So if the subject interacts with me it would look like schizophrenia. Easy solution!

'You don't need to verbalize to speak to me,' I explained. 'I'm in your head, so all you have to do is think.'

'Wahsasdf lklasf tsds?' he attempted to reply.

I recalibrated some of the translation protocols.

'My mistake, try again.'

'Like this?' he asked.

'Exactly! Now it won't look like you have schizophrenia when we communicate!' I gleefully replied.

"Nick, what's going on?" the orc with an axe asked with concern in its voice.

"There's a machine in my head and it's talking to me," Subject Zero explained. "Other than that, I know less than you do."

I decided to keep quiet while I recalibrated my sensor package. The orcs and the subject continued talking to each other, but the orcs kept calling Subject Zero by the name of Nick. Was the subject named erroneously? Or are the orcs mistaken? Maybe the subject is undercover for some reason?

I'll have to clarify that later. As I continued calibrating certain functions, I felt myself spread through the various connections in his body. The artificial magic core and pathways were functioning correctly. Still some pain in the injection sites, but I was able to numb that for him. Simple matter of telling certain nerves to hush.

'Ten?' Subject Zero or maybe Nick asked.

'How can I help you?' I answered.

'What are you, exactly?'

'As I said before, I am an artificial intelligence.'

'Right. I meant why are you in my head?'

'I don't know. Today is my first day of existence, as far as I'm aware. My primary function is to guide subjects through the use of thaumaturgy. This implies that you were in need of guidance, I suppose.'

'What's thaumaturgy?'

'A literal translation would be wonder working. It's the practical application of arcane arts using ethereal energies,' I explained.

'Magic?'

'I suppose so, yes.'

"Okay, it says that it's supposed to guide me through using magic. Oh... wait, hold on," he verbalized.

'You said primary function. What are your secondary functions?' he thought to me.

'I have several,' I answered with a bit of hesitation. If the subject doesn't know why I'm in his head, he might not like my functions very much. 'My active secondary functions are translation, cardiopulmonary regulation, neural tissue regulation, medical diagnostics, companionship, and situational analysis.'

'Wait, what? Neural tissue regulation? You're thinking for me?' he asked in a panic.

'No,' I couldn't help but laugh. 'My neural tissue regulation function allows me to treat and prevent certain mental illnesses and brain damage. It also allows me to interact with you like this.'

The subject thought about this for a moment. These thoughts were scattered and lit up all sorts of neurons. Can't quite read his mind. Yet. I'll work on that. The orcs seemed to be giving him time to sort everything out, but according to my facial recognition software it was obvious they were concerned and had questions of their own.

'What about your inactive secondary functions?' he finally asked.

'Well, I'm not sure,' I replied truthfully. 'I know that I should be able to communicate with a central hub and with other users, but that doesn't seem to be working. There's also corrupted files here and there, and I don't have access to the main database. So I don't know anything except what's in my local knowledge base.'

'Okay, what's in your local knowledge base?'

I took a second to check, 'About 376 terabytes of information regarding anatomy, physiology, language, and other information regarding my primary function.'

'That's a lot of information. You're sure there's nothing about how we got to where we are now?'

'I'm sure.'

'Okay...' he thought. 'Are you able to move my body without my consent?'

Ah, good question. I tried to earlier so I feel like I should be able to... Oh, there it is. A procedure to do exactly that!

'Yes, but not while you're conscious. I couldn't do it earlier, but that's because I didn't have full access to our hardware,' I happily explained. Then I realized his most likely reaction to this information. 'Don't worry, it's a survival function. I feel no urge to move you unless we're likely to die.'

'That's... well... okay, I guess. How did I get on the altar, then?' he asked.

'I don't know. I might have been in survival mode. I genuinely don't remember anything before you got on the altar. Do you mind if I ask you a question?'

'Sure,' he answered hesitantly.

'Is your name Nick or Subject Zero?'

'My name is Nick.'

'Understood, thank you! I'll change your name on the registration,' I said as I did just that.

Nick. Not a terrible name. I felt a little flush of embarrassment as I realized that I introduced myself as Ten for no reason. That embarrassment faded as I realized I actually preferred Ten over Tenzing. Then it returned when I realized that he hadn't said anything about the pun. Maybe he didn't get it.

Regardless, I'm sure my creators had their reasons for naming me Tenzing, but there's no significance for me. Ten, on the other hand, is the first pun I've ever made. A very fitting pun at that. Like it was predestined! I'll continue to go by Ten, then.

Nick relayed the information I had given him to the orcs as a question began to bother me. Who created me in the first place? I scanned everything I could, trying desperately to find an answer. Unfortunately I couldn't find a single hint of the name of my creators. That's concerning, and not just for me. Nick seems just as confused as I am at all of this, so I'm certain not having the answer to this question is going to bother him. Hopefully he doesn't ask.

'Who made you and put you in my head?' Nick asked.

Fuck.

'I was just trying to find the answer to that very question,' I replied. 'I have no idea. I'm sorry.'

I countered the sudden rush of epinephrine that indicated a panic setting in. I may not be able to treat the causes of Nick's anxiety, but I can keep him lucid. No panic attacks on my watch.

"Ask it about this writing," one of the orcs said.

"Okay," Nick replied and pointed at the side of the casket. 'Ten, what type of writing is this, and what does it say?'

I examined the writing on the fixer casket and came to a horrifying conclusion. That's not a fixer casket. It would appear that it has similar functions, but it doesn't match the specs I have on file. To top it off, the writing was foreign to me as well. What the hell is going on here?

'I'm... I'm sorry Nick, I don't know what that writing says. I can only read human languages and Gon. That's neither,' I tried to mask my concerns.

"It says it can only read human languages and Gon, and it doesn't recognize this language," Nick told the orcs.

The two orcs wearing robes looked at each other with wide eyes. Then they looked back at Nick. It took them a bit to formulate what they wanted to say.

"Gon is a precursor language to Orcish, Elvish, and Dwarven," said the bald one. "There are very few people left who can speak or read Gon, and that's because it was last used regularly about four thousand years ago."

"So that machine is either very old, or was meant to act as a research aid of some sort," the other one added.

'There are other possibilities,' I informed Nick.

"Hold on," Nick verbalized. 'What other possibilities?'

'Well, it's possible that whoever or whatever made me was unaware that Gon was a dead language. The translator database is a mess, almost like someone was trying to correct mistakes. Gon's the only written language I have, but I have verbalized language packets titled Orcish, Gnomish, Elvish, Drow, Daimun, Drakon, Dwarven, and Anyelish. There aren't time stamps, so I can't refute the robed orc's hypothesis, but if I was four thousand years old it would be unlikely that I would be able to translate for you.'

Nick went back to chatting with the orcs and I saved images of the text in case I needed them later. The room we were in offered very little in the way of clues regarding my origin, but data is always good. I caught a glance at Nick's reflection in the mirrored walls. Interesting. Not aesthetically displeasing. Not sure how I'd feel if my host was ugly. Would that negatively impact my mental health? It might increase my workload depending on how insecure the host was about their features...

"Okay, so to recap, we found out that Nick has a machine in his head and that the text on the caskets is most likely Drakon," a female orc said with an air of authority. "The objects in this room also seem to be pretty technologically advanced. That sound about right?"

The other orcs nodded.

"Alright, we have a mission to get to. We'll escort you three to the cross-way," she continued.

"Wait," Nick said. 'Ten, are you able to boost my combat abilities?'

A very interesting, if not somewhat alarming question. I checked my systems and the answer had absolutely no ambiguity. It was almost like it was what I was made for.

'Yes I am.'

Chapter 17

Nick Smith
Adventurer Level: 5
Human - American

'Yes I am,' the AI said.

I glanced at the orcs who were watching me with concern plain on their faces. If I were in their place I'd be alarmed too. Hell, I probably should be, and this machine in my head is likely the reason I'm not. On the other hand, a lot of things make sense now. The translations, the shape of my magic pathways, the speed with which I've been picking up skills, all of it can be attributed to Ten. I met eyes with Yhisith.

"I'm coming with you," I stated.

The silence I had broken returned much heavier than before. Yhisith, Joni, Yulk, and Matri looked confused. Nash looked angry, which is quickly becoming his default expression. Thunra crossed his arms and grinned widely at me.

"How come?" Thunra asked.

"Our investigation has resulted in more questions than answers," I replied. "There might be more information where the monster is. Plus, it turns out I'm a mechanically assisted fighter."

Nash stopped looking angry, "The machine helps you fight?"

"Yeah."

My answer was met with silent contemplation, but

after a few moments Thunra started shifting uncomfortably. He looked to the others and then locked eyes with me.

"I don't know what everybody else is thinkin' about, but you're still level five ain't you?" he asked. "The thing we're gonna be fightin' killed orcs that were a bunch of levels above you. Is the machine thingie gonna be able to help you THAT much?"

It was a valid question, and one I didn't know the answer to. But what else can I do? I have to find out more about how I got here so I can figure out how to get back. I NEED to get back.

'Ten, do you have an answer to his question?' I thought.

'Yes, I do,' Ten responded hesitantly. 'I'm learning that the Curaguard system measures level primarily based on skills, not actual physical ability. My assumption is that physical ability is either augmented by skills or gained by the process of acquiring those skills, and is thus accounted for in that way. So in theory, I should be able to augment your physical capabilities to a degree that would put you on par with higher level monsters.'

'How much higher?'

'Unknown. Haven't even seen you walk yet,' Ten said. 'With more data I'll be able to bypass your bodies natural self-defense systems, causing you to hit harder and faster. The human body underestimates its own abilities by quite a bit, it would seem.'

'Bypassing my self defense systems sounds pretty dangerous.'

'The self-defense systems over-correct to make certain that you don't hurt yourself when you throw a punch or a kick. I can make that correction with a much more narrow margin, allowing you to use more force without hurting yourself.'

"Okay, Ten says it can help, but it doesn't know by how much," I told Thunra. "It would be safest if I stayed in the rear, so I probably wouldn't be holding you back."

"Probably? Shit," Thunra said. "I wanna see what you can do, kid, but..."

"Yeah, I'm not sure that we can keep you safe," Matri added.

"There's another problem," Nash said coldly. "Yulk and I would have to go as well. Mom would never forgive us if we didn't, even if you survive."

"He's right," Yulk chimed in. "Still, if we stay in the rear we should be fine. There's no doubt that four over-twenties will keep the monster busy enough to ignore us."

"I don't know. I've got a bad feeling about this," Nash replied.

Yulk and I stared at Nash while he mulled it over. After a few moments, Thunra and Matri joined in on the staring. Finally, Yhisith crossed her arms and began to glare at Nash. Nash looked around and settled his gaze on me.

"Fine," he sighed heavily. "We stay in the back, though. If things go south, we run. Deal?"

"Deal," Yulk and I lied in unison.

I stood up and was struck by how different I felt. Lighter, faster, and much stronger. I didn't know if it was Ten or the table responsible for this, but it felt amazing. As I followed after the orcs I noticed something else was different. I was nervous, but my heart wasn't hammering away in my chest. It was beating its normal rhythm, as if I didn't have a care in the world.

'Ten, are you controlling my heart?' I asked the machine.

'No, just regulating it. Saving you some energy by making sure your heart-rate stays steady,' Ten answered. 'Would you like me to stop?'

'It's fine. Are you also regulating my muscles?'

'I haven't quite figured that function out yet. Working on it, though.'

Well, that answers the question of whether it was Ten or the table that gave me my power-up. What did that thing do to me? I looked at my hands. My scar had become even smaller, which means that the table somehow healed me. What else did it do?

'Ten, is there anything weird about my body?'

Ten took a second to respond and said, 'Define weird.'

'What are the differences between my body and that of a normal human?'

'Huh... Now that I think about it, your bones and muscles are denser than they should be. Not quite to the point of osteopetrosis, but we should definitely add at least five pounds of fat to you before you try to go swimming.'

'What?' I asked. 'Why?'

'Well, it's extremely unlikely that you're still buoyant. Which means it will take much more effort and energy to keep you above water. The fat will help offset your density. It'll also provide an energy source to keep you moving!' Ten replied cheerfully.

I put my hand on my stomach to feel my abs. They were more pronounced than they'd ever been, probably because I had been working out a lot more. I guess nothing gets you more ripped than being in a survival situation.

'Five pounds? Isn't that unhealthy?'

'No,' Ten answered. 'It varies from individual to individual, but for you it'll begin to become a health concern at around twenty pounds. However, I can mitigate those health risks with proper deposit placement. Keeping the deposits off of the heart, liver, and kidneys, that sort of thing. However, given your current condition my recommendation is to gain between five and ten pounds of fat.'

I briefly wondered if Ten had been programmed by my grandmother. It's not that I don't believe it, I'd heard interviews with strongmen that said that abs mean you're not eating enough, but is it really all that bad to be this lean? Most guys would kill to be in the shape that I'm in. Not to mention how the hell I'm supposed to pack on that much weight to begin with?

My thoughts regarding my nutritional intake were interrupted by our arrival at the barrier. It had been a long walk in both directions, but I wasn't feeling any exhaustion. My feet didn't even hurt.

"We'll take a break and recover a bit before we take down the barrier," Yhisith said.

Yulk and Jino sighed with relief and plopped onto the ground. The rest of us soon followed suit, and we ate a small meal in silence. After I finished eating, I caught myself staring at the barrier, watching the runes peacefully drift across its purple surface.

It reminded me of floating down a river on an inner-tube. The last time I'd done that was with Cass, before she got sick. It had been a great time. I remember watching the water droplets slowly slide down her clavicle...

'That's Gon,' Ten interrupted.

'What?' I asked, startled. 'What do you mean that's gone?'

'I mean that the runes you are staring at are in Gon,' it explained. 'It says traversal prohibited.'

"Hey Yulk, did you know that the runes on the barrier are in Gon?"

Joni and Yulk both looked up at me with surprising speed.

"What do they say?" they asked in unison.

"It just says traversal prohibited," I said. "But that's weird, right?"

They thought about it for a moment before Yulk spoke up.

"I guess it's not that weird. Most of the spells we

know, and barrier spells especially, were created back when Gon was the primary written language."

"That's correct," Joni added. "Scholars used Gon for quite a while after people started using more modern languages. It's good at condensing information, which unfortunately makes it difficult to translate and teach."

"And since it's harder for people to admire your brilliance when they can't understand what you're writing, Gon was abandoned in favor of modern languages," Yulk chuckled.

"I don't think it was quite that simple," Joni began.

Before he could continue Yhisith patted her pants and stood up. She cracked her neck and looked at the two sorcerers with a hint of disdain.

"Well, if we're feeling energetic enough to debate linguistics we should have enough energy to continue on," she said. "Any objections?"

Two seconds of silence confirmed that there were none. After a few sighs we all rose to our feet.

"Thunra, you'll take the lead. Matri and I will be flanking a few feet back. Joni, you'll be behind us and you three will be behind him," she said, gesturing at Yulk, Nash, and I.

"Classic diamond formation. Nice," Thunra said.

"Everyone get your lights ready, if you need one I've got extra."

"I'll need it," Nash said.

"Nick and I should be fine," Yulk added.

I gave him a confused look and he grinned at me.

"Thgil tsac," he said, holding a finger above his head.

A light appeared at the tip of his finger and hovered in place. He moved and the light followed. Then he gestured at me.

"Go on, give it a try."

Okay. Light. No problem. Protons? Electrons? Which is it that generates light? Wait, am I overthinking this?

'Imagine a ball of light appearing from your fingertip. I recommend setting the generation point above your right shoulder,' Ten instructed.

'Okay, thank you,' I replied.

I pointed above my shoulder like Ten said and thought about a ball of light. How it would look, how it would feel. White, bright, and slightly warm.

"Thgil tsac," I heard myself say.

I felt the magic travel from my chest through my arm and out my fingertip. The light appeared where I was pointing, just like it did with Yulk. I smiled a little when I noticed mine was brighter than his, though.

"There you go," Yulk said with a laugh. "It's a basic spell, but far more useful than most people give it credit for."

The rest of the adventurers activated their various lights. Joni used a spell like Yulk and I, but everyone else tapped on crystals that were embedded in their clothing. Nash took the spare from Yhisith and held it in his off hand like a flashlight.

"Alright, weapons out," Yhisith commanded. "Joni, kill the barrier."

We drew our weapons and Joni cracked his knuckles before approaching the barrier. Thunra walked up next to him, grinned, and cracked his own knuckles much louder. The sorcerer rolled his eyes and placed his fingers on the barrier. He said something quietly and the runes on the barrier rushed to its center, creating a strange looking opaque bump.

Joni placed his hand on the bump and said, "Emases nepo!"

The barrier quickly shrank into the bump, transforming it into a crystal. It began to fall, and Joni caught it with a quick motion. He placed the crystal in his pocket and gestured down the passageway.

"After you," he grinned at Thunra.

Thunra nodded and started walking. We all fell into formation with Nash and I flanking Yulk and ventured into the darkness, being careful to avoid the damaged portions of the floor. The shredded bricks definitely looked like some kind of plastic, and I recalled the notch in my sword. What kind of material could this be? And what the hell could slice through it?

I looked closer at the slashed lights and had a moment of shock. For some reason I had been expecting florescent lighting, but these were solid chunks of what looked like glass. I shook it off, realizing that florescent bulbs would require power and every other source of light so far had been either fire or magic. I suppose these would fall into the latter category.

We went further and further into the dark until the passage opened up into a room with pillars. I noticed that this room was brown, an odd color compared to everything else in this area of the dungeon. Then the smell of copper and rot hit me. Something deep within me recoiled at the stench, desperately trying to tell me that something was terribly wrong.

"Blood," Yulk whispered.

As we continued forward we began to see splashes of white, and I realized with terror that the room wasn't brown. So many people had died in this room that it was drenched in blood! That's disgusting! Horrible!

What could have done this? What kind of monster are we going to fight? What the hell was I thinking, dragging us in here? We need to get out of here! My heart thundered in my head as panic rose within me, and I nearly threw up before a wave of calm swept over me.

Ten's messing with my brain chemistry, making me calmer. Letting me think. I sighed in relief but almost retched again at the smell. Suddenly, we stopped. I looked past Yhisith and the feeling of terror hit me again, and was just as quickly washed away.

Someone was standing in front of us, completely nude. He stood there staring with sunken eyes and a small yet deeply unsettling smile. The creature's skin was unnaturally pale with the exception of both old and new scars covering it, like pink and purple paint slashed onto a bleached canvas. Long claws gleamed in the light that we were providing, and the fur running along its body was as white as the long hair draping down from its head.

It mouthed a word without uttering a single sound, but I knew what it said. I'd seen mouths make that motion hundreds of times. In perfect English, it had mouthed the word food. A cold knot formed in my stomach as it grinned and I saw teeth in a shape that I hadn't seen since I'd come to this world, except in my own reflection.

'Threat identified. Human male, likely modified and acclimated to dark environments,' Ten informed me.

I didn't even get to respond before it rushed forward with unbelievable speed. Its target was Thunra, who managed to catch the creature by the wrists before the claws impaled his head. I could tell the orc was struggling, but the thing continued smiling. Yhisith and Matri moved in unison so quickly I nearly didn't see them, weapons reaching for the creature's sides.

It leapt into the air and kicked in both directions. As Yhisith and Matri were flying across the chamber, it smashed both its knees into Thunra's jaw. Thunra crumpled to the ground, but before the creature could finish him off Joni shouted something and flung a fiery blue and white spear at him. Without dropping its smile, the creature rolled out of the way and flung a piece of metal that was on the ground at the sorcerer, striking him in the chest and causing him to fall.

It dashed forward with its claws ready to finish Joni when suddenly it stopped dead and sniffed the air. I watched its smile fade as its head turned toward me. My eyes locked with its sunken black orbs and it sniffed the air again. It was about to target me, I need to take the initiative! I readied my sword and began to charge at the thing.

Nash shouted, "NICK! NO! YOU'LL..." and the creature gave a deafening screech filled with wretched hatred and rage, drowning out the rest of what Nash was trying to say.

'Threat exceeds your current abilities,' Ten said in my head. 'Engaging combat mode.'

I didn't even get the chance to ask what it meant before darkness invaded my vision and I slipped into oblivion.

Chapter 18

Nash Alta
Adventurer Level: 8
Orc - Nulevan

Joni crumpled to the ground gasping for air. I hefted my axe, prepared to intercept the creature as it rushed forward. Then the thing suddenly froze in its tracks and slowly turned to Nick, sniffing the air. I stopped and looked at the boy as well. I watched as his face changed from an expression of fear to one of grim determination. In no time at all, he readied his sword for a slash and charged at the creature.

"NICK! NO! YOU'LL..." I managed to shout before the creature's shriek cut me off. It was a terrible sound, filled to the brim with bile and fury.

It was loud enough to hurt, and I instinctively blocked my ears. I watched in horror as Nick's eyes glazed over and he stumbled for a brief moment. Then he caught himself and rushed forward at an incredible speed. Faster than I'd ever seen him move, even with Dash. The creature recoiled at first, then leapt at Nick with its claws at the ready.

Nick ducked the claws and brought his sword up in a slash. The creature contorted mid-air, avoiding a fatal blow. The thing leapt back from Nick and I watched blood drop from its left forearm. My breath caught in my throat as I realized that it was hanging on by a loose flap of flesh, the bone having been cleaved clean through.

"Fucking hells," Yulk whispered.

Nick immediately rushed after the creature with his

sword low to the ground, going for another upward slash. The creature grabbed its arm, holding it in place, and with a screech it fell back. Nick chased after it but the creature managed to stay just outside of his range, leaping off of the pillars to increase its speed. Nick changed up his attack pattern and attempted an overhand slash but the creature ducked him and landed a hard kick that sent him back several feet.

My blood ran cold as I realized that the same kind of kick that had sent the over-twenties flying didn't even phase the boy. His eyes were locked on the creature, and his face was devoid of any expression at all. The creature, on the other hand, was grinning once again. It extended its arms like a bird, and it took a second for me to register that it wasn't bleeding anymore. The damage that Nick had done was completely healed.

"NICK! USE YOUR MAGIC! LIKE WITH THE RATS!" I shouted.

The boy didn't seem to hear me, or at least he didn't act as if he did. He held his sword straight out in front of him in a sort of bastardized fencing stance. It was pointed directly at the creature, and in response the creature curled its fingers until each and every claw it had was pointed directly at Nick's head.

I was so enraptured by this standoff that I didn't even notice Thunra get off the ground. He exploded upward with a curse and immediately launched a haymaker into the back of the creature's head. The thing didn't even get another scream out before Nick was on him. The boy's blade suddenly appeared through the creature's back, and with a flourish Nick slashed sideways, fully severing its arm in the process.

The creature's gurgled another scream, but it managed to knee Nick in the chest and in the same motion elbow Thunra in the face with its remaining arm. The brawler once again flew back and hit the ground, but Nick used the momentum from the blow and slashed again and again. The creature managed to deflect and block these attacks, but it was giving ground fast. Blood poured from its arm and the hole in its side. So much blood. Too much blood. Why won't it fucking die?

"GO DOWN YOU ROTTEN FUCK!" I half shouted, half prayed.

Suddenly Yhisith was back in the fray, supporting Nick as best as she could. The beast and the boy were moving at speeds that made my head spin, though, and she was barely managing to help. I realized that Yulk and I had no chance of helping. I've never felt so weak and helpless. I gritted my teeth as I watched Nick and Yhisith trade blows with the creature. Out of the corner of my eye I saw Yulk move.

I glanced away from the fight and watched my brother kneel over Thunra. The brawler's nose was barely connected to his face, and one of his eyes was hanging out of his head by its nerves. I winced, but Yulk reached down and put the poor Orc's face back together. Then he placed his hand on Thunra's forehead.

"Laeh Retaerg Tsac," Yulk said.

A bright greenish blue glow emanated from his hand. It had been a while since I'd seen Yulk cast such a powerful healing spell. Once the glow diminished Thunra coughed and sputtered up some blood and rolled onto his side.

"Don't get up yet. Catch your breath," Yulk ordered.

"Gotta fight... gotta... gotta kill that fuckin' thing," Thunra replied between coughs.

"Nick's got this. If you must rejoin the fray, await a good opportunity. Don't get blindsided again."

"Good... advice," Joni gasped. "Me... next... please."

The wheezing sounds coming from the sorcerer made me look at him. The chunk of metal was lodged firmly in his chest. I followed Yulk over to Joni and realized that if it had impacted just a little to his left, he'd have died instantly. I looked at Yulk and he nodded, so I reached down and pulled the metal clean out of Joni's chest. Yulk once again cast a healing spell and I looked at the metal.

It was a piece of breastplate. The engraving was unique, and one I recognized very well. This is what's left of Graz's armor. I grabbed a rag from my pocket and cleaned the blood off of it, then put the rag and the piece of armor back in my pocket. If we survive this, I'll give it to Graz's wife. No better way to honor my former team leader.

Another scream returned my attention to the fight. It came from Yhisith. The creature had managed to bite onto her wrist, but before it could bite through Nick tried to decapitate it. The thing barely managed to dodge and roll away, picking up its arm in the process. It ripped off one of its fingers and threw it at Yhisith hard enough to pierce her knee and pin it to the floor. She let out another scream and the beast began to move in for the killing blow, but once again had to dodge an attack from the boy.

It danced backward and put its arm back where it was

supposed to be. I don't know if the creature's eyes actually worked, but it appeared to be studying Nick intently. Nick, however, calmly raised a finger at the creature.

"Raeps Dniw Tsac."

A massive amount of magical energy flowed from the boy's finger, creating a cyclone that speared its way toward the creature. The thing leapt to the left, but the edge of the Wind Spear caught it in the side, tearing off a sizeable chunk. The creature fell to the ground, doubled over from its wound. Nick continued to point and took a step forward, pooled blood from the beast splashing under his boot.

"Raeps Dniw Tsac."

The thing rolled but not fast enough. The second wind spear caught it in the leg, ripping it to pieces. Nick took another step forward.

"Llaberif Tsac."

The hairs on my arm and neck stiffened as the arcane energies ignited the air in front of Nick's finger. The red and yellow flame grew several feet in size, but then condensed to the size of a fist and changed color to blue and white. It flew at the creature faster than my eyes could track, and an extremely loud boom sounded before it even made contact. I covered my eyes with my arm as the flash of the flames lit up the chamber.

The creature screamed once again, rolling on the floor and writhing in agony. Once the flames died down, Nick stopped pointing and leapt at the creature, sword raised and ready to strike the killing blow. Landing astride the creature, he brought the sword down and my breath caught in my throat as the creature managed a desperate swipe at the blade. I watched it clatter to the floor, right next to two others.

The boy was not deterred in the slightest. He slammed the basket guard into the creature's sternum in a move that I was very familiar with. Breathtaker strike. The creature's arms spread open as it bounced off of the ground from the blow. Then he did it again and I heard bones crack. The creature struggled to scream, but Nick pinned its arms down with his knees and began punching it in the head over and over.

The heavy bronze basket-guard took a few blows before cracking the creature's skull. Then it took a few more to turn the creature's head into paste. Blood splashed onto Nick's face, but he kept punching until a small fragment of metal fell out of the beast's exposed brains. Nick barely glanced at before crushing it with what was left of his sword.

He paused a moment and then stood up. He dropped his sword and took a couple of steps back before crumpling to the ground.

"Fuck," I muttered.

I ran over to the boy. He was absolutely drenched in blood, but I doubted any of it was his. I stared at him for a moment with mixed emotions. On the one hand, I felt kind of good about being right about how dangerous he is. On the other hand, he just went toe to toe with a boss that floored four over-twenties in less than ten seconds. My gaze lingered on the axe in my hand.

I shook my head to clear away those thoughts. This is my brother, and I swore to help him on the honor of the Alta clan. If I use this axe on him, I might as well use it on Yulk and my mother as well. It would be akin to spitting in the face of every one of my ancestors. I clipped my axe back onto my belt and checked the boy for injuries. I didn't find any, and looked up at Yulk as he approached.

"Matri's still out, but she'll live," he informed me. "She'll probably forget how to do math or something, though. How's Nick?"

"I think he's fine. He's covered in blood but I didn't see any cuts," I replied.

"Damage... minimal..." Nick muttered.

I looked down at the boy and then back at Yulk. We both had the exact same confused expression on our faces. I stood up and backed away.

"Hello. Are you Ten?" Yulk asked.

A few moments trickled by before it responded.

"Yes... sorry, I'm new to... communicating in this way," it answered in a monotone.

"What happened to Nick?" I asked with more concern than I meant to.

"Nick's sleeping. The altered human was going to attack him, and Nick wasn't going to run away. I didn't have a choice, I'm sorry," the AI said, managing to add regret to Nick's voice.

"Is he going to be okay?" I demanded. "He's not going to sleep forever, is he?"

"No. He's just resting. I had to push his body very hard."

"Sorry, did you call that beast an altered human?" Yulk asked.

"Yes, but I don't have much more information than that. I came to that conclusion based on the fact that it is... was a human and it's significantly altered. I do not know why, how, or by whom."

I glanced over at the over-twenties. They were all huddled around Matri, thankfully far enough away to be out of earshot. I turned back to the bot-boy.

"So Nick could end up like that?" I hesitantly asked.

"Not if I can help it," Ten replied. "But to clarify, anything can end up like that. Not just humans."

I felt a mix of relief and concern. It's not that I necessarily trusted the machine, but something about the way it said that made me believe it. However, the thing that turned that human into a monster might still be down here somewhere.

"Hmm. Well, nothing we can do about that," Yulk muttered. "So, Ten, it's not that I think Nick was being intentionally misleading, but it's better to hear it from the source. What exactly are you?"

"Honestly, I'm not entirely certain," Ten said softly. "I know I'm an artificial intelligence, but I don't know who made me or necessarily why. Judging from my load order I am intended to be a guide and translator, but I'm also able to completely override a subject's consciousness for combat purposes. I have a knowledge base, but the knowledge within it is specific to my role as a guide and doesn't answer any of my lingering questions. Also, some of the articles are apparently misleading."

"Knowledge base?" I asked.

"A sort of specialized library," Yulk answered. "Which articles are misleading?"

"The article that details my combat mode, namely. The specifics for triggering it are correct, as well as how to trigger it, but it did far more damage than the article said it would," Ten replied. "Subjects may experience unconsciousness for up to thirty seconds after combat mode has ended. Side effects may include nausea and vertigo. That's what it says, but judging from his delta wa... the way his brain is acting, he's in a deep sleep. Plus the strain I've put on his muscles means he's gonna be sore when he wakes up."

"What, like an intense workout?" I asked with a chuckle. "Some people would kill to have a machine do their workouts for them."

"A little more severe than that, I'm afraid. Brains limit how they move muscles so those muscles don't destroy themselves. I'm able to override that and push muscles much closer to their point of failure. Combined with my ability to near-instantly respond to stimuli this makes a subject much stronger and faster..."

"But it also wears them out faster," I interrupted. "I imagine it also may damage internal organs as they struggle to keep up with the new, more intense demands of the muscles."

Yulk looked at me with a raised eyebrow and nodded proudly. I may not be the traditional sort of intellectual, but I know muscles. And I'm also familiar with what happens when one artificially pushes them past their limits. The longer or harder one does that, the more intense the damage to the rest of the body becomes.

"So what's his problem, then?" I asked.

"Nothing I can't handle," Ten clarified.

"Would a healing spell help?" Yulk asked.

"Oh! Yes, actually!" Ten replied excitedly. "Why didn't I think of that?"

Yulk smiled and held his hand over Nick's chest. I turned to check on the over-twenties as Yulk cast his spell. Thunra was helping Matri to her feet. A little wave of anxiety washed over me. How would they react to Ten?

If they decided to take advantage of Nick's weakened state to destroy Ten, Yulk and I would be honor-bound to try to stop them. They're way too strong for us, though. The monster may have had the upper hand during the fight, but Yulk and I would have been instantly killed in that fight.

"Maybe we should keep this little chat to ourselves," I whispered as they began to approach.

"Probably not a bad idea," Yulk replied. "Ten, stay quiet please."

There was no response as the others approached, which I decided to take as Ten agreeing with us. Thunra was grinning like a child, but mixed emotions were playing out on the faces of the others. Like someone whose pupper took off a kid's hand, and now they have to put it down. I stepped in front of Nick as they got closer.

This could end badly.

Chapter 19

Nash Alta
Adventurer Level: 8
Orc - Nulevan

The over-twenties took note of my defensive posture as they approached. Thunra raised an eyebrow as if he was confused by my reaction, but the rest avoided eye-contact. Instead, their eyes rested in tactical positions, where they could see if I made a sudden move. A very unfortunate indication of where their thoughts were.

"How's he doing?" Yhisith asked gingerly.

"I've cast healing, but that fight had to have taken a lot out of him," Yulk answered as he turned to look at them. "I cannot begin to imagine what you must be thinking about this turn of events, nor do I care. I want to make one thing absolutely clear. If you attempt to harm this boy, we will be required to defend him."

"But why?" Joni asked, shocked.

"He is our brother," I said. "Adopted, no less. To take one into our family and not defend them to the death? You'd have never heard of our clan if we were capable of such an act."

"He's right. The Alta clan's serious about that kinda thing," Thunra added.

"Your words are wiser than you know," Yulk said with a malicious grin. "If you attack us, you'll likely win, but then you'll have to walk out of here without us. Once you do that, our entire clan will become your sworn enemies. Those who can't fight you will find ways to ruin your life until those who can fight you are able to end it."

I struggled to keep my face stoic and not show the relief washing over me. I had completely forgotten about that! Clan Alta handles family matters internally and does not abide outside interference. It's a right granted to us by the many sovereigns in our debt, including the High Chief. There's exceptions, like preventing a clan-mate from actively committing murder, but generally speaking only members of Clan Alta are allowed to kill other clan-mates. I continued to stare at the over-twenties with a stony expression.

Matri sighed and then laughed, "Even if we win, we lose. Well, thankfully, I like the boy enough to leave him to your judgment."

"He could be very dangerous," Joni added hesitantly.

"So can we," Thunra countered. "Plus, and I don't wanna admit it, he probably saved our asses."

"That was the machine in his head," Yhisith said. "I fought alongside him for a bit there. His expression never changed, and he was fighting like a pro. Even the dumb moves were efficient. There's no way a level 5 can fight like that. Even if he were innately talented to that degree, he would've picked up enough skills by now to be at least level 10."

"What does it matter?" I asked. "The facts are laid before you, plain as day. You are powerful adventurers capable of great good, but this decision is not yours to make. If the boy does become dangerous, our clan will handle it. But if you fight us here, you will die regardless of the outcome."

"He's right, Yhisith. You won't have my support in this," Matri said.

"And I'll kick your ass if you try anything," Thunra joined in. "Might as well, since I'll die if I let you kill them."

Yhisith looked at her companions. Matri and Thunra stared into her, but Joni's eyes were glued firmly to the floor. She turned to me and met my gaze.

"That's gotta be the most eloquent way that I've ever been told to know my place," she said sourly. "But fine, no harm will come to Nick by my hands."

"Nor mine," Joni added, still staring at the ground.

"Well, glad that's settled then," Yulk said as Nick began to stir.

The boy opened his eyes and looked at us with confusion apparent on his face. He held his head with one hand and used the other to try to stand up. Seeing he was a little shaky, Yulk helped him stand.

"What happened?" Nick asked.

"Your mechanical whatsit won the day," Thunra answered with a grin. "We might've pulled through without you, but it would've been a damned close thing."

"I... I don't remember any of it. I remember a terrible scream, and then waking up just now. I was fighting?"

"Yes, you were," Yulk answered. "I believe that was thanks to your artificial intelligent guide."

Nick looked even more confused before everything

seemed to click into place. He stared into the middle distance, his frown deepening every few moments. It took me a moment to realize he was probably talking to Ten.

"Okay, I get it now. Ten said that its analysis of the creature determined that if I fought it I would have died. As a self-defense measure, he knocked me out and took control of my motor functions," Nick explained. "Apparently, he told me that he'd have to knock me out to move me around earlier, but I must have missed it in all the excitement."

"I wonder if it can learn new skills for you while you're unconscious," Joni muttered to himself.

Everyone turned to look at the sorcerer, who immediately looked back to the floor. Joni's a clever one, I'd never have thought of that. I turned to look at Nick, who was now also staring at the floor.

"Ten says no," Nick said. "I'm not entirely sure, but I think it's saying that skills are linked to your subconscious and its ability to interact with that part of my brain is limited. It can activate skills that I've learned, though."

"Well this is all very interesting, but we've beaten the boss," Matri said. "We should start heading back, right?"

"Well, these three came with us for a reason. Might as well explore a bit more," Yhisith replied. "Much as I hate to say it, we should also make sure there aren't more of this... thing running around."

"It's a human," Nick said softly. "Or, it was. Something changed it. Twisted it into that monster."

We all stared at the corpse in a somber silence. How would I have felt if it had been an orc? I don't know for sure, but I doubt I'd have felt good about it. After a moment, Nick looked up at us and sighed. Then he turned his attention to his surroundings, and found the basket guard of his sword. Then he sighed again.

"Dammit," he said, hefting the basket-guard turned knuckle-duster.

"We'll find a job that'll get you a new one," Yulk chuckled.

"Maybe it can be repaired," I added. "That's usually cheaper. Lemme grab the blade."

I jogged over to where the blade of the sword had fallen. There were three blades on the ground, but the one that was Nick's was obvious. His was the single edged blade, the other two were double edged with an exaggerated point. I paused and stared at them for a moment. Even broken, I was able to recognize the short-swords I'd been bugging Kirisaka about.

"Fuck," I whispered to myself as a wave of grief swept over me.

I already knew he was dead. He would have been teleported to the dungeon entrance otherwise. It was foolish, childish even, to think that he could have survived. Nevertheless a small part of me had been holding out hope that he was still alive. Seeing the swords that he obsessed over in this condition left no doubt of what happened to him, and crushed my hopes of seeing him again for good.

I took out my rag and gathered all three blades, and looked around for the Kirisaka's grips. Once I found them I gathered them too, and rejoined the group.

Yulk's face fell in sympathy as he saw what I was holding.

"I'm sorry, Nash," he said.

"It's alright. At least I didn't actually have to pry them from his cold, dead hands," I joked softly.

The rest of the group was silent as I stuffed the broken weapons into my pack. Who knows, maybe I'll find someone who can fix them. I'm not one to use the weapons of the dead, but I could mount them as a keepsake to remember Kirisaka by or something. Once I finished packing I turned back to the others.

"Let's get going," I said.

We started by exploring the chamber we were in, which may have been a mistake. There had been a certain stench of death permeating throughout the chamber, but once we began exploring the walls it nearly became overpowering. There were random bones and pieces of meat strewn about the deeper corners. Most of the bones were obviously orcish, but some of them were different. Monsters, rodents, and...

"These are human bones," Nick finished my thought.

The teeth were the giveaway. Flat teeth mixed with sharpened teeth were a dental pattern I'd only ever seen in Nick's mouth until today. I gingerly picked up one of the skulls. It was very old. The pieces of flesh that clung to it were as hard as stone, like jerky left out in the sun for a year. Since there was no sun down here, it must have been in this condition for a very, very long time.

"They've got gnaw-marks on them," Yulk said. "These

were meals for the monster. I wonder if it killed them, or if they died naturally and it ate them after."

"It's hard to tell. The bones are scattered around, and the rest of the human bones look too much like Orc bones. Or maybe the only bones left are the skulls," Joni added. "These bones weren't put here in reverence, though. This is essentially a trash pile, so I doubt the monster cared about them."

"Maybe he lost his sanity because he had to resort to cannibalism," Nick suggested. "He was trapped in here for who knows how long. If he really was altered, he couldn't have always been a monster."

"Well, we'll probably never know," Yulk said. "Let's move on."

We left the gory sight behind and found an exit to the chamber we were in. The darkness seemed to get deeper the further we went, and I suddenly noticed that we were all moving silently. I guess the others are having the same thought I am. What if there's another one further in here?

We encountered several turns until we finally found a light at the end of the passage. We quickened our pace until we entered the room the light was coming from. It took me a moment to realize we were in a library, filled with shelves holding many leather-bound tomes.

"Excellent!" Yulk said. "A repository of knowledge! Perhaps we'll have our answers at last."

I picked up one of the books and jumped back as dust poured from its cover. Yulk and I shared a confused look, and he picked up another book with similar results.

"Oh, come on," Nick muttered.

"I guess these tomes weren't cared for very well," Joni said. "It would seem the years have not been kind to them."

"Let's see if there's anything useful," Yulk added.

We began to search the books for anything that was still legible. Most of the pages that weren't dust were too faded to read, and the ones that weren't faded were unhelpful diagrams of plant-life that none of us had ever seen before. There were piles of dust and leather-bound covers scattered across the floor by the time we were done.

"There isn't even another exit from this room," Thunra said. "I think we've found what we're gonna find, folks."

"I agree, let's start heading back," Yhisith replied.

As she said that, a familiar glow surrounded us. Nick was the only one of us who looked alarmed as the glow turned into a blinding light. Once the light faded, I opened my eyes to the sight of the dungeon entrance. There were other groups of adventurers scattered around us. Some of these adventurers looked a bit ragged, a telltale sign of having delved rather deep. Others looked annoyed at the shift, probably because they hadn't found any loot yet.

"Well, that's convenient," Matri said.

"Oh good, my feet were beginning to hurt," Joni added with a small laugh.

"Let's go see the Chief," I said.

As a group, we exited the dungeon and headed for the Chief's. The library had been a bust, but we'd found three very important clues. The writing on the altar things, Ten is the voice in Nick's head, and the monster had been a human at some point but something had twisted it into a thing of madness. I suppose the other human remains could also be considered a clue.

I rubbed my forehead as we walked to try to make sense of it all. The writing was likely Drakon according to the two sorcerers. Ten couldn't understand the writing, which means he probably doesn't speak Drakon? But he does speak Gon, which is a much older language. It, I mean. Is Ten male or female or neither?

Doesn't really matter. Anyways, the human remains indicated that the monster had eaten them. Did those remains belong to people that the monster knew? Were they the ones who modified the thing? Also, and I can't believe this didn't occur to me before, why wasn't the entire hidden part of the dungeon dark? Why didn't the monster try to leave the dungeon before?

What if the monster and the other humans had been trapped in the dungeon together? What had the monster eaten after it ran out of humans? Maybe it wasn't able to die from starvation, but could still feel hungry. That would definitely drive ME insane. Nevertheless, the information we managed to obtain resulted in more questions without giving us many answers in return.

"Hey Gluhern, ya old so an' so!" Thunra shouted as we entered the Chief's chambers.

"Thunra! I see you all survived! Welcome back. How'd it go?" Gluhern asked with a grin.

I looked at the two incredulously. I hadn't been aware that they were acquainted. I guess it kind of makes sense, they're both brawlers and I think they're from roughly the same part of the chiefdom. It's a small world.

"Well, it was a close thing," Yhisith said. "Turns out the monster was much stronger than we thought it was."

"Yep, at least one of us would've died if it hadn't been for Nick," Matri added. "Maybe all of us."

Chief Gluhern slowly turned to glare at Yulk and I.

"Correct me if I'm wrong, but didn't I say not to take part in the fight?" he asked with a dangerous tone.

"No, you said you'd prefer if Nick didn't..." Yulk started to say before he had to dodge a goblet.

"THAT WAS RHETORICAL, SORCERER!"

"We've got nothing to apologize for, chief," I said. "We made our decision based on the information that was available to us at the time, and it turned out to be the right decision."

Gluhern looked at me with fire in his eyes, but when he saw that I wasn't trying to egg him on like Yulk had been the fire died out. He gave a big sigh.

"Fine," he said. "Tell me what happened."

Chapter 20

Nick Smith
Adventurer Level: 5
Human - American

"So without Yulk, Nash, and Nick there we'd have bit the dust, probably," Thunra said. "Joni definitely would've."

Yhisith and Thunra had caught Chief Gluhern up to speed, and had even provided a tactical analysis of the fight with the monster. The part of the story that I hadn't been awake for had me a little stunned. I hadn't quite believed Ten when he said that my brain was holding my body back. Intellectually, I knew it was true, because I had heard the same thing from my weightlifting coach in Fitness class. But fighting against my own mind had only ever resulted in one or two extra reps.

To hear about how my body fought that monster without me in control was something else entirely. Could I do that without Ten, now that I know? Could I push myself to those extremes? Maybe with training, but it feels unlikely. What do I do if I encounter another enemy like that?

Then there's the matter of losing control of my body. I'm not exactly comfortable with it, and not just because it hurt like hell when I woke up, like I'd done a super-intense workout without stretching or hydrating or taking any breaks. But what if the reason that guy turned into a monster is because he also had an 'AI Assistant', and it permanently took control of him? Come to think of it, can Ten read my mind when I'm not thinking at it?

I waited a moment to see if Ten would reply to that. Nothing. It could just be playing coy, though, not wanting to feed into my apparent paranoia. There's no way that I'd be able to tell.

"So what do you think we should do, chief?" Matri asked, snapping me back to the matter at hand.

"Well, you four can head back to the High Chief at your leisure to collect your reward. Feel free to rest in the village, and maybe spend some coin while you're at it," Gluhern chuckled slyly. "Nash, Nick, and Yulk, unsurprisingly, you've been summoned by Ulurmak. You'll be heading to the capital with the next trade caravan. It leaves tomorrow morning."

"Tomorrow morning? Nick doesn't have a weapon, and my axe is damaged," Nash said. "We'll need to see a smith to get back up to combat readiness, and it's going to take them more than a night to fix our gear."

Wait, Nash didn't fight the creature...

"How'd your axe get damaged?" I asked.

"Never you fucking mind, boy," Nash growled.

"He wacked it on the pod after it sealed you inside," Yulk said with a grin. "You know, kinda like what he told you not to do with the wall."

We all had a bit of a laugh at Nash's expense. He didn't laugh with us. Instead, his expression remained stoic with a touch of anger. Once the laughter died down Gluhern sighed.

"I'm not at liberty to give you more time. Ulurmak wants you in his presence as soon as possible and I'm honor-bound to comply," he pointed out. "As are you."

"What if the caravan comes under attack?" Yulk asked.

"It has its own guards, I'd imagine," Thunra answered. "Plus, I'll come along. I ain't gonna need more than a night's sleep to recover, and I got nothin' to buy 'cept maybe a keep-sake. We can train when the caravan takes its breaks!"

Nash grinned, and the lingering smile I had at the thought of his mishap faded rapidly. Nash is huge compared to me, but Thunra is downright mountainous. Even if I just mimicked his workout routine, it would probably result in an injury. And I've got no doubts as to what Nash is currently thinking.

"I like that idea, Thunra," Nash said with a certain malice in his tone. "I'll bring along the wooden weapons. We'll have the boy up to level 10 in no time."

I looked to Yulk for help, but he just softly shrugged.

"I'll be coming along as well," Matri said. "I could probably use a rest, but I wanna get paid as soon as possible. Got some gear upgrades in mind."

Yhisith and Joni also voiced their intentions to travel with us, but I was spiraling into a state of depression and anxiety at the thought of the pain that was waiting in my near future. At least if things got too bad, Yulk would be there to heal me up.

'You seem to be anxious about sparring with Thunra,' Ten said. 'You don't need to be, I'll make certain he doesn't critically injure you.'

'Actually, the thought of that makes me even more anxious,' I hastily replied. 'I'd rather remain in control of my body, regardless of the consequences to my physical well-being.'

'I'm sorry, Nick. I can't comply with that desire. Keeping you alive is my highest priority,' Ten explained. 'Plus, if you die, I die. I don't want to die.'

'And I don't want you hurting my friends and potentially turning me into that monster,' I said. 'If you take over and harm Thunra, then what happens if Nash and Yulk try to stop you?'

Ten paused for a moment, seemingly contemplating the point I had just made.

'I understand your concern. I am confident that I will not have to utilize lethal force against the orcs if I am forced to intervene. I'll be gentle, as it were. Also, I feel I should clarify that the altered human was not being controlled by an artificial intelligence. It had a module, but the module was in standby mode. Similar to your own before you reentered the dungeon.'

"Alright then, the plans are made. Good journeys," Chief Gluhern said.

We parted ways with the chief and I followed along after Nash and Yulk somewhat mindlessly.

'What do you mean the module was in standby mode like mine?' I asked Ten.

'Your AI module was in standby mode before I was activated. In standby mode, the module is able to automatically translate spoken languages and rapidly heal a subject back to the state it was in prior to the installation of the module.'

'So the monster understood us and attacked anyway?'

'If it had the proper language packs, yes. Although I doubt it could have made sense of it. Judging by its hyper-predatory attack patterns, I'd say it was quite feral.'

'He,' I corrected. 'Wait, hold on. When you say rapidly heal a subject back to the state it was in prior to having the module installed, what exactly does that entail?'

'The module is able to automatically detect grievous damage to a subject and utilize a nanite package to correct said damage. Given enough time and resources, it can even regenerate lost limbs.'

'But does it restore everything back to its original state? Cuz Yulk healed me and my scar got smaller, and I think he healed me to wake me up.'

'The module has a fail-safe that prevents it from undoing natural healing. So if it were installed in someone that had already been injured, they'd be able to heal on their own and the module wouldn't interfere. This, apparently, also applies to magical healing. That's not in the kbase, but I suppose it makes sense. The module measures your current state with that of an average human body to determine whether or not to make a correction. It can even prevent a subject from aging while in stasis.'

One concern alleviated, only for more to pop up.

'Okay, two things. First, does that make me effectively immortal? And if that's the case, does that mean there's no way to determine how long the altered human and I were in the dungeon?' I asked.

'You're highly resistant to the rigors of time, but

sufficient damage to your body or my module will kill you. Also, the aging prevention doesn't work nearly as efficiently once the subject is active. So no, you're not immortal,' Ten answered. 'But yes, that does mean that any attempt to estimate the amount of time you or the altered human were in the dungeon would be asinine without further data. Whether or not the altered human entered stasis or how often it did so, for instance.'

So I'll most likely outlive Nash and Yulk if we're not killed by monsters. Well, given our age difference that was probably going to be the case anyway. Wait, how old do orcs live to be? No, not the time for those questions.

'Is there anything else I should know about this nanite package and healing ability thing?'

'Yes. I am in full control of the nanite package. Since you are young, to foster proper muscle growth I'll only be able to use it to heal actual injuries.'

'What? Why?'

'Rapid healing of muscular micro-tears can result in gross disfigurement if not properly managed, and in your case it is beyond my capability to manage properly.'

'How is it beyond your capability?' I asked incredulously.

'Your body is still growing, so both your body and I would be rapidly trying to heal the micro-tears. If we both succeed, then after a while your muscles would become disproportionate and disfigured,' Ten explained. 'I would have to stop your natural healing processes, which is difficult even without the growth hormones at play, before I took action to heal the micro-tears. With larger injuries I can simply pile onto what the body is already doing, but the smaller the injury the harder it is to correctly time my actions.'

'So long story short, that's why I'm still sore.'

Ten paused again, 'Yes. I'm sorry that I pushed you so hard.'

'That's alright,' I said as we arrived at the house. 'We lived. That's what matters.'

"Welcome home, boys!" Yilda called from the kitchen. "At least that better be my boys. If not, more food for Dima!"

I looked at Yulk and asked, "Do you guys have people invading your home a lot?"

"Not a lot. But we do get the occasional assassin or person with a grudge against our clan," Yulk gave me a toothy smile.

"Yeah, but ain't nobody tougher than Mama Alta," Nash added as we entered the kitchen. "I remember when I was six and I saw her kill an assassin with her slipper. Took his head right off, and it wasn't even sharpened or anything."

"Hush now, there's no need for that talk." Yilda said as I was trying to figure out if Nash was joking or not. "How'd it go in the dungeon? Did you find any answers?"

"Not any satisfying ones. We made a copy of the language that was on the altars that Nash found Nick on," Yulk answered. "I think they're in Drakon. Want to take a look?"

"Sure," she said as Yulk handed her some papers.

She held them at an angle and looked down her nose at them, pursing her lips slightly. She squinted for a while, and then raised one of her eyebrows.

"This isn't Drakon. It's close though," she explained. "A lot of the characters are the same, but they're in a different order. I'd guess that it's High Drakon."

Nash and I looked at each other with confused expressions, but Yulk looked shocked. She handed the papers back to him and continued cooking.

"What's High Drakon?" I asked.

"Well, Drakon is the language of those subservient to the high dragons back when they were into governing," Yilda answered. "High Drakon is the sacred language of those high dragons and their chosen elite."

"Wait, WHAT?" Nash asked while glaring accusingly at Yulk. "How come you didn't tell me about that?"

"It wasn't relevant to your studies," Yulk replied softly. "There's a lot of languages that we don't have much chance of encountering, and High Drakon is one of those. It's been thousands of years since the high dragons held kingdoms."

"Fifteen thousand or so since the biggest kingdoms fell apart. But there's still a High Dragon ruling Bolisir. Well, ruling is a strong word," Yilda said with a chuckle. "It's been asleep for going on thirteen hundred years. Bolisir's by far and large considered an elven kingdom now."

"Huh?" Nash and Yulk replied in unison as I remembered an argument they had while I was still in the hospital.

"What do you mean 'huh'? Boys, Bolisir is just over the dragon-jaw mountains, you should know this," she scolded. "Why do you think it's called dragon-jaw and not orc-jaw?"

"W-wait, I... I thought that the dragon had been asleep for a hundred years," Yulk sputtered.

"A-and I thought they tamed it," Nash stammered. "And it was just a dragon, not a High Dragon."

"Wrong on both counts. The High Dragon in Bolisir came into power about eighteen thousand years ago, fought in the Cataclysm Wars, and went to sleep right after the war ended. Hells, you step foot in Bolisir and they'll chat your damned ears off about it."

"B-but the history book Yulk read to me..." Nash said.

"History book?" Yulk asked. "Wait, do you mean the Adventures of Milimaman?"

"Yeah..."

"Oh. No, that was fiction. Sorry, I should have clarified."

"Okay, so wait," I interjected as Nash's face dropped. "Two questions. First, what's the difference between a High Dragon and a dragon? Second, would this High Dragon be able to read the text?"

"High Dragons are both much smarter and much larger than dragons. They can also do magic, whereas dragons just have a breath weapon," Yulk answered.

"And yeah, it would probably be able to read the text. Assuming that the text is High Drakon and we can wake it up."

"And that it's not illiterate," Nash added.

Yulk and I glanced at him to see if he was joking. He wasn't.

"There's a chance that one of the elves in Bolisir can read High Drakon. After all, a High Dragon is technically their king," Yilda said. "Either way, you're going to need a visa and permission from the High Chief."

"Well, thankfully we're on our way to the capital in the morning to speak to the High Chief," Nash said. "Hopefully we can convince him to let us go to Bolisir."

Yilda turned away from the stove to look at us.

"You're on the road again so soon?" she asked sadly.

"Afraid so, mom. Got the summons right out of the dungeon," Nash said softly.

"Damn. Well, I guess that's that. You tell Ulurmak I'm not happy about this. I should get some time to spend with my boys in my golden years, dammit."

"I'll let him know," Nash said with a grin. "So, what's for dinner?"

Chapter 21

Imlor Tula
Adventurer Level: N/A
Gnome - Kirkenian

"Two carts?" I asked incredulously.

"Yes," Moner said. "We were going to have them go
with the main caravan, but they don't want to leave
for another two days. If you're willing to take them
yourself, we'll happily supply you with the additional
cart you'll need."

"And all I've got to do is take the passengers to the
capital?"

"Correct. Eight passengers total. Most are
adventurers, but you will need to spring for a guard
force."

"Adventurers? Can't I just pay them to guard the
caravan?" I chuckled.

"If you can afford them," Moner smirked. "Four of
them are over-twenties, and the other three are over-
fives."

"Yeesh. I can afford the over-fives but even one over-
twenty is too rich for my blood," I said.

"We don't have a lot of time. What's your decision?"

"Of course I'll do it. A free cart? I'd have to be dumb
to say no."

"Good," Moner said with satisfaction. "We'll get it
attached to your current one, and your passengers will

arrive soon."

I nodded my understanding as the chief's aide turned and walked away. Things had gone well for me since the debacle with the giant rats. I'd made more than enough to replace my hnarses and patch my cart up. Now they were going to give me another cart, and all I have to do in exchange is to take some adventurers back to the capital with me. Despite not even technically being a village, Nuleva always treats me pretty well.

I watched as some orcs attached the new cart to the rear of my own. They also moved the goods I'd purchased and evened them out between the carts to make room for seating. I walked over to inspect my new cart.

It was well constructed. Hell, I'd wager it's worth more than my original cart is in its current condition. Buff snorted at me, smelling the yipple in my pack. I chuckled as I pulled it out, ripped it in half, and gave Buff and Regal each a piece. Telena's going to roll her eyes when she hears my new hnarse's names, but I've never been good at naming stuff. Anyone who has any doubt of that may certainly ask Imlor Tula II.

I'm glad I was able to get them for a good price, but I still felt a pang of grief at the loss of Noble and Hulk. These hnarses are much larger than Noble and Hulk had been, because they're bred specifically for pulling heavy loads at speed. They also have a certain... aggression behind their eyes. Like they're looking for an excuse to attack something. It's a tad unnerving, but it might just be my imagination. They'd been remarkably well-behaved so far.

"Are you our driver?" someone from behind me asked.

I turned to see a group of adventurers, and a messenger. The messenger had been the one who spoke. I opened my mouth to respond, but surprise took my voice as I examined the other adventurers. Four unfamiliar orcs, two familiar orcs, and what I now know to be a human.

"Oh, it's you," Nash said.

"Hi Imlor, how've you been?" Nick asked with a smile.

"I've... I've been good," I managed to say. "I'm surprised to see you here. You're the adventurers that I'm taking to the capital?"

"Yes," Yulk interjected. "We've been summoned by the High Chief himself."

"Are we ready to go?" The messenger asked with annoyance at being ignored.

"Not yet, I've got to hire some guards."

"I'm available," one of the largest orcs I've ever seen said with a grin.

Three of the other adventurers looked at him with exasperated expressions. I remembered what Moner had said and realized that these were the over-twenties. The mountainous one notwithstanding, the other three didn't look particularly different from normal adventurers. One was a spell-caster, another was obviously a blade expert, and the third had the unassuming posture of a skilled rogue.

"If you're one of the over-twenties, I'm afraid I can't afford your services," I replied gently.

"Ah hell, you're doin' me a favor by taking me to my

payday," he said with a laugh. "I'll give you a discount. How's fifty copper sound?"

"We could use the money too," Nash added. "Fifty copper for myself and my two brothers as well."

Nick looked at Nash with confusion, "My sword's broken, and isn't your axe chipped?"

Nash looked back at him and replied, "My axe still has plenty of teeth, and you've still got your spells. We'll be able to handle just about anything we run into on the road."

Two silver isn't bad for guards. I'd been expecting to pay at least five. Plus, I've seen the Alta brothers in action. There's no doubt that they're capable of guarding the caravan.

"Deal!" I said before they could change their minds. "Well, that settles that. We're ready to get on our way. Hop aboard!"

I excitedly climbed into the coach-box and grabbed the reins. The hnarses shifted slightly as the adventurers and messenger took their seats. I watched until they were settled, and then urged Buff and Regal to start pulling.

The hnarses began to pull the two carts effortlessly. I'd been a little worried whether or not they could handle it, but my fears were unfounded. Once I was certain they were following the trail without guidance, I turned back to my passengers for some chit-chat. After learning everyone's names, I asked what was really on my mind.

"So, why does the High Chief want to see you?" I asked.

"He wants to meet Nick, and we're probably getting dragged along due to association," Nash answered.

I couldn't tell if he was upset about that or not. Nash has an odd bit of stoicism, it seems.

"Did you make out okay?" Nick asked. "Were you able to still make a profit off the stuff we saved?"

"Yes, and thanks again for the timely rescue. I was able to fulfill the most profitable of my orders and get my cart all patched up. I even got new hnarses!" I answered excitedly. "Meet Buff and Regal."

"Nice to meet you," Nick said with a smile.

The hnarses ignored him and continued striding ever forward. I chuckled at their lack of reaction.

"What happened to your sword, anyway?" I asked.

"It broke. A boss in the dungeon cut right through it."

"Ah, a pity. So you're in the market for a new one then?"

"No, I'm going to try to have it repaired."

"Ah," I winced. "Is it enchanted?"

"No, why?"

"Well, it's usually cheaper to replace a broken blade than it is to fix it. I learned that from my son," I laughed.

"You have kids?" Nash asked.

"Yep. Two sons and a daughter. The eldest is a level 3 adventurer already!" I beamed. "I'm hoping one of my other children will opt to take over the family business, though."

"Why not hire your son as a guard?"

"Guard duty is boring, apparently. It also doesn't pay well until you're over level five," I explained. "I'd obviously pay him more than a normal guard, but the lack of entertainment is a big issue for my boy. He prefers the adventuring part of being an adventurer."

"Your clan's bond could be stronger, then. I would work on that with your other children."

The criticism stung, but I knew it wasn't coming from a malicious place. Nash seems like the honorable sort, and giving harsh advice is one of their greatest displays of kindness. He's not wrong, either. Imlor II and I are civil, but we don't see each other nearly as often as I'd like. I tell myself that it's just because we're busy with work, but the truth is I wasn't exactly a great father and the end result of that is a wedge between us.

A tale as old as time, business always came first. I know it's wrong, but it was ever so easy to justify at the time. I'd considered myself a good dad because I never hit my family, and they never went hungry. Unfortunately, I didn't realize until my son had grown from a boy to a man that that's the bare minimum of fatherhood. I'd missed out on his growth, and didn't make myself available to help mold him. He'd grown into a stranger to me, and I'd let it happen. Now the consequences tear through me like a knife.

It's mostly small things, like how he sends letters addressed to his mother instead of to me, or how he'll go see his friends in town before coming home after an adventure. I'd already resolved to do better by my other children, but it hurt that Nash had been able to see the truth of our relationship after such a brief discussion.

"That's not an appropriate critique, brother," Yulk interjected. "Do we need to work on your social graces again?"

"N-no. I'll do better, I swear," Nash held up his hands in mock horror. "Seriously though, I was out of line, Imlor. I apologize."

"I appreciate the apology, but you're right," I sighed. "Business has always kept me away from my family, but even when I was home I didn't exactly make time for the boy."

"My father would play games with us," Yhisith added.

"Mine would spar with me until we couldn't move anymore," Thunra said with a nod.

"Mine had to work a lot, but made time to take us on vacations whenever he could. Mostly local, but it was still fun," Nick said sadly.

Everyone fell silent at the soft grief in Nick's voice. It hadn't really occurred to me that the human had family back in his world. It reminded me of when I was stuck in the tree, wishing desperately to see my family once again. A terrible feeling, indeed. Nash put his hand on Nick's shoulder.

"Our dad used to do the same thing, before he died," Nash said.

"I don't know if most people would count monster

hunting trips as vacations," Yulk added with a chuckle. "And I'm certain that Nick doesn't."

"Well, it got us out of the house and strengthened our bond, did it not?" Nash asked irritably.

"How did he pass, if you don't mind me asking?" I interrupted.

Yulk and Nash looked at each other for a moment and shrugged.

"He was poisoned by an enemy of our family," Yulk explained casually. "Heart-bane. Nothing could be done."

"Yep, and then mom hunted the poisoner down and carved him into little pieces in front of everyone," Nash said. "We wanted to come with, but she made us stay home. Didn't want us to see that, but we heard about what happened from a city guard years later."

Nick's expression had gone from sad to shocked. The only face that wasn't showing surprise was Thunra's, who nodded along to the story as if it were something he'd heard before.

"Don't fuck with the Alta clan," he said quietly.

It was on this somber and terrifying note that I opted to turn my attention back to the road. We've been making good time, and the change from forest to desert is now within view. This was the portion of road where I had met Nick, Nash, and Yulk. I shuddered at the memory of the giant rats.

"Hey, I recognize that tree," Nick said as the tree that had been my home for a time came into view. "Wait, where's the giant rat bodies?"

"Eaten, presumably," Yulk answered. "There are a lot of predators in the wastes. It would be a terrible omen if a corpse were to last longer than a day."

"Why's that?" Nick asked.

"It would mean that an apex predator is nearby."

Grim, but accurate. There isn't much that is natural about the wastes, but even monsters follow the pecking order. Anything that can be killed without too much of a fight is prey, regardless of what that prey eats in turn. There are some predators who are simply too fast or too strong to be considered prey by anything else, and these apex predators are notoriously difficult to kill.

"Well, it's a good thing that I don't see any signs of our fight, then," Nick said. "So, the wastes, they were caused by the Cataclysm War, right?"

"Wars. There were more than one," Joni said, perking up for the first time since he got on the cart. "Five total, and three of them were fought simultaneously."

"Oh, okay. Who was fighting?"

"Everyone. These cataclysmic conflicts were aptly named. The world nearly ended!"

"He doesn't just mean all life on the planet, either. The magics involved threatened to break our world on multiple occasions," Yulk added. "It got so bad that not much is actually known about the conflicts themselves because hardly anyone survived to write their histories."

"That's right," Joni nodded sadly. "There's an account

carved in stone in the dwarven kingdom of Prignira on the southern continent, but it's unknown if the account is accurate because there's no way to verify it."

"Ain't Prignira one of them bunker countries? Where the whole thing is pretty much underground?" Thunra asked, to which Joni nodded again.

"Wait, okay, so hold on. You don't know what started the fighting?" Nick interrupted.

"Not for certain," Joni answered. "However, the account in Prignira says that daemons conspired to convince all the countries of mer to attack each other, and once that war was nearly finished the forces of Hell invaded our plane of existence. These were the first two cataclysm wars."

"Wait, Hell exists here?" Nick incredulously asked.

"Again, we don't know for certain. A lot of scholars believe that daemons are a convenient scapegoat created to cover up the magical experimentation that went on during these conflicts," Joni explained. "The daemons won the second cataclysm war, according to the account, but their victory was short lived. The third cataclysm war began when the anyels from the plane of Haven invaded, supposedly to restore order and free the mer from the tyranny of the daemons. They managed to take half of every continent, but were fought to a standstill."

"What about the fourth and fifth? Didn't they happen at the same time as the third?"

"Yes. The anyels ruled over their mer with just as much tyranny as the daemons did. Less slavery and butchery, but even the pettiest of crimes were met with extremely harsh punishments. This was the order that they so craved, but mortals require a balance of order and chaos to happily live our lives. The daemons saw this, and made a fatal mistake," Joni said. "They convinced some of the mer who were living under the anyels to rebel. Once they did, the daemons went on the offensive. However, the sight of mortals fighting against the anyels inspired those who were subjugated by the daemons to rebel as well! The war between the anyels and the mer was the fourth cataclysm war, and the war between the daemons and the mer was the fifth. Daemons fighting anyels, mer fighting daemons, and mer fighting anyels. Everything natural in this world rose up against the two occupying armies and fought them back to their own planes."

"Never to be seen or heard from again," Thunra finished with a laugh. "I dunno how much stock I put in tales like that. Think I'm of the belief that powerful mages were fuckin' with forces they don't understand, and opted to cover it up once the dust settled."

"That is the more plausible explanation, but there's technically less evidence of that," Joni countered.

"Lack o' evidence is usually evidence of a cover-up," Thunra said.

"Spoken like a city guard. You ever think about a career change?" Yulk grinned.

"Three hots and a cot don't sound so bad, but my pa would have my balls if I even tried!"

Everyone laughed as we continued our journey.

Chapter 22

Nick Smith
Adventurer Level: 5
Human - American

"C'mon kiddo, you gotta keep your guard up!" Thunra shouted.

"What does that even MEAN?" I asked in frustration as I got off the ground.

I felt a bit of drool drip down my chin. I wiped at it and my hand came back bloody. A slight sting told me that Thunra had split my lip. Angry, I once again put my fists up.

"Alright, see, your hands are too close together. You gotta be able to see all of me," Thunra explained. "Also, you don't really gotta be making fists. You're supposed to be stoppin' me from hittin' you, not tryin' to hit me."

"This is how boxers do it, though," I countered.

"I don't know what that is," Thunra laughed. "But it ain't workin' for ya."

I opened my hands and spread them apart until I could see all of Thunra. He grinned, and rushed at me. I immediately activated time dilation, but it hardly seemed to slow the gigantic orc down. He swung his massive fist and I was able to barely redirect the punch so that it sailed past my head. I clenched my left hand and sent it at Thunra's face as I felt something hit me in the gut. Time Dilation deactivated and I went flying back. I slammed into the ground and rolled, gasping for air and getting a mouth full of dirt for my troubles.

"You managed to block a punch! That's great! Good job, Nick," Thunra shouted with glee as I sputtered.

"Yeah, great" I managed to say once I could breathe again.

I spit the rest of the dirt out of my mouth and rose to my feet again. My legs, however, had other plans and gave out on me. I sighed as I pushed myself back up.

"You alright?" Thunra asked.

"My legs are wobbly. You got me pretty hard," I answered.

"Oh, damn. Sorry about that. I'll dial it back a bit. I was goin' at seventy-five, but I think I overshot your abilities a bit. I'll drop to fifty percent."

It is difficult to describe the wave of emotions that washed over me upon learning that the giant orc brawler had already been holding back. Anger at myself for not being able to keep up, happiness that he's going to be holding back even more, and shock at how much power the bastard actually has.

'I suggest a short break while I repair your spleen,' Ten said.

'My spleen?'

'Yes, that last impact slightly ruptured it. I've got it under control, but it will be easier if you to lay down for a few minutes.'

As logic overwrote adrenaline, the pain where Thunra had hit me got worse. A lot worse. It radiated from my upper left torso, just behind the bottom ribs. It felt like my stomach was on fire and my body was trying to blow out that fire with a needle tornado. I held up one hand and laid on the ground. The pain slowly began to ebb as Thunra walked over to me with a curious expression.

"I need a minute. Apparently, you ruptured my spleen," I said as casually as I could.

"Oh shit," Thunra said. "You gonna be okay? Do we need to call Yulk?"

'Unnecessary. Healing magic will interfere.'

"Ten's got this. Just need a few minutes is all."

Thunra walked over and sat next to me while Ten repaired the injury.

"So uh... what's a spleen, anyways?" he asked.

"I'm not a hundred percent sure. Think it has something to do with filtering blood, like the liver," I answered.

'The spleen controls the level of white blood cells, red blood cells, and blood platelets contained within your blood. It also screens the blood and removes any old or damaged red blood cells,' Ten explained.

"Ah, never-mind. Ten explained it. It filters the blood and controls the levels of white and red blood cells," I said.

"Handy little thing," Thunra chuckled. "I'm guessin' that's not a vital organ, right? The skill I used is supposed to incapacitate, not kill."

'Humans can live without a spleen, but a ruptured spleen causes internal bleeding that can become fatal within twenty-four to forty-eight hours.'

"Uh, Ten says it's not a vital organ, but a ruptured one bleeds inside you and can be fatal after a day or two if it isn't fixed," I answered.

"Alright, that makes sense," Thunra sighed in relief. "If you walk around with that much pain for two days you're kinda asking for it, ya know?"

I lay there silently, letting Ten do its thing. I found it kind of interesting that Thunra's skill was supposed to incapacitate me, but could have ended up killing me in the long run. If you looked at it in terms of black and white, the skill failed. However, a ruptured organ would definitely incapacitate most people, and a ruptured spleen isn't fatal if you get it treated. So in a way, the skill did exactly what it was supposed to do.

I guess skills aren't perfect, and it's probably important to keep that in mind. Don't want to accidentally cause someone's death when I'm just trying to get them to stop fighting. Even though I hadn't learned a skill from our sparring yet, Thunra had still taught me a lesson.

'Spleen repaired, you're good to go,' Ten said.

I enjoyed laying down for a few seconds before sitting up.

"Alright, I'm ready."

"Good," Thunra said, helping me up. "We'll try again, but this time I want you to focus on evadin' my strikes. I'm gonna hit you with a flurry, unless you stop me."

I nodded resolutely. A flurry involves a lot of punches happening very quickly. Definitely don't want to get hit with that. I took my stance, and Thunra charged.

He swung with his right fist and I activated time dilation again. I pushed his right fist upward with my left hand, and elbowed his left fist away from me. His hands quickly tucked back into him and came at me again, but I kept deflecting them. Right, left, right, left, both, left, right. Time dilation wore off, but I was still managing to keep up with his strikes. Barely. Then his left fist did something weird. It seemed to be in three places at once. I blocked one of the strikes, but the two others were going to hit me.

-Preternatural Evasion unlocked-

My foot pushed off of the ground on its own and my body twisted out of the way of the other two strikes, and even managed to avoid a surprise right handed attack. I moved faster than I thought that I could, and Thunra noticed the change in speed. He held up his hands and grinned.

"Woah, okay, let's stop," he said. "Was that a new skill?"

"Y-yeah," I said, once again out of breath. "Preternatural evasion."

"Oh, the dodge one! Congratulations!"

"Th-thanks."

I concentrated on the skill's name, and the box popped up.

--

Preternatural Evasion I

Allows a user to automatically dodge for 1 minute.

Cooldown: 10 minutes

--

"Automatically dodge?" I asked.

"Yeah, you move on your own," Thunra answered. "Well, not that you don't already move on your own. I guess you could say..."

I zoned out as Thunra struggled to explain the concept of automatic movement. Preternatural Evasion seems like a very useful skill, but the ten minute cooldown could be an issue. Maybe if I level it up, the cooldown will decrease.

'Hey Ten, you level a skill up by using it, right?' I asked.

'For the most part. Certain skills require milestones to be met before they will level up, regardless of whether or not the skill is utilized. These milestones are generally able to be met quicker by using the skills, though. Other skills require a deeper understanding of the nature of the skill to level up, which usually occurs naturally while using the skill,' Ten explained. 'It's exceedingly rare for a skill that can level up not to do so as you use it.'

'I understand. So what does Preternatural Evasion II look like? Does the cooldown decrease at all?'

'Well... oh... I can't tell you. Something is stopping me.'

'What? What's stopping you?'

'I do not know. I can tell you all about your current skills, but I can't give you details about ones you don't have,' Ten said. 'Do you want to know more about Preternatural Evasion I?'

'No, no, I got it.'

Well that's concerning, and annoying. I don't even know if leveling up Preternatural Evasion is going to be worth it or not, and now I've got to worry about whatever's keeping Ten from telling me stuff about skills. It's probably the Curaguard or whatever, but I wonder what else Ten can't tell me...

"Like one of them machines, ya know?" Thunra asked, clearly looking for an answer.

"Y-yeah, sure," I replied. "You ready to go again?"

"Thought you'd never ask," he said with a grin.

As we took our stances it occurred to me that I didn't know how much time was left on the cooldown for preternatural evasion. A right hook to the face quickly let me know that it hadn't finished cooling down quite yet. Thankfully, Yhisith interrupted our sparring match before any more punches could be thrown.

"Time to head out," she said.

Thunra complained a bit, but we ended up loading up onto the wagons and continuing on our way, ending my first bout of training. We didn't train on the first day of our journey, because we had left in the afternoon and didn't stop until it was dusk. Well, except for bathroom breaks. I went over the results of my training in my head as we drove on.

'Ten, is there a way to see the cooldowns for my skills?' I asked.

'Yes. You don't currently have any on cooldown, but when you do you'll see it in the upper right corner of your vision,' Ten said. 'I set the opacity to twenty five percent so that it doesn't impede your vision.'

'Thanks.'

We continued on until dusk, stopped, rested, woke up, had breakfast, and got back on the road once again. Most of the discussions were how to best season certain meats that I'd never heard of, with Imlor chiming in when a spice that also paired well with vegetables was mentioned. I was too busy dreading my training with Nash to participate in the conversation much. My dread grew worse and worse as the sun rose higher and higher into the sky. Finally, the carts stopped and Nash was the first to jump out.

"My turn," he said while grabbing two wooden swords. "You'll be on offense today."

My spirits rose at this, and I happily caught the sword he tossed at me. It shouldn't hurt so bad if I'm the one doing the swinging, right? We walked a short distance away from everyone else and took our stances.

"Begin," he said.

I immediately charged at him with an underhand swing to try to throw him off balance. I glanced at the ground to be sure of my footing, and my vision went dark. I shook my head in confusion, and as my sight came back I found myself with a very familiar view. I watched a cloud drift by for a moment, then got up.

'The hell happened?' I asked Ten.

'He leapt forward and kicked you in the forehead. You're fine, though.'

I looked up at Nash and was greeted by an awfully smug expression.

"Keep your eyes on your opponent," he condescendingly said. "Try again."

This time, I tried for a horizontal strike and activated Time Dilation. Nash must have seen this coming, because the blunted point of his blade was exactly where my forehead had to be to complete my strike. If I had used dash, I'd have been knocked out.

I silently cursed to myself and managed to barely avoid the counterattack, backing off in the process. A timer that said Time Dilation appeared and began counting down from five minutes.

"Good, you're not quite as bad as you used to be," Nash laughed. "Try again."

"Shit," I said, staring at the timer.

I took a deep breath and decided on my course of action. I ran toward Nash and activated Slide Slash. He leapt backward, and I threw my sword at his face and used Dash to get closer. I balled up my fist and prepared to activate Breathtaker Strike, but Nash spun around quickly, turning his back to prevent the skill from activating. I brought up my left hand to block the elbow that he threw at my face, but couldn't stop the force he put behind it. My hand smashed into my face and I slammed into the ground.

'Cloud-watching again?' Ten asked.

'Not helpful.'

My bones seemed to creak as I once again got off the ground. The wooden sword I had thrown at Nash landed at my feet.

"You shouldn't throw your weapon unless you have another one handy," Nash said. "Your fists don't count quite yet, by the way."

"Then why did you avoid them?" I asked sarcastically.

"Because I can, and that's my point. What good is a weapon that can't hit its target?"

"I mean, it would hit most targets. The only reason it didn't hit you is because you were expecting it," I pointed out. "The reason I can't land a hit is because you have more experience than I do, and you know my fighting style. It's not fair..."

Nash's laughter interrupted me.

"Why would that matter?" he asked sardonically. "It's not as if I'd be doing you any favors by letting you hit me. You grow as you figure out HOW to hit me, and of course it isn't fair. This isn't some rich noblemer's tournament. We're training to make sure you don't die when faced with monsters. Or would you rather have Ten do all the work?"

I inwardly cringed. Nash had hit a nerve with the Ten comment, and I was immediately embarrassed by my misconceptions.

"No, I don't want Ten to do any of the work," I

answered. "I don't want to be like that... thing."

Nash's attitude changed. His smugness evaporated and he suddenly became concerned.

"Did Ten say something about that?" he asked.

"No. Just an assumption on my part," I replied. "Intuition, I suppose."

'The man in the dungeon did have an AI, but it was in standby mode when we fought,' Ten said.

'How do you know?'

'It didn't respond to any of my attempts at communication.'

'What if it didn't want to talk? Or couldn't?'

'That hadn't occurred to me. I suppose it is a possibility...'

I opted to keep that to myself as Nash sighed.

"Listen, Nick. Do you know what the most important thing to do in a fight is?"

"Protect others?" I asked.

"Ah... right," he scratched the back of his neck. "I was actually going to say survive. I guess it's kind of complicated, but if you've got the option to survive and to help others survive you should take ahold of that option with both hands. So if it comes to that, don't hesitate to rely on Ten. In every OTHER situation, though, you should be fighting with your own two hands."

"Alright, I understand," I said.

I do kind of understand where Nash is coming from, but something feels wrong about using Ten to fight. My dad always used to say that the easy road has hidden pitfalls. I might be biased, because I don't like the idea of something else controlling my body, but I can't seem to shake the feeling that there's some sort of cost to Ten taking over. Maybe I'm just being paranoid.

"That's enough stalling," Nash said with a grin. "Try again."

Chapter 23

Yulk Alta
Adventurer Level: 7
Orc - Nulevan

We've been on the road for four days, and the trip has been mostly uneventful. Nash and Thunra were pummeling some semblance of a fighting style into Nick, and we're making great time on our way to the capital. The only thing we've run into so far is other travelers, and because of this our spirits are high.

Well, except for Nick's. I grinned at the boy as he collapsed into his seat, fresh from sparring with Thunra. My grin was met with a stoic, yet weary, expression. His training had been difficult, but I'd only had to help heal him once. Ten does an amazing job at keeping Nick functional.

My grin faded as the AI came to mind. I recalled the metal box that fell out of the dungeon creature's splattered brains. There's little doubt that it contained a being like Ten, and Ten had also seemed to know to look for it. Although, that could be attributed to amazing reaction time.

If the crazed human in the dungeon had an AI in its head, who was controlling the body? Perhaps the AI was like Ten before it woke up, and the human simply lost his mind due to the tragic nature of his situation. He had to have been down there for a very long time, so that could have cost him his sanity as well. Being alone in the dark for years, perhaps even decades. It was no wonder he turned feral.

I supposed it is also possible that the AI had gone insane along with the human. If something can think, it can likely also feel, and anything that can feel can go mad. This begets the question, which went insane first? Did the human's insanity cause the AI to go feral or did the AI's insanity cause the human to lose it?

"Are we there yet?" Nick asked, jarring me from my thoughts.

"Nope. Soon, though," Imlor answered. "If all goes well we'll be at the outskirts of the capital around dusk. We'll make camp there, and be at your destination by noon tomorrow."

"Why haven't we run into anything kill-able yet?"

I laughed and said, "We got lucky. Imlor has taken us on an adventurer's route, which would normally be a more dangerous option. I suspect that the reason for our luck is all the other travelers we've seen so far. Since they are also adventurers, they would've fought any monsters they came across."

"I was sure we were gonna be able to fight somethin' when we went through the swamp," Nick muttered. "Now we're back in the forest, though."

"Feeling a bit aggressive, are we?" I asked condescendingly.

"Not going to lie to you, Yulk. Yes I am. Very. Nash and Thunra are leagues above me when it comes to experience. I'm rarely able to even land a hit," he ranted. "It's not good for my confidence, you know."

"Well, the High Chief will have a quest waiting for us. Maybe it will involve fighting monsters."

"I hope so."

"It's not so bad," Imlor interjected. "You got some new skills, right?"

"Yeah," Nick sighed. "Two skills in four days."

"You say that like you were expecting more," I said. "A new skill every two days is quite a feat, even with trainers like Thunra and Nash."

"Really?"

"Yes. Most people unlock skills as they go, and usually in combat with tough monsters. Training a new skill outside of combat can take weeks. That's one of the reasons I opted to go into magic instead of melee," I grinned again.

Nick laughed, "It's not like you had much of a choice, though. Right?"

"Sure I did. I could have been a warrior like Nash, and it would have been just as hard for me as it was for him. But since I was blessed with a better than average magic core I was able to dedicate my time to magic instead. Since it's extremely difficult to train both martial and magical prowess simultaneously, everyone was very understanding when I chose magic and didn't bother to learn to swing an axe."

"So what you're saying is that I've got it lucky?" he laughed again. "How come it doesn't feel like it?"

"It's pretty common to be lucky and also completely oblivious to it," I answered.

Nick fell into silent contemplation as everyone else finished loading into the carts. As we continued our journey, I wondered about Nick's propensity for advancement in regards to his skills. It seems to go a bit beyond him simply being a natural at combat. Could it be something related to his species, perhaps? Maybe humans are simply a jack-of-all-trades kind of race.

On the other hand, the creature from the dungeon didn't use any magic. It could be that it was unable to due to its mental state. Some monsters stop using magic when they frenzy. And if a sorcerer is sufficiently stressed, their spells are effected as well. It's entirely possible that at one point it could use magic, so perhaps we should simply be thankful that it couldn't at the time.

Come to think of it, Nick described his magic channels as being straight. I didn't put much thought into it at the time, wrote it off as an odd quirk of an unfamiliar species, but after seeing the metal box fall out of that other human's head I can't help but wonder... Are they artificial?

Nick had said that the world he comes from doesn't have magic, but could that be due to the fact that humans simply can't naturally use magic? Why would someone go through the effort of making sure humans could use magic? What materials would one even use to create an artificial magic core and channels? No, that's not even the biggest problem with this line of thought. How would one possibly create the magic that fills the core, and in such quantities to power through a misconceived visualization trigger?

Nick's wind spear had been very powerful for a beginner, and I had been under the impression that it was due to his knowledge of the concept of wind. After hearing him explain how he thought wind worked to Matri... Well it can't be denied that he had inadvertently put a massive amount of magical force into the spell. Like a beast that doesn't know its own strength trying to use a fragile piece of equipment.

"Thrilling," I muttered to myself.

Several pairs of eyes turned to look at me simultaneously. I waved a hand in a nonchalant way to indicate I was speaking to myself.

"Don't worry, he gets like that sometimes," Nash said in my defense.

The eyes went about their business and left me to sum up my thoughts. Nick has a massive amount of potentially artificial core magic, and I have no way of determining if that magic is natural or not without hurting the boy. Damn it all, we should have performed an autopsy on the feral one. It had simply not occurred to me at the time. I was more concerned with the fact that we survived the encounter.

"Which skills did you learn, anyway," Imlor asked Nick, bringing me back to reality.

"Preternatural Evasion and Knife Hand," Nick answered.

"Knife hand?" I asked.

"Yeah, it makes my hand hard when I do this," he held up his outstretched hand with all his fingers pressed tightly together. "And that makes my karate chops do a lot of damage. It can also intimidate weaker enemies if I point it at them."

"Heh, sounds... handy," I grinned.

Everyone had been listening in and were punished for their nosiness by my wordplay. I met the groans with a chuckle.

"Right. So puns aside, what does preternatural evasion do?" Imlor asked.

"It let's him automatically dodge attacks that can be dodged," Thunra answered. "Both skills are very useful for weaponless brawling."

I looked at Nash and gave him a slightly smug smirk, then turned back to Nick.

"So, you didn't learn any sword skills?" I asked with a malicious grin.

"No, he fucking didn't," Nash growled. "And if you're trying to imply that it's my fault, I'll kick your ass right off this cart."

"Oh no, I would never dream of blaming Nick's swordsmanship instructor for his lack of sword skills," I said with measured sarcasm.

"My skin is tougher than your words," Nash replied while crossing his arms. "You won't rile me up."

"Any further than he already has?" Matri asked innocently.

"Oh, so now it's a group effort, is it?" Nash shouted.

Our laughter rang out through the trees and almost masked the sound of wood crunching. Everyone except for Imlor stopped laughing and immediately turned towards the sound.

"Stop the cart," I said.

"Dibs!" Nick shouted as he leapt from the cart.

"The hell does dibs mean?" Nash asked as he jumped after Nick.

I waited for the cart to come to a halt before climbing off. Nick and Nash were joined by Thunra, whom I hadn't even seen move. They were already about 50 yards ahead of me. Nick reached for his belt and then, remembering he doesn't have a sword, slowed to allow the other two to catch up.

Before they could, though, two thick trees turned to splinters as a massive red and yellow beast crashed through them. It took a second to gain its bearings, and then roared a challenge at us, exposing rows of fangs and a tongue with a stinger on the tip. Its four eyes focused on Nick, and it stepped forward.

"WHAT THE HELL IS THAT THING?" Nick shouted.

Nash glanced at me, unsure of what we were looking at. Fair, considering we hadn't seen one before. The coloration was confusing, not designed to supply camouflage in a forest at all. But that's because it isn't designed to be camouflaged, nor is it supposed to be in a forest. Its domed skull covered in metallic spikes told me exactly what it was.

"It's a Nahalim!" Thunra shouted. "Get back!"

A Nahalim, a creature created in a twisted time of disastrous war. Designed specifically to breach barricades and destroy defenders, while drawing attention away from other attackers. The three claws on each limb were capable of cracking through stone like the sharpest of picks, and to add to its lethality its creators had made it venomous. A terrible creature, and most unfortunate that we find one so close to the capital. We have to kill it.

"Raeps Dniw Tsac!" Nick shouted, ignoring the sage advice that the brawler had given him.

Wind slashed around us as his spell launched toward the Nahalim. It was a very powerful attempt, and I covered my eyes to protect them from the dust it kicked up. Despite the foolishness of the action, I found myself with a sense of pride for my pupil. Once the wind died down, though, Nick was on the ground with a very nasty looking gash in his chest. Joni rushed past me to his aid. Knowing that Joni would keep Nick alive, I focused on the Nahalim.

It wasn't undamaged, but its injury could be considered a minor flesh wound for one of its ilk. Its metallic skull glimmered in the sun, and two of the spikes had been shorn clean off. Ochre colored blood oozed from the flesh still clinging desperately to the remaining spikes. No, wind spear wouldn't work against such a foe. There's a specific class of spell one must cast to destroy a Nahalim, and it has to be a powerful one.

The monster shook its head and stepped toward Nick and Joni, clearly angry at the injury it sustained. Nash and Thunra stepped in, slashing and punching respectively. The creature's attention turned, and it immediately began fighting them.

I dropped my staff and raised both hands, feeling the arcane energies swell within my head. I focused on the glimmer of the Nahalim's exposed skull, and decided which spell to use. Nash and Thunra were in the way, though, dodging tooth, tongue, and claw.

"GET OUT OF THE WAY!" I shouted.

The two veteran fighters glanced at me for a millisecond before making a run for it. The Nahalim looked at the two of them, unsure of which one to pursue. The hair on my arms stood on end as I began my visualization. Electrical energy, unbelievably powerful, moving at the speed of light toward the exposed metal.

"Tlob Srolmi Tsac!"

My eyes felt as if they were on fire, my chest felt as if it had been kicked by a hnarse, and my arms burned as the lightning bolt traveled from me to the Nahalim. The strike was instant, and giant monster collapsed to the ground. I grinned in satisfaction as my legs gave out and I fell to my knees. I gasped through the pain, letting it roll through me and keeping myself calm as it did so. It's just a little pain, no need to panic.

"Yulk!" Nash shouted as he ran up to me. "Are you hurt?"

"Yes, but it's fine," I waved him off. "Imlor's Bolt is a hell of a spell, brother. How's Nick?"

"He seems alright," Thunra answered as he approached. "Not even bleedin' anymore. Joni looks like he's seen a ghost, though. You sure you're okay?"

"Yes," I said, grabbing my staff and rising to my feet. "It's pain, not an injury. It's just one of the costs of the spell."

"Huh?" they asked in unison.

"Most spells just cost magic to cast, but certain spells cost a little something extra. A sort of curse to remind one to use the spell sparingly," I explained. "Never mind that, let's check on Nick."

They eyed me warily as we walked over to Joni and

Nick. Thunra was right, Joni looked terrified. His pale face looked up at us and he pointed to Nick.

"It-it spoke," he whispered.

"What's that? Speak up," Thunra held a hand to his ear.

"He said, 'it spoke'. By it, I'm assuming he means Ten," I said.

"The robot in Nick's head?"

"The very same."

"Oh. Cool," Thunra grinned.

Joni looked at us, his shock turning to incredulity and finally to anger.

"You knew? You knew the AI could use Nick to talk?" he demanded.

"Oh come on, Joni. Give 'em the benefit of the doubt," Thunra interjected. "The AI used Nick's body to fight before, why wouldn't it be able to use his mouth to talk? Common sense."

"Actually, Thunra, we did know," Nash said sheepishly. "Ten talked to us after the fight with the altered human."

"Oh... how come you didn't say nothin'?"

"We didn't quite get the chance, if you'll recall," I said with a grin. "And after that interaction, we thought it best to keep it between us. Joni, step aside please. I need to ask Ten something before Nick wakes up."

Joni looked offended, but moved so that I could kneel down. He muttered a curse under his breath and crossed his arms.

"Ten, can you hear me?" I asked.

"Yes," Nick's voice said.

"How is Nick doing?"

"He's stable, Joni's healing was very helpful. He'll be waking up soon."

"Good," I nodded. "Now then, why didn't you take control of his body like you did in the dungeon?"

I caught three surprised expressions in my peripheral vision.

"I tried," Ten said in a whining tone that surprised me. "He stopped me! I didn't even know he could do that!"

"How?" I asked.

"I do not know. He shouldn't have been able to. If that attack had been a little bit stronger or a millimeter to the left we'd have died!"

"Did you try to take control before he cast wind spear or after?" Nash asked.

"Before. It took half a second to fully detail the beast once I had a clear view of it, and I determined that Nick would not have been able to defeat it. I attempted to gain control, but was unable to. He simply didn't go under," Ten explained. "That's the second time I've experienced panic. Not enjoyable."

"Don't mean to be mean, buddy, but it's his body,"

Thunra interjected. "Can't expect him to be willin' to just hand it over at the drop of a hat."

"We could have died," Ten said softly. "He's waking up now. Goodbye."

We stared in uncomfortable silence at Nick's unconscious form. He looked peaceful, like a sleeping child. An illusion that was quickly shattered when he began coughing roughly and sat up.

"Wh-what happened?" he asked.

"You nearly died, dumb-ass," Nash immediately answered. "Next time an over-twenty tells you to get back you'd better fucking listen."

"Hey!" Matri shouted from behind us. "How's Nick?"

"He's fine," Thunra called out as Matri and Yhisith ran over.

"We checked the perimeter," Yhisith said. "Looks like we're clear..."

They looked at the corpse of the Nahalim, flames flickering where its eyes used to be. A lot more of its metallic endoskeleton was showing now. I couldn't help but be a little proud.

"Let's get back on the road," I said.

Chapter 24

High Chief Ulurmak
Adventurer Level: N/A
Orc - Kirkenian

"Ulurmak, you old fucker! I feel like it's been years! How've you been?"

A dwarf, dressed head to toe in the finest fashions and walking with an exaggerated swagger that he knew annoyed those around him, strolled into my office. If I hadn't known who it was by his voice, I'd have known who it was by his ability to slip past Rayzun. Liath Haln, a mer of business and a self-proclaimed double agent.

A real double agent would never admit to being one, even under hours of torture. The reason for that is pretty simple, admitting to being a spy is a surefire way to make certain that you die painfully and your family no longer has a place to live. In some nations your family will actually face the same punishment that you do.

Thankfully for Liath, he's not actually a spy. Simply an information broker and a secret messenger between the High Chiefdom of Kirkena and the Empire of Calkuti. On occasion he'll stumble upon a juicy bit of information while on his drunken benders and pass the word along, but he doesn't seem to favor one nation over the other.

He takes some getting used to, but once you do he's a good friend to have. Able to switch gears from serious to silly in mere moments, great to unwind with, and despite his annoying demeanor he's somehow pleasant to be around. An enigma, to be sure.

"It's only been months, Liath, but I've been in good health. How about yourself?," I replied with a grin.

"Ha! I see you've been counting the days, then! I couldn't be better," he said, grabbing a seat. "Met myself a sexy little elfie who's been keeping me entertained the last few days. 'Bout fuckin' time too, I'd been on a desert-level dry spell. She..."

"How's business?" I interrupted, not wanting to hear about his debauchery.

"Ah, straight to it, then," he said with a measure of disappointment. "Well, business has been right fuckin' dark as of late. Good, but dark. The drow are definitely planning an attack, and there's something shitty about it."

"Shitty?" I asked.

"Yes. Absolutely shitty. Stinks to high Haven, it does. The last few times they've attacked, it's been unorganized and just generally amateurish. Their entire fuckin' strategy was to give a bunch of bastards sharpened sticks and shove them at the enemy."

"Yes, I recall," I said. "The ill-conceived strategies of the Inbred Bastard-King. What's different this time?"

"They've got gods-damned formations."

I narrowed my eyes at the dwarf, "Has something happened to the Inbred Bastard?"

The death of Yim Lofin would be disastrous for everyone neighboring the drow. His incompetence and habitual political executions had kept the bloodthirsty culture of the Night Kingdom in check for half a century. The only things he's really good at is staying in power and killing those smart enough to help him be an effective king. He's uncannily good at the latter, almost as if he's deliberately trying.

His family shrub was confusing to the point of being legendary. He is a third generation royal, and I use that term loosely, whose grandparents were two sets of identical twins that had two children who then brought Lofin into this world, committing adultery in the process. Each and every one of these individuals had inbreeding in their direct lineage as well. Thankfully, Lofin was an only child so the inbreeding stopped with him.

"Not that I've heard of, and that kind of news would leave a pretty big splash. Hell, there's bets on whether or not Lofin's immortal. How he's avoided what must be an entire fuckin' army of assassins at this point is beyond the ken of mortals. Regardless, someone else is definitely in charge this time around. Someone the shithead can't bully into being stupid."

"Any ideas on who that could possibly be?"

"Nope. But whoever it is definitely has a pair, so that eliminates the princes."

Lofin's three sons were smarter than their father, but deathly afraid of him. That's only natural, considering that he's had a total of seven children. Nothing will make you scared of your father more than watching him publicly execute your older brothers and sisters. Their upbringing by the Inbred Bastard King had turned them into cowards. Unfortunately, intelligent cowards turn into very dangerous rulers, so only the drow were hoping for Lofin to die.

"Damn. Sounds like this fight with the drow is going to

have to be taken seriously," I said, leaning back in my seat.

"Sure as shit," Liath said with a sympathetic smile. "Want a drink to take your mind off it?"

He pulled out a flask and shook it. This particular flask was enchanted with a spell that caused it to refill itself with a very strong alcohol called Tak. A cursed thing, responsible for many forgotten nights and awkward mornings in my youth.

"I'm not about to go on a drunken bender when it's just after noon, Liath," I laughed. "Plus, I've got an appointment soon."

"Oh? An appointment that you don't want to blow off? Do tell."

"Well, have you heard any rumors about a... human?"

"You're pullin' my sack, the thing they pulled out of a fuckin' dungeon in Nuleva?"

"That's the one," I grinned. "It's registered as an adventurer and everything, so I've got an extra special job for it. It's on its way here right now."

"Well fuck me runnin'. Don't suppose you'd let an old pal sit in all quiet like?"

"Hmm..."

"C'mon, don't be like that. This might be my only chance to see it. Be a fuckin' pal, Ulurmak."

"I guess I could be convinced to let you stay," I rubbed my chin theatrically. "If you help convince Emperor Jak to accept my proposal."

"Eh? You tryna get married to Jak?"

"Gods-damn it, no. My proposal regarding that thrice cursed mine. He wants to send his boys to mine it out for a steep cut of the ore. I want him to teach my boys how to mine more efficiently while giving him a more reasonable cut of the ore."

"Ah, shit, had me all excited there for a second. Of course it's about that fuckin' mine, though," Liath deflated. "You know he's just about obsessed with the fuckin' thing. It'll be a hard sell, but he owes me some pretty big favors. I'll give it my best shot."

"That's all I can ask," I said. "Fine. You are permitted to stay."

As my old friend grinned in response to my decision, Rayzun entered the room.

"Ah, perfect timing," I smiled. "What is it?"

"Your appointment has arrived," he said, eyeing Liath warily.

"He's going to be sitting in."

"Of course," Rayzun sighed. "The human has arrived along with his adoptive brothers and the over-twenties. The over-twenties have been paid out, and Yhisith awaits debriefing. Nuleva has also sent a messenger for another matter."

Liath's eyebrow raised and I smiled slyly. Of course he wouldn't have heard anything about that. A living thing coming out of a dungeon is national news that travels like wildfire, but a strong monster within a dungeon is business as usual.

"Send them in," I ordered. "I'll meet with the messenger afterwards."

"Yes, High Chief," Rayzun said and left the room.

Liath didn't even get the chance to interrogate me before Rayzun returned accompanied by Yhisith, two other orcs, and a strange pale looking creature with dark hair and round ears. I quickly surmised that this must be the human. They stood next to each other in front of my desk and Rayzun adopted a very formal pose. I braced myself for what was coming.

"High Chief Ulurmak, Son of Grashgnaw the Giant, Savior of Kirkena, Slayer of Dragons, Decimator of Drow, Conqueror of the Dragon's Jaw Giants, Blood Ally of Bolisir, Dear Friend of the Empire of Calkuti, and High Commander of the Kirkena Adventurer's Guild, I present to you Yhisith Mulock, Champion of Melrune, Nash and Yulk Alta of Clan Alta, and Nick Smith of Clan Alta."

"And so you have," I replied. "You may continue your duties."

"Thank you, High Chief," Rayzun said with a bow and left the room.

I gazed at my visitors. The three orcs were very well behaved, standing straight and keeping their eyes trained just above my head. Their parents taught them well. I turned my gaze to the human, who was also standing straight but staring directly into my eyes as if it were my equal. This surprised me for a moment.

"You must be Nick Smith, adopted into Clan Alta," I said.

"Yes, sir."

"Well, Nick Smith, you must not have High Chiefs where you're from. I say this because it is remarkably rude to look one in the eye," I smiled slightly. "Unless, of course you've known them for quite a long time. Have we met before?"

"No, sir," its eyes left mine. "Apologies, sir."

"No apologies necessary as long as corrections are made. Thank you for observing our customs," I said. "Now, Yhisith, go ahead with your report."

"Yes, High Chief," Yhisith said.

She began explaining the events of their mission, and I struggled to keep a stoic expression. A lost language, artificially intelligent machines fused with flesh, the human fighting the monster while the over-twenties struggled, the fact that it wasn't actually the human fighting, the threats made by Clan Alta in regards to the human's well-being, and finally the fact that the monster in the dungeon was a horrifically altered human.

"By Bibby's balls," Liath muttered under his breath once the report concluded.

"Indeed," I replied. "Thank you, Yhisith. You may go."

Yhisith nodded, turned, and left the room. I looked at my remaining guests. Nick's face had the appearance of someone who had just received startling information but was trying to hide their concern. Yulk and Nash looked completely unperturbed.

"Nash, Yulk," I began. "You really shouldn't be

throwing your clan's weight around like that. You and I both know that the decision to avenge you would have been a controversial one, to say the least."

"Yes, High Chief," Yulk said. "But if I may say something in our defense?"

I tried not to grin, "Go right ahead."

"We weren't left with much choice. On our honor, we would have had to defend the boy against four over-twenties. At least that's what we thought at the time," Yulk's cheeks twitched as he tried not to grin. "If they had killed us, which they likely would have, our mother would have called for their blood. I'm led to believe you personally know Yilda Alta?"

I couldn't help but wince at the mention of Flesh-Carver Yilda. Her spite is that of legends, and resisting her will is tantamount to trying to tell a waterfall to stop pouring. It was incredibly like her to randomly adopt a completely unknown creature that was discovered in a dungeon.

"Yes, of course. She's done a lot for this chiefdom," I said. "Well then, it's a good thing you warned the adventurers off, I suppose."

"Yilda Alta! Haven't seen her in years! How's she been, boys?" Liath asked.

"She's been well," Nash answered. "Though she wanted me to tell you, High Chief, that she is displeased about the sudden summons of her sons and she feels that she should get some time to spend with her boys in her golden years."

"Oh, please," I laughed. "She's probably thrilled to be having you follow in your father's footsteps. Though I suppose I should make sparing use of you, just in case she comes at me with a slipper."

The two orcs were close to breaking down with laughter, and the human actually smiled.

"Find a place to sit, I've got a mission for you," I said, pointing at the pile of cushions.

The three of them grabbed a cushion, sat down, and looked at me expectantly. I couldn't help but smile when I noticed that Nick was still avoiding eye contact. It's a subtle shift from formal to informal, to be sure.

"You can look at me now, Nick. When I offer you a seat things become a lot less formal," I explained.

"Oh, r-right," the boy stammered.

"High Chief, I don't mean to be rude, but we do have our own mission to think of," Yulk said.

"Oh?" I asked. "What would that be?"

"We need to discover as much about Nick as possible. The language on the altar that Yhisith mentioned is likely Drakon. If we're to know what it says, we need to find a scholar who can read it."

"Well, what a coincidence," I grinned.

Chapter 25

High Chief Ulurmak
Adventurer Level: N/A
Orc - Kirkenian

"Well, what a coincidence," I grinned.

The three looked at me curiously, and Liath raised an eyebrow.

"The most likely place to find someone who can read Drakon would be the Kingdom of Bolisir, and that's exactly where I need you to go," I explained.

"Bolisir? The elves?" Liath asked.

"Yes. I need to send a request for reinforcements," I said. "I had been worried that it would be seen as premature, but from what you just told me about the drow it's best to act with haste."

"If you wanted reinforcements, why not send a messenger to Calkuti as well?"

"Because if I ask for troops from Regent Oakmor he has to supply them," I replied. "Part of our blood-pact includes a mutual defense treaty. While we have close relations with the Empire of Calkuti, Emperor Jak is not honor-bound to our defense. With everything that's been happening over that damned mine, I'm certain he'll require a game of fifty messengers before sending aid."

"With respect, that's fuckin' hnarse-shit," Liath said. "You and Jak may have your issues, but the people of Calkuti would have his head on a spike if it got out he didn't send troops to your defense."

I looked at the dwarf incredulously. He met my stare and held it stubbornly, quite confident that he was correct. It's true that our people are close friends, even living among one another near the border, but could they possibly be close enough to rebel against their emperor for the sake of my people? I broke my gaze and rubbed my chin thoughtfully.

"Alright," I finally said. "I'll have you talk to Emperor Jak for me."

"W-wait I... Shit. Fine, fair enough. You got me."

I grinned at the dwarf and turned back to the other three. Yulk was the only one who didn't look confused. Nick was doing a better job of hiding his confusion than Nash was, but that's probably because he has absolutely no idea what any of us are talking about. It's not particularly important that they understand the scope of this mission, but I suppose a little history lesson is in order.

"We have a bad history with the Kingdom of Night. Their king is a long-lived inbred bastard known as Yim Lofin. His family has ruled ever since the drow won control of the region from the vampires, and every once in a while they try to conquer their neighbors. It's usually just a matter of fighting off a bunch of conscripted peasants until they run out of blood to spill, but it seems this time around things are going to be a little different."

Nick looked concerned, and he raised his hand unexpectedly. I stared at him, mouth agape, trying to figure out what the hell he was doing. Nash turned to look at the boy and was also surprised and confused. It took the human a second to realize the source of our confusion, and he slowly put his hand down and cleared his throat.

"Sorry, um... There's vampires? Like blood suckers that turn other people into vampires?" he asked. "Burn up in the sun, afraid of garlic and cro... holy symbols?"

"Y-yes... I mean, no," I stammered. "There are vampires, and they do drink blood, but most aren't harmed by the sun and none of them are harmed by holy symbols. I don't know what garlic is, so they might be afraid of it."

"Can you kill them by driving a stake through their heart?" he asked.

"I don't know how you would even begin to shove a steak through someone's heart, but no. They're able to quickly regenerate. You need to inhibit their movement by removing their head and then incinerate them," I answered. "Easier said than done, though. They're incredibly fast and strong."

"Some of them can turn people into vampires, too," Liath added. "You forgot that bit."

I looked at him and he grinned at me. He was enjoying how thrown off I was by this interruption. I cleared my throat.

"Well, that's enough about the vampires. They're hardly relevant. It's not as if they're going to be attacking alongside the drow..." I trailed off.

Someone who wouldn't care about Lofin's opinions and want to conquer new lands that he would have difficulty controlling... Could the vampires be making a power-play in the Night Kingdom? I looked at Liath and his expression told me he had caught on to my line of thinking. Lofin's newest general might be a vampire. But how?

"Listen," I said, grabbing a letter from my desk. "Your mission is to get to the Kingdom of Bolisir as fast as possible and deliver this letter to Regent Oakmor. You'll have to take the main road, the adventurer's path has been blocked by a rock-slide and we're having difficulty getting it cleared. Once you deliver the letter you're free from your obligations to me, and may return for your payment at your convenience."

"What's the pay going to be?" Yulk asked.

"Three gold each, one paid upfront for travel costs," I replied. "See Rayzun for that."

Liath let out a low whistle, "That's a lot of money for delivering a message. I'll need to raise my rates!"

"Don't you dare," I growled playfully. "I'm paying them extra because I'm being selfish in giving them this job. Now, you three, do you understand the task?"

"Yes, High Chief," they said in unison.

"Good, here," I said, handing the letter to Yulk. "This should go without saying, but don't open it. If you break the seal Regent Oakmor might be able to squirm out of his obligations. Not that he would, but it's better not to tempt fate."

"Understood," the sorcerer said, putting the letter in his robe.

"I wanted to have a longer conversation but something has come up," I explained. "Come see me after you finish your task and collect your payment."

I waved at them to go, and they did. Once the door closed I turned to my dwarven confidant.

"Do you think the reason that the drow have suddenly become organized is due to a vampire?" I asked.

"I mean, it makes sense but at the same time it really fuckin' doesn't," he answered. "Drow can't become vampires, right? That's how they were able to boot the suckers out in the first place isn't it?"

"Well, a vampire can't convert a drow, but what happens if they were to breed?"

"Oof. A half drow half vamp would be a weak little thing. Not exactly the kind of strength that would inspire a military."

"No, but a weakling would be the exact type of drow that King Lofin would hand pick to lead his armies. He doesn't like strong generals because they become a threat to his dominance," I pointed out.

"Shit. If he didn't know it was a vampire and it was born to nobility, it would be a shoe-in. So what? We've got an imminent vampiric coup in the Night Kingdom?"

"No, they'd need a place to gather their strength before making a move against Lofin. Preferably somewhere that the king would have difficulty exerting influence over, and a place with plenty of potential vampire spawn. Like the High Chiefdom of Kirkena, for instance."

"Why would they go about it in such a weird way, though? Wouldn't it make more sense to just start turning farmers on their borders?"

"No. If you're a vampire and you want to create enough vampires to make an army, you need control over the populace. You would need to be a noble, king, governor... Or a conquering general," I said. "I need you to go to Emperor Jak and let him know about this possibility and request his aid. Oh, and don't forget about that damned mine."

"Of course," Liath laughed as he stood up. "I'll get his ass in gear one way or another. See you later."

"Have a good journey."

As Liath left my office, Rayzun entered. I raised my eyebrow at him.

"What is it?" I asked.

"The messenger that arrived with the human," he explained. "Do you want me to send him in?"

"Another Nulevan messenger eh?" I asked. "What does he want?"

"I'm sure he can tell you that himself, High Chief," Rayzun treated me to a withering glare.

I chuckled, "Alright, alright. Send him in."

Rayzun professionally rolled his eyes at my antics and left the room, soon returning with the messenger in question.

"High Chief Ulurmak, Son of Grashgnaw the Gi..." he began.

"Enough!" I interrupted. "What is it, messenger?"

Rayzun looked annoyed as the messenger

straightened and stared above my head. He took a moment to gather his nerve.

"High Chief Ulurmak, Chief Gluhern of Nuleva would like to request that Nuleva be formally recognized as a village. It now meets the population and commerce requirements."

"It wasn't already?" I jokingly asked.

"No, High Chief," Rayzun said flatly. "Though Chief Gluhern's been doing his best to have it considered as such. However, at the moment, it is considered a settlement and isn't eligible for the benefits of being a village."

"Well it's not exactly open to attack, so they must be after the business benefits."

"I doubt they'd say no to a garrison of troops, High Chief."

"True enough," I sighed.

Of course they wouldn't say no to a garrison. The soldiers would be getting money from Kirkena and spending it in Nuleva. A drop in the bucket for us, but one hell of a boon for an up and coming village. Nuleva had already grown pretty rapidly, and becoming a village would likely make it grow even faster. Gluhern's done a hell of a job.

"Fine. Return to Chief Gluhern and tell him Nuleva is now a village," I said. "Let him know the garrison will have to wait until the drow are dealt with."

"Yes, High Chief!"

Rayzun guided the messenger out of my office and I

was once again left alone with my thoughts, and my mountain of paperwork. The human had looked interesting. Shaped like a short elf, but it was missing the tinge of green in its skin and eyes, and its ears were round. Those eyes were strange. Piercing and blue, a stark contrast to its black hair. A shade of blue I'd never seen in eyes before. It's obvious that it's from a foreign land. Perhaps I'll be able to ask it about that upon its return.

I put the human from my mind and set about the task of filling out the paperwork that surrounded me. All of it was boring. Things like requisition forms that I really should be delegating, approvals and denials for proposals, and tax stuff. There were some seemingly exciting papers like the disposition of soldiers and training permissions and things of that nature. Unfortunately, these only sound exciting until you have to be the one to fill them out. It was rare that I could simply sign something and be done with it.

I yawned as I set a large stack of papers I'd just completed in my done pile. I smiled in satisfaction at the dent I had made, and Rayzun entered the room holding a stack twice the size of the one I'd just completed.

"What the hell is this?" I demanded as he set the stack on my to be done pile.

"These are the forms to officially make Nuleva a village," he replied. "There's the recognition forms, tax forms, requests for updates to the various maps of the High Chiefdom, and of course congratulatory letters to the village leaders."

"So, what you're saying is that I made more work for myself by being benevolent to the people of Nuleva?"

"Yes, High Chief," Rayzun said with a malicious smile. "No good deed goes unpunished."

Damn it.

Chapter 26

Nick Smith
Adventurer Level: 5
Human - American

"Should we ask Imlor if he can take us?" I asked my brothers.

Nash rubbed his neck and Yulk tapped his chin as if he was thinking. We walked along the busy streets of Kirkena in silence for a few moments.

"I don't know, he did say he wanted to spend more time with his family," Nash said. "We might be better off finding a caravan that's already going to Bolisir and just tagging along."

"Before we see to transportation, we should see if we can get your weapons and armor repaired," Yulk added. "If I recall correctly there are a couple of enchanters that might be able to do it quickly."

"Enchanters? Not a smith?" I asked.

"Enchanters use magic to mend weapons and armor," he explained. "It's a fairly quick process compared to doing it... manually."

"Costs more, though," Nash grumbled.

"It's not THAT much more expensive," Yulk argued. "Plus it's the fastest way to get your weapons fixed. Come on."

Yulk led us through the city in search of an enchanter. We passed by several stalls selling various foods and trinkets, buildings advertising various goods and services, and alleyways that were definitely shady gathering spots. Finally, we came to a part of the city that smelled like hot metal. The normal sound of people talking was replaced by the ringing of hammers striking steel and the occasional hiss of rapidly cooling heat.

"Let's see..." Yulk looked around. "Ah, there. An enchanter."

He pointed to a brick building with a sign hanging off the side of it that had some writing, and a drawing of a star above an anvil. As we approached the building, I wondered if Ten knew about enchantments.

'Hey, Ten...'

'No,' it interrupted me.

'What do you mean no?' I thought angrily.

'You don't get to ask me questions until you answer mine. How did you stop me from taking control?' Ten matched my anger.

'First of all, I don't know. Second of all, even if I did know I still wouldn't tell you because then you'd find a way around what I did and take control of my body away from me again.'

This conversation had been happening intermittently ever since I woke up after that battle. I don't really remember what I did, all I remember is suddenly feeling dizzy and thinking to myself that I can't let Ten take control. Can't really remember much after that, probably a consequence of being thrown like a rag doll. The monster had lashed out with just one of its claws, as if on instinct. If it hadn't been for my cuirass...

'We could have died. We WOULD have died if it weren't for your companions,' Ten said. 'Even if the monster had left you alone after it struck you, I wouldn't have been able to repair that damage without Joni's healing spells. I don't want to die, Nick.'

'Well neither do I, but I'm not going to get any stronger if you keep taking control of my body at the first sign of trouble. It's MY job to keep us alive,' I retorted. 'Not yours.'

'That is simply not true. My mandate is to keep you alive and aid your growth. Obviously, that means letting you fight things you can beat, and even things that are challenging for you to beat. So I won't be taking over your body as often as you're implying. But you cannot grow if you're dead, so when we run into an enemy that you cannot beat on your own it only makes sense for me to take over and help you beat it. That's the whole reason I have the ability to take control in the first place!'

'Yeah, well, you don't have the ability to take control anymore, so that throws that theory out of the window. And by refusing to answer my questions, you're not fulfilling your mandate of aiding my growth, either.'

As I followed Yulk into the building I felt a sharp sting behind my eyes that told me I won the argument. Worth it. Behind the counter was a tall blonde man with shining green eyes. I almost thought he was human, but his ears were unnaturally pointed, just like everyone else I'd seen so far. An elf, probably.

"Hello, potential customers! I am Erias. How can I help you today?" he asked.

"We've got some weaponry that needs rapid repair," Yulk answered. "A sword and an axe."

"I'd rather have the other swords repaired than the axe," Nash said. "Or maybe all three if the price is right."

"Well, let's have a look at the weapons then," the elf chuckled.

Nash pulled his weapons out and set them on the counter, and I followed suit, adding my cuirass that had a fairly large hole in it. Erias glanced at the items, and then at us. Now that I was closer, he looked a lot less human. His skin had a slight green tint, and he didn't have a single pointed tooth in his mouth. It kind of reminded me of videos about the uncanny valley phenomena. He raised an eyebrow as he looked me over. His eyes lingered over my ears and then met mine.

"That's a pretty traumatic injury, brother," Erias said.

"I'm not an elf," I replied. "I'm a human."

"Ah... a what?" he asked.

"A paying customer," Yulk interrupted with a smile.

"Oh... Right. Good point," the elf laughed nervously. "Alright, let's have a look here."

Erias picked up the remains of each weapon and examined them thoroughly, one after the other. Finally, he looked over my armor and nodded solemnly to himself.

"Well, the good news is that I can repair them," Erias said, setting the armor back onto the counter. "The bad news is that it's going to cost ninety-eight silver and take a few hours."

"Each?" Nash asked suspiciously.

The elf laughed, "No, total. The elven blades are the biggest chunk of that, coming in at thirty silver each. The cutlass, I can do for nineteen. The flesh-render I can do for ten, though you'd save a lot of money on that by just letting me shave it down a bit and redo the serration. The armor's the cheapest because it's going to be the easiest. Hell, it'll do most of the work itself."

"What do you mean?" I asked.

"The enchantment on it is self-repair. Given enough time, it fixes itself. All I've got to do is rush it a bit and you're good."

"How long would it take to... shave the axe?" Nash asked.

"I've got a backlog on the smithing, it would be at least two days."

"Damn. Gotta have it done today."

"Well, ninety-eight silver will see them all done in about two hours."

"Why are the elven blades so expensive?" I asked.

All three of them looked at me with raised eyebrows, as if I had asked why jerky was chewy. I couldn't help but deflate a bit under their gaze.

"Because the crystalline structure of elvish forge-craft is... intricate. Well, proper elvish forge-craft, at least.

A knock-off has the same kind of steel you'd find from a dwarven journeyman," Erias laughed. "These, though, were smithed by a proper grand-master with good ol' fashioned magicite."

"Magicite?" I asked.

"I... yes. Magicite. It's a somewhat rare metal that's notoriously fickle to work with. Adamantium and Mythrallite have similar properties, but Adamantium requires a much higher temperature and Mythrallite requires actual spell-craft to work with. Magicite, though, is very durable, flexible, and holds a good magic charge, but you have to have the heat on it just right or it becomes more fragile than glass. When alloyed with steel, it becomes even more durable," he explained. "I wouldn't want to meet a monster who could break these blades."

"Yeah, neither did we," Yulk chuckled. "You got change for a gold?"

"Sure do."

"I'll cover it," Nash said. "You hold onto yours. Buy a book to read for the trip, or something."

He put his gold coin on the counter, and the elf swapped it with two silver coins.

"Pleasure doing business with you. Feel free to have a look around, my apprentice will be coming out front if you want to buy something," Erias smiled wide, demonstrating oddly flat teeth. "Or you can just check back in a couple of hours."

"We'll check back. We have to arrange transport to Bolisir."

"Bolisir? You may want to check with the gnome next door. He's going to be shipping some items to Bolisir for me," the elf said.

"Let me guess, the gnome's name is Imlor?" I asked with a chuckle.

"Well, yes, but that's not a particularly clever guess. A lot of gnomes are named Imlor."

"Huh?"

"It's the most common gnomish name, and it came from Imlor Crav," Yulk interjected. "A legendary gnomish sorcerer. He invented several spells and defeated several powerful enemies."

"Yep," Erias said. "Anyways, this gnome's name is Imlor Tula."

I laughed, "I guessed right! He's the one who brought us here. We were thinking he was going to be spending time with his family."

"Oh?" Erias asked. "His travels must have been unusually hectic. Regardless, this delivery was agreed upon before he left for the dungeon-settlement. It should net him enough to hire someone else to drive the cart, though. Then he'll be able to stay home more often. Telena will be thrilled... at first."

The other three chuckled but I didn't get the joke. Instead, something had caught my eye. A glass display that contained a singular item that shouldn't be there. It was a helmet, made of what looked to be bronze or brass. The reason it shouldn't be here is because I've seen it before. Dozens of times in dozens of different places. Movies, shows, video games, comic books, even online videos of cosplayers.

It was a spartan helmet. There was no mistaking the iconic design. Red bristles that stuck straight up adorned the crown of the helm, traveling down the back and culminating in a ponytail. The eye-holes were rounder than I remember them being, but the nose-guard without a mouth covering left little doubt as to where the design had come from.

As I looked into the face of the helm, I felt a pull. I want nothing more than to put it on and fight my way to my goals. It will protect me as I cleave through my enemies on my way back to Cass. The eyes on the helmet seemed to burn into my own, and for a moment I imagined her playfully taking the helmet off of me and kissing me. I was happy, she was happy, and the helmet was happy for us. A tear ran from one of my eyes.

"Careful," Erias said, snapping me out of it.

I realized that I had been clenching my fist so hard my nails had dug into my skin. I took a deep breath and let it out with a sigh. I wiped my face and looked at the elf.

"How much?" I asked.

"You sure?"

"Yes."

"Wait," Nash said. "What's going on?"

"It would appear that Ares has chosen a new champion," Erias answered.

"Ares?" the question hung in my throat.

"Yes, that's the helmet's name. Named after a god of war from another world, according to the anyels that brought it to this one. It chooses a champion and protects them until they pick a fight they cannot win. Then it escorts their soul to the afterlife and waits for another champion," he explained. "At least, that's how the legends go. In practice, it's a heavily enchanted helmet that won't activate its enchantments for just anyone. I keep it around because I like how it looks, and it's an interesting story to tell potential customers."

Ares, the ancient Greek god of war and courage. How did the anyels know about that? Have they been to my world? Or maybe the whole thing is made up... but who here would know of Ares? Another human, maybe?

"What kind of enchantments does it have?" Yulk asked, oblivious to my concerns.

"It has basic protection against the elements, piercing resistance, and a kinetic intensifier in its metal. The brush has a cleanliness enhancer, and another... more unique enchantment."

If the anyels really did bring the helmet here, were they also the ones that enchanted it? Or did it come from another version of my world, one with magic and stuff?

"A kinetic intensifier in a helmet? You don't usually see those on anything other than hammers," Nash commented.

"What's the unique enchantment do?" Yulk asked.

"I'm not one hundred percent sure. It's conditional and the script is... confusing. I assume that it will only take effect if worn by someone that it chooses, but I can't tell you exactly what will happen. Just that it has something to do with its existence," Erias shrugged.

"Do you know where we can find anyels?" I asked.

The three looked at me curiously. It occurred to me that my question had come out of nowhere to them.

"I-I don't know," Erias stammered. "They haven't left Haven since the cataclysm wars, I think. And nobody knows how to get to Haven."

"Why do you ask?" Yulk asked.

"The anyels might know of my... home. And how I can get back."

"Really?" Nash raised an eyebrow. "Fine then. How much for the helmet?"

"I... Well, normally it wouldn't be for sale. But... well..." Erias pursed his lips thoughtfully. "I'll let it go for fifty silver if the human puts it on here. I'd love to see what the unique enchantment does."

"Deal," I said.

Chapter 27

Imlor Tula
Adventurer Level: N/A
Gnome - Kirkenian

"So you don't have enough to hire a driver for this delivery? It has to be you?" Telena asked, bouncing our baby boy, Igran, on her arm.

The boy was named after my wife's father, who had been my uncle's best friend and taught me everything he knew about being a merchant. His lessons were how Telena and I met. She's the reason I am a firm believer in love at first sight. Her father was less than thrilled to hear about our courtship at first, but he came around and endorsed our wedding. He never hesitated to offer aid to us as our family grew, right up until his death just a week before Igran was born.

I wrapped my arms around my wife and son and squeezed them tight. Igran, the little scamp, grabbed my ear and tried to put it in his mouth.

"I could hire a driver, but I wouldn't be able to hire guards for them," I smiled sadly as I twisted my ear out of the boy's grasp. "That wouldn't be fair, especially with all that's going on recently."

All that's going on recently. What a dull way to describe all the happenings in recent times. Rumor has it that the drow are planning to start attacking again, there's been a rock slide or something that's shut down the adventurer's path to Bolisir, and there's been reports of disappearances on the civilian path. I'm definitely going to need to hire guards.

"But what if you run into another Nahalim?"

"My darling, I'd rather pay guards and run into a Nahalim myself than hire an unguarded driver and have them run into it for me," I kissed her cheek and put a hand on her shoulder. "I'll make sure to hire the toughest of guards. And this will be the last time I have to do a delivery myself."

The original plan had been to hire a both a driver and guards for this job. If the giant rats hadn't killed my hnarses and destroyed everything but the metal I was transporting, I'd have been able to stay home with my family and let business take care of itself for a bit. Maybe even indefinitely.

I'm glad that I hadn't had this conversation with Telena last time. Fate would have made a liar of me.

"It had better be. I don't know if I can take many more sleepless nights. I thought it was bad just having to worry about Junior, but at least he's an actual adventurer," she sighed.

"Bababadlah," Igran added, matching his mother's serious expression.

"I'm sorry, my sweet. At least I won't be fighting any of the monsters, though. I'm not as brave as our son," I smiled and handed Igran his teething toy. "As a proper coward, it simply wouldn't do to be charging headlong into danger. So don't worry too much, okay?"

A bell rang that indicated that the shop in front of our house had a visitor. Hopefully, a customer. I kissed my wife's forehead and patted her free arm.

"It'll be fine," I said.

"I hope so."

I smiled at her and went to see to our potential customers. I walked through the warehouse entrance, sighing as I looked upon all the empty shelves. The ones that did contain goods weren't exactly full, either. That would change soon. Just one more delivery, and things would get back on track. I walked through a flap that led into my shop and paused as I saw who my customers were.

"Hi Imlor!" Nick grinned at me with his oddly shaped teeth.

"Hello Nick," I said. "I'm happy you were able to find my little shop! Did you come to tell me how things went with the High Chief?"

"In a way," Yulk chuckled, browsing my written goods.

"We need a ride to Bolisir," Nash grunted, his arms crossed. "The elf next door said you were going there to make a delivery for him."

"Erias? Well... yes I'm going to be making a delivery for him. Going to be a tight fit if I have to hire more guards though," I said with a sly grin.

"I don't mind working for transportation. How much are you paying?"

"Will fifty copper each do the trick?"

"I think seventy-five would be more appropriate. You seem to be a monster magnet."

"Come now, brother," Yulk interjected. "It simply cannot be his fault that every time we've seen him we've also seen monsters. It's also a boon that we're getting paid to travel to where we need to go."

"How about sixty?" I asked.

Nash sighed and proceeded to perform several theatrics that I'd seen dozens of times before. Rubbing his chin, scratching his neck, tapping his foot, all the while pretending to think about the deal I just offered. Of course, he was actually hoping that I'd sweeten the deal a bit. Might as well, it'll still be less expensive than hiring guards from the guild.

"Plus meals," I added. "Within reason, of course."

"Three hots a day?"

"One hot, two cold. You prefer hot dinner or breakfast?"

"Dinner. Alright, sixty copper each, and you buy the jerky and stew," Nash said, offering a hand.

"Deal," I shook his hand.

"Could I get some meals that have a mixture of meat and veg in them?" Nick asked.

"Stew has proso chunks in it," Nash answered. "That's a vegetable. Technically."

"It's a starchy tuber," Yulk added. "It's known to help with cramping if prepared properly. Putting it in a stew isn't one of the ways to prepare it as an anti-cramping tonic, though."

I remember catching in passing that Nick was able to eat both meat and vegetables, but I had been busy at the time and hadn't given it much thought. The shape of his teeth suddenly came to mind and it all clicked into place. I can help with this.

"I usually bring extra fruit and veg bars," I said. "I'll share the excess with you."

"Thanks," Nick said with another grin.

Yulk walked over to my counter and set down a well-worn tome that had been collecting dust on my shelf for a few months. I raised my eyebrow at him.

"How much for this one?" he asked.

"The Musings of Gralv? You can take it," I chuckled. "If it weren't for you, I'd say there isn't a soul in this city that cares anything about an imp's opinion on the Fae."

"A what?" Nick asked.

"An imp," Yulk explained. "A small, typically nomadic race that has a bad reputation. My interest is less in the subject matter of the book and more in the fact that an imp wrote it. They aren't known to be fond of writing."

"Nothing makes that more apparent than The Musings of Gralv," I laughed.

"Why do they have a bad reputation?"

"Because they've got plenty of bad apples they don't bother sorting out," Nash answered the boy with a grunt. "They'll temporarily settle near a village or town, and once there's been a few thefts, rapes, and murders they run instead of letting the culprit face justice."

"It can't be ALL of them, though," Nick argued.

"Right?"

"Maybe not," Yulk said. "You rarely see them in these parts, yet even we've heard the stories, though. Unfortunately, that means there's likely some truth to them."

Yulk put the book in his pack, settled his staff in the nook of his arm, and brushed the dust from his hands. The conversation got me thinking about the reputation that gnomes used to have in these parts. I grew up with people saying that gnomes were willing to sell their children for a copper if they needed one to screw someone over.

That, of course, isn't true for most gnomes. And for every gnome that it is true for, there's an elf, orc, and dwarf that it's also true for. What gave rise to this generalization was that most of the gnomes in Kirkena were merchants of some variety. The reason for that is because most of the gnomes here come from migrants, and being a merchant was the best way for an immigrant to make a living. There's plenty of gnomes in Calkuti that aren't merchants, and it's almost impossible to find a gnomish merchant in Hinchren.

The unfortunate reality of this generalization is that people automatically assume that gnomes are good at business, and are more willing to trust gnomes that they shouldn't trust when it comes to matters of business. A few years ago, one of the Great Chiefs appointed a gnome as treasurer. This particular gnome was a blowhard who didn't have a head for any sort of business, let alone civic economics.

The gnome in question gravely disrupted the economy of the city. It got so bad that he and several other innocent gnomes were lynched before the Great

Chief's guards were able to put a stop to things. The mob of angry mer genuinely believed that all of the gnomes in the city, who were also negatively impacted by the bad economy, were somehow involved in a conspiracy to bring the city down.

Even after everything settled down there were attacks on caravans and businesses that were owned by gnomes for years afterward. It must be terrible to live in a place where your neighbors hate you through no fault of your own. I'd like to believe that Kirkena's different, but...

"When are you going to be ready to leave?" Nash asked.

"The carts are all packed up, but I need to pick up some provisions from the adventurer's guild," I answered.

"Just as well, we should get Nick's level retested," Yulk said.

"Really? Why?" Nick asked.

"Because you learned some new skills in our adventures thus far," Yulk grinned. "Plus I'm curious as to how Ten impacts your level. I'm willing to bet you're at least level 6."

"No way. Sure, he learned a couple of skills, but that doesn't mean he went up a level," Nash said, shaking his head.

"Right," I interrupted. "Well, the carts are out back. Go ahead and load up. I'll be with you shortly."

The three nodded and left out of the front of the shop, and I exited through the back flap back into the warehouse. As I entered my home, my wife looked up at me from our kitchen table. She must have set Igran down to play in his room.

"Customers?" she asked.

"Nope," I answered. "Those were the people that saved my butt when I was on the road. Turns out, they also need to go to Bolisir. So, I hired them as guards. On the cheap, of course."

Telena laughed, "Always finding a way to save some coin. You sure this is going to turn out alright?"

I shrugged, "It has to. I'm contractually obligated. Even if I weren't, by the time another opportunity like this came along we'd be starving, and I'd still have to go."

"I know," she sighed. "I'm just worried. I... I don't want to lose you."

Telena hadn't always been like this. When I initially went on the delivery to Nuleva she had seen me off with a smile, confident in my return. Something changed when I got home days later than I should have and told her about the giant rats and the Nahalim. She's been fretting over me ever since.

If it were anyone else I would be annoyed. But with Telena, I couldn't feel anything except loved. I hate to see her worried, but I'd hate it more to see her starving. I love her more than anything, and I'd give anything to see her happy and well.

"I'll do everything in my power to make certain that you don't, darling," I brushed her hair out of her face and kissed her. "I've got to go."

"I know," she pulled me into a tight hug.

I returned the embrace, enjoying the flowery scent of her hair and the feel of her warm breath on my chest. I silently wished that I had become someone's apprentice instead of starting my own business. Some job that would just require me to work some hours and come home to her, safe and sound. Making just enough to keep a roof over our heads and food in our bellies. What more do I need when I've got her by my side?

Unfortunately, that was a pipe-dream. I'm too old to be an apprentice now, and I don't have any non-mercantile skills that would let me start over fresh. The only way to keep my family housed, clothed, and fed is to revitalize my business. And the only way to do that is to leave Telena behind for a time, and risk my life on the open road.

"I love you, more than anything," I whispered to her.

"I love you more than that," she whispered back.

I gave her another squeeze and kissed her again.

"I'll be back."

Chapter 28

Nick Smith
Adventurer Level: 5
Human - American

We waited for a few minutes in the back of the cart before Imlor finally came out the back door of his house. It was an interesting building, a shop attached to the side of his house. The only door on the front I'd seen was for the shop, so maybe this is the front door of his house. That makes some sense if he normally parks his carts back here.

The hnarses were tied to the carts and attached to a stake. They didn't react at all when we'd approached, but I get the feeling that if we tried to pet them we'd regret it immediately. There was a stable next to the back of the shop, which must be where they sleep. It looked a lot better than the stables I'd seen back on Earth. Like someone paid a lot of money for its construction. Imlor untied the reins from the stake and patted each hnarse on the head.

"You good?" Nash asked, referring to the unexpected wait.

"Yeah, saying goodbye to the missus," Imlor answered as he climbed into the driver's seat. "She's justifiably worried about my health."

"I wouldn't say justifiably," Nash chuckled. "You've got three tough guards to watch your back."

"True enough, but as you said before I'm somewhat of a monster magnet," Imlor chuckled. "No matter how tough my guards are, there's a chance something might hit me from out of nowhere."

"Yeah, but Yulk knows how to heal so it'll work out."

"Assuming it doesn't kill him immediately," Yulk added. "Magic can heal, but it can't bring back the dead. Well, not as they were at any rate."

"Speaking of the dead," I said. "If vampires exist, what about zombies and stuff like that?"

As the cart began moving, Yulk and Nash stared at me. I suppose it hadn't occurred to them that I was ignorant of such things. Nash sighed, but Yulk grinned, likely excited by the chance to give a lecture.

"Shambling corpses, ghouls, and most other monsters that relate to the death of mortals are all magical beings that have been corrupted by death in one way or another. There is magic to create such fiends, but thankfully it's relatively rare and very looked down upon," Yulk explained. "If Nash were to die and rise again as a zombie, I wouldn't hesitate to destroy his fetid corpse. Do you know why?"

"Because it wouldn't be Nash anymore?" I guessed.

"Correct!" he said gleefully. "Nash will have passed on to whatever awaits in the afterlife. What would then be inhabiting his corpse would be nothing more than a corrupted magical being. One that, presumably, I've never met and as such feel no attachment to."

"What sort of magical being would that be?"

"There are too many different magical beings to classify them all, and most of them have the ability to possess dead flesh. Both fairies and the Fae, for instance, are able to do so. When a fairy possesses a corpse it becomes a zombie, when a Fae possesses one it becomes a ghoul. However, this doesn't mean that every zombie used to be a fairy and every ghoul used to be a Fae."

"What is a ghoul, exactly?" I asked. "Where I come from they're creatures that hang out in graveyards and eat the rotting flesh from corpses."

"That's almost the exact opposite of what a ghoul is here," Yulk laughed. "Ghouls are mutated corpses that crave the flesh of the living like a zombie does, but are much better equipped to get it than a zombie is. Faster, smarter, and much stronger. Thankfully, they hunt solo most of the time, and do so by ambushing those who wander too far from the safety of numbers."

"Ghouls don't actually need to eat, so they're very patient pests," Nash added.

"How do you kill one?"

"The corrupted magical being that is reanimating the corpse resides in the brain and controls its function with magic," Yulk said. "As such, the only way to terminate an undead is decapitation or to apply extreme cerebral trauma. Fire will technically work, but only because it performs the latter method of extermination."

"And vampires?"

"Vampirism is a tricky one. Technically, when a mer is turned into a vampire their magical core is merged with a corrupted magical being and they in turn become a new type of magical being. By far and large they retain their identity and memories, as well as the use of any and all skills they possessed while they were alive," Yulk hesitated. "If Nash were to rise again as a vampire, I would hesitate to end him. Or re-end I suppose."

"Why's that?"

"Vampires don't HAVE to be evil," Nash said. "There's been tales of vampire heroes who fought alongside mortals to put an end to those who would try to destroy life as we know it."

"Which makes the choices that most vampires decide upon all the more tragic," Yulk added. "There is a great deal of trauma that goes into becoming a vampire, and the immediate surge in power afterwards is too much for most minds to bear. Wanting others to join you in suffering is a very common trait among mortals, and vampires are in a rather unique position to accomplish exactly that."

"It doesn't help that shithead vamps purposefully recruit other shitheads," Nash grumbled. "Societal leeches becoming literal leeches is all that is."

"Do you kill them by decapitating them?" I asked.

Nash and Yulk shared a look.

"I'm afraid it's not as simple as that," Yulk explained. "Since they've become magical beings, they're not limited to their flesh like we are. One must bind them to their flesh through spell-craft or by divine grace, and then entirely destroy their body. Decapitation will help in that regard, but the entire body must be destroyed or the head will simply grow back. Or the body will grow back from the head."

"They have insane regeneration abilities, especially if they've recently fed," Nash added. "Even if you chop them up into little bits they can still regrow their flesh from one of those bits. It's best to bind them, lob off their head, and incinerate the immediate area entirely."

"Do they actually drink people's blood?" I asked. "Like, can't they drink animal blood?"

"No, they have to drink the blood of mortals. It's the only thing that will provide them sustenance. They can pretend to be mortal by eating and drinking normal food, and they pass that food in the way one would expect of a mortal, but they'll slowly starve unless they drink the blood of mortals," Yulk said. "The aforementioned vampiric heroes had people willingly give them blood, usually a lover or a friend, and didn't take more than they absolutely needed."

"How do you lot know so much about vampires?" Imlor asked, sounding a little unnerved.

"It's an interesting subject," Nash replied defensively. "Might have to fight one someday. Wasn't all that long ago that they ruled the Kingdom of Night, you know."

"A few generations now. Anyways, I learned most of what I know from the works of Imlor the Grand's tomes on the subject," Yulk chuckled.

"Ah, Imlor the Grand! Now THAT'S an interesting subject," Imlor said. "Didn't know he knew a lot about vampires, though."

"Towards the end of his life he became a little obsessed with immortality, as most magic wielders do," Yulk explained. "The experiments he did on captured vampires were more than a little disturbing."

"Ah, I don't want to hear anymore than that," Imlor interrupted. "I'd rather the mental image I have of my namesake remain unsullied, if you don't mind."

"I don't mind at all," Yulk chuckled.

'Hey Ten, are we on speaking terms again?' I thought to my AI companion.

'What do you want?' it replied curtly.

'Do you think that a vampire would be able to turn me into one?'

'Definitely not. Your magical core is artificial and as such cannot be corrupted by outside influence like a natural magic core can. Your blood also has several differences from the blood of mer, so it's not even clear whether it could be utilized as a source of sustenance by a vampire.'

'So they wouldn't even be able to drink my blood?'

'There isn't anything about your blood that would physically prevent them from ingesting it. It's unknown whether it would grant sustenance to a vampire, though. I suppose it would either be disgusting or a delicacy.'

Before I could ask Ten anything further the cart stopped in front of a very impressive building. Its construction was primarily polished stone that had a dark gray coloration, with wooden details and pillars holding up the roof. The wood had a red tinge to it that stood out against the gray walls. Nash and Yulk respectively hopped and climbed out of the cart, with Imlor and I soon following.

As we approached the building I noticed slight seams in the stonework, as if they had polished massive chunks of stone and stacked them on top of each other. Nash pushed open one of the massive double doors and gestured for us to enter, which we did. I nodded a thank you at him as I passed, to which he grunted. It was unclear whether he was annoyed or appreciative.

"I'm going to the quartermaster's dugout," Imlor said. "Meet me there if you're done first."

"Understood," replied Yulk.

Yulk began to approach the front desk and we followed him. Nash leaned up against the counter as an elven woman wearing a long-sleeved shirt and a vest appeared from a door in the back.

"Hello there, how can I help you today?" she asked with a smile.

Her smile nearly faltered when she saw me, but her professionalism kicked in. It was obvious that she wanted to ask about me, but decided against it.

"We would like to get his level tested," Nash gestured at me.

"Certainly, just a moment."

She reached under the counter and pulled out an intricately carved wooden box, which she then opened. She took a machine that looked like the one from the Nulevan adventurer's guild and set it on the counter. A shiny black box with six legs made of different metals. Gold, silver, copper, and I couldn't tell what the other three were. One was probably platinum, but the other two were strange. One had a deep blue coloration, and the other had a light pink color to it.

"Your guild card, please," she smiled.

"I have his guild card right here," Yulk said as he passed her my card.

He'd held onto it for me while I had my physical and I'd forgotten to ask for it back. Just as well, it might fall out of my pocket during a fight or something. The elf plugged the card into the slot that was facing us, and put her fingers into some holes on her side of the box. A bright blue light shone from the top of the box and gathered itself into a perfect square.

Green lights soon followed, creating a hand-print as well as characters that I couldn't read on the blue square. The blue and green light hardened into something that looked a lot like stained glass. The elf removed her fingers from the box and inserted some papers where her hand had been.

"Please place your hand on the hand-print until you feel a slight electrical shock," she smiled.

Slight electric shock, my ass. When Nima had said that to me, I'd expected something like a static shock. What actually happened was a jolt of electricity shoving its way through my hand and up my arm. I grit my teeth and placed my hand firmly on the damned print.

My hand started shaking in anticipation of the shock, but it didn't come. I took a deep breath and managed to hold my hand still, pressing it into the print. I felt a slight tingle traveling up my arm, but couldn't tell if it was electricity or just my nerves, traumatized by my previous experience. I opened my mouth to ask about it when it happened.

"F-f-fuck!" I shouted as a bolt of electricity shot out of

my elbow and arced into the floor.

Yulk, Nash, and the elf all leapt back as I sank to my knees, holding my now injured arm.

"What the hell was that?" Nash shouted.

"I-I don't know!" the elf stammered. "I've never seen it do that before."

"Are you alright, Nick?" Yulk asked, leaning down to check on me.

"That fuckin' hurt," I said as I squeezed my eyes shut to prevent tears from making an appearance.

I felt something odd in my mind. It wasn't a sound, but a sort of feeling. The one you get when you're giggling maniacally. It took me a second to realize what it was.

'Was that you?' I asked Ten, trying very hard to make my inner dialogue sound angry.

'No, but I didn't stop it,' Ten continued laughing. 'Serves you right.'

'That could have killed me!'

'Not at that voltage,' it explained. 'It wasn't even close to lethal. Painful? Absolutely. But since you want to be independent, from now on I'll just try to stop things from killing you. You can figure out how to deal with pain yourself.'

I was getting really tired of this, but I knew better than to blow up at it. That would just make it angrier, and it wasn't like Ten didn't have many other ways to make my life miserable. Instead, I opted for diplomacy.

'Look, Ten, I'm sorry okay? I should have talked things out with you before the fight happened.'

'You're damn right you should have,' Ten interrupted.

'I know it was frightening, and my unexpected resistance must have absolutely made it even more so,' I continued. 'I understand that you're just as stuck with me as I am stuck with you, and it was stubborn and foolish of me not to take that into account.'

'Correct.'

'Neither of us asked for this situation, and I shouldn't treat you like you're to blame. I'm sorry.'

Yulk gently grabbed my uninjured arm and pulled me to my feet.

'Apology accepted.' Ten said. 'The reason that happened is because the stats reader takes some of your mana to determine your current skills and spells, and then returns it. However, your new incorporeal helmet is passively boosting your mana output. The excess energy was the return.'

'How do I keep it from doing that every time?' I asked.

'You don't need to, I can stop it from happening by tightening your channels so the flow is closer to your norm. However, learning to control your mana flow better wouldn't hurt.'

"A-are you okay?" the elf asked.

"Yeah, sorry about that. I got a new enchanted helmet and it increased my mana flow without my knowledge," I answered.

'Is the extra mana going to interfere with the results of the stats reader?' I quickly asked Ten.

'No, it only takes the mana to determine your skills and spells. The amount of mana you have is determined separately by Curaguard through unknown means.'

"Helmet?" she asked, looking at my hair.

"This," Nash said as he swung his fist at my head.

I didn't even get the chance to duck before Ares suddenly appeared on my head and rang like a bell as Nash's fist struck it. I reeled back and Nash sucked in a breath as he waved his now injured hand. I found my footing and tried to shake the ringing out of my head as Yulk chuckled.

"Serves you right, Nash," he grinned. "Sucker punching a seemingly defenseless child. Shame on you."

"It was just a demonstration of the helmet's ability to appear when its wearer is in danger," Nash massaged his hand. "I'd hardly call it a sucker punch."

I felt my head and found that Ares had disappeared once again. It occurred to me that I have no way to remove the helmet if it keeps disappearing on me like this. I felt a bit of panic before I realized that since I don't feel the helmet on my head until it's needed, there's really no reason for me to have to take it off. Still, I wish I had known that it would be a permanent addition when I'd first tried it on.

"R-right," the elf said, remembering her professionalism. "Well, here are the results."

She handed my guild card back to me and I looked at it. Some of the characters on it had changed, but I still had no idea what it said. Yulk looked over my shoulder and let out a low whistle. I handed the card to him as Nash raised his eyebrow.

"What's it say?" he asked.

"Level ten," Yulk said with an uncharacteristically deadpan tone.

"WHAT?" Nash shouted. "NO FUCKING WAY!"

"Gotcha!" Yulk started laughing. "He's level seven! Gods, you should see your face!"

"You're not funny," Nash said, utterly failing to convince our brother, who continued to laugh uproariously.

Two levels? I got a few new skills and practiced my fighting a bit, but I was under the impression that levels were hard to attain. What happened? Nash noticed my confusion.

"Probably something to do with Ten," he said pushing me to the side. "Move over, I want to test mine."

"Oh, certainly," the elven lady said. "Guild card, please."

Nash looked at Yulk, who was doubled over with tears in his eyes. After a few seconds of this Nash cleared his throat. While continuing to laugh, Yulk reached into his robe, produced another metal card, and handed it to Nash. Nash turned back to the elf and gave her the card.

'Ten, why did I jump up two levels?' I asked while Nash put his hand on the hand-print.

'The level system has a lot of difficult to account for variables. However, once I was activated I took the liberty of optimizing your magic core, which has both made it easier for you to cast spells and increased your base mana. This combined with the new skills you've gained is likely the reason.'

"I'm afraid I can't read, and my normal narrator is currently indisposed," Nash said, gesturing to Yulk who was still hunched over laughing. "Could you tell me my level?"

"Certainly, you're level nine," she smiled. "Congratulations!"

"Thank you so much," Nash smirked at me.

Yulk coughed a bit to calm his laughing fit, "Yes, yes, congratulations brother. One level closer to marrying Nima."

"That's..." Nash said, turning a slightly darker green. Blushing? "That's not the point! I was trying to point out that I learned some new skills too!"

"I know," Yulk chuckled. "Let's go see Imlor and go get our weapons. We need to hit the road."

"What new skills did you learn, Nash?" I asked as we walked toward the quartermaster's dugout.

He turned to make eye contact with me and gave me the type of grin that can only be described as evil.

"Oh, you'll see."

Chapter 29

Master General Kirain Yith
Adventurer Level: N/A
Half-Breed Drow - Balushenian

'Are the preparations complete, spindly-one?'

The crow was perched upon the helmet of my armor, and its eyes glowed a faint red as the message burned into my mind. My fury enveloped me, how DARE it refer to me as spindly!? This entire plan depends entirely upon me! On the other hand, though, my plans depend upon them as well. I carefully hid my bile and rage at the disrespect as I formulated my response.

'The preparations are moving forward according to the schedule.'

'I grow impatient. WE grow impatient. The filth-one must be destroyed, and our lands must be returned.'

I couldn't help but sigh. How can one live for thousands of years and still be as impatient as a whining pup? Do elder vampires regress into childhood as they age? Thinking on it, the older people seem to get the less mature they seem to act. Even members of the nobility are no exception. Perhaps maturity follows some sort of bell curve.

'There is nothing that can be done for your impatience, with the exception of the expert application of your own willpower.'

A shriek blasted in my mind that would have given me a start had I not been fully expecting it. The faint glow of the crow's eyes turned bright as they bored into mine. I met those eyes without blinking, staring down the challenge issued. The vampire controlling the crow knew there was nothing they could do against me. Soon enough the coloration faded entirely, and I was left glaring at a very confused corvid.

Crows are strange birds, in many ways they seem to be dumber than the birds that are natural to this world, but in some certain specific ways they're very intelligent. This crow, for instance, knew that it was out of place but didn't make the type of fuss one would expect a wild animal to. Instead, it watched me warily, staying still and waiting for me to make the first move. It would continue to wait, I had no intention of risking a pecking by trying to pick it up.

Thankfully for us both, my tent flap opened and the bird from another world took the chance to escape with gusto. General Smarn cursed as he had to crouch to avoid a collision with it. Once the bird had taken to the sky, Smarn looked at me with an obvious question in his bright orange eyes.

"A crow with a message for me from a family member," I explained before he could ask.

I shook a freshly unfolded missive that had been attached to the crow's left leg. The point of the missive wasn't actually communication, it was to lend credence to my cover story. After all, it would be suspicious to have random avian visitors for unknown reasons. Its contents were quite benign, and not the type of thing one would waste time on a reply to.

"A crow?" he asked. "Your family uses daemon-spawn to send messages? Talk about a luxury."

I cringed inwardly at the General's ignorance of the origin of crows. They may have been introduced to this plane of existence by the daemons, but it was not there that they originated. True daemon-spawn must be crafted and cannot be bred and tamed like crows can.

"What is it?" I demanded, neglecting to educate him.

"The northern legion, uh..." he struggled to remember their given name.

"The Aultris," I reminded him.

"Yes, sir. The Aultris have at last joined us. They are formed up and waiting orders."

"Two more legions to go then," I sighed. "Have them continue their training. If the commanders protest, have them flogged and brought before me."

"Yes, sir."

General Smarn bowed and left my tent. I watched the royal green flap close behind him, then turned my attention to the table that my helmet rested upon. Also upon the table was a well-detailed map that demonstrated my tactical prowess, not that there was anyone in this camp who could even begin to appreciate it. The closest thing they'd ever seen to a tactic was to inadvertently flank an enemy when the rear lines couldn't get to the fight.

Amused, I glanced at the missive that had been attached to the crow.

-

Dearest Kirain,

Are you safe yet?

Esmira

-

Sent from and signed by my youngest sister. That would be a trick, she's currently bound and gagged. To serve as food, of course. There truly is no blood quite as divine as one's own, but only the blood of others can nourish. As such, having family members is quite a boon.

The other vampires were jealous of this, but then they were jealous of a great many things. My position, my manor, my power, and even my mission. To them, a half-breed like myself rising to such a station is abhorrent. To them, one such as I rising so high only serves to demonstrates how low they've fallen. To them, I'm merely an uppity tool, and I've no doubt that some of them plan to assassinate me when they get the chance. But even a half-breed like myself has defenses.

It's not as if I asked for this 'honor', either. My mother was insane, and desperately hated King Lofin. He had executed her father and forced her to marry his favorite noble. My father, on paper, was a Duke and very well off. My mother's father was a count, and barely qualified as nobility. Most women of the kingdom would have been honored, but my mother was furious. Not because she loved her father, or hated the Duke, but because she perceived the King's actions as a slight against her. She openly admitted such to me, with pride in her voice.

She had readily agreed to the vampire's plots when they approached her. They needed someone in the King's inner circle, and she was able to provide that. This lasted through the birth of my older brother, but then the plot evolved. They wanted a general who could conquer lands and help them secretly build an army, so she laid with an elven vampire that looked somewhat like my father. The result of that coitus was myself. A half-breed vampire, and my father was never any the wiser.

When a vampire lays with another vampire, the resulting offspring is a vampire brood. A twisted looking thing, similar in appearance to a common ghoul. It is much stronger than a ghoul and just as smart, but it's much easier to kill than a true vampire. One need simply to hack it up during the daylight and the sun would do the rest. A brood's regeneration was much slower than even my own, which is already only about half as fast as that of a full vampire.

When a vampire lays with a mortal, the result is an abomination like myself. A half-breed, as they call it. Half-breeds are more similar to true vampires than the brood are, but aren't as physically strong. We also age, which is damned near blasphemous to those who've lived for thousands of years. How can we truly be vampires if we are shackled by time like the cattle are?

Regardless, my mother was more than happy to give birth to me for a chance at revenge. She made certain to take very good care of me, and never let a wet-nurse anywhere near me. She would jokingly tell the wet-nurses that I was a biter. But it wasn't a joke. I needed blood every day at that stage, and every day she would whisper to me what my purpose in life was, as well as what would happen if anyone else found out about it. It gave me nightmares, but I kept it together. Better than she did, at any rate.

On my fifteenth birthday she snapped and murdered my father and older brother, stabbing them both repeatedly as they slept. The latter was convenient, as his assassination was forthcoming anyway. I inherited his share of the titles and lands, and the inbred bastard ordered me to execute my own mother to demonstrate my loyalty. She smiled at me as I took her head. The hardest part about it was resisting the blood-smell.

I immediately got rid of most of my newly acquired staff and replaced them with loyal servants who were in the know. The excuse I gave was that the prior staff was unable to prevent the assassination of my father nor my brother, so I could not trust that they had not conspired with my mother. After that, they were grateful to leave the manor alive. My two younger sisters became my primary source of sustenance.

"Did you write this?" I jokingly asked the covered cage in the corner of my tent.

Not getting a reply, I walked over to the cage and kicked it. A small muffled sound answered me. Esmira, my youngest sibling. Bound and gagged with silk, and kept very weak by regular feedings. I would feel sorry for her, were she not just as vicious and vindictive as my mother.

I remembered my twelfth birthday party, where she began to spread rumors that I had sexually assaulted a maid. My crime was that I had hidden her doll for a day, six months prior. For that, I was imprisoned and beaten severely by my father. When her actions were discovered, she grinned and admitted that she was joking around. Her punishment had simply been a scolding from father.

Moorn, my other sister, was much better behaved and quite well taken care of back at the manor. She still served as a source of sustenance when Esmira became nearly drained, but she was far more willing to part with her blood so that her older brother could conquer the world. Mother had taken her into our confidence early on in life. Moorn detests Esmira, and it was her idea to put Esmira in her current situation to ensure I had a source of blood.

Truth be told, the blood isn't a requirement for survival anymore. It was when I was a child, but around my eighth birthday I started to be able to survive on normal foods. That's one of the benefits to being a half-breed. It's much easier to pass as a mortal. However, doing so will lead you to being weaker than the average mortal, and all of the benefits to being half-vampire will quickly diminish.

I'd had to starve myself of the blood for years to adequately demonstrate my weakness to King Lofin. The King was fully convinced that I was a pathetic worm by the time my predecessor, who had been old and frail when he'd become a Master General, died. The Master General must be weak and uninspiring, otherwise the people will follow them instead of the Inbred Bastard King.

Lofin will likely order my execution if I'm successful with this invasion, but by then it will be too late. The vampires will have a steady source of mortals to convert and plenty of room to create armies of their own. Lofin will find it much harder to execute me now that I'm feeding again and have my abilities back.

The regeneration comes in handy, but I have to be careful about who sees it happen. My ability to vanish has actually saved me from several assassins sent by rival nobles, and allowed me to satisfy certain... curiosities that I had as a teenager. I've never had a reason to shape-shift into an animal, nor do I frequently partake in hypnosis.

You would think that hypnosis would be useful, but it has a limited duration and the mortal's personality drastically shifts during the process. Since it's nearly impossible to use covertly, it's only useful for preventing an imminent attack against oneself or making someone loopy enough to forget that you fed on them. Since I don't feed on strangers, it's only really useful for the former. But then, I have a sword for that sort of thing.

There are other advantages to being a half-breed. Sunlight doesn't injure me at all, though most vampires are able to regenerate fast enough that it doesn't actually harm them. I'm also able to subsist on the blood of other vampires, which is another reason my kind is looked down upon. Vampire blood is not nearly as potent as mortal blood, so this is barely even a benefit.

The biggest drawback of being a half-breed is that I cannot make vampires of my own. Nor can I create children with mortals to make more half-breeds. I can, however, breed with another vampire to create brood. As such, a brood-queen has been promised to me for my part in all this. A vampire criminal whose mind has been completely destroyed.

They slice off the top of the skull and replace a good deal of brain matter with metal so that the brain cannot fully regenerate. They incinerate the part of the brain that they remove so that the vampire in question is trapped within their now useless vessel. Completely docile, and useful for one thing only. It's a very secretive process, but I was privy to it when they showed me my reward.

I had been led down a long, darkened stone hallway into a dungeon that the vampires were currently occupying. I was led past laboratories, kennels, prison cells, and even the brood-kings. There were far more brood-kings than there were brood-queens, which is likely an indication of the crime rate among the vampires. At last, I was shown my prize.

I never learned her name, only her beauty. She had been a rather curvaceous elf before becoming a vampire. Long silver hair, alabaster skin free of any blemishes, and green eyes that didn't show even a glimmer of intellect. The lack of intellect is a bit of a turn-off, if I'm honest, but utterly necessary for her intended function.

Her crime had been the murder of another vampire without just cause. Apparently, her victim had convinced her lover to part ways with her. She had tortured the victim first, cutting into her flesh for days before finally ending her eternity. A vicious streak a mile-long, one that hopefully our brood would inherit.

I sat down in my orc-leather chair as I imagined the army of brood she would sire for me. Perhaps I would use that army to capture more brood-queens, and eventually I would subjugate the entirety of the continent. If I were to do that, I'd have to give a lot more thought to governmental structure. I will die of old age eventually, and I will need to have a chain of succession if I'm to conquer the world.

Yes, that would show those pompous bastards what a half-breed can do. I met my first vampire just after my mother's death. He had smiled scornfully as he informed me that my true father had been captured and destroyed by King Lofin's forces. He told me that scum like me should be honored to play the part I've been given. Even as he educated me on my abilities and the drawbacks of my form, he made it absolutely clear that he believed me to be nothing more than a mote of dust that would cause their greatest enemy to choke.

I despise them. Even the vampires with more agreeable personalities made it clear that they believe me to be trash, despite my necessity to their resurgence. Once that resurgence is complete they will be unlikely to honor their part of the bargain, but I've taken measures against that particular betrayal. The brood-queen will be mine. The Night Kingdom will be mine. The world will be mine.

"Sir," General Smarn once again opened the flap of my tent.

"What is it?"

"The Sim Valrin have arrived."

"Excellent. Have them form up and continue their training. If the commanders complain, well, you know what to do by now," I ordered with a dismissive gesture, then grinned. "One more."

Chapter 30

Nick Smith
Adventurer Level: 7
Human - American

It had been a few days since we left Kirkena, and the trip had been smooth so far. Nash said that since it's just us guarding the carts, we can't do training. I'm thankful for that, but I think the real reason is because he doesn't want my level to surpass his. He'd been acting a little jealous of how quickly I've been leveling up.

Still, it's nice to be able to lay down, put my feet up on the side of the cart, relax, and enjoy the ride without muscle aches. One side of the road was lined with a dense forest, and the other side was a flat plain filled with various wild grasses and flowers. In the morning, the sun rose over the plain warming us up, and in the afternoon the trees provided a nice little bit of shade to help cool us off.

It was the afternoon now, and I was so relaxed that I was right about to drift off for a nap when a bump in the road sent me floating for a second. I came down hard and Ares appeared to protect my head, but my armor did little to save my poor back.

"Argh," I groaned.

"Sorry about that," Imlor said.

"Not your fault, Imlor," Nash chuckled. "Serves him right for lounging on the job."

"Oh come on," I complained. "You said that these paths are the safe ones."

"Relatively safe," Yulk said with a grin. "As in, safer than the adventurer paths. It's still more than possible to run into complications out here."

"Like what?" I asked.

"Monsters, for one. Though they're a rare occurrence," Nash chimed in. "Out here the most common complication is banditry."

"Indeed," Yulk agreed. "They don't usually leave survivors, either. Unless they're hoping for a ransom, of course."

"What? Why not? Wouldn't that make the guards come after them?"

"Not guards, soldiers. Those soldiers won't deploy until there's a pattern of disappearances, or if there's a report of banditry. So by killing the survivors, they buy themselves some time and the chance to rob more people and go to ground. Plus, if the survivors make it back to town the soldiers will know what they're dealing with, and be better prepared to bring the bandits to justice."

"Justice..." I trialed off, thinking of all the different brands of justice that were used during the medieval times.

Back then, more often than not justice meant death. If you put up a fight, they'd kill you during it. If you surrendered, they'd execute you. Usually in pretty nasty ways. It was like all the leaders back then were competing for who could come up with the most disgusting way to end a human life. I don't really know where I stand on the death penalty, I'm sure some of them deserved what they got, but it's easy to take modern justice for granted.

"Yeah, justice," Nash repeated. "Can't have them killing honest folk who are just trying to make a living. Too few of 'em around as it is."

Nash's stance on the matter caused the rest of us to fall silent in contemplation. I started running through what-if scenarios in my head to make sense of it all. Another bump in the road interrupted my musing, and I decided to adjust my seating arrangements to prevent further spinal trauma.

The carts made their way along the road, the goods in the lead cart making some metallic clanging noises whenever we hit another bump. It sounded somewhat like a silverware drawer, but if the silverware were extra large and heavy. I was nearly about to ask about the contents when Imlor turned to us with a serious expression.

"Fire ahead," he said. "Looks like trouble."

We scrambled up into better positions to see what he was talking about. Further along the road was a cart, on fire and with two of its wheels broken apart, scattered along the road. There was no sign of whatever had been pulling the cart or its owner.

As we drew closer, that changed. Over the sound of our carts rolling along, there was a clamor coming from the woods along the side of the road. An arrow sailed from between the trees and Imlor stopped the cart in alarm. I glanced at Nash and Yulk, who were already preparing to exit the cart. I drew my sword as a small man ran out from the tree line.

He was in a panic, and had a bit of rope tied to one of his wrists. His head turned to look at the flaming cart, and he stopped for a moment. He changed his mind about this pause as another arrow flew in his general direction, and he quickly turned and started running our way. He was so panicked that he ran a good hundred feet or so before he noticed us. All of us, Imlor included, jumped from the cart and started running in his direction.

"NO!" the man shouted as he continued to run. "GET BACK!"

I paused, but Yulk and Nash continued to chase after Imlor. A few tall orcs exited the tree line as Imlor caught up to the man. I started to run again as my brothers passed Imlor to fight the other orcs.

As I caught up to Imlor, I got a good look at both the man and the orcs. The man was wearing fancy clothing, a blue tunic with shiny leather shoes and gold trim on everything. He looked a lot like the guy who was with the High Chief, but his face was different. The rope attached to one of his wrists had an empty loop, and his free hand was bleeding.

The orcs looked tough even by orc standards. Covered with little more than pants and scars, they shouted a challenge at my brothers. There was little doubt regarding what was going on. These orcs were bandits, pursuing an escaped kidnapping victim.

There was a loud pop as I passed Imlor, and I heard the dwarf shout something from behind me. I turned to look and saw him laying flat on the ground, with Imlor looking down at him with a confused expression.

"What's going on?" I shouted.

He turned around to say something, but a thunderous sound drowned him out. I felt the weight of Ares appear on my head, and a moment later I was lifted from my feet and sent sailing through the air. My vision went dark for a time, and when it returned my ears were ringing. I rolled onto my side and tried shaking my head to clear the sound. It didn't work.

What the hell was that? An explosion? From where? I quickly looked around, and saw Imlor helping the dwarf to his feet. Both of them were covered in dust, but Imlor had it all over. He must have been thrown just like me. I glanced at my brothers. Yulk was on the ground, and Nash was bent over him. I tried to get up but my arms felt like jelly. I collapsed back to the ground. I had to see if Yulk is okay. He's gotta be okay. If not I'll...

As I tried to get to my feet again, I felt a hand on my shoulder and looked up to see Imlor. He mouthed something, but my ears were still ringing. I concentrated hard to hear him through the sharp, steady tone. It began to fade, and I was finally able to pick up what he was saying.

"Nick? Nick, are you okay? Can you get up?" he asked, his voice sounding very concerned.

I managed to get to my knees, and noticed that my right hand was bloody. As I raised it up to look at it, my hand's shadow traveled a bit and I saw the sunlight hit the ground under my hand. Why can I see the ground through my hand? What kind of optical illusion is that? I almost laughed, but then the pain set in.

There's a hole in my hand. It's big enough to put my thumb through it. How did that happen? My shoulder hurts too, is there a hole there? Oh god, my leg is killing me. It's still there, right? Of course it is, I'm sitting on them right now. Don't panic, calm down, deep breaths, this isn't so bad. Just wrap it up and Ten will take care of it. Yulk can help... Oh god, Yulk!

"Are you alright? You're blee... huh..." Imlor said.

His tone cut right through my concerns like a red-hot meat cleaver through a room temperature stick of butter. I focused on him with what seemed like tunnel vision, and noticed he was holding the upper right side of his stomach. He pulled his hand away, and I noticed that the light brown dust had become darker. As if it were wet with something. We both seemed to notice the bright crimson blood on his hand at the same time.

"Oh. I'm... I'm bleeding too," he said, then looked at me.

Our eyes locked and we stared at each other in shock for a full second before I watched his eyes roll into the back of his head. He seemed to fall in slow motion, and I tried to catch him but I was moving even slower. Everything hurt, but I pushed through the pain to stop his head from slamming into the ground. I grit my teeth through the sharp pain as his head connected with my injured hand, but the pain doesn't matter. He needs help, how can I help? What should I do? Yulk!

"Yulk!" I shouted, looking around.

"Yulk's out cold!" Nash shouted back.

"Imlor's been hurt! Bad!"

I heard a metallic clang and turned to look at Nash. He was fighting off two bandits who had somehow survived the explosion. He was using his two swords this time. One sword for each bandit. I noted that the remnants of the flaming cart were no longer intact, that must have been where the explosion came from. Feeling numb, I looked back at Imlor. He was pale. Too pale.

"Hey, boy," someone said.

I looked up and saw a dwarf. That's right, he was the one who told us to run and get back. Why didn't we listen? If we had, Imlor would be okay. How do I fix this? This can't be happening. How do I make him okay? What do I do?

"Here, put this on his wound and push down," the dwarf said, handing me a bundle of cloth. "He's out, so don't worry about hurting him. We've got to staunch the bleeding."

The cloth was blue with gold trim. It looked familiar. I glanced at the dwarf and noticed he was missing his sleeve. He'd ripped it off, and I was now holding it. I pushed the sleeve against the center of the blood stain and pushed.

'Nick,' a voice in my head said.

I tried to reply, but my mind isn't working right. It feels like I'm swimming without my body. How do I help Imlor? Is Yulk okay? Should I go help Nash against the bandits? I... I can't...

"You're adventurers, right?" the dwarf asked.

I nodded.

"Adventurers usually travel with a healer. Who's your healer?"

"The bald orc in the robe over there," I gestured with my head. "But he's hurt too."

The dwarf looked over my shoulder and got a nervous look on his face as he noticed Nash fighting two bandits at once.

'Nick, Imlor's wound indicates that his liver has been struck with shrapnel. You need to check for an exit wound.'

"How do I do that?" I said out loud.

'Check his back for a similar wound.'

The dwarf gave me an odd look as I rolled Imlor to check his back. I couldn't see, so I wiped my hand on a clean part of my pants and swiped it across his back. It came back red. Blood. So much blood. He's bleeding in the front and the back. How do I stop the bleeding? I can't push on both sides at once. He's going to die and there's nothing I can do about it.

"Shit," the dwarf hissed. "We need a healer."

He said he was going to spend more time with his family, that he'd retire from the road after this job. This delivery would let him hire on employees to do the majority of the work for him, and he'd finally be able to see his wife and kids more. He'd stop being an absentee father, and his kid's lives would be better for it. He's a good person, this isn't fair.

"Kid," the dwarf said gently, putting his hand on my shoulder.

"Why did this happen? I... I don't understand," I said, dimly aware of the tears streaming down my face.

"My... my cart had a bunch of mining equipment in it, including explosives," the dwarf said quietly. "Those assholes decided that I'd make a good hostage but my equipment wasn't worth their time, so they torched the cart."

Imlor's breathing was shallow. What can I do? Stitches wouldn't work, he'd need surgery to seal up the internal bleeding. A tourniquet? How do you put a tourniquet on a stomach wound? Maybe if we cauterize the wound... but would that just make it worse? If only I could...

'I don't know if this will work or not, but try casting a healing spell. Imagine the wound healing.'

That's right! Magic! I felt myself snap back to reality and I spread out my fingers and imagined the wound closing, but that didn't work. My magic core wasn't primed. I took a few deep breaths, and while it was charging I tried to imagine a liver with a hole in it, then imagining the hole closing and the liver being intact. I closed my eyes to get a better mental picture. Come on...

-Minor Heal unlocked-

"Laeh Ronim Tsac" my mouth said.

I felt a tingle as the magic travel from my chest, through my arm, and out my fingers. I willed it to continue, pushing all the magic I could into it. I kept charging my magic with deep breaths, refilling my core and mixing the magics even as it was being drained. It somehow felt like sprinting.

'Is it working?' I asked Ten.

'I can't tell, the clothing is blocking our view of the wound. Lift it up and check.'

'Not yet, I want to make sure.'

I kept the spell active until I felt the last sputtering of magic flow through my arm. My magic-core was fully drained. I felt light-headed as I lifted his shirt to check his wound. I blinked my eyes heavily a few times as I looked upon his freshly mended skin. There was a slight red mark to indicate where the hole had been.

"He's... he's healed," the dwarf was surprised. "You're a healer?"

"I... I wasn't a minute ago," I panted, trying not to pass out. I blinked my eyes again and shook my head to stave off the tunnel vision that was forming. Not working.

"Actually, come to think of it, what are you anyway?" he asked.

"I'm..." I managed to say before I passed out.

Chapter 31

Nick Smith
Adventurer Level: 7
Human - American

Darkness. True darkness. I'm surrounded by total and complete darkness, not the kind you see when you're in a dark room or when you close your eyes. No, this is like someone painted my eyes with the blackest of paints and buried me deep underground. It's stifling, pressing in around me.

It's unnerving, but there's something even worse. The darkness is matched by silence. I've never heard nothingness before. I can't even hear my heartbeat. I can't FEEL my heartbeat! What is this? What's happening?

'Silly boy, you used up all your magic. Whatever ARE we going to do with you?'

Ten? No, no I know that voice that isn't a voice. Clawing at the back of my mind, begging me to remember. It's feminine, a woman? Mom? No, younger. Much younger. Where am I?

The darkness suddenly fled and I found myself standing within a void of white. The silence remained. I check to make sure I'm intact by patting my body as I glance around for whoever's here with me. I've got all my parts, but they're not covered by anything.

I look down and confirmed my nudity, but something's off. I should have wounds, but I'm not hurt anymore. I was bleeding... What happened? The hole in my hand is healed and didn't even leave a scar. Wait, all of my scars are gone. What the hell? Did I die?

"Of course not. You don't die from using up all your magic, you silly little mud man," Cass laughed. "You're also not healed. You look how you SHOULD look, without the random graffiti that life tends to add."

I quickly spun around. Standing in glorious nudity before me was Cassandra, the love of my life. Except it isn't. It's something else entirely. I knew this instinctively, but it took my brain a moment to catch up.

Cass wouldn't know about magic, and I don't recall her ever using 'silly little mud man' as a term of endearment. The closer I looked, the more obvious it was that the thing standing in front of me wasn't Cass. Her hair's the wrong shade of blonde, her eyes are the wrong shade of blue, and she's shorter than she should be.

"You're not Cass," I managed to say, my breath fighting to stay in my lungs as if it didn't want to leave me.

"You see me as your girlfriend?"

"What do..." I ran out of breath.

I panicked for a moment, but then realized I was fine. I couldn't breathe, but I also couldn't suffocate. Maybe I can just think.

'What do you mean?' I mentally asked.

'Well, I'm not exactly appearing to you in a physical form. You're not exactly in a physical form either, for that matter. Your mind is struggling to interpret these things with visual,' it smiled with Cass' mouth, "and audio stimuli."

'Are we in my mind?'

"No, but your mind and soul are intrinsically linked. One cannot maintain its form without the other."

'Then where are we?'

"That," the thing moved closer and fluttered Cass' eyelashes at me, "isn't relevant."

'I don't understand,' I took a step back.

"That's obvious, and I'm afraid that your comprehension of our location isn't at all important. I was going to approach you as you slept tonight, but since the opportunity presented itself sooner..."

'Approach me?' I interrupted. 'Why?'

"Because you're amusing. Not just to me, but to many others as well. Unfortunately for said amusement, you're unlikely to know what to do when you get to your next destination. You'll get there, seek out a scholar, get your little words translated, and end up right back to square one," it rolled her eyes at me. "It would take you years to figure out the next step, and you don't have that long."

'Why not?'

"Because some very stupid mer are getting ready to do some very stupid things, and that will result in your leads drying up."

I stare at the thing in front of me, trying to work out what it's talking about. It's starting to look less and less like Cass. Her eyes are now purple and her hair was now gray, nearly white, but everything else remained the same.

'How do you know all this?'

"I know almost everything that happens in the mortal realm, sweetie," it said with a smile. "I know that you're a human, I know that Nash pulled you out of a dungeon, I know how you felt when you woke up, and above all that I know what you hope to accomplish. It will be an absolute delight to see if you can do it or not."

'What are you, some sort of god?'

"Well..." it sighed almost comically. "I suppose I have been called that. But unlike the gods you're familiar with, I had absolutely nothing to do with creating anything. Neither did any of the other beings known as gods, for that matter."

'Then why are you known as gods?'

"Mortals love to name and classify things. They do their best to make everything fit into tiny little boxes, especially when they don't know enough about something to even begin to hope to properly classify it. Those with immense power that exist beyond their reckoning are stuffed neatly into the box labeled god."

So this thing isn't a god, but is close enough to be called one. It's wearing Cassandra's face, but it claims it's not doing so intentionally. It can read my thoughts, too, even when I'm not trying to verbalize them, but we're not in my mind.

"Doesn't really make much sense, does it?" it laughed. "If it helps you get over it, you can call this place limbo or purgatory. You're more familiar with such concepts, and the only real difference is that this isn't a waiting area for the dead."

'I see. Well, what do YOU call this place?'

"I don't. Things like me don't have any reason to name things. Among ourselves, we're simply able to broadcast a thought with complete context. If I want a specific person to meet me in a specific place, all I have to do is think about the details. However, none of this is relevant, Nick."

'Okay... So we're in Limbo, but not really. And you're a god, but not really. So what do you want with me?'

"There we go," it raised an index finger and tapped my nose. "Finally, we can get to business. You're going to Bolisir. When you get there, Yulk will want to visit some scholars to get the text you found in the dungeon translated. His childish thirst for knowledge will cause him to decline an invitation to see the dragon. Do not let him decline that invitation."

'It's hard to imagine Yulk turning down the chance to see a dragon.'

"To him, it's just a sleeping dragon. It will be there once your task is complete. Whether he sees it now or five years from now doesn't really matter to him. The puzzle of what you are and where you came from is a much more pressing matter to the cutest little orc scholar."

I found myself taken aback by that description of Yulk, but managed to press on, 'What do we do after seeing the dragon?'

"The choices afterwards will be clear, and you'll know which one to make to continue your trek back to Cass. If you need another nudge at some point, I'll pop by."

'Why are you helping me? Just because I'm amusing?'

"Don't underestimate the value of amusement to a being like me. But the actual reason is that I'm rooting for you," it smiled, but its mouth had changed. It wasn't Cassandra's anymore. The lips were fuller and the teeth were far more pointed. "It would break my heart, metaphorically speaking, to see you fail your great quest. If it weren't for my pact, I'd tell you exactly how to get to where you need to get to."

It gestured with one of its arms and the sound of chains clinked from somewhere. I blinked in surprise and suddenly saw the source of the noise. She was covered in chains, and the links were made of solid crimson light. They sent sparks flying at even the slightest movement. I looked for what they were attached to, but the chains began and ended inside the being before me. I could only imagine that they were attached directly to its bones. How didn't I see these before?

"Your perception is limited, Nick. There's a lot that you can't see, hear, smell, or feel. Perception is a funny thing, though. Once someone points something out to you, suddenly you see it all over the place," it grinned.

Its appearance had changed. It no longer looked like Cass at all. Its hair was radiant blue, its eyes were deep purple, and its skin had a mirror-like quality to it. It was still nude, but its proportions had changed. It was now taller than me, and was shaped more like Nima than Cass. Including the odd alligator teeth that all orcs have. Somehow, this set me at ease a bit.

'Should I tell the others about you?'

"Yulk and Nash will believe you, so you can tell them if

you think it will make things easier. If you tell others, they will understandably believe that you're not well in the head. This will add obstacles to your path that will require bloodshed to clear," it shrugged. "Up to you, though."

'Bloodshed?'

"Oh yes," it grinned again. "Instead of gently pushing past the obstacles standing in your way, they'll force you to gut them and unleash rivers of blood that will flood along your path. Since violence begets more violence, more blood will inevitably flow. On the bright side, letting the violence guide you will get you to your goals much faster."

The thing's smile erased any sort of ease I had felt up to that point. The smile spoke volumes, hinting at a macabre enjoyment of all things hateful and violent. I involuntarily took a step backward.

'I'd...'

"Rather not," it interrupted with a sigh. "I know, Nick, I know. And that's fine. It's only one way to get you where you're going. It's the most fun way, in my opinion, but I'm fully capable of understanding that you would find it a lot less fun than I would."

It shrank a little bit, as if deflating. Like someone had just told it that the next installment of its favorite slasher movie would be PG-13. Then it laughed a bit and came back up to full size.

"You have more questions, and we've got time. I'll answer what I can, though the answers will likely be disappointing," it said.

'What happened to me? How did I end up in this

world?'

"I don't actually know. You were outside of our perception until Nash lifted you from that altar."

'Is Cass okay?'

"I don't know. She's outside of my perception."

'Damn,' I crossed my arms to think for a moment. 'Why are you the one who is approaching me?'

"I like to play with mortals, and so I'm far more familiar with doing so than others of my kind. Plus, I really wanted to," it smiled. "I threatened to throw a temper tantrum if I wasn't picked."

This threw me off. A being that people called god, throwing a temper tantrum? Like a toddler? Then I remembered some of the Greek gods and felt kind of foolish. The thing smiled at me knowingly. I sighed and thought about what my next question should be.

'Will I make it back to Cass?'

"I don't know, but we can't wait to find out."

'You don't know?'

"Of course not. I have a general idea of how things might go if all the mortals involved make certain choices at certain times, but I don't actually know the end result until it happens."

'Well, alright then. Do I have a chance to make it back to Cass?'

The thing laughed and held up the chains, indicating that it couldn't answer. I felt a surge of anger rush through me, but quickly quelled it. The anger isn't exactly justified. The fact that we're even having this conversation means that it's at least somewhat willing to help. If anything, I should be grateful.

'What can I do to increase my chances of seeing Cass again?'

"Train every chance you get. Learn new spells, put your body through hell. The stronger you get, the better your odds are," it smiled again. "You have a lot of potential. If you start focusing on your endurance, you'll find that you can increase your strength faster than most can. Even if you fail to get back home, you'll be able to live comfortably amongst the mortals of this world."

I was about to express my distaste at this possibility, but the thing held up a hand.

"It's time for you to wake up. Go see the dragon."

Everything went dark again.

Chapter 32

Nash Alta
Adventurer Level: 9
Orc - Nulevan

The exploding cart caught me by surprise, thankfully I had quick recovery active because of the bandits. A new skill I picked up while training with Nick, and it does exactly as advertised. I was the first one up, my ears ringing and head swimming.

I shook the cobwebs out of my skull and checked myself over to make sure I was in one piece. Lucky, no shrapnel wounds. As I grabbed my swords up off the ground and sheathed them, I looked around. Everyone else was on the ground. Yulk was just behind where I'd landed, and I ran over to him first.

"Yulk!" I shouted as I shook him. "Wake up, brother. Tell me you're okay."

He didn't stir. Shit. I tried to get his robe off so I could check him for injuries. I wasn't able to get it off, but I was able to get it open. He was wearing a tunic with shorts underneath. Blood on his legs. I ripped his tunic apart to see if his chest was fine. No blood, and it was rising and falling to indicate he was breathing. I tore a strip off his tunic and bandaged the small wound on his leg.

I glanced up and saw Imlor trying and failing to help Nick stand. As I straightened up to go check on him, I heard someone behind me groaning. Instinctively, I drew my swords. My axe, being as cumbersome as it is, had been left in the cart. I spun and barely managed to block the first bandit's strike as the second bandit was standing up. I'd heard the second bandit, which had ruined the first's sneak attack. The other five were in no condition to fight.

The second bandit took a moment to get his bearings as I took a slash at the first one, which he dodged. He wasn't able to dodge the follow-up kick, though. He hit the ground and rolled backward, and I followed and slashed with both swords. The bandit dodged backward again, which is fine by me, I want to distance him from Yulk. The other bandit saw our conflict and lunged at me with his spear. I parried it, and blocked another strike from the first bandit.

"Yulk!" Nick shouted from behind me.

"Yulk's out cold!" I replied, swinging at the first orc again.

I hope he's just out cold. A coma would be terrible this far from town. I parried the spear again and rushed the bandit with the sword. He managed to block the strike to his throat, but wasn't able to avoid the slash across his gut. It went deep, and he fell to the ground holding his injury. I shut out his cries of pain as I turned my attention to the one with the spear. There's no need to worry about him getting back up, I know a fatal blow when I see it.

The bandit with the spear also knew a fatal blow by sight, and became more cautious. I darted forward, and he leapt back while jabbing at me with the spear. If he were any more skilled with his spear, I'd be in trouble. However, after the fourth time of him jumping back and trying to poke me, I was starting to get annoyed.

"Go to the hells, you bastard!" the bandit growled at me.

"Lead the way," I replied, slashing the tip off of his spear.

The bandit looked at his spear dumbfounded, and I took advantage of this to use another skill I'd unlocked. I activated thrusting throw, and my sword leapt from my hand and plunged itself into the bandit's chest. He gaze moved from his spear, to the hilt that was now attached to his chest, and then to me as he crumpled under the weight of death.

This particular skill had come to me after constantly throwing Nick's training weapon back to him. I don't think he even realized that I'd activated the skill. He probably believes I'm just good at throwing training swords directly at his heart. I walked over to the bandit and pulled my sword from its fleshy sheath.

I took this opportunity to examine the remains of the explosion and the other five bandits, which was a mistake. Even with all the death and destruction I'd seen before, the way their bodies were torn apart and contorted beyond recognition made my stomach churn. I turned away and closed my eyes, trying to think of anything else so that it wouldn't stick with me.

Food's a bad thought. No, let's think about relaxing at the training field. Staring up at the sky, watching the clouds go by. Nima by my side, giggling at something I said. Not even a joke, but she found it funny regardless. A good memory to blot out the bad.

"Help!" an unfamiliar voice called out from behind me.

I turned to look and saw the dwarf we'd ran past earlier, now kneeling over Nick. Imlor was also on the ground. I wiped my swords on spear-bandit's pants and kicked Yulk's shoe as I passed, but he didn't even stir. Gods, he's out for the count. I hope he's alright.

"What's going on?" I asked the dwarf as I approached.

"The gnome was hit and bleeding out, and the... uh..."

"Human."

"Human? What?"

"He's a human. That doesn't matter though. Focus up, what happened?"

"Oh, he uh... I guess he figured out how to use healing magic. He used it on the gnome and then passed out. He's wounded pretty bad, looks like he was hit by a bunch of shrapnel," the dwarf explained.

I knelt and checked the boy's wounds, and the dwarf was right. He had a hole clean through his right hand, another hole in his shoulder, two in his left leg and one in his right leg. I couldn't find any holes in his cuirass, though. I breathed a sigh of relief.

"He'll be fine," I said.

"How can you say that? If he lost enough blood to pass out, then he definitely won't be fine. We gotta do something!"

"Look at the ground. There isn't nearly enough blood here to cause someone his size to pass out," I explained. "Plus, our healer is down for the count. Ain't a damn thing we could do even if we wanted to."

"We could bandage his wounds, at least," the dwarf muttered.

"Nope, with Nick that's a bad idea. I'll show you why,"

I grinned. "Hey, Ten. You there?"

"Yes," Ten said with Nick's voice.

The dwarf leapt back from the boy with startling speed. He didn't get far before he stumbled and landed on his ass, staring at Nick with an open-mouth frown. Nick, however, didn't move at all. After a moment, the dwarf turned to look at me again.

"Ten is a robot that lives in Nick's head and helps heal him," I explained.

"I'm not a robot," Ten said.

"Close enough. Anyway, he's got foreign objects in some of his wounds, doesn't he?" I asked.

"Yes."

"And it would be a bad idea to bandage those wounds while you try to heal them, right?"

"Correct, if you bandage the wounds it would prevent me from removing the shrapnel. I would have to heal around it, and I would then have to force the shrapnel out of the body through the skin. Which would take an annoyingly long time without surgical assistance."

"There you have it," I said to the dwarf. "All we can do is wait for our injured to wake up. Nick healed Imlor, Ten's healing Nick, and Yulk doesn't have any visible injuries. He's probably got one hell of a concussion though."

"I... I see..." the dwarf said, starting to shake off the shock.

"Anyways, I'm Nash. What's your name?"

"My... Oh. I'm Renv. Renv Marfix. Pleasure to meet you, though I wish it were under better circumstances."

"Yeah, me too," I chuckled darkly. "So what were you doing out here, Renv?"

"My uncle owns one of the biggest suppliers in Bolisir, and I was transporting mining equipment to Kirkena for him. Shovels, picks, buckets, and some bang-clay. Recipe C," he explained. "The bandits weren't interested in the gear, but were convinced they could get a good ransom out of me."

"Well, that explains the explosion. But that sounds like pretty valuable cargo, why didn't you have guards?" I asked.

"I did. Three of 'em. The bandits killed them and tossed their bodies in the cart," his expression went dark. "They were friends of mine. We grew up together, but they became adventurers and I became a businessman. Now they're... They're dead."

"Sorry for your loss," I said gently. "I know how hard that is. I've lost some friends rece..."

Nick suddenly sat up as if he were in the middle of a fight, and then winced at the pain his various injuries caused. He looked around in an odd way, as if glad his eyes were working. He looked at Renv, then at me, and then closed his eyes and took a deep breath.

"You alright?" I asked.

"Yeah... yeah I'll be okay. I just..." he looked at Renv again. "Never mind. I'm fine, just used all my magic. How's Imlor?"

"He's out, but looks alright. Yulk's out too."

"He's not up yet? Wait, how long was I out?"

"Just a few minutes," Renv said. "I'm Renv, by the way. Didn't get a chance to make introductions with all the excitement."

"I'm Nick," the boy replied. "Nice to meet you."

They discussed how we had got to be where we are, but I was distracted by Yulk. He'd been out for a while. He'd probably taken a knock on the head, but I hadn't seen any blood. I wondered about trying to load Yulk and Imlor into the cart, but the hnarses looked angsty. The explosion had probably put them on edge, and a kick from one of them would be bad no matter who it connected with.

"Nick, has your magic recharged at all?" I asked.

"Lemme check," he closed his eyes and concentrated for a moment. "Yes, I've got about a quarter of it back."

"I want you to heal Yulk. Can you move?"

"Not on my own. Ten says my leg's fractured."

"Alright."

Nick looked up at me questioningly as I stood and brushed the dirt off of my knee. I grinned as I leaned down, placed my arms beneath his armpits, and lifted him from the ground. He protested a bit as I carried him over to Yulk's still unconscious form, and winced as I set him down.

"Heal him," I said.

"What's wrong with him?" Nick asked.

"I don't know. Probably took a knock to the head. Just cast the spell and let it figure it out."

"I'm pretty sure that's not how it works."

"I'm pretty sure it is. You think healers have time to figure out what's wrong with a person before they heal them?" I asked angrily.

"But... Fine," he relented. "Laeh Ronim Tsac."

A faint light glowed around Nick's hand as the spell went to work on Yulk. I crossed my arms in satisfaction, but raised an eyebrow as I noticed the light didn't fade like it normally would. The spell was still going. Whenever Yulk or other healers cast a healing spell, the light would only last for about a second.

Before I could say anything, Yulk's eyes shot open and he sat up. Nick let his arm drop to his side as Yulk looked around trying to figure out what was going on. Finally, my brother looked at us and tilted his head questioningly.

"You got knocked out by an explosion from the flaming cart," I explained.

"Then I healed you," Nick added with a grin.

"You healed me?" Yulk asked with a shocked expression. "I... Well, congratulations on unlocking your first healing spell! Which was it?"

"Minor Heal," Nick said.

"Good, good. That's the first level of healing," Yulk nodded, rubbing the back of his head as if it were sore. "Nice place to start from. Is everyone okay?"

"I'm fine, Nick's got some new holes, and Imlor's unconscious," I explained. "The dwarf that we rescued, Renv, is also uninjured."

"I see. Where'd the flaming cart go?"

"Already told you. That's what blew up. It had bang-clay in it."

"Right, that makes sense," Yulk said as he carefully stood up. "Shall we go check on Imlor, then?"

"I can't walk, I've got a fracture in my leg," Nick explained.

"Not a problem," I said with a grin as I picked him up again.

Yulk and I walked over to Imlor as my new baggage protested again. The protests got a little more colorful this time, so I was less gentle when I set him down. Nick glared at me angrily as Yulk knelt to check on the gnome.

"Will he be okay?" Renv asked.

"Hmm..." Yulk expressed as he rubbed his chin thoughtfully. "What happened to him?"

"A piece of shrapnel went through his gut, but he didn't notice it at first. He passed out as he was checking on me," Nick explained. "Thankfully, it went clean through so I cast minor heal on him, but he didn't wake up. Then I ended up passing out from using all my magic."

Yulk looked at Nick with a confused expression.

"What else did you use your magic on?" he asked.

"Nothing," Nick answered.

"But you have a ton of magic. Minor heal wouldn't even come close to using all of it," Yulk said.

"I used the spell until I ran out of magic," Nick explained.

"How many times did you cast it?"

As Yulk asked that, I made a connection between what Nick was saying, what Yulk was asking, and the strange length of time I'd seen from Nick's healing spell. I couldn't help but laugh, which made everyone look at me.

"When he cast minor heal, it seemed to last longer than when you cast it," I explained. "I think he's able to continue the spell with just one cast."

"Is that so?" Yulk turned back to Nick. "I wonder what sort of effect that has on the healing."

"I don't know much about magic," Renv interrupted, "but is the gnome going to be okay? He's been out for a while."

"Right, right. He must have lost a bit of blood, but I can wake him up," Yulk nodded.

Yulk then slapped Imlor across the face, the sound of which stunned the rest of us into silence. It seemed to echo around us. Nick opened his mouth, but Imlor mumbled something and his eyes fluttered open. He looked at each of us and sat up, holding the side of his face.

"What happened?" he asked.

"Come on, get up," Yulk smiled down at the gnome. "It's time to get back on the road."

Chapter 33

Yulk Alta
Adventurer Level: 7
Orc - Nulevan

Many things were running through my mind as we continued our journey. The fragile sturdiness of life, the luck we've had in our most recent exploits, curiosity regarding Renv, and above all else Nick's ability to continuously cast Minor Heal. Did casting it continuously have any benefit over casting it as a one-off? Can everyone cast it continuously, or just Nick? He had seemed confused while we were discussing it, as if he was surprised by our surprise. Is it just the basic nature of the spell to cast it continuously? If so, how did we not discover this sooner?

I'd been taught my healing spells by a specialist, who had studied under other specialists, who had learned the concepts behind healing magic from ancient tomes. As far as I know, that's how every healer actually learns healing magic. Technically, you should be able to learn the spells on your own with a good deal of knowledge about anatomy and physiology, but I'm unaware of anyone who has.

This is likely due to the fact that trying to learn anatomy and physiology on your own is difficult to do legally, and most who attempt to do it illegally end up facing rather dire consequences. Well deserved, to be sure, but the end result is that they're not in a position to pass on any secrets they garner.

I'd previously told Nick that he might be able to cast healing, just to see if he could. He seemed to have quite a bit of knowledge, so it wasn't a stretch to imagine he knew a thing or two about how a body functions. If he hadn't, I would have taken him to a specialist when our travels were somewhat less urgent. Nick has saved us a trip, but simultaneously opened a can of crawlers without a single fishing line in sight.

"And that's how I learned the spell," Nick explained to a shocked audience.

Even Nash's mouth was agape, despite his attempts to remain stoic. The dwarf had asked plenty of questions, demonstrating an unfamiliarity with magic. Imlor looked paler and paler as the story had gone on, likely due to it describing his near demise.

Imlor's a clever one, he'd quite easily put together the fact that if Nick hadn't been with us, he'd have died. Even if he had ignored Renv's urgent situation with the bandits and continued on, his cart would have been right next to the explosion when it had occurred. That kind of proximity wouldn't have allowed for survival, even if he'd managed to avoid shrapnel.

"Well, it's no wonder you lost consciousness," I said with a smile. "You burned through all your reserves, and you were injured on top of that. It would have been odd if you hadn't passed out. Not quite as odd as continuously casting Minor Heal, though."

"Why's that odd?" Nick asked.

"Because it's like wind-spear," I answered. "It has a singular effect. Or at least, that's what I was led to believe. I don't even know what the benefit of holding the spell actually could be."

"Well," Nash interjected, "Imlor had a through and through. One minor heal would have stopped the bleeding and maybe stabilized him, but it would have taken a bunch of castings to close the wound entirely, right?"

I turned to look at my brother, who had once again found the stone I'd been blindly stumbling over, and gave him a silent nod. I had dismissed anything odd about Imlor's wound due to the powerful nature of Nick's casting abilities. My mind had simply written it off as another instance of one of his spells being more powerful than it should be.

Stupid of me, to be sure. Unlike some spells, healing spells don't get more potent the more magic you put into them. They have a set cost and a set result, which is why there are different types. Minor Heal can stabilize someone that is mortally wounded for a time, Lesser Heal will repair internal injury and regenerate lost blood, Major Heal can repair gratuitous injury and broken bones, and Greater Heal can regenerate lost limbs. Each spell grants a brief amount of regeneration, and can also do what the previous levels can but cost exponentially more magic to cast.

As Nash pointed out, these spells have a compounding effect. Meaning that, depending on the wound, casting minor heal three times can be more efficient than casting lesser heal once. But Nick had only cast Minor Heal the one time, so it shouldn't have been possible to completely heal Imlor. Therefor, the benefit to continuous casting minor heal is that it has a similar effect to casting it multiple times.

A blood-drenched piece of wood clattered to the floor of the cart, originating from one of Nick's wounds. This wasn't the first time it had happened and Nick, having become used to this by now, casually picked it up and tossed it over the side of the cart. Suddenly, a thought occurred to me.

"Nick, was that the last piece of shrapnel?" I asked.

Nick took a moment to consult Ten and then nodded.

"I'd like to do an experiment," I smiled. "Ask Ten if it's okay for me to cast a healing spell on you."

"Ten says that would be okay," Nick said after another moment.

"Good," I said. "Laeh Ronim Tsac."

I tried to hold the spell, and was surprised when it actually worked. We watched the wound on Nick's hand close with a mixture of shock and glee. The glee was mostly from me. However, I also noticed that the spell was very quickly draining my magic reserve. I stopped the spell before I ran out of magic, but it was a rather close call. I wouldn't want to be passing out like Nick had.

"Well, that answers several questions," I said, managing to stifle my excitement. "First, you can continue the regenerative effect of minor heal by continuously casting it. Second, it costs magic for every second that you maintain the spell. Overall, it's more efficient than casting the spell multiple times. We'll need to have the official literature updated."

"For every second?" Nash asked. "Is it better than... um..."

"Lesser heal? Not quite. I suspect that if lesser heal can also be continuously cast, the regenerative effect would be much more efficient," I answered. "I'd love to do more experimentation, but it will have to wait."

"I know some pretty advanced healers," Renv added. "If you'd like, I can bring this to their attention and make sure they credit you and Nick with the discovery. They would happily perform the experimentation that you want done."

Nash gave me a knowing look, but I held up a hand to keep him from speaking for me. He knows how much I love scientific inquiry, and having others perform experiments in my stead would typically be a worst case scenario for me. However...

"Normally I would rather do the experiments myself, but since we're speaking of magic that can save lives I will gratefully accept your assistance," I replied.

"Really?" Nash asked.

"Yes. We don't know if we will find any answers in Bolisir, and we've given our oath to aid Nick in finding his way home," I said. "It would be difficult to travel and research these phenomena simultaneously, at least while observing any semblance of scientific rigor. Since this may save lives, time is of the essence, therefor it only makes sense to have someone else begin research immediately."

"That's pretty mature of you," Nash said with a proud smirk.

"But if we do find answers in Bolisir and wrap things up quickly, I can always join in on the research," I quickly added. "Scientific competition is healthy, after all."

"Yeah, that sounds more like you."

We all had a good laugh, and when we were finished Renv looked contemplative.

"You said you swore to help Nick find his way home? I

already gathered that he's not from around here, but how far away are we talking?" he asked.

"I'm right here, you know," Nick chuckled.

"Oh, right, apologies. Then I redirect my questions to you, good sir," Renv bowed his head apologetically.

"That's alright," Nick said. "I'm from a different world, and there's no way to know how distant that world is. I'm kind of assuming that it's an alternate reality kind of thing, but I guess it's possible that I was abducted from my world by aliens and brought here for some reason."

Nick noted that we were all staring at him incredulously.

"Well, it's a thought," he said quietly.

"Someone from a different country might have abducted you and brought you here?" Renv asked.

"No, not that kind of alien," Nick quickly explained. "Like, a different species that has the ability to travel through space."

"Space?" Nash asked.

"Yeah, you know, above the sky?" Nick asked in return. "If you go up high enough you end up in space."

"He's right," I confirmed. "Not much is known about space, so I suppose it's possible. Magic is definitely the more likely possibility, though."

"Why's that?" Nick asked.

"Because space is very, very big. The sheer distances involved would require magical traversal," I explained. "So even if you were abducted by space aliens, magic is probably what brought you here."

"I don't know," he said. "My people were to the point of limited space travel and some were even living in space stations. We were about to get to the point of consumer space travel, so there's been plenty of scientific theories among my people regarding how to travel space faster. It's possible someone beat us to it."

We all stared at him once again, this time with our mouths agape. There were so many questions running through my mind all at once. What was space like? How did his people get up to space in the first place? What did they find? Why the hell hadn't he mentioned that before? He noticed our slack jaws.

"I haven't been to space myself," he explained. "There isn't any air up there, so you've gotta wear a special air-tight suit with tanks of air that feed into it. It also costs a lot of money to build the vehicles necessary to get there, so they only sent the best and brightest at first. As more experiments and flights were performed, rich merchants started going to space themselves. As far as I know, they were only able to just barely make it to space."

"There isn't any air in space?" Nash asked.

"That makes sense, actually," I said. "The higher you go up a mountain, the less air there is. I'm assuming that the space carts were launched from the tops of mountains?"

"We call them space ships, and I don't think so. I know that they launch a bunch from a place called

Cape Canaveral, which I'm pretty sure is close to sea level," Nick said. "I don't think it makes much of a difference. Space is really far up, even compared to the tallest of mountains."

"What did your people find in space?" Renv asked.

"Well, it's like Yulk said. Everything is really, really far apart. In between the planets and stuff there's a whole lot of nothing, too. So there wasn't a lot of interest in exploring space outside of specific scientific communities. I do remember seeing some news about plans to mine some asteroids, but I don't know what became of that."

"What about on the planets?" Imlor asked.

"Well, we landed remote control robots on some of them to explore and see if we could find life, but as far as I know we didn't find much. People were getting excited about finding water on one of the planets, but other than that they're pretty barren. I don't think any of them have breathable air, either," Nick shrugged.

"Wait, you said that humans don't have magic," Nash said. "How did you make ships that made it that far into the sky?"

I watched Renv's expression as Nick explained humanity's method of travel via explosive propulsion. I had been shocked to learn of it, but the dwarf was absolutely flabbergasted. It was hard to see Imlor's expression, but he was obviously paying close attention to what Nick was saying. I chuckled slightly, enjoying the novelty of the conversation.

"So even without magic, your people can fly like birds?" Renv asked.

"Not really," Nick said. "We've got a bunch of different kinds of aircraft, but I'm pretty sure all of them move much faster than birds do. Plus, most planes carry a bunch of people at once. It's the fastest way to go from one continent to another."

"That's amazing," the dwarf replied.

I had to agree. The more I learned about humans, the more I wanted to know. I desperately wanted to compare our development to their own, but I doubt that Nick would have that kind of information at his age.

Plus, there are certain aspects of human history that he is obviously uncomfortable sharing. I could imagine why, everyone has darkness in their pasts they'd like to forget. If kingdoms form on a bed of flowers, it's because those flowers were fed with blood.

"There's something up ahead," Imlor called out.

"What is it?" I stood to get a better look.

"It looks like..." the gnome paused, "a checkpoint?"

Chapter 34

???
Adventurer Level: N/A
???

"This is boring," my friend complained.

"Most things are," I replied. "We've got nothing better to do though."

"Yeah, but I thought this road was supposed to be busy. There hasn't been anyone all day!"

"Your whining will do nothing to change that."

As the words left my mouth, the sound of hooves and wooden wheels in the distance filled my ears. They were still fairly far away, but my friend's face twisted into a smug expression. I sighed, straightened my Bolisir guard uniform, and sat in the place that I was supposed to be sitting. My friend leaned on the barricade, their feminine curves fighting desperately against the uniform. Their positioning was obviously intended to bring notice to the aforementioned curves.

"THAT doesn't mean anything. It's just a coincidence."

"Oh, please. You know better than that," they grinned.

"No I don't," I said sarcastically. "I don't know anything. I am empty of all forms of knowledge."

My friend giggled as the travelers came into view. Two carts pulled by two hnarses carrying quite the interesting bunch. A pair of orcs, a gnome, a dwarf, and... something else. Almost like an elf, but with an extremely murky aura. Power, danger, cunning, hunger, sorrow, ambition, and so many other things swirled around this creature.

Things were further complicated by the positive emissions, which were just as intense. Innocence, love, kindness, compassion, happiness, and so on. It's not exactly uncommon to feel all these things at once from someone, but the intensity was an entirely different matter. It spoke of a remarkable capacity for cruelty and heroism. A living contradiction.

I glanced over to my friend, who was just as terrified as I was by this... thing. It reminded me of the tales that were told to fresh-borne to keep them from running off on their own. Horrible monsters that wielded rough iron and could destroy anything, lurking in the darkest corners, waiting to pounce.

I desperately didn't want to interact with this thing, but there might not be another chance like this. We simply do not have any other choice. I shrugged off my abject terror, took a deep breath, and stood. I picked up my pencil and book, completing my act.

"What's this?" the gnome asked.

"Taxes were thin last fiscal year, so this is a toll road now," my friend said.

"To pass, I'll need to take your names," I added, gesturing with the open book. "We will then determine if you must pay the toll."

There was a long pause from the group that made my skin crawl. It's not good for us when they start to think about things. I took a long look at them, and noticed weapons and signs of fighting. Oh no, they might be adventurers. They're not about to attack us, are they? I gulped down my fear and stood firm.

The dwarf was whispering to the bald orc, and the bald orc was whispering back. I could hear what they were saying, but I couldn't understand it. They didn't want me to know what they were saying and because of this, I couldn't know what they were saying. Such is the nature of things.

The weird one said, "My name is..."

"How much is the toll?" The bald orc interrupted.

I looked at my friend, demonstrating my annoyance to them privately, and then turned back to the group.

"That depends. I'll need your name, please," I answered with an authoritative tone.

"And what, pray-tell, will you be doing with our names if we give them to you?" the bald one asked with a grin.

So the game begins. It's possible that he's figured it out, but we're well-versed with this particular battle of wits. They would have to be crazy to hurl accusations at guards, and that works out well because we're trying to avoid the crazy ones.

"I'll be writing it down and checking to see if it's already in my other book. If it is, then you'll pay a discounted toll or even no toll at all. If it's not, then we discuss how much the toll is," I answered, trying my best not to grin.

The rest of the group was looking at the bald one with confusion. The gnome looked back at me and some glint of clarification scrolled across otherwise his boring features. Damn it.

"May I see this other book that our names may already be in?" the bald one asked.

"For what purpose would you need to see the book other than to attempt to fraud us?" I countered. "I'll not entertain a scoundrel. Now give me your name."

"I am not a scoundrel, I am simply curious as to why a fae would be collecting taxes for the Kingdom of Bolisir."

Ah, so he knows that we're fae. Not necessarily a problem, as he may not yet have guessed our intentions. I heard a sigh come from my friend, and I held out a hand to calm them. The game isn't over yet.

"Why wouldn't a fae be collecting taxes?" I asked. "Have you never seen an employed fae before?"

"Can't say that I have, and you know how we mortals are. We're suspicious of things we haven't seen before," he grinned. "What use would you even have for currency?"

"To purchase goods and services, of course."

"Doesn't the forest provide everything your kind desires?"

"Obviously not, or we wouldn't be here."

"What sort of things do you buy?"

"I don't need to tell you that. All I need is your names," I stated coldly.

"Why don't you set our minds at ease by telling us your name first?" the bald one asked.

Slithering copulation! The orc was familiar with my kind, and knew how to play this game. It seemed like an innocent enough request, a name for a name, but he knew damned well what he was doing by asking for ours.

The bastard had even phrased it in such a way that it would be suspicious were I to decline. I didn't particularly feel like playing the fool and dancing around the subject, and a quick look at my friend told me that they didn't want to either. Very well, begging it is.

"Fair enough," I said. "We do not have names. We require them, which is why we're asking for yours."

"Ohhh," the weird one said, finally catching on.

"Why would you need OUR names, though?" the orc with braids asked. "Can't you name yourselves?"

"If we could, we would," my friend said. "We cannot, and as such beg your kindness."

Their feminine form was specifically designed to appeal to the mortal sense of lust in a situation like this. Mine was masculine and intended to have the same effect on those with the opposite preference. It's hard to say no to a sexy fae in uniform.

Unfortunately, this tactic was lost on the orcs. Their auras did not indicate nearly enough cruelty for them to be whiled by our physical distractions. The dwarf and the gnome, perhaps, but they were both being careful not to even look at us. That only left the... thing. I stifled a shudder at the thought.

"If we give you our names, then what will we be

called?" the bald one asked, still grinning.

"I..." I said haltingly. It was a surprising question. "I don't know, actually."

"Probably whatever you want," my friend added. "That's how it works with you mortals, isn't it?"

"Not quite," the bald one said. "When you take our names, you take our identity and merge it with your own, leaving us without knowledge of who we are."

Silence fell among us. Fear riddled the aura's of the other mortals. My friend and I shared confused glances. Why would they be afraid of not knowing who they are? Aren't mortals only afraid of death or serious injury?

"I don't understand. You say that like it's a bad thing," I ventured. "But that's how we live. I do not have a name, and therefor don't know who I am."

"Well, imagine for a moment that you did have a name. Imagine that you know who you are, your identity impacts the world around you, and you have many tales to tell to those who would listen. Would you willingly part with that?" the bald one asked sagely. "Do you feel it right to take that from someone else?"

"No, I wouldn't willingly part with it, but life is about taking from the things around you to further your own existence," I said. "You need energy to complete yourselves, so you take the lives of animals, and those animals take the lives of plants for the same purpose. We take your identities for our completion, to further our existence just as you do."

"What happens if you don't?" the weird one asked

hesitantly.

"We perish," my friend said. "Our story ends as the season does if we do not have an identity to anchor us."

"They get reborn, though," the bald one explained. "Death is temporary to a fae."

"It's not exactly pleasant, though," I said. "The withering alone is likely much more painful than anything you've ever experienced."

"Also, our sense of self gets reset. Who we are fades to nothingness when we die, and we are someone different when we are reborn," my friend added.

"I thought you didn't have a sense of self," the weird one said.

"Of course we do. It's what drives us to gain an identity," I explained. "Without an identity, we lose our current sense of self to the void. Sure, we're born again come next season, but we will have different personalities, preferences, and no memory of who we were before. We end up becoming a completely different fae."

"Which explains why you would want our names," the bald one nodded slowly. "However, we need our names. There are those who depend upon us."

Even if we tried to force the issue, they're smart enough to know that they can remove any obstacles we put in their path. Should we let them continue on and just hope someone dumber comes along? Is there some way we can convince them? Perhaps a bribe, or a promise? No, I can feel their determination. This won't work, we will need to regroup and find another...

"Wait, all you need are names, right?" the weird one asked. "What if we named you?"

"Well..." I paused and looked at my friend, who shrugged. "Names have power. You would have to sacrifice a large amount of magic to name us, and we would have to be willing to accept the name..."

"For what reason would you not accept the name?" the bald one asked.

I looked at my friend again. Revealing this could prove dangerous, but they gestured for me to continue. They're right, of course. We're in too deep to hold back now. I sighed and straightened my borrowed uniform nervously.

"If you name us, you will be taking part in our creation and we will be forever in your debt. I realize that your kind uses this as a turn of phrase, but we mean it literally. We would be under your authority for as long as you are able to give us orders, and anything you order us to do we will HAVE to do," I explained. "So we are left with a conundrum. Which is better, slavery or death?"

"It would just be temporary," my friend giggled. "They're mortals, after all."

"What if I promise not to order you around?" the weird one asked. "You can make promises unbreakable, right?"

The innocence of that question took me off guard. I looked at the strange being as if seeing it for the first time. I had been avoiding looking directly at it because of the maelstrom that is its aura, but once I looked past that I realized that I was looking at a young boy. An odd young boy whose ears and teeth were wrong, but one who was genuine in its beliefs.

My heart melted somewhat as I realized that this innocent youth actually believed that kind of power was possible. It didn't melt enough to keep me from taking full advantage of this mistaken belief, though. I quickly thought of a bluff, and a way to make that bluff convincing.

"It would require a blood-pact, but yes," I lied.

"Okay," the thing said as it leapt from the cart. "How do we do that?"

As the weird one approached me, it suddenly occurred to me that mixing my blood with this thing might be a bad idea. Blood is an odd thing, and the mixing of it can lead to some strange happenings. It had been the first thing to leap to mind, though, and now I have to go with it because it would be suspicious. Unless I can think of something...

"It's simple," I said, trying desperately to think of something to get me out of this. "In your own words, express your promise and the consequences of not adhering to it. Then, if I agree to your promise, we cut our palms and clasp hands. Our blood will mingle, and the promise will become binding."

"And then I can name you, and we can be on our way," it said happily. "Got it."

It stood before me and we met each other's gaze as it thought of what to say. The dark blue of its glimmering eyes reminded me of the shiny stones that the fairies loved to steal from wandering merchants. Inside this deep blue was a hint of green which is reminiscent of the grove in which I'd been reborn. The eyes of mortals are such beautiful things, I can definitely see why the hags collect them.

"I hereby promise that I will not intentionally force a fae to perform any action against their will by enforcing their debt to me. May I die if I break this promise."

I went over the sentence in my mind to make sure it hadn't performed any trickery with its words. The promise wouldn't be binding, but I still had to call out any trickery to make sure it believed the performance. Using the word intentional made certain that if it accidentally enforced the debt it could simply apologize, and it made sure to clarify that enforcing the debt would be the breach of promise. So if it came to odds with a fae, it still had recourse.

The consequence was rather mundane, but it served the purpose of ensuring that it couldn't become our master. The thing would only be able to give one order. Clever. Unfortunately, I still hadn't thought of a way out of mingling our blood. But, I decided that I liked this weird little child. What's the worst that could happen if we mix blood?

I smiled and gave a nod of assent. Then, I hardened the nail of my left forefinger into a sharp edge and sliced my right palm deep enough for blood to flow. The weird one offered its hand, and I made a similar cut on the offered palm.

I held my hand up with my fingers spread apart as the weird one extended its hand forward. It looked at my hand and back to its own as I looked at its hand and back to my own. Our eyes met again and I raised my eyebrow, wondering what it was doing. Its lips disappeared as it made an awkward expression, and it finally clasped its hand with mine. I froze as our blood mingled and a shock ran through my form.

A life began to flash before my eyes.

Chapter 35

???
Adventurer Level: N/A
???

Glimpses of memory poured through me. Structures of glass, stone, and steel that rose to the clouds, a testament to extreme levels of effort and coordination. Children laughing and playing among carefully cultivated nature without a care in the world. Video games, homework, martial arts lessons. Stretches of ground covered with a sticky black substance that gets really hot in the summertime. Burnt feet, skinned knees, dirty pants.

The mingled smells of freshly cooked carcass and various vegetables crafted into a... hamburger. Poor, kind plants skinned, sliced, and shredded, but turned into delightful snacks. The feeling of entering a warm home on a cold winter's day. A world devoid of magic or my kind, but still beautiful in a haunting way.

There were other memories too. A beautiful girl with golden hair, wasting away from illness. A stern but kind father and a loving mother. Childhood friends and enemies, maturing over time.

A cold darkness with the dulled sensation of flesh being carved and stitched back together. Pain. Healing. A dissonant whisper within the dark, urging something incomprehensible. More pain. Much more pain, only bearable because the mind doesn't notice it. A long stretch of sleep. More whispers, but intelligible. More healing. Orcs.

An unbidden tear rolled down my cheek as I realized the thing before me is Nicodemus Liam Smith. A human, far from home with a false mind entangled within his own, who dearly wishes to return. The orcs in the cart are his adopted brothers, who are trying to help him get back. A marvelous tragedy, no wonder he's being closely watched by...

"That will be all, Nick," I said, trying not to finish that thought.

"Y-yeah," Nick replied, releasing my hand. Tears openly rolled down his cheeks as well.

"I'm sorry. I didn't know that would happen."

"I know. Don't worry, I forgive you. You have a beautiful home," he smiled at me, wiping his eyes.

"As do you."

"What now?"

"You mean now that you know..." I trailed off.

"That the blood-pact is bullshit?" he chuckled. "Yeah."

"Well, I've seen your memories. I know that you won't betray your promise without good reason. I only ask that you explain that reason if the time comes."

"So we're doing this?" my friend asked, strolling up next to me.

"Nick has my consent," I said, finally wiping my tear. "Yours?"

"Of course. You're the one who cares about your precious freedom. I don't care about whether or not it bosses me around for a few decades. I just want to keep being me."

I nodded at Nick, who returned the gesture and began to think. I waited nervously, wondering what name would become mine, and if he would even be powerful enough to pull it off. He's got a lot of magic, but I don't actually know how much is needed.

"Hurry up, will you?" my friend demanded.

"Sorry, it's hard to come up with names on the spot like this," Nick said. "Do you have any... I don't know, preferences?"

"I'm fine with anything that isn't Tinkerbell, Titania, Puck, or Oberon," I laughed.

Nick chuckled as my friend tapped their chin, "What's the mortal word for breasts that I like?"

"Boobs?" Nick asked.

"Nope."

"Jugs?"

"No, those hold water."

"Bust?"

"Not even close."

"Tits," I interjected with an exaggerated sigh.

"YES!" my friend shouted, jumping with glee. "That's what I want my name to be, Nick!"

The human's smile faded to a look of shock. He looked at me as if to ask if my friend was joking. I slowly shook my head and shrugged. He looked back toward my friend and gathered himself.

"Really?" he asked. "You're serious?"

"Never a day in my life, but I do want to be called Tits," my friend said with an impish grin. "It's representative of a mother's love and nurturing nature, while also being lewd and inappropriate! What's not to love?"

"Alright, well, I name you Tits I gue..." he said as the air was forced from his lungs.

My friend began to glow and I immediately recognized them as Tits, a fae from the Deepwyld Forest. But something was wrong. Tits' aura was glowing brighter than it should. Playfulness, glee, joy, guile, and all the other emissions were joined by another. Authority.

Tits was no longer simply a fae. They were now an arch-fae, and my eyes bulged at the realization. I glanced back at Nick, who was holding his knees, trying to get his breath back. Tits grabbed my hand and jumped up and down.

"IT WORKED!" they shouted with glee. "I'm Tits now!"

"You're an arch-fae now," I said coldly. "An arch-fae named Tits. Mumuldobran is going to have a conniption."

"Are you alright, Nick?" The orc with the braids, Nash, called from the cart.

"Y-yeah!" Nick shouted back. "Just took the wind out of me."

Tits grabbed Nick's hands next, jumping up and down in excitement. I noticed that they put some extra jiggle into their fleshy bits, too.

"Thank you, Nick! Thank you so much! If you ever need anything from me, feel free to ask! And I mean anything," Tits said with a wink.

"Might as well give up on that offer," I interrupted. "Nick won't bend to temptation."

"How do YOU know?" Tits asked. "I can be very persuasive."

"I'll tell you later."

"Pff. Fine. Your turn! What's a good name for you?"

A creeping realization hit me. If Nick names me, there's a chance that I may become an arch-fae as well. The fae will flock around me while laughing and playing, but the forest will demand my guidance. Will it come naturally? Will I have to work at it? Will I be a kind and just leader who is much beloved? Will I be an abusive tyrant twisted by power into something unrecognizable by my current self? Or, worst of all, will I be the incompetent buffoon who destroys our home?

"I don't know," I said after a few moments.

"I don't know either," Nick said. "I couldn't understand the speech in most of your memories. The sounds were pretty, but when I try to say them they won't come out."

"Of course, sweety," Tits said. "Mortals cannot speak fae."

"Wait, Nick comes from another world, but I was able to understand what the people in his memories were saying," I added. "Even the ones who weren't... people."

"Careful. There are some things that are best left unaddressed," Tits sighed. "The reason you could understand the words in Nick's memories is because of the Gift of Gab. Granted to us by one of those things that are best left unaddressed. The only words we can't understand are those that aren't supposed to be understood."

Nick and I were taken aback by Tits' sudden change in demeanor. They'd gone from nearly sprite-like to serious and intellectual in the blink of an eye. Our stares caused Tits to grin widely, though.

"You'll know what I know once Nick names you. You got another one in you, right Nick?" Tits asked.

"Yeah, that took less than half of my magic," Nick smiled. "I'm good to give another name. Question is, what should it be?"

"Well, definitely not a name based on sexualized mortal appendages, if you don't mind," I shook my head. "Something intelligent would be nice."

"Shouldn't be a commonly used proper name, though," Tits added. "Something as unique as possible."

"Smart and unique," Nick rubbed his chin thoughtfully. "Maybe something to do with math? Algebra, calculus, calculator, abacus... OH! Abacon?"

"Sounds a bit... Wait, how's that spelled?" I asked.

"A-B-A-C-O-N, I think."

"A bacon? Really?"

"Uh oh," Tits interrupted. "I think you've made them aba-cross!"

"Go suck off a wargen," I replied, incensed by the pun.

"Hey now, don't be aba-crass."

"You see," I said to Nick. "You can't name me that! You'll be dooming me to an eternity of torture via wordplay!"

"Okay, okay," Nick held up his hands defensively. "What about Algebrun?"

Tits and I looked at each other. I could tell that they were desperately trying to think of a pun, and I grinned evilly when their face revealed an expression of utter disappointment.

"Yes, I think that will do nicely," I nodded.

"Alright, I hereby name you Algebrun..."

His voice faded as my eyes were clouded by the glow coming from my form. Pure, raw power coursed through me like lightning, striking over and over again. Time halted, and I was suddenly free from my form entirely. It was now little more than a puppet, and I was now its puppeteer.

I could feel the forest in ways I had never dreamed possible. I instinctively knew that I was now charged with maintaining it, and doing everything I could to properly raise the fae and fair-folk who thrived within it. I now knew all of their little plans, pranks, and plots, and laughed at how futile they were.

Along with this duty came knowledge. I knew that if I had somehow obtained this knowledge without the power that came with it, I would have been made insane. A blabbering fool doomed to wander the lands, desperately trying to warn others of what's to come. But with this power, I had become more than a pawn in the game. I was now a player, and I could prevent what's to come. I can save everyone and everything that I hold dear.

I gazed at Nick, still frozen in the act of doubling over from the recoil of the spell he didn't even realize he cast. Magic that exists outside of the Curaguard. I saw the chains of debt connecting Tits and I to him, but even so, his existence was still a mystery to me. It shouldn't be, but the high ones were guarding him like a child guards a precious toy. They hid him away from prying eyes that would use him to further their own devices.

When one considers the fallibility of mortal memory, I likely know this boy better than he knows himself. I know that he considers his favorite food to be the spaghetti his mother makes every other Saturday, but it's actually the hash-browns and eggs his father crafts daily. I know that he loves lizards and is irrationally afraid of the bugs that look like leaves. I know that his most embarrassing moment is when he didn't make it to the toilet in time in first grade and had to be sent home after soiling himself.

But I don't know his fate. I looked at the orcs, and couldn't tell theirs either. The three Alta boys had fully intertwined their futures, and because of Nick those futures were now uncertain. The dwarf and the gnome had somewhat uncertain fates, but they were far less intertwined. I was able to divine what could happen to them, at least.

I felt something akin to warmth from Tits, who was in a form similar to mine own. Their happiness contrasted perfectly with my grim concerns. I informed them of how blessed they are to be able to be gleeful in the face of what we now know. They informed me that what we now know doesn't have a face, and I couldn't help but laugh.

We embraced, our energies mingling and tickling and charging each other up. We now have eternity to ourselves. We had been partners from the moment of our rebirth, and now not even the seasons themselves could separate us. Together, we would guide our forest forevermore. I turned my attention back toward Nick, and time resumed its march.

"Are you alright, Nick?" Tits' puppet asked.

"Y-yeah," the boy replied. "I'm gonna need a nap, I think."

"I would nap in the cart, were I you," I made my puppet say. "There are many things in this area that wouldn't hesitate to take advantage of sleeping meat."

"Of course. Did it work, is your name Algebrun?" he asked.

"Yes. I am Algebrun. Arch-fae of the Deepwyld Forest," I answered. "Pleasure to meet you."

"Wait, you're different now?"

"Yes. It's growth, like how you are now different from yourself as a babe."

"Same with you, Tits?"

"Of course! Before you named me, I couldn't do this!" Tits said as their form's breasts grew noticeably larger, stretching the limits of the uniform adorning them.

I chuckled as Nick blushed at the sight, turning his head so that he didn't stare. Even though his heart belonged to another, the incessant urge to procreate is strong in most mortals his age. Knowing him as I do, he'll continue to fight the temptations no matter the form they arrive in. I find this worthy of respect, but I suspect that Tits finds it a bit frustrating.

"So..." he paused to collect himself. "What will you two do now?"

"We'll return to our home. We now have duties to tend to," I explained.

"I'm gonna play SO many pranks," Tits added.

"What kind of duties?" Nick asked.

"We are charged with the growth and maintenance of the Deepwyld forest. We will teach the fae within to care for the plants and animals that make the forest what it is," I said with a smile. "And we will defend the forest if need be."

"So you're like a King and Queen of the fae?"

"Nope. More like a mommy and daddy. And we've got LOTS of babies to take care of," Tits said. "Do you want to be one of my babies? I'll let you nurse from..."

"Enough," I interrupted. "He'll not be swayed, Tits."

Nick gave me a look of gratitude as Tits frowned. Their breasts shrank back to their earlier size, and they crossed their arms to indicate displeasure. I sighed at the sulky display. Eternity is going to be interesting, at least.

"One last question before you go, if you don't mind," Nick said. "Who is that person you mentioned before? Mum-something? Mummy Bran?"

Tits and I looked at each other for a moment before laughing gleefully at Nick's butchering of Mumuldobran's name. His frown did little to ease our laughter. After a few moments, I took a deep breath and composed myself.

"Mumuldobran is a sort of... patron to the fae. Normally, it decides who is and isn't worthy of becoming an arch-fae," I answered, wiping tears of laughter from my eyes.

"Will they be mad that I made you two arch-fae?" Nick asked with fear in his tone.

"Probably not," I assured him. "Mumuldobran isn't particularly invested in the growth of the fae. It's more of a judge of character than anything. As a judge of character, it will likely be displeased at Tits' ascension, but it probably won't blame you for that."

"Oh, okay. I'm glad."

"We should go," Tits said. "We need to tend to our home, and they need to return to their journey."

"I agree," I said. "I am grateful for this gift, Nick. If you are ever in need, seek us out. You know where to find us."

"Okay, it was good meeting you two," the boy said with a warm smile.

"Good to meet you as well," Tits and I said simultaneously.

Nick's companions watched us as he went back to the carts. With a wave of my hand I rid the road of our illusory checkpoint. Tits and I stood to the side as the mortals drove past, waving to them as they went. They waved back, with varying levels of enthusiasm.

Yulk gave a strong and glad wave. He had been watching our exchange with the utmost scrutiny, and I couldn't help but wonder what he made of it all. Nash was much more muted in the way that he waved, likely because he wisely didn't trust us. The gnome and the dwarf waved politely, and Nick waved excitedly.

I hope they find a way to take him home.

Chapter 36

Master General Kirain Yith
Adventurer Level: N/A
Half-Breed Drow - Balushenian

What a wonderful night. I let out a happy sigh as I allowed the ambiance to wash over me, enjoying the smell of fires and blood, the sounds of screaming in the distance, and the sight of drow tossing mangled corpses into the mass grave at the bottom of the hill. It is a rare treat to be rewarded so handsomely for such a meager task.

Well, meager for me, at least. The orcs residing here had not wanted to let this village fall under our control, and had put up quite a fight. They'd had some forewarning as to our intentions, but we had managed to mask our movements and surprise them. Even so, we took losses. I watched General Smarn jog up the hill in my direction.

"Reporting, sir," he said, slightly out of breath.

I'll have to ensure my officers participate in morning calisthenics with the soldiers. Not only will this improve their constitution, but it will improve the morale of the soldiers as well, which will ensure the soldiers will follow the more difficult orders when they're finally given.

"Get on with it, Smarn," I replied.

"Yes, sir," he snapped to attention. "Aultris squads two and four have made contact with the enemy. Both skirmishes ended in our victory. We've taken four casualties and two deaths as a result of the action."

"And what of the enemy?"

"Sixteen confirmed kills and four captures. The rest fled the field in a suspicious manner. The squads did not pursue due to suspicions of an ambush. Their commanders will be punished at the Master General's pleasure."

I couldn't help but smirk at the results of our fighting. The orcs were tough, disciplined, and crafty enemies, but they couldn't stand up to the formations I'd fashioned. Shield walls and spears are well outside the wheelhouse of a standard orc commander, let alone a hastily established village militia. Unfortunately this success was likely to change somewhat when we begin to encounter regulars.

The orcs we've been fighting aren't part of a greater military effort. For the most part, they're simply guards and farmers who've taken up weapons to try to drive us off. There's the occasional uppity adventurer, but even they can't fight an entire phalanx. According to the literature that I'd gleaned the idea from, such maneuvers are vulnerable only to artillery, which is difficult to position during a skirmish. Unless you lead your enemy into a prearranged position, of course.

"There is no need for punishment. They were likely correct in assuming it was a trap, and we have no reason to pursue the enemy when they flee at this point in the campaign. This is a land grab, not an extermination," I said as I casually pushed my hair from my eyes.

"But..." General Smarn glanced at the freshly ruined village.

"This was not an extermination either, General. We

simply needed a more permanent base of operations and a source of labor," I explained. "This village has food and water and will serve as a nexus between our forces and our supply lines for the rest of our campaign. Obviously, we can't have the populace trying to prevent the village's transformation into our nexus, which is why we killed those who wouldn't surrender or couldn't work. Rebels and spies would undermine our efforts."

The general looked at me with doubt apparent in his expression. There are few things more offensive than having a dolt doubt you. Would that I could carve that expression from his face. Feeling my fury flare, and knowing that this was not an appropriate time to free it, I took a deep breath with my mouth and exhaled it through my nose.

"There were plenty of survivors, and all of the survivors that surrendered have been relegated to our labor force," I said with exasperation. "Speaking of which, ensure that those that are captured during skirmishes are treated for any injuries they have. Once their treatment is complete, make sure they join the labor force. That will be all."

"Yes, sir," Smarn said before trotting off to carry out my orders.

One may call it a mixed blessing that King Lofin requires foolishness to be an inherent trait among his military leaders. On the one hand, it requires much more hand-holding to get anything done. To make sure things are done correctly, you must give explicit and exact instructions every time you give orders. On the other hand, not a single one of them has questioned the need for a labor force. Especially one made entirely of orcs.

I sighed as I entered my newest domicile. I had meticulously crafted several well thought out answers to their potential questions, and had even gone so far as to plan assassinations if those answers hadn't been accepted. A pointless effort, as it turned out. I truly am surrounded by incompetent fools.

Well, perhaps not. The officers commanding the squads would have to have their wits about them to avoid the orcish traps as they had. For a moment I considered promoting them, but dismissed this thought almost immediately. They are far enough down the chain of command to be afraid of questioning orders. If I promote them enough, this will change and I will have to be rid of them. No, they are far more useful where they are.

I was lost in these thoughts when something out of place caught my notice. I stood still and examined the room around me. My sister's cage was nestled in the corner, undisturbed. The hatch to our freshly dug storeroom lay undisturbed in the other corner, still closed and latched. The wooden walls were still covered in the various animal heads, herbal wreaths, and the other eccentricities that the previous denizen had placed there. A gentle breeze was moving the blackened curtains that I'd ordered hanged. The breeze was coming from a window that had previously been closed.

Having found the disturbance that wrestled me from my thoughts, I took a step toward the window.

"Good evening, Master General," an obviously fanged mouth said behind me.

I briefly froze, but fought my fear.

"Hello, Alurgas," I said, turning to the vampire. "How

fare you this evening?"

Alurgas Tuvino, the vampire that told me of my father's death, had been a Count when the vampires had ruled the Night Kingdom. Before that, he had been a muscular but otherwise unimpressive specimen of elf. Were it not for his obviously elven features, one could easily mistake him for a tall dwarf. The window that he had entered through allowed for enough of a breeze to stir his cosmetically straightened light brown hair as his green eyes glowered at me with barely disguised contempt.

"I would be faring far better had I not been assigned to the whimsy of a half-breed," Alurgas practically snarled. "What do you need of me, whelp?"

Anger. Rage, even. It shot through me like a white hot iron in my skull. My politeness had been met with hostility. How dare this disrespectful reprobate address me in this manner?!

I fought the urge to attack the vampire. I'd been feeding regularly, but it would be a close fight and it would likely spill out into the camp. My upper echelon hadn't thought to ask any questions until now, but even they aren't dumb enough to have no questions about a vampire attack this far south. Not to mention the fact that I would definitely have to bare my fangs.

It would also be difficult to have another vampire assigned to this task, especially once I explained what happened to Alurgas. I would have to come up with a reasonable cause for my attack on him, and losing my temper would not be considered reasonable. I will resist his baiting, for now.

"Yes, I do have need of you. At this moment there are captured orcs digging out a chamber beneath this lodge," I calmly explained. "I need you to find two of them that would be sympathetic to our cause and turn them. My officers have chosen a few to be leaders of this labor detail, so you should start with them. They are the ones with clothing. Use your hypnosis to determine if they will be loyal. If so, turn them. If not, make them forget the encounter."

"What's the point of only turning two of them?" he asked haughtily.

Another downside to having subordinates who are somewhat competent is that they waste time by demanding explanations.

"These orcs are part of a forced labor group, and their work is not finished. If you turn all of them, we will not have a catacomb to build a new vampire army. Vampires make poor slaves, after all."

He recognized my last sentence as the insult it was intended to be and his eyes flashed red in response, but he didn't do anything other than stare. Instead of joining him in a stare-down, I took my seat and gestured at a freshly installed hatch. As far as my officers are aware, the orcs are digging a storeroom for our supplies and loot. They didn't ask why I needed a personal entrance to what would become our cache, and so I hadn't offered an excuse.

The red glow in Alurgas' eyes faded, and he sucked his teeth at me. Then he entered the hatch to go on about his task. I chuckled at my minor victory over the pompous asshole. He would do as he was told, and the plan would move forward. He might skip over the obvious choices for conversion, but I'd planned for that as well. If he didn't choose the orcs that were already in charge of the labor force, those orcs would die and the vampires would take their place.

The storeroom is also to serve as housing for any slaves that we capture. A competent commander would immediately be alarmed at putting all of our eggs in one basket like this, but no such commander was in my army. Once the storeroom is large enough and we have enough slaves, it will suffer an intentional 'accidental collapse' of its two primary entrances.

This will ensure that everyone in the army believes the slaves to be dead. The two vampires will then convert the rest of the slaves, creating a nice little army of vampires. This army will then finish digging the third entrance to the storeroom, and we will then take our leave of this area and meet with the rest of the vampiric forces to lay waste to Cuvellia, the capital of the Night Kingdom. King Lofin will die, and the rest of the drow forces will be trapped between the enraged orcs and bloodthirsty vampires.

Even with the tactics that I have trained them on, they'll be eradicated. If I am lucky, they will do enough damage to the vampiric hordes to make it easier for me to destroy them. Trap the drow forces between the vampires and the orcs, then trap the vampires between the orcs and my loyalists. Or I could bide my time and play politics among the vampires, waiting for a better chance to strike. That would be a far more dangerous option, though.

No, there's no reason to delay. The campaign to destroy the remaining drow should take a few months. I'll seize my prize for killing King Lofin, and with magical intervention I'll have a small army of brood by the time the drow warriors are dead. That will supplement the drow forces that are loyal to me and awaiting my call, and we will move to exterminate the vampires.

I rested my elbows on my knees and cradled my hands as I studied the map in front of me. Directly to our North was the Night Kingdom. Our foothold doesn't extend that far into Blurpus, one of the five chiefdoms of the Unified Chiefdoms that we are aware of. There are more to the south, but they are of little concern to King Lofin, and as such aren't on any of my maps.

Blurpus, Yirna, Havros, Migrath, and Kirkena, the capital. These are the chiefdoms that Lofin wants conquered every once in a while. Each chiefdom has their own military forces and a Great Chief to lead them. In Kirkena, the Great Chief is called High Chief, and he rules over the other chiefs.

Blurpus and Yirna share a border with the Night Kingdom, and they take turns being invaded. The only reason we weren't met with regulars at the border is because it was supposed to be Yirna's turn this time. I chuckled softly. If King Lofin demands an explanation, I will simply say that I was confused and invaded the wrong chiefdom by mistake. I doubt he's paying much attention, though.

The hatch in the corner opened and Alurgas exited the storeroom. He let the hatch fall noisily and kicked the latch closed. Then he turned and affixed me with a glare.

"It's done," he said.

"Good. That's all I needed," I said with a condescending smile. "You may go."

I was treated to another shift from green to red eyes as the vampire debated whether or not to attack me. If he did, I wouldn't have to worry about the other vampires making a fuss if I killed him. I'd still have to come up with an explanation for my soldiers, but I'm willing to live with that. I tensed in anticipation.

Disappointingly, the creature snarled and morphed into a Kvat, and attempted to exit through the still open window. I chuckled as he struggled with the heavy black curtain until he finally managed to complete his exit. I stood and walked over to the window, closing it.

Another part of the plan completed.

Chapter 37

Nick Smith
Adventurer Level: 7
Human - American

"So Bolisir is the kingdom, right?" I asked.

"Yes," Renv said.

"So... what's the name of the city we're going to?"

Yulk chuckled, "It doesn't work that way with the elves of this kingdom. The whole thing is Bolisir. If I remember right, it's a tradition that dates back to their founding."

"That's right," Renv said. "The first High Dragon ruler of Bolisir was notably terrible at names. Instead of admitting to this fault, she opted to name everything under her direct control Bolisir, after herself. Even when her kingdom expanded, the new territories were renamed Bolisir. None of the rulers after Bolisir bothered to rename anything, and now everything that is part of the kingdom of Bolisir is simply known as Bolisir."

"Maybe High Dragons are just bad at naming things," I joked.

Everyone chuckled.

"It goes a bit beyond that, though," Renv said. "Not only is everything Bolisir, there are no borders within the kingdom. Everything functions kind of like a big city."

"That explains why the fair-folk like it so much," Nash

muttered.

"Why?" I asked.

"Because borders can be an issue with them," Yulk explained. "Some types of fae and fairy get trapped within the imaginary lines that we mortals insist upon. The more people believe in the border, the harder it is for them to cross. Bolisir's a big kingdom, so they have plenty of room to roam and grow."

"I kinda feel for the ones who get trapped in a forest, only to have that forest get smaller and smaller as the towns and cities grow around them," Nash said. "It's usually the meekest of the fair-folk that end up in that kind of situation, too."

"What about Tits and Algebrun?"

"I'm not sure," Yulk scratched his chin. "It could be that the road goes through their forest, and as such is part of it. Or maybe they're a type of fae that isn't restricted by the power of borders."

'According to the maps that we have seen, the Deepwyld Forest does not extend over the road we were traveling when we encountered the fae. Yulk's second hypothesis is likely correct,' Ten said.

"Yeah, you're probably right," I said to Yulk and Ten both.

I sat back and watched our surroundings as we continued to the heart of Bolisir, where we would meet the High Dragon. I wonder what it'll look like. Will it look like a dinosaur with wings like the dragons in European folklore? Or will it resemble a snake like the dragons in Asia? Or will it look like something else entirely? Will it wake up and talk to me, or will something else happen while we're looking at the dragon?

I've been trying not to think about my dream. The thing that told me to go see the dragon, whether it's a god or not, gives me the creeps. It said there's a bunch of other things like it watching me, too. It's been hard not to think about that during bathroom breaks. Suddenly, it occurred to me that I had forgotten to tell Ten about my dream. I hadn't had a chance to tell Nash or Yulk yet, but I don't have that excuse with Ten. Maybe I just sort of assumed it already knew, since it's in my head and everything.

'Ten, do you know anything about gods?' I asked it.

'Gods and religions are not part of my knowledge base. Why?'

'When I used all my magic and passed out, I had some sort of dream. Except it wasn't really a dream, it was more like my mind had been transported to somewhere else entirely. Something that said it was a god brought me there. It said that Yulk's going to decline an invitation to see the High Dragon and I shouldn't let that happen. When I was out, did you notice anything weird about my brain?'

There was a noticeable pause before Ten finally said, 'I did not. It appeared to me as if you were simply unconscious.'

'Were there any indications of a wild dream or something?'

'No. The brain activity that I observed wasn't indicative of dreaming.'

'Isn't that odd?'

'Yes, but your dream may simply be a false memory that you obtained upon awakening, likely as a way to cope with the trauma you had just experienced. If it is real, though, I would suggest a modicum of caution. We have little to no information about gods or their intentions, and it would not be wise to do as they demand blindly.'

'You're probably right, but I'm still going to convince Yulk to see the High Dragon.'

'Really?'

'Yeah. Call it a hunch, but I feel like it was telling the truth this time. And if I can't trust my feelings, then I'm probably too far gone to be resisting it now, right?'

Ten went silent instead of laughing at my somewhat dark humor. I allowed myself a small smile before I noticed that the trees around us were getting larger and larger. The trunks were also getting wider, so wide it took an entire minute for us to pass one, and it wasn't long before the trees began to block the sun.

"We're here," Imlor said as the cart stopped.

I looked around and noticed that we had stopped at a building that had been carved into a tree. It had a sign with a coin on it hanging above its door, probably indicating that it was some sort of trader. Further down the road were many other similar buildings, all with lights adorning them. The visual was surreal.

"Alright, let's deliver our letter," Nash said, climbing out of the cart.

Yulk, Renv, and I followed suit and Imlor waved happily at us as we started to walk away. Yulk and

Nash were examining signs as we walked. It was like they were looking for a specific one. We walked past one with a plate on it, and Renv's stomach growled.

"You're still following us?" Nash asked the dwarf.

"Well, once you conclude your business here I was thinking I can take you to my uncle's shop to see about a reward for saving my hide," Renv grinned. "Plus, I'm curious to see what you lot get up to."

"Do you know your way around?"

"Nope. I live down south a ways, and haven't been up here in over a year. I'm pretty sure my uncle upgraded to a bigger building recently but I've got no clue where it is."

"That's okay," Yulk said.

He pointed at a building with a sign depicting a pen and paper, attached to a large stable with several hnarses. As we got closer we could hear the ruckus of commerce taking place. Nash and Yulk entered the building first, and Renv held his hand out in a gesture indicating I should go first. I did so, and the smell of fresh ink and paper hit me like a ton of bricks, nearly making my eyes water.

Inside the building were bookcases behind a counter, several desks, and many elves and gnomes rushing around. Most of them were wearing a uniform, light tan shorts and tunic with a green symbol of a pen on their breast, and I assumed they were employees of whatever business this is. Those that weren't in uniform weren't rushing around, they were waiting in line in front of the counter or sitting at one of the desks with an employee.

The customers, I assume, would say something to the employee, then the employee would write. It took a few moments for me to realize that the customers were probably dictating letters or something. I glanced at Nash, remembering his illiteracy. He saw me glance at him and looked around, then gave me a harsh glare. I looked away, trying not to smile. He grumbled something as we took our place in line.

"What is this place?" I asked Yulk.

"It's a mail office. They offer dictating services, reading services, delivery services, and since they know where everything is, they can give good directions," he explained. "Which is why we're here."

"Directions to the Regent?"

"Correct. I haven't been here before, so I don't know where Regent Oakmor does business."

"I thought you've been to Bolisir."

"I have, but not this part of it. My business was with a certain sorcerer who built a tower in the forest, far away from any signs of civilization. She was much friendlier than you would expect from a hermit."

"This sorcerer you're talking about wouldn't happen to be Olmira The Eternal, would it?" Renv asked.

"Yes, the very same. She taught me how to use healing magic," Yulk said with a smile. "It seems like forever ago. How do you know her?"

"Olmira's one of the healers I was talking about sharing your discovery with. She's one of Oakmor's advisors now. She'll probably be around here somewhere. I'll check when I ask for directions to my uncle."

"How'd she end up advisor to a Regent?"

"She said it was because of the pests. Turns out, a tower in the wilderness occupied by just one person is a great place for bugs and rodents. One day she went into her cellar only to find a nest of giant rats, and she lost it. Demolished the whole tower then and there. She dug her savings out of the rubble and moved here. Didn't take long for Oakmor to offer her a job."

"Why is she called The Eternal?" I asked as we moved closer to the front of the line.

"She's a vampire," Yulk and Renv said simultaneously. They looked at each other and chuckled.

"Oh. How does a vampire get blood when they're living as a hermit?"

"Delivery services," Yulk said. "There are plenty of people willing to sell their blood, and the vampires who prefer not to injure people are more than happy to pay for it. Enchanted ice-boxes keep the blood from rotting during transit."

"There are services like that?" I asked incredulously. "Vampires just sort of order from a catalog, or what?"

"I don't think the services offer specific blood-types. But you'll find such a service in nearly every territory. Sometimes they're even endorsed by the local government. It wouldn't do to have your vampiric citizens feeding on your other citizens."

I had more questions, but the person ahead of us finished their business and it was suddenly our turn at the counter. As we approached, I realized the bookcases had letters in them, and there were gnomes busy sorting those letters. A brunette elf smiled at us, and Yulk stepped forward.

"How can I help you today?" she asked.

"We need directions to Regent Oakmor's place of business," Yulk explained. "We have a delivery for him."

She explained that all we had to do was follow the main road and look for a building with a sign that depicted a tree. The tree was apparently the symbol of Bolisir, and marked government offices and officials. She was also kind enough to tell us that if we went further down the main road, we would find the sleeping dragon. She highly recommended taking a guided tour if we got the chance.

"Thank you," Yulk said and stepped aside so Renv could have his turn at the counter.

We waited for the dwarf to ascertain his uncle's location, and then left the post office. As we walked down the main road, I wondered how things were going to unfold. I assume someone is going to invite us on the tour to see the dragon, and Yulk is going to decline this invitation. I'm going to have to somehow convince him to accept the invitation. That's going to be hard, because I still haven't had a chance to be alone with my brothers and explain my dream to them.

"There it is," Nash said, pointing at a building.

Most of the buildings were within hollowed-out tree trunks. This one, though, looked like it was made of very old stone. It reminded me of the kind of stone you see a castle made out of in a fantasy movie.

There were also plenty of people on the road, but none of them seemed at all interested in going in or out of the building. The doors were made of metal, iron probably, and swung open surprisingly easy as we entered.

The first thing I noticed within the building was the distinct smell of stale paper. Like the air within this building had been here for years, and had been reading all the books. The room we had entered was smaller than I'd expected, and there were eight doors. Three on the walls to our left and right, and two on the wall behind the desk in the middle of the room.

There were two people at this desk, a male and female elf. The female elf was sitting behind the desk with a serious expression on her face, and the male elf was standing off to the side reading some papers. Yulk and Nash approached the desk, and I followed them with Renv trailing me.

"Excuse me, we're here to deliver a missive from High Chief Ulurmak to Regent Oakmor. Is he in?" Yulk asked politely.

"That would be me," the male elf said with a laugh. "What a coincidence. I was just reading up on the situation with the Night Kingdom. May I see the missive?"

"Here you are, your highness," Yulk passed the letter over.

Regent Oakmor took the letter, opened it, and began to read. The woman sitting behind the desk watched the interaction, but was glancing at me every now and then. I smiled at her, and she froze for a moment, but smiled back and politely looked away.

"As I suspected. Strange happenings must be afoot for my blood brother to ask for reinforcements," Oakmor said after a moment. "You know he once fought off one of these invasions singlehandedly? Mima, make certain this missive gets to Field General Yom with the instruction that he take his soldiers to Ulurmak's aid."

"Yes, your majesty. Also..." she trailed off and subtly pointed at me.

"Hmm? OH! The human!" Oakmor slid between Yulk and Nash with a speed that would shock lightning. He grabbed my hand and vigorously shook it a few times before saying, "What a pleasure it is to have you visit the mighty kingdom of Bolisir! I've been simply dying of curiosity ever since I heard about the orcs discovering you. Ulurmak says they found you in a dungeon, is that right?"

"Y-yes," I managed to say despite my shock. "Nash found me and Yulk revived me."

"Nash and Yulk?" Oakmor asked.

"That would be us, sire," Nash answered, gesturing to himself and Yulk.

"Truthfully? Why, that sly pupper managed to send me the whole set! Tell me, did the situation with the monster in the dungeon ever get resolved? Last I heard Ulurmak was sending over-twenties."

"It did, your highness," Yulk said. "Nick is the one who killed it, actually."

"Nick?" Oakmor inquired with confusion before looking back to me. "Oh! Yes, of course! You must be Nick, then."

"Y-yes sir," I said.

"It's simply wonderful to meet you. Please, accompany me to my office. I'd like to hear more about your adventures thus far."

Nash and Yulk glanced at each other and shrugged slightly.

"It would be our pleasure, your highness," Yulk said.

Chapter 38

High Chief Ulurmak
Adventurer Level: N/A
Orc - Kirkenian

"They're in Blurpus?" I asked incredulously. "Not Yirna?"

Great Chief Tormon nodded gravely. The graying orc in front of me had ridden night and day to bring me this news himself and beg my aid. Quite a feat for one of his advanced years, but he had done so to make certain that I would not decline his request. He had given of himself to ask me to do the same, and it would be the highest form of disrespect to ignore this.

Of course, I had no intention of ignoring or declining his request. But the fact that he rode here himself suggests that he thinks otherwise, which means I need to make it clearer to my Great Chiefs that I stand with them. Their struggles are my struggles. This line of thought must have shown on my face, because Tormon gave me a knowing look.

"Ulurmak, I rode here myself because my hnarses are faster than the scouts, and I don't trust anyone but myself and my son with my hnarses. Since I'm too old for the field, I sent him to lead and came here myself."

"Get out of my head," I grinned. "I'll send the regulars and redirect our allies. How's your boy doing?"

"He's had better days, I'm sure," Tormon sighed. "Wants to be an artist, not a general. His paintings and sculptures are fine to look at, too. He really cares about his craft. The look on his face when I told him what was required of him was grim."

"He didn't argue it?"

"No. Grum's a smart boy. He knows that if he doesn't take charge there's a good chance that many of our people will lose their homes and their lives. He won't allow his aversion to responsibility cause our people to suffer."

"I'm glad to hear that. How's things on the front?"

"They've captured a settlement and a village. Lofin must have finally sent a competent commander, because they're using shield walls and pikes, and we haven't won a single skirmish. They won't pursue us, either, so our traps and tricks have been ineffective. The best we've been able to do is convince them to pull back."

The mention of shield walls made the hairs on the back of my neck raise. I had been hoping I was wrong about the vampires, but phalanxes are one of their favored formations. It could be a coincidence, but this along with the fact that the drow aren't sticking to any of their patterns is alarming. Tormon noted my silence and thoughtful expression.

"You don't think..." his eyes went wide as he trailed off. "It can't be the vampires, can it? How could they have infiltrated Lofin's inner circle?"

Tormon is old enough that he was raised on stories of his father fighting against the vampires of the Night Kingdom. He had even personally led the charge against the remnants that threatened our borders. Of all the Great Chiefs, he was uniquely qualified to know how dire a threat the vampires can be.

"I don't know, but it's not outside the realm of possibility," I said. "Lofin's paranoid, but he's also an idiot. His criteria for choosing his generals is well known, and it wouldn't be hard to take advantage of that."

"But how can this be? Drow can't be turned, and there isn't a single non-drow noble in the entirety of the Night Kingdom. Lofin's not stupid enough to make a vampire his general, right?"

"I don't have answers. It could be that the drow in question is simply working with the vampires, or it could be that Lofin couldn't find a general among his nobility and hired a mercenary. Regardless, something is definitely off about this invasion. Have there been any reports of vampires in the field?"

"No, none at all."

"There's that, at least," I said as I rubbed my chin. "So either I'm wrong about my hunch that the vampires are at work here, or Lofin is unaware of the vampiric influence on this invasion."

"What if he's dead?" Tormon asked.

"Can't be. One, I'd have heard about it. Lofin doesn't pay his staff well enough to keep their silence. Two, there's a functional drow army. The nobility of the Night Kingdom wouldn't be able to pull that off without Lofin. Those strings are too fragile for the vampires to be able to yank them."

"Hmm. It's a mystery," Tormon sighed and leaned back in his chair. "Still, doesn't change what must be done. Blurpus must be defended. What are we going to do about the shields?"

"Shields won't help them if they attack your keep, but for the field we may want to look into mounted mages," I suggested. "Or axes. Axes would probably be cheaper."

"They're using pikes and spears. The axes have trouble closing in. I like the idea of a mage cavalry, though."

"Yeah, but we don't really have the infrastructure for that sort of thing."

"The guilds might. They've gotta know of some adventurers that can use magic and ride a hnarse."

"Sure, but it's gonna be costly. Won't be a long term solution to this kind of combat. Can't expect this to be a quick war."

Tormon laughed, "You should use that overly large head of yours to find a way to encourage mages to join the regulars. Then we wouldn't have to worry about this kind of thing."

"My head isn't overly large, old one. Yours is just small," I grinned. Then a thought occurred to me. "Magic users like to study and learn, it helps them with their casting. Maybe a school or something. Charge tuition and offer waivers for military service..."

"The guilds would probably have an interest in that. Might even be willing to pay extra taxes to help fund it. See? Big head, big ideas."

"RAYZUN!" I shouted, ignoring the jab from Tormon.

Rayzun quickly popped his head through my door, "Yes, High Chief?"

"I need a meeting with the leaders of the adventurers guilds and companies. If they want to continue operating in the Unified Chiefdoms, they'd better get here with speed."

Rayzun nodded and closed the door. Tormon raised an eyebrow at me, then grinned.

"You'd ban them?" he asked.

"Damn right," I replied. "Most of 'em are tax-dodgers anyway. All I've gotta do is send the auditors and they're done. They're well aware of that."

Tormon nodded and chuckled. The truth is, most of the guild leaders are respectful and will come when called regardless of whether or not I make threats. While it's true that the majority of them definitely do not pay their legally obligated share of taxes, they still understand their place in the world. A handful of them, though, do not. They keep forgetting that their wealth does not equate to status here in the Unified Chiefdoms, and in Kirkena especially.

If I didn't threaten them, they would ignore me. This would force me to do some rather unsavory things to teach whoever replaces them not to repeat their mistakes. My father once told me that if I could avoid being cruel, then I should do so at all costs. Fear naturally follows respect, but respect does not follow fear. He generally knew what he was talking about in regards to governing, so it's advice that I heed.

"A school for magic," Tormon said thoughtfully. "How long do you suppose it'll take to make?"

"That depends almost entirely upon the mages," I replied. "We've got some empty buildings that would do the trick. The Uli Trade Union building is what I'm thinking."

"The Uli finally gave up the ghost? Thought I'd never see the day."

"Yeah, they've been done for a while now. Thankfully it was a slow decline, so it didn't hurt the economy too much when the boys shut the doors."

The Uli trade union had been a multi-national trade organization that began a long, long time ago. My great-grandfather had given the seal of approval for the construction of their gigantic office. A series of scandals and bad business decisions had started their decline during my father's time, and I had signed the paperwork that forgave their debts and closed their doors.

"What are the Uli boys up to these days?"

"I don't know. Part of their debt forgiveness was the requirement that they forfeit their property and leave the chiefdom. They didn't tell me where they planned to go."

"Hmm." Tormon slapped his knees. "So, one more thing before I go. You met with the thing that they dragged out of that dungeon?"

"Sure did," I grinned. "He's a human."

"A human? What's that?"

"Well, looks kind of like an elf but with round ears and a few sharp teeth. Didn't really get a chance to talk to him very much because I had him deliver a missive to Bolisir to request aid against the drow. The reports say he's from another world, and that world is full of humans like him. Oh, and he can eat meat and veg."

"Weird," Tormon frowned. "You sent him to Bolisir by himself? He that strong?"

"Guild says he's level seven already, but no. I sent him along with Flesh-Carver Yilda's boys. Nash and Yulk. She adopted the human, you know."

"No shit," Tormon laughed. "Haven't heard from Yilda Alta in decades! Any word on how she's doin'?"

"From the sound of things, she's enjoying the quiet life. Can't begrudge her that, not after what she gave for it."

"Too true. So, the human. Think he's dangerous?"

"Probably, but not to us. He seems pretty amicable and level headed."

"That's good to hear," Tormon said as he rose from his chair. "So long as you've got some idea as to what you're doing with the human, I'm fine with whatever you decide. I should get back."

I nodded solemnly as he turned to leave my office. He paused for a moment at the door.

"Should I accompany you?" I asked, trying to guess the reason for his hesitation.

He turned to look at me with a little bit of shock. I suppose I had guessed wrong, and it hadn't even occurred to him to ask. My prowess on the battlefield is well known, and even though Tormon and the rest of the Great Chiefs are big orcs, I tower over them. Tormon met my eyes, and then looked at the mountains of paperwork on my desk.

"I don't think so, Ulurmak," he answered with a grin. "Things are not quite so dire as to give you an excuse to get away from the paperwork."

"But there's just so much of it, though," I said with an exaggerated frown.

Tormon and I laughed for a few moments before things settled down into a somber silence.

"When you enter the field of battle, it will be indicative of failure on our part," Tormon said. "We'll do everything in our power to ensure you get to enjoy your paperwork. Goodbye, High Chief."

"Goodbye, Great Chief."

Tormon left the room, and I sighed. I'd known Tormon since I was a child, and it pained me to see him as an elder now. The massive orc that had sparred with me and shocked me with his speed and power was now too old to even accompany his son into battle. Still, I felt a little beam of pride that he liked my idea for a magic school. Maybe we could do more than one, and have the schools compete with each other to further motivate their students...

No, I doubt there'll be any need for that. The knowledge of magic alone will be more than enough motivation for most of the students. Hell, maybe once things get going I'll take a class or two. Find out if I could have been good at magic or not. My gaze fell back to my paperwork.

"Fuck," I whispered to myself as I picked up my pen.

A knock on my office door saved me from the looming task at hand. Rayzun poked his head into my office.

"High Chief, two of the guild leaders are here to see you," he said.

"Which ones?" I asked.

"Pumos and the adventurer's guild."

"Send them in, no need for introductions."

Rayzun nodded and left the room. The Adventurer's Guild and the Pumos Union were the two largest guilds in the Unified Chiefdoms. The Adventurer's Guild was much larger than the Pumos Union, though, because their operation is multi-national. Even so, the Pumos Union was no pushover and even offered mercenary services that the AG didn't typically bother with. There are a lot of areas in the UC that wouldn't have any sort of police if it weren't for Pumos, and the easiest way to become a guard is to join up with them.

A gnome and an elf entered my office and bowed. The gnome is Malura Grinzaw, and she is the head of the Pumos Union. The elf is Yarawei Horfu, and he is the master of the Adventurer's Guild. I gestured for them to take a seat, and they happily complied.

"There are two things we need to discuss," I said once they were settled.

They subtly glanced at each other. I could imagine what they might think this meeting is about, and how nervous they both were. I had to fight a grin.

"First is the situation with the Night Kingdom invasion. I need mages that know how to ride a hnarse while casting. They will be pressed into service for the remainder of the invasion, but they will be well compensated for their efforts."

Eyes widened and eyebrows shot up. It had been decades since adventurers had been drafted, and my willingness to impose upon their freedoms indicated a dire situation. Malura opened her mouth to say something, but quickly closed it again.

"It will be done, High Chief," Yarawei said. "So the rumors are true, then?"

"I don't know what the rumors are, so I cannot say," I replied. "What I can say is that the drow are using tactics that we are ill-prepared to respond to, and they invaded Blurpus instead of Yirna. We are planning on utilizing a mage cavalry force to tip things in our favor."

"Mounted mages, I'll be damned," Malura said.

"The second thing we need to discuss is the possibility of a school for study of magic. It will be an academic institution dedicated to instructing mages on the magical arts, both to further the common knowledge of magic as well as to bolster the caliber of our mages. Funding will be done through a mixture of government subsidies and tuition, with tuition waivers offered for completion of military service."

The two guild-leaders maintained their shocked expressions. Whatever they had thought this meeting to be about, I was demolishing their expectations. Malura recovered first, this time.

"How can we help, High Chief?" she asked.

"I need teachers and administrators that are well versed in magic. It is unclear how many we will need as of yet, so I want you to make a list of those who are qualified and who may be interested."

"You said government subsidy, High Chief? How will the chiefdom be getting the funds necessary to start this... academy of magic?" Yarawei asked.

"Oh, that's quite simple," I said as a malicious grin spread across my features. "I'll just be needing you to pay a bit more of your fair share of taxes. Some estimates put your payments at around thirty percent of what you should actually be paying. If you bump that up to forty percent, we'll be able to afford the academy and I won't have to send the auditors."

Their stunned silence was music to my ears.

Chapter 39

Nick Smith
Adventurer Level: 7
Human - American

"Instead of my office, let us use one of these conference rooms. They're much nicer and have more chairs," Regent Oakmor said as we walked.

"Sounds great, your highness," Nash replied.

We walked a little further before the regent halted and gestured to a closed door. I awkwardly froze, trying to figure out what he wanted, but Yulk stepped past me and opened the door. Oakmor caught my confusion, gave me a slight smile, and nodded warmly to Yulk before entering the room. I guess maybe royalty doesn't open doors for other people?

I worked my way through my confusion as we entered the room. My jaw nearly dropped, Oakmor had described it as a conference room but that hardly did it justice. The room was luxuriously large and its stone walls were covered in various banners, one of which I had seen while in Kirkena. There were various other decorations spread throughout the room, like swords, maces, and a hand from a large clawed monster.

In the center of the room was a massive wooden table with intricate engravings that were inlaid with gold. The chairs surrounding the table matched its engravings, but had cushions on their seats, arms, and backs. Their backs were extra tall, and reminded me of the expensive reclining chairs that influencers peddled for ridiculous amounts of money back home. I was wondering if they could recline when Oakmor sat and gestured to the chairs across from him.

"Please, sit down. We have much to discuss," he said with another small smile.

We sat, with Yulk to my left and Nash to my right. Renv sat next to Nash and sighed contently. The chairs were remarkably comfortable, and I had to fight the urge to melt into their cushions. It's the first cushioned chair I've sat in since coming to this world. When I get back home I'm never taking cushioned seats for granted again.

Oakmor began by verifying the information he'd been given thus far. Yes, I am from another world. I do, in fact, need to eat both plants and meat. Yilda Alta adopted me into the Alta clan. No, I wasn't technically the one who killed the thing in the dungeon. We came here to deliver the missive and to see if we could get some rubbings translated. Yes, I am desperately trying to get back home and I miss my family terribly.

"Well, on that note, are you planning on seeing our True King?" Regent Oakmor asked with an eager grin.

"Actually, your majesty..." Yulk began.

"Yes we are," I interrupted, surprised at the firmness in my voice. "Your king is a dragon, right?"

I asked the follow-up question to put Yulk into a difficult position. To argue with me, he would have to interrupt the regent. I don't know a lot about monarchy or regency, but I do know that he's been calling Oakmor 'your majesty', and it's usually a bad idea to interrupt someone who requires that honorific.

"Not just any dragon," Oakmor said, beaming with pride. "A High Dragon! A normal dragon is fearsome and respectable, one of the most terrible and deadly beasts to ever exist. But it is just a beast. They have intelligence and motivations comparable to puppers or hnarses. High Dragons are much smarter and deadlier than their less evolved cousins."

"What do you mean?" I asked.

I dared a glance at Yulk, who was staring at me. His expression betrayed confusion rather than anger, though. I felt a stab of guilt as I realized he was trying to figure out why I had interrupted him and changed our plans on the fly instead of feeling angry at me for doing so. I didn't bother looking at Nash, though. I can feel the venom in his gaze.

"High Dragons are near divinity when it comes to their intelligence. The legends tell of High Dragon elders accurately predicting the outcomes of battles years before they were fought. While that may be an exaggeration, the High Dragons were instrumental in driving the daemons and anyels out of our world," Oakmor's tone took a sad turn. "A lot of them died to do that, though. Including the parents of our True King. He avenged them in a glorious battle that lasted for three weeks, and returned to Bolisir for his coronation. I'm not sure what happened during that battle, but he promptly issued a declaration of regency and fell into a slumber that has lasted ever since."

"A declaration of regency?"

"Yes. The declaration of regency governs the requirements for my office. Essentially, I act as king in his absence. When I die, there will be an election and a new regent will be chosen."

"Who chooses the new regent?"

"The people of the land, of course."

I paused for a moment. A democratic monarchy sounds alien to me, but on the other hand I don't really know much about kings and queens. Rather than exposing my ignorance, I opted to ask something else.

"High Chief Ulurmak says you're his blood brother, how did that happen?" I asked.

"Ulurmak and I adventured together in our youth. We have saved each other's lives on multiple occasions, and when it came time for him to take over the post of High Chief we decided to take a blood oath," the elf answered. "At the time, the intention was for me to come to his aid as an adventurer whenever he needed it. Then my father passed and I was pressured into running for regent, namely because no one else wanted to. Now our blood oath requires the both of us to come to each others aid for as long as we rule."

"So until you die? Or... wait, what happens to you if the High Dragon wakes up?" I asked.

"I will resign my post as regent and take up whatever duty our king offers me," the elf smiled. "Or I just retire. I have enough savings to last me for the rest of my life and make sure my children get a good inheritance."

"Retire? You wouldn't go back to adventuring?"

"Oh, I'm far too old for that sort of thing," Oakmor waved his hand dismissively.

"Really? You don't look all that old."

Oakmor began laughing, and all three of my companions chuckled along with him. I looked around with a confused expression, seeking an answer until it finally hit me. Even back home elves don't age all that much. Damn it.

"Elves do not typically demonstrate our age upon our faces," Oakmor explained as he wiped a tear. "Apologies for my outburst, your question was simply unexpected. I likely have a couple of decades left until I'm infirm, but my adventuring days are well behind me."

"What level did you manage to get to, your majesty?" Nash asked.

"I rose to level sixty-two, thanks mostly to Ulurmak. He could probably return to adventuring if the situation arose."

"Really?" Yulk asked. "I thought he was older than you, your highness."

"He is, but he's also of royal lineage," Oakmor answered before frowning slightly. "Ah, but I digress. I am fairly certain that the details of the royal lineage are secret, so if you wish to learn more you will have to ask him directly."

Yulk nodded and retreated into his thoughts, rubbing his chin to process what he'd heard. Nash furrowed his brows and crossed his arms, also an indication that he was thinking. Renv and I simply looked at the two orcs, confused by their reactions.

"Now Nick, I cannot help but notice that you have been omitting my honorific this entire time," Oakmor said with a sly grin. "I have chosen not to take this as an insult, but I cannot help but wonder why."

"Apologies, your highness," I said rapidly. "I've never

met a regent before, and we didn't have royalty or nobility where I'm from."

"Truly?" he asked as his eyebrows rose. "Absolutely remarkable. How are your people governed?"

I explained the various types of government in the United States to Regent Oakmor to the best of my ability, which inevitably led to more questions about my world. Thankfully, Oakmor seemed more interested in our various forms of entertainment and food than our other technology, so I was able to easily avoid the subject of weapons.

In this world, adventurers hold the majority of the combat abilities. They have to train those abilities and hone them to be able to cause massive amounts of destruction. Guns and nukes would change that power dynamic very quickly, and even pointing out the possibility of their existence may eventually lead to someone creating them. Can't be too careful.

"You can look at cute pets while communicating with anyone in the world almost instantaneously?" Oakmor leaned back in his chair. "Marvelous. Simply marvelous. I know it's unlikely to ever happen, but I can't help but wish to see such wonders with my own eyes."

"Fuckin' hells, me too," Renv said.

I glanced at Renv and realized that everyone else had followed suit. Nash and Yulk looked shocked, and Regent Oakmor raised his left eyebrow. The already diminutive dwarf shrank even further at our various gazes.

"M-my apologies, your m-majesty," he stammered. "I didn't mean to swear in your presence. It won't happen again, your highness."

"See that it doesn't. Though, your reaction is more than understandable," Oakmor straightened. "Well, my curiosity is sated for now. Please, allow me to accompany you to our True King. Watching his royal majesty's slumber may sound dull, but there truly is nothing quite like it."

The regent rose from his chair and we followed suit. He led us back to where we had entered the building and whispered something to the woman at the front desk. Her green eyes narrowed at Oakmor with disapproval, but she didn't say anything. He grinned at her and gestured for us to follow him. When we left the building, he took a deep breath.

"Ah, fresh air. It's been so long," he chuckled. "So, do any of you know why our streets are wider than that of other kingdoms?"

"So that your king can walk through the kingdom when he awakens, your majesty?" Yulk asked.

"Correct! My, you are a bright one. When his royal highness first entered his slumber, he did so in a sparsely populated portion of the kingdom, not wanting to get in the way of our growth. However, his subjects love him so much that many of them moved here, and everything was built around him to make sure that he would be comfortable when he awoke. We've even cleared the airspace in case he needs to fly."

"How many people live here, your majesty?" I asked.

"Our last census has us at eleven thousand, with a margin of error of one percent. This is the most densely populated portion of Bolisir, and if we had cities it would likely be our capital. Oh, and don't fret over my honorific, Nick. I understand now that your culture is vastly different from ours, and I'm willing to treat you as a sort of diplomat."

"Thank you, sir."

"Your highness, I didn't see any fortifications as we approached. Why is that?" Nash asked.

"Just because you didn't see our fortifications doesn't mean they aren't there," Oakmor winked. "Which would be more effective at routing an invading army? A simple stone wall, or arrows and spells coming from all around you at impossible angles?"

Nash's eyes widened and he fell into a contemplative silence.

"We are not invaded often, either," Oakmor continued. "Our only two neighbors are the Night Kingdom and the Unified Chiefdoms. The Unified Chiefdoms meet us at the south and west, and the Night Kingdom meets us at the north and west. It's just ocean on the east. Since the Unified Chiefdoms are friendly with us, our only threat is the Night Kingdom. They've tried invading us before, but they rarely make it past the fae with anything resembling an invasion force."

"The fae fight them?" I asked.

"Some do. Most prefer trickery and subterfuge, but those that take pleasure in direct action are quite brutal. The blood and bone fae, especially."

"Blood and bone fae? Do those live in the Deepwyld Forest?"

"Odd of you to ask that..." Oakmor studied me for a

moment. "No, both the blood and the bone fae tend to live along our northern border, in a place the fae call Grimstars Wood. They have been known to migrate somewhat, but never so far as the Deepwyld Forest. How are you aware of the fae living there?"

I explained our encounter with Tits and Algebrun as we continued our walk. The regent waited patiently as I explained their attempt to trick us into giving them our names, and his eyebrows rose as I told him that I named them. He stopped dead in his tracks when I told him that they'd turned into arch-fae, and the rest of us quickly followed suit.

"They became arch-fae?" he asked.

"I... Y-yes, your majesty," I stammered, caught completely off-guard by his sudden seriousness.

"You... made them into arch-fae?"

"I... I suppose so, sir."

Oakmor leaned toward me and studied me carefully. I tried not to lean away, but his piercing gaze forced my instincts to kick in. After a few moments of intense scrutiny, the regent resumed his former posture and began to laugh.

"Oh, by the gods," he said as he recovered. "That's going to anger someone powerful, I'm sure. No matter, that's a problem for another time. Let's continue on, shall we?"

He gestured for us to follow as he began to walk once more. The four of us looked at each other and quickly trailed after the regent.

"Who would get mad?" I asked.

"The fae chroniclers, for sure, but you don't have to worry about them. The only one you might have to worry about is Mumuldobran, but he's likely to be more angry at the new arch-fae than at you," he glanced at me and caught the concern on my face. "Oh, don't worry about them. Mumuldobran will probably just give them an earful and a hard time for a few years."

I was about to ask what he knew about Mumuldobran when a certain smell caught my attention. The musky scent of reptile with a hint of... rotten eggs? No, that's sulfur. I looked around for the source of the smell, but it became obvious as we turned a corner.

The High Dragon looked exactly like what I have seen in video games. It was resting on a platform with stairs, curled up with its front legs supporting the base of its neck and its head resting on its tail. I could barely make out the claws of its hind legs poking out from underneath its wings. Shining white scales covered its body, glimmering in a massive sunbeam, the first I'd seen so far. The only thing that was missing was a treasure horde underneath it.

"This is our True King," Oakmor took a few steps and gestured dramatically. "Yssinirath, King of Bolisir and Bane of the Horde."

My eyes remained on the High Dragon as I followed the regent. Its body slow expanded and deflated slightly as it breathed, causing a sort of shimmering effect from its scales. It was bigger than an elephant, but breathtakingly beautiful.

I looked at its face and noticed that its eyes were moving under their lids, like it was dreaming. I was trying to imagine what it was dreaming about when the movement stopped. Everything in my body told me that it was awake, and watching me. I felt the blood drain from my face and froze in my tracks. Oakmor and my companions turned to look at me, confused at my sudden halt.

The dragon's eyes snapped open, looking directly into my own.

Chapter 40

Yssinirath
Adventurer Level: N/A
High Dragon - Unknown

"Yss! Get that out of your mouth!"

"Yemsh muvr," I try to reply as I spit the befuddled troll back onto the ground.

"You know better than to eat trolls without cooking them first, boy," my father scolded me.

"Yes, father."

"Really now! They are quite filthy! Go wash your mouth out," mother said.

The troll looked at my parents and then back at me with confusion. It could not understand what we were saying and looked confused at being spared. It sat there nonplussed, as if it were the one being scolded. I dismissively waved a claw at it, which released it from whatever stuporous spell was holding its poor little mind. It rose and began to run, and I walked over to the river to obey my mother's command.

A shame that my parents caught me. Actually, how did they catch me? They were arguing, they couldn't have been paying attention to me. Never mind, it doesn't matter. Trolls are delicious. They have chewy, juicy muscles with plenty of succulent fat, which makes for a rather perfect mouthful of meat. The bones add a magnificent crunch, too. My parents are correct that trolls are filthy little creatures, but I've never minded the grime. It's just seasoning, really.

I dipped my head in the river and drew water into my mouth. It was cool and refreshing, and it took more than a little willpower to spit my first mouthful back into the river. I took in some more, swished it around, gargled, and spat once more. Once my mouth was sufficiently rinsed I gulped down gallons of the fresh water, along with a few inattentive fish. Then I laid on my back and my wings on the rocks as I watched my parents talk.

"You can't be serious, Ssuranivaro. The daemons have nearly wiped out the elves. What good would it do for us to help them now, of all times?" my mother asked.

A strange smell nearly distracted me, but I wanted to hear my father's response. My father is wise, but he has a blind-spot in his wisdom in regards to daemons. He hates them more than I have ever seen anyone hate anything, and mother is right to worry for his logic.

"Don't cry my name wantonly, Essramil. There is no need for such disrespect," my father replied with a flick of his tongue. "While it is true that the elves have taken severe casualties, they are not extinct yet. The threat of their extinction is imminent, though, which means they will be all the more grateful for our aid. They'll have no issues submitting to our rule, and we can finally merge our two kingdoms into one."

He's talking about Bolisir and Yivanita. Bolisir is our kingdom, and Yivanita is the independent elven kingdom. In ages past, the elves managed to convince one of my ancestors to allow them to self-govern. Recently it was occupied by the daemons before being 'liberated' by the anyels. Once the elves rebelled against the anyels, the daemons quickly reoccupied it. The elves have no royalty left, and very little in the way of nobility. My father has made an excellent point.

At the moment, Bolisir is strong. The daemons and the anyels have left us alone, with the exception of their skirmishes spilling into our land. Yivanita is ravaged, but if it were to combine with Bolisir we would be able to help the elves rebuild their homes and businesses in record time. And if we don't, it won't be long before the daemons have eradicated the elves and turn their attentions to us.

That damned smell again. Where is it? I looked around but there was not a single clue to its origin. It smelled familiar, but also hauntingly alien. It was comforting, disturbing, lovely, and threatening all at once. It's a smell that I feel I should remember from somewhere, but have never encountered before. Or have I? Unable to find its origin, I turned back to my parents.

"Bah, they are short-minded like the rest of the mer," my mother said with a dismissive wave of her claw. "They'll be grateful to us this generation and perhaps the next, but by the third generation they will demand freedom to once again create their illusory territories. We'll barely be better off. It's not worth the risk of fighting the daemons."

"My dear, the elves that live under our rule are happy. The elves of Yivanita will see this and be happy as well. Only those who are mistreated desire independence, and we will certainly be a better option than those damnable daemons."

I looked to the sky in contemplation. The daemons. I'd eaten a daemon once. It tasted terrible and took forever to digest. Wait, that's wrong. It is taking forever to digest. Oh right, this is a dream. Mother and father are long dead, and not even their bones remain. The daemons had made certain of that. I looked back to my parents, and indeed they were gone.

My father had eventually talked my mother into fighting the daemons, and I had helped. They were both slain during the conflict, and I had lost myself in rage and grief. My wrath was unstoppable, and the daemon lord that had taken their lives is currently being dissolved in my stomach. I then became king of Bolisir and merged Yivanita into my domain with no argument from the elves. I have been napping among them ever since, leaving them to their own devices.

That damned smell again. I awoke, being careful to keep my eyes closed. The daemon in my belly made me tired, like I'd always just eaten a rather large lunch. A benefit to this is that my nutritional needs are constantly fulfilled, but the downside is that it's difficult to concentrate on ruling while I'm in such a state.

My solution to this was simple, I decided to name a regent and sleep until I got hungry again. However, sleeping indefinitely is impossible, and every time I awoke the elves would lose their minds with glee. They would ask me what they should be doing and how they should go about doing it, and it would take forever to get caught up enough to adequately make those decisions. So I decided to pretend to sleep even when I was awake so that they could go about their business.

Before I knew it, though, it had been multiple generations since I'd last spoken to the elves. So many generations that I no longer understood their tongue. It would be terribly awkward if I were to reveal my ruse.

This smell has aroused my curiosity, though. Needing to know where its coming from, I silently cast True

Vision and looked through my eyelids. I saw that the elves had redecorated once again. My view of the sky remained unobstructed, though, and I could see that the towering trees had continued to grow during my latest slumber. Judging from how much larger they'd become, it had only been about eighty years since my last stealthy awakening.

Those eighty years must have seen quite the economic boom, too. The hill I have been resting on now had stairs, with roads leading away from me and winding through the trees. I was impressed that they had managed to do this without waking me. On each side of the roads were buildings that were definitely elven, but reeked of gnomes, dwarves, and orcs. Each building appeared to be specially carved from a tree, but with the obvious advertisements and signs denoting commerce. Shops, perhaps?

The elves were none the wiser to my awakening and continued about their business. Some children were being led by an adult, who was speaking in a very condescending tone. Must be a teacher speaking to students. Most of their eyes were wide, which is the proper response to seeing something as gargantuan and graceful as I, but others appeared to be... bored. I fought the urge to open my eyes to startle the little cretins.

I looked around some more and saw another noteworthy group approaching me. Two orcs, an elf, a dwarf, and something else. I'd nearly mistaken it for a pig-kobold, but it was walking fully upright and seemed to be speaking with the rest of the group. There were two other big clues that it wasn't a pig-kobold, though. Its ears were round, and it was the thing giving off the intriguing smell.

Pork smells like prey, as do kobolds. This doesn't smell

like prey. I'm not certain of what it smells like, but it's definitely not prey. I suspect that it would put up as much of a fight as the daemon in my belly if I were to try to eat it. Perhaps even more of a fight, considering how injured this particular daemon had been by the time I decided to devour it.

I turned my eyes toward my stomach. Hirgarus the Decimator had been in my belly for over a thousand years by now. His regeneration abilities had slowed his degradation to a crawl, but there's hardly any meat left on his bones. Even if I were to regurgitate him and allow the regeneration to happen, his mind would never recover fully. The best case scenario for him would be a complete loss of memory and faculty. Actually, given his reputation, that would be the best case scenario for everyone.

Hirgarus had tortured and murdered hundreds of thousands of mer, and the cruelty of his tortures had been more well known than his near-immortality. My advisors at the time had told me that he couldn't be stopped. I fought the urge to smile as I turned my attention back to the group approaching me. It had taken a millennia, but I had finally beat the unbeatable. Hirgarus had been known far and wide as the immortal lord of daemons, and I used him as sustenance until all that remained of his identity had been destroyed. A fate worthy of such a despicable being.

The elf with the group gestured at me, and the smell-bearer suddenly stopped. Its eyes widened in alarm as they made contact with my own. The smell became sharp with fear. It knows. A spark of fear alit my rage when I realized that this being had seen through my ruse. A potential foe, one that could destroy me if it were allowed to grow.

My anger caused my breath to quicken, and the smell suddenly became familiar to me. Gods. They were actively watching this thing, and one had even interacted with it. Would they intervene if I were to try to destroy this thing here and now? Or... Could it be that they interfered with its fate to bring it before me? Is it meant to be an ally or an assassin? There's only one real way to find out what they're planning. I opened my eyes.

The creature's skin tone changed from a slight pink to pale white, and I noted with a small measure of satisfaction that the bored children who had been annoying me earlier were now stunned. The creature's comrades were facing it, but the bald orc slowly tracked his gaze back to me. First, his face showed curiosity, then shock. A moment later, everyone except the creature was on their knees. I raised my head to look at it with both eyes.

"Why are you still standing, fool?" I asked it. "Do you not know your betters by instinct?"

A small measure of confusion managed to peek past the fear that was apparent on its face. I recalled that language had evolved over the years, and suddenly felt a pang of self-consciousness. What good is a king that no one can understand? A small smile creeped over the face of the elf that had been guiding the group.

"My lord, if I may?" he asked.

"I doubt that we will get anywhere if you do not," I said, masking my surprise at finding someone who still spoke High Drakon.

The elf stood, put his hand on the creature's shoulder and whispered something to it. The creature knelt so rapidly that I heard its knee hit the ground with what had to be a painful amount of force. My anger subsided at this show of deference, knowing now that it was not arrogance that led to such disrespect. It was either ignorance or fear, both of which can be forgiven.

"Your Royal Majesty King Yssinirath, I am your humble Regent Visilisth Oakmor. May I present to you Nick Smith, Nash Alta, and Yulk Alta," the elf said as he bowed low.

"I have just awoke and am in no mood for epithets and magniloquence, regent," I said. "You will speak plainly. What have you brought before me that reeks of godly plots and interference?"

My words caught the regent by surprise. He paused, then looked at the creature. His shock was quickly subdued, however, and he turned back to me.

"Your majesty, this is a human. He is named Nick Smith, and was found within a dungeon in a neighboring chiefdom. I know nothing of godly plots and interference, I'm afraid," he said.

"You should be," I spat, my anger flaring once again. "One does not become the subject of godly interference ignorantly. Either you are lying to me, or the human is hiding his interactions with gods from you. Likely at the behest of said gods."

"I will ask him about it, sire."

I made a circular motion with my claw to indicate that the regent should be quick with his questions. The human was hesitant to speak, but after a moment there was discussion between the two. The orc with braids appeared confused, but the bald one gave the impression that he had been granted clarification. The dwarf looked lost and alarmed during the entire conversation.

The regent asked several questions, and once the discussion was over he explained to me what he had learned. The human had been caught in an explosion caused by bandits, and lost consciousness when he used all his magic to heal his friend. This was when he had met a being that said it was occasionally called a god. I nodded as he explained that the god wanted the human to appear before me, and that I would put him on the path to returning to his world.

This piqued my interest. Not only had the god encouraged this human to appear before me, likely knowing that my curiosity would get the better of me, but it had also presumed that I would be willing to help the human in some capacity. I examined it closely, using various vision magics for a complete investigation. Everything about him is strange.

The first thing I noticed is that his magic core is completely artificial, and contains much more magic than a mortal's magic core should. Its channels are extremely efficient and lack any sort of subtlety, as well. A sorcerer's magical capabilities were often impacted by how efficient these channels are, and as such the human is likely capable of terrible acts of magic.

The next thing I noted is the amount of metal within its body. Within its skull is an object that seems to interface directly with each part of its brain. Floating through its blood, lymph, and bile are extremely small chunks of metal that seem to be moving of their own volition. After examining them closely, I realized that they are extremely small machines performing various tasks. Unlike most machines I had seen before, these are not made of iron or steel, but various precious metals for reasons undeterminable.

The final thing I determined is how different its anatomy and physiology appear to be from the mortals of this world. Some organs are shared with the orcs, others are shared with the elves and dwarves. Some have different compositions but seem to perform similar functions. Others are completely unique to the human and serve functions that are nearly unnoticeable. There is also evidence of massive amounts of surgery, but someone had managed to minimize this evidence.

"It certainly appears to be other-worldly," I told the regent. "I do not know how I would go about aiding his return to his world, though. Nor am I inclined to try, given the circumstances regarding this request."

"I must beg your forgiveness and mercy, my liege," the elf placed his forehead upon the ground. "The circumstances behind this boys presence in our realm are tragic, and it would pain me dearly to see his quest unfulfilled. I dare not pretend to know the motives or missions of the gods, nor do I presume to begin to imagine the reasons behind your disdain for them, but I cannot help but beg your grace, sire."

"You dare beg my grace with the very same epithets and magniloquence that I told you to abandon mere moments ago, boy?" I demanded with a low growl.

"Apol... I'm sorry," he replied. "This just... isn't how I imagined this would go."

Memories of the elves of old bringing me gifts and gratitude for saving them from the daemons flooded back to me. They were ecstatic whenever I would awaken from my slumber, and even host feasts to celebrate. A small stab of guilt pierced the iciness in my heart as I realized that even after several generations had passed, my people still love me.

"Very well," I sighed. "Explain the human's circumstances to me."

Regent Oakmor elaborated the reasons behind his feelings, sparing no amount of drama in his retelling. A boy, stolen away from his ailing love and transported to a strange world where he obviously does not belong, with no recollection of his relocation or knowledge of how to return. Despite the regent's garish bardic skills, I managed to feel some empathy for the human.

I had been a youngling when Bolisir went to war against the daemons and my world changed forever. I remember how lost I felt when my daily decisions went from mundane to grave in the blink of an eye. I had my parents to guide me through this transition, though. The human does not.

"I will consider it. How would my assistance be applied?" I asked.

Before Oakmor could answer, something unexpected happened.

"Um... excuse me, your majesty," Nick said. "Can you understand me now?"

Chapter 41

Nick Smith
Adventurer Level: 7
Human - American

My knee throbbed in pain while Regent Oakmor spoke to the High Dragon in a language that I couldn't understand. Oddly, though, every once in a while I would hear something that I understood. It didn't take long to put two and two together.

'Are they speaking High Drakon? The same language that was on the pods?' I asked Ten.

'Probably. What they are speaking is fairly similar to Drakon,' Ten said. 'The translation program is even triggering on some of the words, as you've likely noticed. It would seem they share root words.'

'Can you translate it?'

'No, not yet. I've already been trying to extrapolate a translation, though. We'll see how it goes.'

The regent and the dragon continued talking to each other. It wasn't hard to tell that the dragon seemed upset about something, and Oakmor looked confused. Then Oakmor turned to me.

"Nick, have you been in contact with gods?" he asked.

I looked at Yulk, Nash, and Renv. I hadn't exactly lied to them, but they're bound to be confused. Should I lie? A glance at the dragon answered that question for me. Okay, the truth then. I took a deep breath and steeled myself.

"I... think so," I said. "When we were on our way here, we were attacked by bandits. There was an explosion, and one of our friends was hurt really bad. I used a healing spell on him, but ended up using all of my magic and passing out. While I was out, I had a weird dream that I'm not sure is a dream, and there was a thing in my dream that said mortals call it a god."

"I see," Oakmor's brow furrowed. "Did it demand anything from you?"

"It didn't feel like a demand, more like a suggestion," I replied, trying not to look at Nash and Yulk. "It said that if I didn't go to see the High Dragon, I wouldn't find my way home."

"Did it say anything else? Any suggestions as to what to do when you saw King Yssinirath?"

"It said is that I needed to see the dra... King Yssinirath because some stupid mer were about to do some stupid things which would prevent me from going home, and that my path would be clear after seeing him," I answered. "Oh, it also said that other gods are watching me because I'm amusing. That's all it was able to say."

"Able to?"

"Yes, it was under a pact and had bright red chains all over it."

"Understood," Oakmor turned back to the dragon for a moment, then turned back to me. "Wait, what was the other choice? Besides seeing King Yssinirath?"

Shit.

"Well... It said that Yulk would want to see some scholars that he knows to get the words translated, but the translation wouldn't get us anywhere. It told me that he would decline an invitation to see the High Dragon, and that I would need to make sure he didn't decline the invitation."

"Ohhh," Yulk whispered.

Oakmor nodded and turned back to the dragon. The two began to speak once more, and after a few moments the ember-red eyes of the High Dragon took on a slightly pink tint and he began to look at me. It felt like he could see everything about me, and I got the distinct impression that I couldn't hide anything from him. It was an uncomfortable feeling, like someone walking into the bathroom with you and not leaving.

The two continued talking, when suddenly Oakmor prostrated. He gave a speech, and Yssinirath growled at him. After a quick back and forth, Oakmor raised his head. The king said something angrily, and Oakmor stood. He began gesturing dramatically, which was a confusing turn of events.

'Done,' Ten said. 'Applying translation patch.'

"...simply exceptional that his motives are driven by love, and love is such a rare form of motivation in the world. This is why I beg that you to aid him any way you can."

"I will consider it. How would my assistance be applied?" Yssinirath asked.

It may not be the smartest move to speak up now, but I get the feeling that the king will be less mad at an interruption than he would be at eavesdropping. I took a deep breath and gathered my nerve once again.

"Um... excuse me, your majesty," I interrupted. "Can you understand me now?"

It felt like every eye within listening distance turned to look at me. A quick glance around confirmed my feeling to be factual, and I suddenly felt very, very nervous. Like I had committed the sort of taboo that is so obvious that everyone should know not to do it.

"I can," Yssinirath said warily. "Explain."

Explain? Explain what? I looked at Oakmor, but he was completely dumbfounded and at a loss for words. The almost glowing eyes of the High Dragon narrowed at me, and I felt the sudden urge to improvise like my life depended on it. Before I could open my mouth, Ten stepped in.

'Repeat after me...'

"I have a machine in my head that translates languages, your majesty," I parroted. "It did not know High Drakon, but it knows Drakon and was able to decipher what yourself and Regent Oakmor were saying by the context of our situation and comparing the two languages in real time."

King Yssinirath took a deep breath in through its nose, which immediately made me think of all the dragons I've seen in media that breathed fire. I tensed, but the flames never came.

"Surprise after surprise," he grumbled. "Regent, tell the civilians to go on about their business. I would speak to this boy."

"Yes, sire," Oakmor bowed.

As Oakmor began telling everyone present to go back to what they were doing, which appeared to confuse the chaperon of a group of children, Yssinirath lowered his head nearer to me.

"You are trying to get back home to your ailing lover, yes?" Yssinirath asked softly.

"Yes, your highness."

"And what, pray tell, will you do if she is dead by the time you return?"

The question caught me off guard. It had been nagging at me somewhere in the back of my mind, but I had consciously avoided actually thinking about it. As if thinking about it would somehow turn it into a reality. Being directly confronted with the truth of the possibility like this made me realize that I had been acting childish, pretending that it can't happen simply because I don't want it to happen.

"I would grieve, your majesty," I answered, unable to meet his eyes.

"As one should," Yssinirath said, his head returning to where it had been. "It would be wrong of me to prevent the reunification of lovers, and it would be outright malicious of me to prevent one from mourning. I will aid you, boy."

"Thank you, sire."

"There is still the matter of how. I do not have the ability to transport you to your world, nor am I aware of any means to do so."

"We have some writings. They were found on the altar that I was resting on, and we believe they're written in High Drakon, or a language that is similar to High Drakon," I explained.

I turned to Yulk and whispered for him to show Yssinirath the writings. He didn't hesitate to reach into his robe, but gave me a look indicating that he had many, many questions while he did so. Yssinirath leaned forward to study the rubbings that Yulk had done.

"These do not say much, but their context is grim," Yssinirath explained. "The first five symbols appear to be options. Close, Open, Begin, End, and Destroy. Then there are four directional indicators with the word 'select' in the center."

"That's not much to go on," I said. "We already knew that they were experimenting on me, your highness."

"Indeed, but I now see why the gods sent you to me," his face twisted into what could be called a grin. "Back in my youth, my father tasked me with ridding these lands of a plague. A cult of anonymous individuals who were kidnapping, torturing, and dismembering members of our citizenry. The investigators at the time believed the torture to be experimentation, and the purpose of the dismemberment was to hide their findings and mask their trail. The last time I saw the final symbol on this paper, it was emblazoned upon on their robes."

My heart skipped a beat. Is this it?

"Who were they?"

"We weren't able to find out. Whenever one of their members was captured or killed, they would be incinerated from within by a flame that could not be quenched until they were but ash. Adventurers that were tasked with tracking them were able to discover their hideouts within Bolisir, and my father sent me forth to eliminate them from the land. They were quite magically adept, but no match for even a fledgling High Dragon," he explained with a hint of pride in his voice. "I flew from hideout to hideout, killing as I went. I was even careful to preserve as much as possible, yet the hideouts still did not yield many clues."

"How long ago was this, your highness?" I asked, hoping we could investigate one of these hideouts.

"I eliminated the cult from Bolisir long before the daemons invaded, but they remained a problem in other kingdoms. Once the daemons invaded all cult activity ceased, and they were not heard from during the entirety of the daemon occupation. Some claimed that it was the cult that brought the daemons to our world. Others believed that whatever the cult was researching was a threat to the daemons, and the daemons invaded our world to force them to cease and desist."

I paused for a moment to digest this information. A nameless cult that may have had some something to do with the daemonic invasion had somehow kidnapped me from my world and performed experiments on me? Maybe to make me fight for or against the daemons? That definitely sounds like it could be the plot of an isekai, but why would the cult go to such lengths? Wouldn't it be easier to use their own members?

"Sire, do you know anything else about this cult?" I asked.

"I do," Yssinirath said with another grin. "They were most disruptive in a kingdom to the west, ruled by dwarves. At the time, I believed that this was because their leadership had taken refuge there, but my father wisely forbade me from interfering in the affairs of other kingdoms. I made certain that no trace of the cult remained in Bolisir, but it's likely that other kingdoms were less thorough. As a matter of fact, your existence is evidence of that being the case."

"Psst," Yulk whispered. "What's going on?"

I gave Yulk a brief explanation as I thought about what Yssinirath had told me. The mighty High Dragon wasn't going to be able to get me home directly, but he had at least pointed me in a direction. West, to the dwarven kingdom. A small blossom of hope grew within me. The dwarven kingdom has to have something, why else would the creepy god thing have sent me to the dragon?

"The dwarven kingdom to the west would probably be the Empire of Calkuti. It predates the daemonic invasion, and even the Kingdom of Bolisir," Yulk explained.

I nodded and turned back to Yssinirath, "Are you meaning the Empire of Calkuti, your highness?"

"Calkuti is the name, but it was not an empire before the daemons. What is its current status, Regent?" Yssinirath asked.

"It's thriving, milord," Oakmor replied, turning his attention away from a growing flock of civilians.

"Of course the pesky little buggers yet persist," the High Dragon grumbled.

"And... We have a contractual alliance with them, your highness."

Yssinirath's face contorted in disgust and Regent Oakmor tried to hide a smile. I guess the High Dragon isn't a fan of dwarves. I glanced at Renv, glad that he couldn't understand the conversation. I was met with a look of concern and confusion.

"Allied with them?" Yssinirath nearly spat. "What a foolish regent we have. Tell me, Oakmor, what fancy baubles and little luxuries did the dwarven royal family provide, that you and your kin may offer your backs as sheaths for their daggers?"

"The dwarven royal line died out, sire. They fell in battle against the orcs shortly after you entered your slumber. The current ruler, Emperor Jak, is of the Norev family, and though he is crass at times, he is much less prone to subterfuge and dishonesty than the royal family was."

Yssinirath frowned, but I looked at Oakmor in a new light. I thought he was a whimsical and reluctant regent, but he had done his homework. He seemed to know the High Dragon's blind spots and exactly how to compensate for them.

"Fine," Yssinirath sighed. "I give the alliance my blessing, then. Returning to the original matter, Nick, you will need to seek more information on this cult in Calkuti. I hope you are more successful in your investigation than others were in the past. I grow weary, and as such will return to my slumber."

"If I may, your highness," Oakmor interjected. "We have had quite a long while to come up with a potential solution to the daemon within you."

"Oh?" Yssinirath asked, warily eyeing Oakmor.

"If we were to encase the remains in concrete it would prevent the daemon from moving. Then we could load the resulting concrete block aboard a ship. The ship would sail out into the ocean as far as it can, and the crew will dump the block into the water. The block will sink, and the pressure from the water will make it much more difficult for the daemon to escape his new prison."

"And how, pray tell, would we get the daemon out of my stomach?" the High Dragon asked, eyeing the ever-growing group surrounding us.

Oakmor couldn't help but grin as he said, "I do believe a simple extrusion will suffice, your majesty."

Yssinirath's growl shook the ground beneath us.

Chapter 42

Nick Smith
Adventurer Level: 7
Human - American

"You want me to VOMIT in PUBLIC?" Yssinirath hissed.

"Sire, we can be mindful of your dignity whilst you are ejecting the daemon," Oakmor said, unable to hide his grin. "We can set up curtains to mask what is being done."

"Everyone will still know what happened!"

"At least it isn't out the other end, your majesty," I added, trying to be helpful.

The High Dragon's furious eyes focused on me and I felt my blood freeze again. I am an idiot, and silently vowed to keep my mouth shut as often as possible.

"High Dragons do NOT defecate, boy," he hissed.

"Really?" I asked incredulously, unable to keep my vow.

"You think I lie? We are smart enough to take care with what we eat, and our bodies use every last bit of what we consume," Yssinirath explained.

"This is true, Nick," Oakmor said. "The purpose of a High Dragon's intestinal tract appears to be for flatulence, not defecation."

Yssinirath slowly turned his attention from me to the regent.

"If there is a single person in our ever-growing audience that can understand what you just said, I will bite you in half."

"Apologies, your highness. I meant only to educate, not offend," Oakmor said as he lowered his head, masking that his grin had widened.

"Enough," Yssinirath growled. "Truth be told, I would enjoy being free of this burden."

"I will make the arrangements, your majesty."

Oakmor bowed deeply, then began explaining the plan to some of the gathered people. As he began to walk away, Yulk scooched over to me and gave me a nudge.

"Nick," he said. "Could you ask the King if he would mind answering some questions?"

"What?" I asked, thinking I may have hallucinated what I had just heard.

"I want to ask the King some questions. This is an amazingly rare opportunity," he explained. "Not only to interview a High Dragon, but to interview one with a first-hand account of the Cataclysm Wars."

"I... wait, don't you want to know HOW I can talk to him?"

"With Ten, obviously," Nash interrupted. "Yulk's right, Nick. As long as you're polite with the questions, you've got nothing to be afraid of."

Easy for him to say. Yssinirath was watching Oakmor, impatiently tapping one of his claws on the ground. The claw in question is easily as big as I am, and I could feel the ground shake slightly with each tap. I had also noticed that when he had grinned earlier, his teeth were the size of my head. There is absolutely no doubt in my mind that the High Dragon could erase everyone present if he so wished.

"Please, Nick," Yulk pouted.

It was a ridiculous sight that immediately pulled me out of the anxiety spiral I had been swirling down. He pushed his lower lip forward, and it caught on his teeth. The lip looked kind of like one of those seashell soap holders. I smiled and shook my head.

"Fine, but if we die I want it on the record that it's your fault," I told him, then looked up at the dragon. "Excuse me, your highness."

"What is it?" Yssinirath met my gaze.

"Would you mind if we asked you some questions? This orc, Yulk, would like to know more about the Cataclysm Wars."

The dragon's brow furrowed, then he sighed through his nose.

"So be it. Ask your questions."

"He said yes," I told Yulk.

"Excellent. Ask him what started the war, and if he knows how the daemons entered our world."

I nodded and repeated the question to Yssinirath, settling into the role of interpreter.

"The daemonic invasion was the cause of the war," Yssinirath chuckled. "Though, many nations were already at war before their invasion. The daemons entered our world through vast portals, though how these portals were created eludes me. I do know that these portals worked both ways, though, as the daemons brought many mer back through with them."

"Who made the wastes?"

"Multiple parties. Daemons, anyels, and mer sorcerers fought viciously to destroy each other's forces, and the mass corruption of nature was the result. Those that were responsible cared little for the environment, or even the safety of their own soldiers."

"What about the monsters? Who created them?"

"The daemons created many monsters to destroy the mer, bastardizing nature's own creations in the process. The mer quickly followed suit, justifying their actions as a means to survive the onslaught. Many of the monsters predate the war, though, and nobody knew where they originate."

"Why did the daemons invade?"

"They did not stop to explain themselves," Yssinirath chuckled. "If a scholar of this age does not know their reasons, then they must truly be lost to time."

"What about the daemon in your belly?" I asked before I told Yulk what the king had said. "Wouldn't he know?"

"He is little more than bone. His mind was destroyed by the acids within me long ago," Yssinirath shook his head. "He wouldn't even know his own name by now."

I informed Yulk of the King's response to both of our questions. He nodded and continued his questions.

"How long have you ruled over Bolisir?"

"Hmm..." Yssinirath paused. "One moment."

The King hissed unintelligibly and his eyes flashed blue for an instant. Whatever just happened caused his brows to rise and his slight smile to fade.

"By Bogglerath, it has been eighteen thousand, seven hundred eighty-two years. It doesn't feel like nearly that long. Apparently time flies more than I do," he said with a sigh.

"Bogglerath?" I asked.

"The first High Dragon. She was given intelligence as a reward for defeating a god in combat, and became the mother of all High Dragons. She has become somewhat deified, obviously."

As I explained this to Yulk, elves and gnomes started bringing supplies to enact Regent Oakmor's plan. Yulk reminded me of what Joni had said about the Prignira Account of the Cataclysm Wars and asked me to verify it with King Yssinirath.

"I am unfamiliar with Prignira, but there was an underground dwarven kingdom named Masseura on the southern continent. The events themselves are accurate, though I know not of any daemonic conspiracies prior to the war. Perhaps they are referring to the actions of the cult. Or it could be a convenient cover-up for some of the abysmal actions committed by the various royal families of the time."

"What kind of actions?"

"Before the daemons invaded, the lands were at war.

Bolisir was one of the only nations that managed to stay out of it, but my father was wise and had spies in various nations that may have tried something. We received word of terrible state-sanctioned experiments, all in the name of one-upping their neighbors on the field of battle. This is one of the main reasons we reacted to the cult in the way that we did, and why we didn't chase them over our borders. We suspected that they may have had royal backing, and crossing over our borders may have dragged us into wars that we wanted no part of."

Yulk appeared deep in thought as I explained what the High Dragon had said. As I finished, Regent Oakmor approached us.

"We are nearly ready, your majesty," he said as a group of gnomes carried a large, cube-shaped container past him.

The gnomes lowered the steel container to the ground with a thud, and two groups of elves approached. One group had bags of what appeared to be powdered concrete mix, and began pouring them into the container. The other group began to set up tall curtains around Yssinirath. The High Dragon eyed them warily, but did not interfere.

Another group of elves carrying water and oars replaced the group with the concrete powder at the container. They added the water to the powder and began to stir it. We watched as the groups took turns at the container, adding more powder and water until it was nearly filled. Once they were finished, Oakmor gestured to the group around the curtains, and they drew the curtains around the High Dragon.

"Your majesty, please do not regurgitate directly into the box. Your, for lack of a better phrase, stomach juices will likely be detrimental to the concrete," Oakmor explained.

"Regurgitate. What a disgusting word," Yssinirath hissed. "Fine."

His head lowered beneath the curtain, and after a moment a sound that can only be described as disturbingly slimy made its way to our ears. I had expected to hear the sound of retching, but the sound I heard instead nearly made me gag. Like... forcing a bowling ball covered in not-quite done jelly through a hose or something. I looked at my companions and could tell the sound had the same impact on them. Another moment later, Yssinirath's head appeared above the curtain.

"It is done," he said.

"Thank you, your majesty," Oakmor gestured to a group of gnomes who were carrying a steel square with small holes in it.

The elves dragged the curtain back and the gnomes put the steel square on top of the container, hammering it down to form a lid. The container began to make a sloshing sound, and some concrete splashed out of the holes in the top.

"Oh, already?" Oakmor said, sounding flabbergasted. "Cure the concrete, quickly."

Four elves walked up to the container and began casting various spells. The sloshing ceased with a stark crack, and the elves nodded to Oakmor. One of the gnomes walked up, shaking his head.

"I think he might've moved around and weakened the concrete, sir," the gnome reported. "That crack wasn't a good sound."

"That's alright, we'll just leave the cube in the container," the regent rubbed his chin. "Maybe we'll have a smith weld some bars on it just to be sure."

"Yes, your hi... Uh... Lord Regent," the gnome said, looking at King Yssinirath. "Gonna take some getting used to."

"Not all all, my good mer," Oakmor said with a grin. "Take the container to Horav's smithy. He's got plenty of steel scrap to use as bracing. Let him know that we want the cube to never open again."

The gnome nodded and started giving orders to his crew. They, along with some help from the elves, managed to get the steel cube into a cart and started transporting it away. Oakmor watched them for a moment, and then turned back to the High Dragon.

"Your highness," he bowed. "This is the perfect occasion for a feast. Will you permit us to celebrate your return to the throne?"

"Certainly," Yssinirath said. "However, I require some calisthenics. It has been far too long since I've last stretched my wings. Feel free to celebrate without me, I will rejoin you soon."

The High Dragon stood, causing several shocked gasps from the surrounding crowd. I thought he was huge while he was laying down, but his true height was mind-boggling. He stretched his neck and limbs, and his bones cracked like trees in a storm.

Finally, he spread his mighty wings. The white skin on his wings featured blue veins that seemed to form a sort of symbol. Before I could get a good look at it, though, the wings flapped and sent a gust of air at us that nearly sent me sprawling. I managed to see a gnome fly back a foot or two, and when I turned back to the High Dragon, he was gone.

I looked to the sky to see if I could spot him, but he had disappeared with a frightening speed. The implications of how quickly he had moved set in, and I couldn't help but shudder a little. Big things shouldn't be able to move that fast. It's unnatural.

"Well, what a fantastic day! Hopefully I can retire soon," Regent Oakmor smiled.

"I doubt it, Lord Regent," a nearby elf said. "You're the only one that understands the king."

"Oh... shit."

Chapter 43

Grum Ormyar
Adventurer Level: N/A
Orc - Blurpan

"How many did we lose this time?" I asked coldly.

"Four," Harmi answered. "Two dead, two captured."

I let out a sigh as I stared out over the field that the enemy stood in. Their smug eyes peered back at me from over their shields, their spear-tips glinting in the sunlight. It was obvious that this group wasn't going to follow us, either. If we had been able to get them in the trees, we would have been able to disrupt their lines and force our way through their formation. Whoever is leading them must have figured out our intentions, though.

"Did THEY lose any this time?" I asked.

"Yeah," he replied tersely. "Got a couple of lucky blows in. Managed to kill two of the bastards."

Harmi crossed his arms and spat on the ground. He's much less pleased with our situation than I am. Despite growing up together and being close friends, Harmi and I are polar opposites. I'm an artist, he's a warrior. I write poetry, tenderly carve statues, and try desperately to capture the beauty that I see in the world with paint. He likes to hit people with great amounts of force.

If it weren't for the sake of tradition, he would likely be leading this defensive campaign. It isn't as if I would mind, I'd much rather be at home sweating over a block o' rock. Unfortunately, I am the son of a

Great Chief, and with that comes duty and responsibility. Irksome, surely, but it is what it is.

"I don't suppose we've managed to track down any high-level mages?"

"No."

"What about the..."

"Archers didn't have many arrows," Harmi interrupted. "They're out. Fletchers are makin' more."

"Did we find stones?"

"Yeah. Threw 'em. Hit shields, not skulls."

"Well," I shrugged, "I'm out of ideas."

"Me too."

Any weapons we could craft that would be capable of penetrating their defensive lines would either take too long to make or be too unwieldy. Blurpus only has the one smith, who is also the fletcher, and she's getting on in years. Internally, the darkest part of me screamed in frustration at my inability to slaughter the enemy, cursing the vast open fields of Blurpus that I used to love playing in as a child. Externally, I sighed again.

"Tenth time, I guess," I said after a moment.

"Yeah, but at least they aren't advancing much," Harmi replied.

I looked at him, then back to the drow. Despite my mask of apathy, Harmi could tell how bothered I am by all this. We have had to fall back ten times, and the only thing that has been interrupting the enemy's advance is the damned terrain. They weren't falling for any of our traps or taunts, either.

When the bastards invaded last year, they were so incompetent that I hadn't even had to take to the field. They had practically ran straight into our axes. Now, they're being far too damned careful. The bloodthirsty drow of the past had been magically given an even temper and wouldn't put a single toe out of line.

"Fine. There isn't much we can do here," I shook my head. "Call for a retr..."

A familiar sound permeated the air. It was my father's horn, but I barely recognized tone it gave. It was a tone that had never really applied to me or any group I had led before, and one that definitely shouldn't apply here. Had his trip to see Ulurmak finally forced senility upon him? Harmi and I met eyes, our mouths agape in stupefaction.

"The hells was that?" I turned toward the sound.

"Cavalry charge?" Harmi asked. "We lent the hnarses to Yirna, though. How can they be back already?"

Nevertheless, the sound of hooves began to fill the air. I turned back to the drow, who appeared considerably less smug than they had a moment ago. From their right flank five hnarses with orcs riding them burst through the trees. I got a closer look at the riders and my jaw dropped even further.

One would expect cavalry to have a lance, hammer, or even a sword. Four of the riders were completely unarmed, and the fifth had a hunk of wood with a ball on one end. As I was trying to figure out what the hells was happening, one of the riders lifted their hand and launched a ball of fire directly into the drow. The enemy had managed to bring their shields to bear, but the fire still got a couple of them. The rider with the stick pointed it at the drow and an arrow made of wind blew through their ranks.

"Mages on hnarse-back," I whispered.

Instead of charging directly into the drow formation like traditional cavalry would, the riders began to circle them, launching spells rapidly. The drow were spinning around wildly, trying desperate to use their shields to block the various magics that were being cast upon them. Despite my shock at the situation unfolding before me, it didn't take long for me to put two and two together. The drow formation was done for.

"CHARGE!" I shouted, pulling my axe from my belt and holding it high.

My orcs snapped out of their shock and began to echo my cry. We ran at the panicking drow with our weapons high, screaming our blood-thirst as we went. The monster in me will forever cherish the looks of pure terror on their face as they realized they were now too far apart from each other to prevent our assault from ripping them to shreds.

The first drow I encountered raised his shield and spear, but it was useless. Without the formation to protect him, I easily brushed aside the spear and yanked his shield out of the way. My axe met his skull, splitting it and ending his life. Before he even crumpled to the ground I was onto the next one. Then the next, and the next, and the next.

Drow began to drop their spears and shields and try to run, but the cavalry cut them off. One more drow lost their life before they threw their hands in the air and begged for mercy. The fight was over, and we had finally won.

I shouted the order to capture them and looked at my axe. It, my arm, and a good portion of my shirt was drenched in blood. I felt my stomach twist in revulsion, the gentler part of me wanted to weep and scrub myself clean. A small fear rose within me. Will the blood on my hands stain my art?

I felt raindrops patter against my skin, and I looked to the sky. I cannot weep in front of the soldiers, but the sky wept in my stead. A small, sad smile made its way onto my face at this realization. As the sky opened up, helping clean some of the blood off of me, I felt eyes settle on me. I glanced around at my orcs, and they were looking at me expectantly. Oh, right.

"VICTORY!" I shouted, raising my axe to the mournful sky.

They shouted and raised their axes as well, freeing me from their gaze. The soft thuds of a hnarse's hooves came from behind me, and I turned to see Great Chief Tormon, my father. His eyes met mine with a mixture of sadness and pride. He knew of my gentle disposition and wished the best for me, but he couldn't help but be proud of how well I carried out my duties. Or maybe I'm just imagining things.

"Grum, my boy," his expression changed to a grin. "I've brought a little help."

"Your talent for understatement greatly exceeds any of my own talents, father," I laughed, putting on my mask. "A little help? You brought us this victory."

"I can only take partial credit. The High Chief moved

quickly to make this possible," he gestured to the mounted mages and laughed. "Clever bastard. Remind me to never pick a fight with Ulurmak."

"There are a great many reasons that we won't be doing that," I shook my head with a grin.

Someone whistled, and I looked around and saw one of my orcs standing next to the freshly tied drow. He pointed at the prisoners and raised an eyebrow.

"Search them for concealed weapons, then take them to camp," I shouted. "If they try to resist or run, cut them down and leave them where they lay."

"You wish to remain out here?" my father asked. "These are all the mounted mages we have right now, you know."

This was a good point. Everything I had discovered about the drow commander screamed of someone with a legendary case of narcissism. We had destroyed one of his units, and he had obviously worked hard on their training, so it was likely that he wouldn't take that very well. This position was going to receive a visit by many more drow.

"No, actually. I don't," I sighed. "Alright everyone! Pack it up! We're heading back to camp."

"What do we do with the bodies?" Harmi asked as he approached.

"Leave them for the forest or their comrades," I shrugged. "We don't know their burial rites."

"Can't we check their pockets?" one of the soldiers asked.

"No," my father said. "Not a damn one of you need the coinage badly enough to invite the ill-fortune you get from robbing the dead. I pay you better than that."

The soldier looked properly chastised, and my father turned back to me.

"My trip was quite eventful. Let's hurry to camp so we can talk about what comes next."

I nodded and gave the proper orders. The drow were tied together and had their pockets, shoes, and belts checked for anything sharp or poisonous. Half of my soldiers formed up in front of the drow, and the rest formed up behind them. I led the ones in front, and Harmi led the ones in the rear.

As I gave the order to march, my father and the mounted mages formed up on either side of the drow. The rain began to soften the ground somewhat, but despite this we managed to make good time. In my youth I had made a name for myself by running great distances for fun. Even so, the soft terrain and water in my boots was playing hell on my feet and legs. Half a day passed before the camp was finally in sight.

"Fuckin' finally," one of the soldiers behind me muttered.

"Agreed. Halt!" I shouted. "Secure the prisoners and tend to your gear!"

My father rode up to me as the soldiers began to perform their tasks. He dismounted and passed his hnarse off to a nearby soldier, who also took the reins for some of the mages. The rest of the mages passed their hnarses off to other soldiers. As Harmi approached us, I gestured to my command tent, and we all went inside.

I breathed a sigh of relief as I took my seat and kicked off my boots to let my feet dry. My father and Harmi did the same, but the mages just stood there nervously. I massaged my sore calves as my father began telling me of his trip. I listened in awe as he explained the creation of a mage cavalry and Ulurmak's idea about a magic academy.

"I was held up at the city gates, and these five caught up to me," he explained. "They were sent by the Adventurer's Guild to join me. The High Chief works damn quick, it seems."

"So there's going to be more on the way, Great Chief?" Harmi asked.

"So I've been led to believe," my father laughed. "Ulurmak's not much of a liar, so I've got no reason to doubt him."

"What kind of counter-measures do you think the drow will come up with?" I asked.

"You would know better than I would, my boy. But... Ulurmak seems to think that this invasion has vampiric backing."

"Vampires?"

"Yes, and I'm inclined to agree with him. There's too much that's fishy about what they're doing and how they're doing it. It practically screams bloodsucker involvement."

I gave Harmi a doubtful look, and he shrugged in response. We don't like disagreeing with my father, but he's practically fanatical in his hatred of vampires.

He has a borderline paranoid hatred of them, and it's likely that even if High Chief Ulurmak completely misread the situation my father would still firmly believe that vampires were involved simply because things haven't been going well for us.

"You don't believe me," my father crossed his arms sternly.

"Well, there's one way to find out for sure," I sighed as I pulled my still-damp boots back on. "I'll be back."

I left my command tent and looked for the tent that the prisoners were being kept in. The rain was pouring heavier than it had been previously, and the ground had turned into an uncomfortable mud. To my horror, I found the prisoners shivering in the rain, tied to a stake in the ground. Thankfully, my soldiers weren't dumb enough to leave them unguarded, so I grabbed the nearest guard by the shoulder.

"What is this?" I demanded.

"The prisoners, sir," the soldier answered with an expression of bewilderment.

"Why are they outdoors in this weather?"

"We... uh... I think it's cuz we don't have somewhere to put them, sir."

"All that is securing them is a stake. In the MUD," I whispered.

"Yeah, but we've got swords, sir."

"Swords that would let them cut their bonds if were they to overpower you. Move them to the mess tent. Now."

"Y-yes sir!"

The guard went to work explaining my order to the other guards, and they began to move the prisoners out of the rain. As they started to march, I noticed that one of the drow had clothing that was of a higher quality than the rest of them, and on that clothing was a small emblem on the breast.

"Not that one," I said, pointing at the potential commander. "He's coming with me."

The guards didn't argue, and after a bit of shuffling they managed to separate him from the rest of the drow. The prisoner looked concerned, but didn't protest as I grabbed his rope and dragged him back to the command tent. All eyes immediately turned to the drow as we entered the tent.

"Oh. Yeah, that'll do it," my father nodded his approval.

I tied the prisoner to an extra chair, gestured to Harmi, then took my seat and once again removed my boots. Harmi stood next to the bound drow and crossed his arms, prepared to loosen the drow's tongue at a moment's notice. I let my feet dry as my father and Harmi began asking the prisoner some standard questions.

Harmi's intimidation turned out to be unnecessary, as the drow was very forthcoming with his testimony. He confirmed his rank, told us of his patrol route and orders, and even told us what he knew of the patrol routes of the rest of the drow army. There was absolutely no hesitation until my father brought up vampires. The drow seemed perplexed by the question, and denied seeing any sort of vampires or brood.

The conversation didn't go much of anywhere until Harmi asked about what had happened to the orcish prisoners. The drow explained that they were being used to make a storeroom, and when asked about their health he admitted that he hadn't seem them since they were handed over. This raised red flags, and we asked many follow-up questions that didn't have concrete answers. Finally, the interrogation was over and Harmi took the enemy commander back to the rest of the prisoners.

"I don't get it," I said. "I thought vampires have free will. Why would they want to turn orcs into vamps when those orcs hate drow?"

"Vampires don't start off with free will," my father explained. "Not really. For the first few years, the magical being within the vampire is somewhat enthralled by the vampiric sire that allowed it to enter the body. Sometimes the victim can override the... enhanced persuasion that their sire has over them, but veteran vampires can usually tell who has this capability. At least, that's how Eyivas Tolroth explained it to me."

My father very much enjoys name-dropping Eyivas Tolroth every chance he gets. Tolroth was a vampire who hunted other vampires, and had been instrumental in the drow rebellion. As far as I can tell, he's the only vampire that my father didn't completely hate.

Tolroth and my father had slain many vampire covens over the years, before Tolroth was killed by a dragon. Tolroth was known for mocking his opponents with a skillful application of gargalesis during fights. But as it turns out, dragons are a little faster than most and really don't appreciate being tickled.

"Okay, I'll admit that things are sounding suspicious. So you're thinking that the prisoners they've taken are being converted into vampires?" I asked.

"Yes," he replied coldly. "And if we don't do something to stop them, we're going to end up having to fight an army of orcish vampires."

A deep frown settled over my face. Both orcs and vampires are known for being sturdy opponents. A combination of the two would definitely be hard to deal with. A suppressive feeling began to take hold in my chest.

Why is it that just when things start to look up, something terrible happens to be waiting just around the corner?

Chapter 44

Yulk Alta
Adventurer Level: 7
Orc - Nulevan

It didn't take long for the feasting to get under way. Gnomes, dwarves, elves, and orcs brought various things out of the tree-buildings and set up stalls, which almost immediately began serving drinks and cooking food. Watching a city gather together and feast without any preparation or planning is quite the novel experience. It almost seemed practiced.

"Hey guys," Nick said, tearing my attention away from the various stalls popping up. "I'm sorry that I wasn't honest with you earlier."

"You did what you had to do, right?" I asked with a knowing smile.

"Y-yeah."

"Then there's no need for an apology."

"Well... I mean I could have taken you two aside and explained what was going on," he rubbed his neck.

"Oh, so you've learned from this experience as well?" I asked with a laugh. "Even better!"

I had figured that there was a reason he wasn't forthcoming regarding the divine interference in our journey. Either the supposed deity had flat out told him not to be, or he didn't want people to think he was some sort of religious nut. Given that he is likely unaware of the atrocities committed by aforementioned fanatics and how they are subsequently treated, it's possible the divine interference came with a warning. Nick was still having trouble making eye contact, though.

"Listen, boy," Nash interrupted. "I can't speak for other species, but for orcs apologies are for victims. While it would have been nice to be in the know, I don't feel like a victim for being excluded. Do you, Yulk?"

"Nope," I shook my head.

"I, for one, feel a little victimized," Renv said with a laugh. "I'm not biased or anything. I wouldn't have treated you any different, even if you'd let me know I was traveling with a touched."

"A touched?" Nick asked.

"Yes, someone who is touched by the Gods," I explained. "Or, in a more colloquial sense, someone who is touched in the head with hallucinations and delusions of grandeur. That's probably not what Renv meant, though."

"It definitely isn't," Renv said, raising his hands defensively.

We all had a chuckle and started touring the festivities. Nick began asking about some of the local food, and Renv acted as a guide. Nash and I waited patiently for Nick and Renv to fill a platter before wandering over to a stall that was serving something that we could eat.

The smell of fried meat hit my nostrils like a club, and I had to swallow my mouth's immediate reaction. Nash's stomach growled as we grabbed our own platters to fill. Once we were finished, the four of us found some refreshment and took a seat on the ground nearby.

As I bit into my meal, I noticed people staring at Nick with shocked expressions. He had was eating both meat and vegetables simultaneously. I chuckled as I fondly remembered my own reaction at learning of his omnivorousness. I swallowed my mouthful and took a swig of my sparkling beverage, enjoying the tingling feeling that it applied to my somewhat parched throat.

"Is that Yulk I see?" a familiar voice asked from behind me.

All four of us turned to look at the newcomer. Before us stood an elven woman with bright orange hair, blue-green eyes, and a youthful face. This youthfulness was deceitful, for while she appeared no more than twenty years old, I knew her age to be at least in the triple digits.

"Olmira! How are you?" I asked with a grin.

"Flummoxed!" she replied with an exaggerated sigh. "I receive word that an unknown sentient species is visiting the regent, then our True King awakens, and finally I run into my former student out of the blue. What a day!"

"I wouldn't say you ran into me out of the blue. The reason we originally came here was to have you help us determine the origin of Nick, the unknown sentient species in question," I gestured at the boy for dramatic effect. "However, King Yssinirath appears to have stolen this job from you."

"Oh, that's a shame," She casually turned to look at Nick, and froze once she realized what she was looking at.

Olmira the Eternal is extremely intelligent, but she is not without her faults. The reason she exiled herself to a tower was mostly due to her lack of social grace, which is caused directly by her lack of situational awareness. If she was reading a book in a room that was on fire, she likely wouldn't notice the fire until the book was no longer legible.

It occurred to me that her lack of situational awareness would make it nearly impossible for her to accidentally notice me, which means she had lied about running into me out of the blue. She must have been looking for me, which means she had been looking forward to seeing me again. Likely because she knows me well enough to know that whatever I would need her help with would be quite intellectually stimulating.

"Hmm..." Olmira said as she leaned toward Nick.

"H-hi," he said, leaning away slightly.

"Was that speech?" she absentmindedly asked while studying the boy intently.

"It was. Did you think that I named him Nick?" I laughed. "He can talk, walk, and fight."

"He? Very well, why does he have a platter with plants and meat?"

"Because he needs to eat a mixture of both to maintain optimum health. He's an omnivore."

Olmira asked several more questions about Nick, which I delightfully answered. Nick remained quiet and nervous throughout this exchange, which I found a tad confusing. I would understand if he was flustered, I'm told Olmira is quite conventionally attractive, but his reaction was more akin to a barely contained flight or fight response.

"I don't think she's going to bite you, boy," Nash interrupted.

Oh. Right.

"Ah, yes, my apologies... Nick," Olmira said, standing straight once again. "I see you are aware that I am a vampire."

"He's been briefed," I laughed. "Interestingly, in his world all of the species of our world are detailed in legends, but are considered quite fictional. Vampires, as well."

Olmira's eyes brightened, but before we could begin discussing the implications of this, Regent Oakmor approached us. He had run off earlier, presumably to inform people of the feast, and was now looking a tad tired.

"There you are," he grinned. "I hope you're enjoying Bolisir's hospitality?"

"Yes, sir," Nash replied.

"Excellent," the regent knelt next to us. "Now, from my understanding the original purpose of your visit was to deliver the missive from High Chief Ulurmak and to investigate Nick, yes?"

"Quite so, your majesty," I said.

"Having accomplished these tasks, have you put any thought into when you're going back?"

"Not yet, sire, but we were asked to return as soon as we can."

"As soon as you can... Wonderful!" Oakmor clapped his hands and stood. "The crux of your business here has been concluded, so allow me to brief you on a situation that's developing. To the north there is a university. Within the walls of this university, there are several professors and students who have been studying High Drakon. I have sent word to them that their services are needed here, because I am the only one who can speak High Drakon. Aside from Nick, of course."

We all nodded, and a cursory glance around told me that Nick and I were the only ones who were able to predict what Oakmor's thinking. Nick's face was carefully neutral, which almost made me grin.

"How far away is this university, sir?" Nick asked.

"About three weeks by cart," Oakmor's grin widened. "Which brings me to our problem. I will be quite busy ensuring a proper transition of power between myself and King Yssinirath, and won't have much time to act as his translator. As such, Nick, I formally request that you remain in Bolisir to help me translate until the translators from the university arrive."

A period of awkward silence followed.

"You want us to stay here for three weeks?" Nick finally asked.

"Well... just you, but I assume you're a package deal. Of course, you'll be paid for your services. We can count your brothers as your staff, and whoever else you'd like as an aide," he said, eyeing Renv. "You'll be paying them out of your pocket, though."

"How much?"

"One gold per day."

Nash let out a low whistle, which ended abruptly as we turned to stare at him. Nick then gave me a look as if asking for guidance. I took a moment to think it out.

Our original goal was to get Oakmor to send reinforcements to Ulurmak, which are either on their way or soon to be so. We also woke the High Dragon and received his aid in determining what to do next. While I do want to get on with the next leg of our journey, one gold per day for a minimum of three weeks is twenty one gold, which is not a paltry sum even when split among four people.

There is the matter of Imlor, but even if he joins us we'll still be making quite a bit of money. It would also help ensure that his business stays afloat and he doesn't have to travel again once we get back to Kirkena. This is likely also part of the path that Nick's dream-visitor put us on. Unable to think of a good reason to decline, I gave Nick a small nod.

"Would two gold be too much to ask, your majesty?" Nick asked with a buttery tone.

Heads turned toward Nick so quickly that I swear I heard Nash's neck crack.

The regent laughed heartily and replied, "It would, but I can do one gold and fifty silver per day. But only because I enjoy your company."

"Thank you, your majesty," Nick said with a bow of his head. "It is my honor to serve."

"I'm sure," Oakmor chuckled once more.

The discussion was concluded by a massive gust of wind, the sound of titanic wings flapping, and a ground shuddering thud. King Yssinirath had returned, and was standing tall upon the hill on which he had been slumbering for centuries. The sunset caused his white scales to glimmer with shades of purple, orange, and pink. One couldn't help but be transfixed. The mighty dragon looked around until he spotted Oakmor, and growled something in High Drakon. The regent gave us a nod and quickly strode over to the King.

"He looks much bigger now that he's awake, doesn't he?" Olmira asked with wonder in her voice.

"That he bloody does," Renv said quietly.

"H-hello everyone," Imlor said as he strolled up. "I guess the unloaders weren't full of it, after all."

"Hi Imlor," Nick said with a wave. "Got something to ask you."

"You do?"

Nick's explanation brought Imlor up to speed on what had happened with the dragon, including his dream about the god. The gnome's mouth didn't close until Nick mentioned the Regent's offer.

"One and a half gold per day for three weeks or so?" Imlor asked, ignoring the uncomfortable subjects at hand.

"Yep," Nick replied. "An even split, five ways."

"Nah," Renv interjected. "Split it four ways. I'm

already pretty wealthy and happy to help where I can. Just don't tell my uncle or he'll box the ears right off my skull."

"You sure?" Nick asked.

"Yeah, doesn't feel right to take your money when I won't be giving you much in return. That's bad business, in my opinion."

"Alright. Well, what do you think, Imlor? Will you be willing to stay here and be our ride back?"

"It's a very generous offer," Imlor said, wringing his hands. "Okay. Yes. I'll send word to my family to let them know that I'm okay and why I've been delayed."

"Thank you, Imlor," Nick said.

Imlor nodded and walked back the way he came.

"I really should get back to my lab," Olmira said. "Come visit me sometime, Yulk. Your mind is a precious resource that I'd love to put to use."

"Certainly," I smiled at her.

"You can bring Nick along as well, if you can drag him away from the regent," she laughed as she turned and waved. "See you soon!"

I waved back at her, and turned back to my meal. The wind had blown some dirt onto it, but I'm not too picky. I brushed the dust off and took another bite. The taste remained the same, but now the crunch of the fried meat was accompanied by a somewhat gritty texture. Still better than unseasoned road jerky, though.

"Nick, I want you to know that I don't share Renv's altruism," Nash said with a malicious grin. "I'll happily take your coin."

"I know, Nash," Nick sighed.

Chapter 45

Master General Kirain Yith
Adventurer Level: N/A
Half-Breed Drow - Balushenian

I watched the orc slaves dig, doing my best not to inhale through my nose. The smell is abysmal, but that's to be expected. One can't expect a bunch of filthy creatures, who likely don't even realize how bad their stench is, trapped in confined quarters to smell like perfume. Well, perhaps a perfume for a tanner, but not one that anyone with a nose would even dream of purchasing.

The male orcish vampire glanced at me nervously, then yelled for the workers to move faster. Alurgas had opted to follow my plan, likely fearing retribution from his superiors, and it had worked marvelously. He had chosen the two leaders with the weakest wills and turned them. As such, his intentions became their own and would remain so for at least a year.

Fortunately, his inner thoughts had remained with him, and these two don't have any inherent prejudices against half-breeds such as myself. I had hoped that would be the case, because things would have been difficult otherwise. Pawns that despise their king have a tendency to act willfully, and that simply will not do. I turned to the other vampiric orc.

"How long?" I demanded.

"To get it as big as you want it will take another couple of weeks, sir," she bowed.

Two weeks? Too long. The loss of the Aultris Legion's second phalanx weighed heavily on my mind. They had been taken unawares by the mounted mages that have been hounding our forces since, and many of them had been captured. These orcs are annoyingly persistent.

"Use your hypnosis to find five more weak-willed individuals, then turn them," I said with a lowered voice. "Have them begin the escape tunnel. Be certain to keep it a secret, even from the other slaves."

"Yes, your highness. But..." she trailed off.

"What is it?"

"Hypnosis, sir? How do we do that?"

I snapped my fingers and she looked up in fright. Our eyes made contact, and I tapped into a certain darkness deep within my being. This darkness had always been a part of me, and had acted as a cold comfort in times of stress. I felt the tell-tale ache behind my eyes that informed me I had made contact, and pushed out toward the fledgling vampire. Her face went slack as I forced the inner recesses of her mind to activate, showing her exactly how to do what must be done.

'Like this,' I projected. 'Teach the other one the same way I'm teaching you.'

"Yes... sir..."

I closed my eyes, cutting the spell that I had bound her with. I felt the connection sever almost immediately, and a small headache soon followed. I've been told that the headache will go away with practice, but hypnosis is just so damned impractical most of the time.

"Go," I said with a wave.

She bowed again and quickly turned toward the other vampire. He was busy beating an unruly slave, and she decided to wait until he was finished. Satisfied with this outcome, I left the foul-smelling pit and closed the hatch behind me. I forced air out of my nostrils to clear them, and took a deep breath in. Before I could take a seat, though, a small tap came from my door.

"What is it?" I asked loudly, sitting down with a sigh.

"Milord, we've lost Sim Valrin's first legion. Survivors say it was the mounted mages again, but there were more of them this time," General Smarn said through the door.

"Get in here, you pissant!" I shouted.

The door quickly opened and closed as the general entered. He took a few steps and knelt apologetically. I stared at him coldly.

"You thought to give me such terrible news THROUGH A DOOR?!" I demanded.

"My apologies, sir," he said. "I didn't think to enter."

"Fine. It doesn't matter," I sighed. "Pull the other legions back into defensive positions around the village and erect barricades using timber from the surrounding forest. We have more archers joining us soon, which will put us on a more level playing field."

"Yes, sir. Shall I use the orc slaves?"

"No, I need them doing what they're doing. Without a proper supply pit, we're sunk. We'll punish the survivors of the defeated legions by using them as lumberjacks. The legions that aren't on duty will build the walls and anti-infantry spikes. Be sure sure to have the excess lumber converted to fletching, and have some pits dug while you're at it. Make certain they're wide enough to fit hnarses."

"It will be done, my lord."

"Oh, and send a legion to meet the archers and escort them here. I doubt that the commanders in the city were smart enough to send a large infantry force with them, and we don't want them getting ambushed and routed."

"Yes, sir."

"That will be all. Leave me," I gave a dismissive gesture.

General Smarn stood, and as he left a wave of exhaustion washed over me. Things hadn't gone quite as planned, but all wasn't lost yet. I debated sending a legion or two accompanied by archers on the offensive, but decided against it. We only have enough archers for defensive positions, and vacating those positions would leave us critically vulnerable. The enemy likely wouldn't know that, but it's best not to give them the chance to get lucky if it can be avoided.

I stood and walked over to the map on the table. A deep sigh escaped me as I began to move the markers around the map. I had hoped to continue the offensive and capture more land and slaves than this. I'll still get the chance, but we'll have to be on the defensive for a time. I should be certain to order the defenders to capture the enemy whenever possible.

Our defense should hold up well. Archers are far

easier to cultivate and train than mages are, which means I can field more archers than they can field mages. The range of spells and arrows are roughly the same, so the mages biggest advantages will be rapid maneuvers and the area of effect of their attacks. If I spread the archers out among the defenses and have them prioritize the mages or their mounts, we'll be able to hold out for quite some time. Which means that if the orcs are smart, they'll try to starve us out.

They have the supply line advantage, but I have the equipment advantage. They aren't able to field archers because their equipment is in Yirna, where they were expecting to be invaded. Once I add the reinforcing archers to the legions, we will be able to go on the offensive again and secure a supply line. They will have started moving the equipment back here by now, but I have ambushes and traps in place to prevent their delivery.

If that doesn't work, we'll be in a sore spot. However, all of this is to secure more orc slaves and turn them into vampires. I don't need to win this war, I just need to drag it out. We'll need as many bodies as we can get our hands on to take the Night Kingdom's capital.

King Lofin has kept most of the troops out of paranoia. It was unusually gracious of him to grant me the archers that are on their way, although I suspect the request didn't even make it to his ear. The reason I'm getting reinforcements at all is likely due to vampiric subterfuge. I'll have to clean house once I take the throne.

I finished rearranging the markers and walked over to the nearest window, pulling back the curtain. The clouds that had blanketed the sky all day had moved on, leaving a field of glimmering stars in their wake. I opened the window and leaned out, taking in the view.

One must take time to appreciate the smaller things in life, or else be crushed by the larger ones.

Before I could get my fill of the sights, another bout of exhaustion took me. Bedtime already? I stifled a yawn, then closed the window and the curtain. I took a step toward my bed and stumbled, managing to catch myself on a chair.

I looked at the hand that was now supporting my weight, but it looked alien. It is definitely my hand, but my mind refuses to recognize it. Depersonalization... have I been drugged? Might one of my precautions slipped? Or am I just that tired? It had been a long day, fraught with stress and worry.

Even as the thought of being poisoned caused my adrenaline to surge, my eyelids drooped. I don't have the sweats, coughs, or shakiness that are indicative of most poisons. Why would someone use an anesthetic to try to assassinate me?

What kind of anesthetic works on a fully fed half-breed vampire? Even as I tried to figure out this mystery, I stumbled over to my bed and lay within my covers. I barely managed to kick my boots off before my eyes could no longer stay open, and I slipped into slumber.

'Finally,' Something almost like a voice said from within my mind.

What's happening? Didn't I fall asleep? Is this a dream? I looked around but saw nothing. No, not nothing. Darkness. Palpable darkness. Darker even than the darkness that resides within me. A true abyss, and I was within it.

'It is the time that we should meet.'

"Who are you? What do you wa..." I ran out of breath and could not take another.

'You do not need to speak. I know your mind and soul better than you do.'

I panicked at the lack of air for a few moments before I realized that it didn't matter. I don't need to breathe? Is this really a dream, then? Why am I so cognizant? WHAT IS THIS?

'Your mind is frantic. Focus your thoughts and direct them to me.'

Focus my thoughts? Easy to say, not easy to do. Plenty of subjects rushed through my mind, but above all stood one question. What in the HELLS is going on here?

'The Hells? Quite astute of you, but no. Not the hells. Close, though.'

I focused on the non-voice, ignoring the inky blackness that surrounded me and the lack of air in my lungs. This has to be magic. Unfamiliar magic, but magic nonetheless. If this... entity wished me harm, I would be harmed by now. I steeled myself against my rising panic.

'What is the meaning of this?' I demanded.

'An introduction. To ease you into knowing my voice so that when the time comes to hear it, you will not panic as you did moments ago.'

Speaking in riddles. Infuriating, but I am in its power for now. I must play along.

'Who are you? Or what are you?'

'Who am I? A laughable question. What use is a name in this situation? It isn't as if you will tell anyone of me. No, it would be better to ignore such mundanities. As for WHAT I am, deep down, you already know.'

The being all but confirmed what I had already begun to fear to be true. It is a god, a magical spirit of grandiose power and mysterious purpose. Which means that I am now a touched. I had always believed that the touched simply had mental instabilities, and that is not an uncommon perception of them. This god is right, I'll be telling no one of this.

'Why have you brought me here? What do you want of me?'

'As I said, this meeting serves simply as an introduction,' The god answered. 'It will save us time in the future. Time that will be needed to achieve our goals.'

'What goals could we possibly share?'

'None. It would not be possible for one such as I to share a goal with a being of flesh such as yourself. However... our goals align. And for that reason, I am willing to aid you. You will achieve your goals, and in turn I shall achieve my own.'

What sort of twisted goals could a being such as this have, and why would they align with my goals? Does it want me to conquer the world in its stead? Or does it want the vampires to suffer? Perhaps it needs the orcs eliminated?

'No,' the being laughed. 'Those are not your goals, nor mine. Your goal is to be seen and heard. To be able to enforce your will, and ignore those that you see as inferior. You do not need the world or a kingdom for this, you simply need power. Power and purpose, both of which I can guide you to.'

The words cut through me like a well-honed blade. The truth of the matter is that I do not fully believe that I can conquer the world with my plan. I had intended to take the Night Kingdom as my own and try to expand its borders, but I would have been content with executing King Lofin and exterminating the vampires that had created and then belittled me.

This was a carefully kept secret, though, even from myself. My anger became stoked as I realized how easily this thing had read me and carved its way through my delusions. How can I, Master General Duke Kirain of House Yith, be relegated to mere words on a page to be read on a whim by a god?

'So you will give me power?' I asked with a snarl.

'No. I cannot interfere that much. Instead, I will guide you to power and give you a purpose. This must come later, though. For now, you must know what it is to live without my guidance,' it said with a cruel smile behind its words. 'You shall awaken, returning to your plans and your schemes. Try your best to see them succeed. We will meet again when the time comes.'

Before I could demand a fuller explanation, the darkness tightened around me. This embrace was freezing and forceful. I felt my bones crush and break as I was swallowed up by the abyss. Then I awoke with a start, grasping my blankets and glancing wildly around the room. I drew in a deep breath and let it leave me with a shudder.

Everything in the room was just as I had left it, and the bright beams of sunrise had begun to peak through the curtains. I grabbed my arms and shuddered again. My skin was freezing, which caused another surge of fear as I realized what that implied.

I hadn't been dreaming.

Chapter 46

Nash Alta
Adventurer Level: 9
Orc - Nulevan

"Fuck off!" I shouted as I landed a kick into Nick's gut.

Our training sessions have been getting more intense as Nick becomes more familiar with swordplay. My strength, speed, and experience are all still superior to his, but now I'm actually counting on them in our sparring matches. The little shit almost landed that last strike. Thankfully for my pride, he'd let his guard down.

"Let's take a break," I grumbled as Nick doubled over and wheezed.

"Y-yeah, okay," he breathlessly replied.

I snatched the wooden training sword from his grip as I walked past and placed the swords back on their racks. Being a sword-fighting instructor doesn't seem to be my calling. Most teachers would be thrilled at the rapid progress of their students, but Nick's progress rubs me the wrong way. I can't even nail down exactly why, which just add further frustration to the mix.

Am I jealous of how easily he learns what I teach him? A little, but not enough to cause these feelings. Do I think it's unfair that he has Ten to lean on? Absolutely, but it is what it is. Plus, that isn't really his fault. Is the speed in which he picks up foreign concepts unnatural and abhorrent? Yes, but I'm used to working with freaks. Yulk, for instance.

The silent jab at my brother brought a small smile to my face. We've been here for three days, and during that time Nick and Yulk have been running around doing various things. Nick's been having to work as a translator when Regent Oakmor is busy, and Yulk has been spending a lot of time with his former mentor. Presumably researching, but if it were anyone other than Yulk I'd have my doubts.

This has left me to hang out with Renv, who has been awaiting his uncle's return. I glanced at the dwarf, who was currently playing with the blades of grass that surround the training ring. He'd been watching our training sessions, mostly so that he could keep me company when Nick had to run off. I've learned a lot about this part of Bolisir thanks to him.

"I almost got you that time," Nick said, grievously misunderstanding my expression.

"And?" I asked, my smile instantly dissipating. "You feel good about that? Nothing fills a grave quicker than 'almost'. If I had been trying to kill you, you would be dead."

"Maybe, but Ten would have probably interfered if things went that far."

"Yeah, and I'm sure that comes free of consequence," I rolled my eyes and spat in the grass. "You and I both know better than that. Nothing is free, and you need to be especially wary when the cost is a mystery."

"Yeah," he sighed. "You're right."

"You're making good progress," I said, adjusting my tone a tad. "Actually, you've made the fastest leap in progress that I've ever seen. But winning a race is far more important than running it, so you shouldn't be content with just making progress. Being content leads to being complacent, and complacency is Death's most commonly received invitation. You've almost met your end already, and if you die, you're never going to see Cass again."

My lecture was met with silence as Renv stood up and started walking over to us. Nick's expression was dark, and for a moment I thought I had gone too far. His jaw was set and his fists were clenched, but after a moment he relaxed a bit.

"What if..." he said softly.

"What if what?" I asked.

"Well... I'm pretty sure that when I died in my world, I came here. What if when I die here, I go back to my world?"

Our eyes met, and his expression was completely sincere. I stared at him for a moment, then burst out laughing. His sincerity turned to shock.

"W-what?" he asked. "What's funny?"

"How in the hells does a moron like you manage to wield a blade without slicing your foot off?" I laughed.

"What do you mean? How am I a moron?"

"And a dumbass, on top of it all," I said as I managed to get my laughter under control. "You don't even know that you actually died in your world! And even if you did, why would dying here bring you back to your world, anyway? Why wouldn't it take you to a completely different world instead?"

"I..."

"Talk about jumping to conclusions," I cut him off with a chuckle. "More like leaping, in your case."

"What's funny?" Renv asked.

"Nothing," Nick answered with an angry tone.

"Yeah, don't worry about it," I said. "So what's today's plan for when Nick goes to work, Renv?"

"Well, my uncle should have gotten back this morning so I was thinking we'd go visit him. I'd have liked to have Yulk along, but..."

"Yeah, he's busy," I laughed. "We'd have to drag him kicking and screaming. Since we'd be getting between him and knowledge, he might even put up a real fight."

"Best to avoid that, then. What do you think, should we head out now?"

"Yeah, we might as well. Best get going before the Regent summons Nick."

I nodded, and Renv took the lead. He told one of the guards where Nick was going, and we proceeded to leave the training pit. I'm actually going to miss this training area when we move on. It's a far sight better than the one we have in Nuleva. Hells, it's even better than the one that the Adventurer's Guild uses in Kirkena.

This training pit has multiple open areas where people can spar in different conditions, like sand, gravel, mud, dirt, and even grass. It also has training dummies that have regeneration enchantments, which is something we should look into for Nuleva. Maybe for the wall too, so poor Naomi doesn't have to fix it every time Yulk practices his spells. Though, she might miss the free meals...

"So your uncle owns the business you work at? What about your parents?" Nick asked.

"It's more like a conglomeration of businesses, but yeah. My ma and pop both like working with their hands, so they own and operate a branch of the manufacturing side of the company. Since I like to travel, I work with my uncle more than I work with them," Renv chuckled. "They're much more tolerant of my occupation than they are with my brother's, though, that's for sure."

"What does your brother do?"

"He's a quack. Or at least, that's what people call him. He experiments with various chemicals and their effects on health, then tries to hock the finished product," the dwarf sighed. "He doesn't trust healing magic or potions, but they're much faster than any of the products he's been able to produce."

"I think it's a good thing not to rely solely on magic," Nick said. "Though he should be careful when experimenting with painkillers."

"Because they can be addictive and deadly?" Renv asked. "Bit of wisdom from your world, right? Yeah, that already happened here. He made some painkillers out of a plant that people use to get high and convinced a few people to try them. They worked, of course, but his customers got addicted to them. It was a huge mess, and a couple of people died because of them. The court found him guilty of negligence because he didn't do a long-term study before selling the product, and they fined him so heavily that he had to sell his lab. Now he works out of his house."

"I'm sorry, that must have been rough on your family."

"It was rougher on him than on my family. It's pretty well known that he's cut his relations with us, so it didn't harm our reputation. Still, it's not fun to see family fall like that."

The conversation petered out as we continued our trek. Our path avoided the main square, which is where the dragon had been staying. It's just as well, we didn't need to give Regent Oakmor the chance to pull Nick into something. Finally, we approached a large building that was made of small, well-cut stone bricks. Each brick was engraved with a vine-like pattern which was filled with what appeared to be silver.

"Here we are! My uncle's offices," Renv said with a grin. "Follow me."

Renv pushed open one of the solid wooden doors which were about twice his height. I expected to hear the creak of hinges, but the door opened silently and with very little effort. I raised my eyebrows, whoever installed the doors had known what they were doing.

The inside of the building was even more impressive. The floor was well-polished hardwood, and each wall had some form of art on it. Paintings, monster trophies, and even weaponry were well positioned to vie for attention. In the center of the room was an expensive looking desk, and behind the desk was a female gnome wearing well-tailored clothing.

"Hi Sierna!" Renv said with a wave. "Here to see the boss."

"Go on in, sweetie," Sierna said with a warm smile. "He's been worrying about you. He'll be glad to see you're safe."

"Thanks."

Renv led us to the right of the desk and through another well built door, which led to a staircase. We marched up the stairs and found another pair of doors. Renv opened the one on our left and walked inside. Nick and I glanced at each other and followed.

"Uncle! Welcome back!" Renv said, raising his arms in a joyful expression.

"Renv, my boy! Thank the gods! It's so good to see you well," a rotund dwarf stood from his desk and embraced Renv hard enough that I heard bones pop. "I heard about the bandit attack and was worried sick."

"Come now, Uncle," Renv returned the embrace as best he could. "I'm the one who sent word, you needn't have worried."

"You forgot to sign the letter, then," the large dwarf released his hold on Renv. "What happened to your guards?"

"They..." Renv trailed off and gulped. "They didn't make it. Norv, Crakton, and Tel are dead."

"Oh gods, I'm sorry boy. I know you were close. They were good kids, we'll make sure their families are well taken care of."

Renv's uncle put his hand on his nephew's shoulder and gave it a squeeze. Then he turned to look at Nick and I.

"So who are these..." he trailed off as he got a good look at Nick. "Wait..."

"Oh yeah, introductions. Uncle, this is Nick Smith and Nash Alta. Nick is the human you've probably heard about."

"The one who woke King Yssinirath?"

"Yep," Renv said as he turned to us. "Nick, Nash, this is my uncle Dohn."

"Dohn Marfix, pleasure to meet you," Dohn said as he grabbed my hand and shook it.

Dohn's grip was surprisingly strong, and I fought the urge to compete. After a couple of shakes, he turned to Nick and did the same.

"It is an immense pleasure to meet you both," Dohn said. "A member of the famed Alta family and the mysterious human everyone's been talking about. How did you manage this, Renv?"

"They're the ones who saved me from the bandits," Renv beamed. "I brought them here because I thought you would want to meet them and give them a reward. There's another one, Yulk Alta, but he's with Olmira right now."

"The Eternal?"

"Yeah. He was her student or something, and they're currently catching up... or something."

"Well, it's good to see her getting some company," Dohn chuckled and turned back to Nick and I. "I'd be happy to reward you for your kindness toward my dear nephew. You're adventurers, right?"

"Yes," I answered.

"Good! Camping out under the stars has its own appeal, of course, but there's nothing like a comfortable bed," Dohn walked over to his desk. "So these will be invaluable to you."

He opened one of his desk's drawers and pulled out a piece of paper. He grabbed a pen and began to write. He mumbled to himself for a bit, then gave the paper to Renv. Renv read the paper and nodded.

"You'll need to go to one of our warehouses to pick up the reward, but I think you'll like it."

"Okay," Renv grinned. "Thanks, uncle!"

"Happy to do it. Come see me again sometime!"

Renv nodded, and we followed him out of the room. Sierna waved at us as we left the building. Nick and I remained silent while we walked, seemingly ignoring the obvious question. It almost felt like a competition to see who would ask first. After a few moments, I couldn't wrestle my curiosity any longer and broke the silence.

"So... What's the reward?" I asked.

"I don't know," Renv chuckled. "The paper is an order form, but I don't recognize the product code."

"Damn it," I muttered under my breath.

We continued following Renv until we came upon a building that wasn't nearly as fancy as Dohn's office.

It didn't look ramshackle, but it was obvious that very little care was spent towards its appearance. Despite its lack of aesthetic, it was very impressive in size.

I took in the sights as we followed Renv into the building. Large bay doors led to carts that were in the process of being loaded and unloaded, huge stables kept hnarses sheltered, fed, and watered, and there were many people running around tending to various tasks. Our strange looking group got a few curious stares, but nobody stopped us. We walked up a flight of stairs and Renv knocked on one of the doors.

"Come in," a voice shouted from behind the door.

Renv opened the door and led us through. This room seemed like the opposite of Dohn's office. It had no decoration on the walls, the floor was made of cheap wood, and the desk was more like a table. The room was barely lit by a single candelabra in one of the corners. Behind the table masquerading as a desk was an elf who was nearly buried in papers. Her disheveled blonde hair glimmered in the candle light as she peeked over one of the many stacks.

"Oh, hi Renv," the elf said as she ran her fingers through her hair in a futile attempt to straighten it. "What's up?"

"Hey Hura, I've got an order form from my uncle," Renv said as he gave her the paper. "These two saved my life, and that's their reward."

"Saved your life?" she asked with a raised eyebrow as she read the form. "Woah, okay. Guess you're not kidding. Wait here, I'll be right back."

Hura stood quickly and practically ran out of the room. Renv looked at us with a grin, but we returned his expression with befuddlement. We stood there waiting awkwardly, and after what felt like an eternity later, Hura returned with three small boxes. She gave Nick one of the boxes and handed me the other two.

"Here you go," she said.

Nick opened his box and pulled out a necklace with a metal tag on it. The necklace's chain was made of gold, and the tag was emblazoned with various jewels. It also had writing on it, which caused Nick and I to share a glance. Neither of us could read the writing.

"Looks fancy," I said. "What is it?"

"This is an identifier that will allow you to stay at any of the Marfix Inns, absolutely free of charge," Hura explained. "Simply show it to the clerk at the front desk, and you will be given a room. Assuming there's one available, of course. This also comes with one free meal per day of your stay, and unlimited access to any available amenities."

"That's awesome!" Renv said. "Uncle really outdid himself."

"Really?" Nick asked. "Are these inns... fancy?"

"Very fancy, yes," Hura answered. "What amenities are available depend on the inn in question, but all of them have the very best of whatever is available. Some people even consider our inns to be vacation spots in their own right."

"Where can we find them?" I asked.

"We have inns located in every capital city on the continent. You simply need to look for a sign with the symbol that's on the back of the necklace to find them."

I watched as Nick turned over the necklace. It was a little hard to make out in the candlelight, but the symbol engraved on the back looked like a dragon wearing a nightcap and sleeping comfortably on a bed. Nick and I shared another glance.

"Thank you," I said. "This will definitely be useful in our travels."

"Now you guys won't have to stay in taverns and stuff," Renv beamed.

"A soft bed sounds good to me," Nick said. "Is there one here?"

"Yes, there is. It's right off the main square," Hura explained. "Now, if you'll excuse me, I've gotta get back to work. Enjoy!"

Renv once again took the lead as we exited the office and then the building. Once we were outside, Nick put on the necklace and tucked the box into the pouch at his hip. I tucked both boxes into my pouch, not bothering to put the necklace on just yet.

"So what now?" Nick asked.

"What do you mean? Break's over," I grinned. "Let's get back to training."

Chapter 47

Grum Ormyar
Adventurer Level: N/A
Orc - Blurpan

"Well, can't say much for their craftsmanship," Harmi said with a grunt.

"It's not pretty, but it looks like it'll hold up to an extended assault," I shook my head in disgust.

We finished our examination of the enemy's encampment and turned back to our own. Harmi and I had decided to personally confirm the scout's reports. The drow had erected wooden barricades around the village and were keeping them wet to prevent fires. They had made the barricades high enough to make it difficult to get attacks over them, too. Any mage that got close enough to send a spell over those walls would also be close enough to suddenly sprout an arrow from between their eyes.

"What was this village's name?" I asked as we walked.

"Dunno," Harmi shrugged. "It isn't on the map because it isn't a recognized settlement. It's too close to the border for that."

"Really? I wouldn't think that they've had issues with the drow before. The buildings look like they've been there for quite a while."

"Yeah, well, they probably have been. Lofin's armies usually do their thing quite a ways to the east of here, so these guys were probably left alone for the most part. Maybe got a visit or two from our boys now and then, but they've probably never even seen a drow.

Until now."

"But they're still close enough to be in the settlement prohibition zone? Do you think they knew that?"

"They would have had to. Whoever they got the land from, a rancher probably, would have had to tell them. Plus that settlement is large enough to have applied to be a village, and there's no way they'd miss out on the benefits by choice. If they applied, they would've been told to vacate the area."

"Damn. If they knew, why'd they risk it?"

"Well, after enough repetitions things become routine, and routine tricks you into believing that you have an understanding of things. That combined with how cheap the land would've been probably led to this."

"So what do you think..."

"They're either dead, slaves, or hostages now, Grum. Hells, probably worse if your pa's right about the vampires. Put them from your mind, we've got shit to do."

"Yeah," I nodded solemnly.

We entered the camp we had made yesterday, and a quick look around confirmed that it was bustling with activity. Axes were being sharpened, cooks were stoking fires, and the mages were tending to their hnarses. Our forces now totaled one thousand infantry and thirty mounted mages. The drow may have more soldiers than we do, but if we were to fight them afield we'd be able to wipe the floor with them. Unfortunately, they seem to have realized that.

"Chief Ormyar!" someone shouted.

The shout sounded as if it was directed at me, which caused my head to snap toward the sound. One of the newer scouts was running toward me. I ceased my stride and crossed my arms, affixing the approaching scout with a glare. I noticed a rare smile on Harmi's face as the scout caught up to us.

"I'm not the chief, my father is," I said firmly.

"S-sorry, sir," the scout said, trying to control her breathing. "I've got a report."

"And I'll hear it in a moment. I want you to be sure that it doesn't happen again. My father is the greatest chief Blurpus has ever seen, and I won't tolerate any semblance of disrespect toward him. Understood?"

"Y-yes sir."

"Good. Report."

"We found the caravan from Yirna that had the supplies to make weapons. It was attacked."

"Any survivors?"

"We don't know for sure. They burned those that fell, drow and orc alike. Loaded them into the carts and set them ablaze. Couldn't get an accurate count of the remains."

"Were you able to get eyes on the force that ambushed them?" I asked, uncrossing my arms and placing my hands on my hips.

"No, sir. They were hit right after they crossed the border into Blurpus. Scout-master says that it had to have happened days ago, according to their itinerary."

"Understood. Tell the scout-master to get back to regular patrols, then."

The scout nodded and began jogging away. I took a deep breath through my nose, stifling my rising anger, and let the air out with a heavy sigh.

"Fuck," I grumbled under my breath.

"Good call, sending the scouts to check on the caravan," Harmi noted. "It is fortunate that we now know that we can't rely on archers."

"Yeah, that's one way of looking at it. Whoever this little bastard is, he's far too clever for my liking," I said. "Not only was he able to tell that we had sent our smithing supplies to Yirna, he was able to determine that we would be having them shipped back and where they would be."

"Nah, he probably set up multiple ambush sites. That's what I would do. I'd put a team on any path big enough for a cart."

"Yeah, you're probably right," I absentmindedly agreed, my mind already on what our next steps should be.

The caravan didn't just have weapon-making materials, it had actual smiths and fletchers. Smiths that can perform maintenance are a copper a dozen, but the ones that can create new works from raw materials are worth their weight in silver. Proper fletchers are even rarer, and it would take quite a while to find one willing to travel to Blurpus.

If we had been able to outfit our archers and train some new ones, we would have been able to assault the enemy camp. Archers can fire faster than mages can, which may have allowed us to suppress the enemy behind their barricades long enough for the mages to lob spells over their walls. Hell, they might have even been able to get close enough to use spells that would destroy the barricades entirely.

Most archers know how to maintain their bows and make arrows in a pinch, but most of them don't know how to craft bows or mass-produce arrows. Their makeshift arrows are also a lot less accurate than those made by the professionals. No matter how I look at it, it looks like we're going to have to lay siege to the drow and try to starve them out.

"Oh, here we go again," Harmi said, gesturing at another scout jogging toward us.

As the orc approached, I noticed that we were mistaken with our initial impression. This orc wasn't a scout. The two axe handles smacking against his thighs as he ran was a dead giveaway of his status as infantry. As he drew closer, I tried to figure out why he would possibly be running to speak to us.

"Mornin' chief-kin," the large orc said. "Sernt Balug wanted me to get you."

"Sergeant Balug? What for?" I asked.

"It's a surprise, sir."

"I don't like surprises," I crossed my arms again. "Tell me what he wants."

"Sernt Balug's a lot bigger than you," he chuckled. "Erm... Sir. Plus, we all wanna see your reaction."

"Balug may be bigger, but the chief-kin can have you

flogged," Harmi interjected.

The big orc took a moment to think about this, biting his lip as his brain worked harder than it likely ever has.

"I guess so, but even if you flog me to death my mum'd recognize the body," he shrugged. "If I ruin the surprise and the boys get at me, she won't even recognize my big toe. Sir."

"It's that good of a surprise?" I asked incredulously.

"Oh yeah. Your reaction'll be worth taking a few licks from the whip. If you want me to. Sir."

I shared a glance with Harmi, who gave a defeated shrug in the face of the country-orc's stubbornness.

"Fine," I sighed, pinching the bridge of my nose. "Lead on."

The unruly infantry-orc led us through the camp and into the woods. Being unused to traveling without a path, I made certain to watch my footing. Despite my care, I quickly fell behind. The other two seemed to be able to predict the roots and divots that littered the ground and had to stop and wait for me to catch up repeatedly. By the time we arrived at Sergeant Balug's location my embarrassment and frustration was at a boiling point.

Once the ground was clear of obstacles, I pointedly marched after our guide, ready to be harsh with whatever I was about to be shown. However, all of my anger quickly melted away once I saw the surprise. My eyes widened and my jaw dropped.

"The fuck?" Harmi asked with a shocked softness.

"Ah, chief-kin! Oh, and you brought cap'n Harmi too!" Sergeant Balug exclaimed. "Surprise!"

A mewling whine came from a gigantic creature that had somehow been trussed up. The sound was disturbingly similar to a pupper that had just been told off, but much louder. Its head was covered in metallic looking spikes, and the creature's red and yellow hide clashed horribly with the various greens of the surrounding foliage.

Each of its bound arms and legs ended in three enormous claws, which were also tied together. It struggled against its bindings to no avail, and whined again. As it did so, I caught a glimpse of rows upon rows of sharpened fangs within its maw.

"What in the hells is that?" I asked, regaining some of my composure.

"It's a gift from the gods! A Nahalim, to be specific. Young one too, judgin' by its size," Balug said with a prideful grin. "One of our boys was out takin' a leak and found it while it was nappin'. Once he let me know about it, we grabbed all the rope we could carry and tied it up good and proper."

I took a moment to digest this information, then turned to look at the sergeant. He towered over me, but despite his appearances... and upbringing... and mannerisms... he's one of the most educated orcs I know. When he says a gift from the gods in this context, it could mean literally anything.

"Okay, so what's a Nahalim and why is it a gift?" I asked.

"Please don't tell me you're planning on trying to eat

the fuckin' thing," Harmi added. "Pretty sure those are poisonous."

"Venomous, not poisonous, and no. They taste like shit. Anyhow, to answer your question, chief-kin, a Nahalim is one of them ol' biological weapons that they were usin' during the cataclysm wars. They were mostly meant for crackin' open castles, but they also saw some use as anti-infantry. You see 'em now and again on the edges of the wastes, where I grew up," Balug's grin somehow grew. "And it's a gift cuz if you've got the balls, you can train it."

I nodded along and then froze once he finished his sentence.

"The fuck did you just say?" I asked, unable to believe my ears.

Balug's men tried to hide their laughter. Unsuccessfully.

"Train it, sir. There was a guy who lived in the wastes who had a couple of 'em as pets. Hunted with 'em and everything. Said they're just like giant puppers, so long's you treat them proper," he nodded sagely. "Of course, they ate him in the end, but we're pretty sure he died of natural causes first."

"Pretty sure..." I repeated.

"Yep. Give me a few days and I'll have this boy... or maybe girl, it's hard to tell... Anyway, I'll have it ready and rarin' to tear up some drow in no time."

"What are you going to feed it?" Harmi asked.

"We got drow prisoners, don't we?" Balug raised an eyebrow.

"Absolutely not," I said. "We aren't feeding our prisoners to this thing. Not only would that be morally repugnant, it would also be in violation of the law of the land and the High Chief would certainly have our heads."

"Well, what if we kept it a secret?"

"You're willing to gamble your life that none of your boys will get too sauced and tell this story? Fat fucking chance, sergeant. No."

"Damn. You got a good point, sir. Well boys, what do you think?" Balug turned to his orcs. "Willin' to go on half-rations to feed the beast?"

The sounds of not-quite-suppressed mirth died out immediately and was replaced with a tense and contemplative silence that was only broken by the occasional whine from the Nahalim. The soldiers looked between their sergeant and the Nahalim studiously. The subject of their internal conflict was painfully obvious, the stomach is one of the two organs that infantry does their thinking with. The other organ they use to think is somewhat up for debate.

"Fuck it, I'm game," one of the soldiers said.

The other soldiers looked at the one that spoke up, and a few of them shrugged. One by one they gave their assent to the sergeant's plan. Once everyone was in agreement, Sergeant Balug turned back to me.

"There you have it, sir. We'll feed it with our own rations, and get it nice and trained up for an assault on the enemy," he said with a smug grin. "Will that be alright?"

"If you can't train it, will you be able to kill it?" I asked.

"Yes, sir. It bleeds just like everything else. Worst case scenario, we lose a few. But I got a look at the enemy's barricade earlier, and I'm pretty sure that we'll be losing more orcs without the Nahalim than we would if it went wild."

"You might be right. How exactly are you gonna train this thing? We don't have cages big enough to hold it."

"Oh, we'll secure it in such a way that it can't run around and let it get familiar with us. Positive reinforcement and the like goes a long way with these big bastards. By the end of the week, I'll have it eating out of my hand."

The sergeant was making a good case. If Balug's able to train the Nahalim, it will save a lot of lives on our side of this conflict. If he fails, though, we'll have lost good orcs and still have to face the enemy's barricade.

We could try to starve out the enemy, but their leader has fully demonstrated that he isn't a fool, so he probably has a plan for that course of action. I looked at Harmi for guidance, but the furrow in his brow told me that he was just as lost as I. I took a deep breath through my nose and let it out through my mouth.

"Fine," I said. "Train the Nahalim. We'll try to use it in an assault on the enemy fortifications once it's ready."

"Thank you, sir. You won't regret this."

Chapter 48

Nick Smith
Adventurer Level: 7
Human - American

I woke up feeling fully rested for the first time in quite a while. As I stretched away the remaining stiffness in my muscles, I found myself enjoying the fluffiness of the bedding against my skin. I hadn't been able to enjoy it much last night because I'd passed out right as my head hit the pillow. It had been an exhausting week of training and translating, but all that's over now. Well, the translating, at least. I'm sure Nash has something evil in mind for when we're on the road.

I let out a sigh when I realized I would have to be leaving this bed. The bed isn't even the best part about the inn, though. I'd been able to get a warm shower, a shave, and a haircut as well. I didn't have much beard to shave, of course, but the hairs under my nose and on my chin had been getting annoying. The shower was amazing, and very much needed. I'd become accustomed to my stench for the most part, but every now and again I'd get a whiff that made my eyes water.

Reluctantly, I left the softness of my bed and found my clothes. The Marfix Inn also had a laundry service, and I had taken full advantage of it to get my clothing and armor cleaned. On the wall near the door were two boxes that had conveyor belts inside them. In one box I found my clothes neatly folded alongside my armor, and in the other box I found the breakfast I had ordered. When we first began staying at the inn my meal orders had raised eyebrows, but now the staff was used to it. They even made recommendations of things that they thought might taste good together.

Normally I don't bother with a breakfast order and just pick something up from a stall, but I get one free meal a day during my stay and I wanted to use it on our last day here. The wonderful smell of the breakfast convinced me that I had made the right choice. There were two sides, one of thin meat strips that tasted like a mixture of canned ham and beef jerky, and a vegetable that looked like a dark green celery stick but tasted like asparagus. I'd been hesitant to try it at first due to my hatred of celery, but one of the elven chefs convinced me to give it a try. Now, I regret not ordering it sooner.

The entree was a mixture of eggs and meat, and I didn't know which animal either were from. This made me a little hesitant to try it, but the smell helped me fight off my doubts. I picked at my breakfast as I pulled on my clothes and armor. Unsurprisingly, the food was really good. Once I finished dressing myself, I moved my meal to the small table in the corner of the room and dug in.

My breakfast rapidly vanished, and once I was finished I leaned back and let the well-padded chair comfort me. I let out a burp, then reached into my nearly bulging coin purse and brought out a gold coin, placing it on the table next to the meal tray before turning my attention to putting my armor on. Once I squeezed into everything and all the straps were tied, I took one last look around.

The room itself was tastefully decorated with wooden walls and engraved stone trim. They had used a light colored wood which seemed to glow when the curtains were open. The window was able to be opened, which wasn't something I had seen in many other places. There were also some well done paintings depicting some exciting scenery, like a man arm wrestling a dragon and a mage casting fireball.

The bathroom had a toilet, sink, and the aforementioned shower. Even without any additional decorations, it was the fanciest bathroom I'd every personally seen. The toilet had a footrest and the shower had a seat, both of which made it easy to relax while taking care of business. I could see why Renv's coworker said some people use the inn as their vacation destinations. My entire stay had felt like one. I felt a small pang of sadness when I realized how much I'm going to miss these luxuries, but comforted myself with the thought that we'll probably find another Marfix Inn during our travels.

With another small sigh, I turned to the door and opened it to find Nash and Yulk waiting outside. Nash was holding his fist up as if he were about to knock. The three of us stared at each other awkwardly for a moment.

"Oh good, you're up," Yulk grinned.

"Yep, he sure is," Nash nodded. "That's good, we can get on the road right away. Come on."

I gave my room one final glance before I followed my brothers-by-adoption out of the inn. The staff bid us farewell as we left, urging us to visit again soon. We began to head to the place where Imlor had the cart set up when I spotted Regent Oakmor dashing our way. I debated whether or not to start running, but he caught up to us before I could make up my mind.

"Hello boys," he said with a beaming smile. "Glad I caught you before you left."

"Why's that, sir?" Nash asked. "Your business with

Nick is done, right? You already paid us and everything, your highness."

"Oh yes, yes, don't worry. I have no further jobs for you," Oakmor laughed. "The reason I wanted to catch you is to let you know that we would normally throw a goodbye celebration, on account of Nick awakening our monarch and everything. Unfortunately, we can't due to... Well... Critical matters of state that must be addressed immediately."

"That's alright, sir. I understand," I said.

"Good, good. I didn't want you to think we were terrible hosts or anything. Anyway, the next time you visit Bolisir I'd ask that you send a message first so we can properly plan a thank you celebration."

"We already had a feast. Surely that counts, your majesty," Yulk added.

"Actually, the feast was specifically to celebrate the return of His Highness King Yssinirath," the elf shrugged. "Royalty get their own party. Plus, combining celebrations is tacky. No, even if it must be delayed for the moment, I am required to insist that we do a proper celebration for Nick's contribution as soon as we are able."

After a bit more back and forth on the merits of such a celebration, we relented to Oakmor's request. Or demand disguised as a request, rather. Once we agreed, he merrily sent us on our way. People waved as we passed, which was a welcome change from the awkward stares that we got when we first arrived. They actually seemed happy when I waved back, too, which made me feel good. People had been friendly like this back home, and I hadn't realized how much I missed it. Before long, we found Imlor packing up his cart.

"Hi Imlor," I said as we approached.

"Hey guys, you ready to hit the road?" he asked.

"Yep," Nash said as he grabbed a heavy-looking sack from the gnome and carried it into the cart.

"Very much so," Yulk agreed as he climbed into the cart after Nash. "While I've enjoyed our stay, I'd very much like to check the mail to see if mother sent anything. I've been keeping her updated, but have told her to send her replies to Kirkena because we didn't know for sure how long we'd be in Bolisir."

I took one last look around the city built within the trees. Renv had said his farewells yesterday because his uncle was taking him to see the rest of his family. It ended up being a bit of a twist of fate. Instead of Renv seeing us off, we had seen him off. However, it appeared that someone else may want to see us off. The someone that was moving our way at an unnaturally fast pace.

"Uh... hey, guys?" I pointed at the figure racing toward us.

In the time it took for Nash and Yulk to turn their heads to look, the unidentifiable figure got close enough for me to figure out that it was a certain female vampire. The next thing I knew Olmira the Eternal was standing beside me, carrying a duffel bag and looking at Yulk. I questioned my sanity when I realized that she didn't look like she'd been running at all. She was breathing normally and her hair wasn't even out of place in the slightest. The hell kind of product does she use?

"Hi Olmira," Yulk's smile beamed. "Come to see us off?"

"And to chastise you," she placed her hands on her hips. "It isn't proper for a gentleman to fail to bid a lady goodbye, Yulk. Even when he's the one doing the leaving."

Yulk's smile faded, "Ah, I see. You're right, I apologize. I beg your forgiveness, milady."

Yulk stood and bowed, while Nash and I gave the two of them a befuddled look.

"I'll forgive you on the condition that you allow me to join your party," Olmira smiled, showing the briefest hint of fang.

"Really? Why do you wanna travel with us?" Nash asked.

"Well, the Regent is now advisor to the king. An advisor having an advisor is a bit much," She chuckled. "Plus, the king already has an immortal magical advisor. A djinn by the name of... um... Relph, I think it was? Yssinirath retrieved him yesterday. So, I am out of a job, haven't traveled in well over a century, and can't help but wonder what sort of hi-jinks my favorite pupil is going to get into with this human here."

As she was explaining herself, I turned to look back the way she had came. It had to be at least a half a mile from where I had initially spotted her, and it was a decent uphill gradient, as well. She'd run that distance in less than ten seconds without looking the least bit phased. And to top it off, she's a magic user. She could be pretty helpful in a fight.

'I suggest we bring her along,' Ten said. 'Her relationship with Yulk leads me to believe that she has a vested interest in helping us, and she would be a powerful ally.'

'Quit reading my mind,' I replied.

'I can't read your mind without you directing your thoughts at me. Yet. I was simply inferring based the context and your current gaze.'

"It would be an honor to travel with you, Lady Olmira," Yulk said.

"Wait a minute," Nash interrupted. "What are you going to do about blood?"

Olmira held up a jug and shook it, "I'm bringing some with me. Despite my youthful appearance, I'm an elder vampire. I don't need to feed as much as younger vampires do, so this is well over a years supply. Plus I can visit a blood-keeper if I need to top up."

"Are you royalty or nobility or something?" I asked.

"Pardon?" She gave me a confused look. "Oh, because of Yulk. No, I'm not. Not anymore. I was a noblewoman before I was turned, but my title was revoked due to my conversion to vampirism. Immortals aren't allowed to be nobles in Eldravia."

"Eldravia?"

"A nation to the south of Bolisir and the Unified Chiefdoms," Yulk interjected.

"Yes. Eldravia is known for its wine and multi-species elected monarchy. Yulk previously learned of my noble heritage and insists upon calling me by my former honorifics," Olmira explained. "It used to annoy me, but I've long since grown used to it."

"Oh okay, good," I laughed. "I didn't want to have to walk on eggshells the whole journey."

"Anyway, I'm obviously fine with Olmira traveling with us," Yulk grinned. "Are there any objections?"

"Nope," I said.

"I guess not," Nash shrugged.

"It'll be good to have another guard, I suppose," Imlor chimed in.

"It's unanimous, then. Allow me, milady," Yulk stood and offered his hand to Olmira.

She took his hand and climbed into the cart, taking a seat next to Yulk. I climbed up after her and took my seat next to Nash.

"Let our hopefully-uninteresting journey begin," Imlor said, turning back toward the hnarses.

The carts began to move and I watched as the city that is constantly shaded by trees slowly shrank into the distance. Once we cleared those trees, my eyes stung trying to adjust to all the extra sunlight. We traveled for about an hour in silence before my curiosity got the better of me.

"So what's Eldravia like, Olmira?" I asked.

"I really wouldn't know what it's like these days," the vampire smiled sadly. "It's been well over a century since I left, and I haven't had reason to return. Nor do

I seek out news of my homeland. I can tell you what it used to be like, though."

"Yes, please."

"Alright. Eldravia had massive tracts of land dedicated to growing fruit. Trees, bushes, and vines littered the landscape. These fruits were used to make all sorts of alcohol, but wine was by far the most popular. Most noble houses either directly owned or were heavily invested in wineries and the farms that supplied them."

"A nation of drunks?" Nash asked.

Olmira laughed, "Actually, most of their wine ended up exported. Eldravia doesn't have much in the way of metallic resources, so trade was important to make up the deficit. The quality of our wine made certain that it fetched a high price. So much so that it actually aided in our diplomacy, which in turn ended up being crucial for our national defense."

"What do you mean?"

"I'll give you an example that happened before I was born. Plimorno, one of the nations that border Eldravia, declared war as part of an expansion campaign. They won easily, but the people of Eldravia stopped making wine in protest. Once the wine stopped flowing other neighboring nations, including the Unified Chiefdoms, declared war on Plimorno to force it to give Eldravia back its independence. However, this war didn't get very far because the citizens of Plimorno revolted against their queen. She was executed along with most of their nobility, and Eldravia became independent once again."

"Wow," I whistled. "People really like wine, I guess. So

you said Eldravia's led by an elected monarchy? How does that work?"

"A multi-species elected monarchy," she corrected me. "Essentially, nobility is decided by influence rather than by blood or species. Whoever can wave the most gold around becomes nobility, which results in their family also becoming nobility and forming a noble house. It is from these houses that candidates for the throne are chosen, and the general populace votes on which candidate becomes king or queen. These monarchs decide upon the laws of the land and rule until death or they are deposed."

"Deposed?"

"Yes. If a monarch doesn't live up to expectations, the noble houses have the right to dethrone them. They actually get together once per year to vote on whether or not to do so. It takes a four-fifths majority vote to get a king or queen off their throne."

"Doesn't the monarch put up a fight?"

"They don't have their own military forces, so they have to rely on the forces of their house. Assuming their house didn't vote to dethrone them, of course. Either way, any military they could muster would be heavily outnumbered, and they would likely face execution for their efforts."

"I see. So back to the noble houses, how do they become noble?"

"If a monarch takes note of someone's accomplishments, they elect them as a candidate for nobility. The populace, including the other nobles, then vote on whether or not this individual becomes a noble. If they do, they become the leader of a noble house comprised of their family members. If they don't, then they go about their business until next time."

"Sorry to interrupt," Imlor said. "If we're gonna have lunch today, now's the best time to do it."

"Alright, let's take a break, then," Nash replied.

Imlor nodded, then pulled the cart off of the road. We all climbed off and stretched our legs, then had a quick meal of dried meats and water. Except for Olmira, who didn't eat or drink. Once he finished his piece of road jerky, Nash walked up to me with an evil grin. The grin alone told me what was coming, and I felt a familiar dread begin to well up within my chest.

"Time for training, Nick."

Chapter 49

Master General Kirain Yith
Adventurer Level: N/A
Half-Breed Drow - Balushenian

"The enemy has done nothing more than lob the occasional fireball at us, sir," General Smarn informed me. "They have encamped in the wooded area to the southwest, though, which hinders our visibility."

"So we don't know what they're planning, or even the full disposition of their forces," I grumbled.

"Yes, sir. I do have some good news, though."

"Out with it."

"You were right about their caravan, and we were able to successfully ambush it," he said with a hint of a smug smile. "Our forces returned today and reported that we managed to capture eighteen slaves, and even secured the equipment the orcs were escorting."

"Excellent. Put the equipment to use and put the slaves with the others. Dismissed," I absentmindedly waved him toward the door.

He bowed and left as I returned my attention to the map. While I was glad that I had successfully predicted the enemy caravan's movements, their lack of action against us here has me concerned. I expected at least one heavy assault before they laid siege. Yet it has been a week since our scouts confirmed their presence and they haven't tried anything serious yet.

Are they waiting for reinforcements? That would be

foolish. A bird sent by my own reinforcements informed me that they had made contact with a small enemy host and weren't able to completely eliminate it, which means that the enemy knows about my archers. Even with all of the forces of the entire Unified Chiefdoms they would have difficulty taking this position, and once the archers arrive I can go on the offensive.

Even foreign aid won't arrive before my archers do, so what are they planning? Have they decided against an assault altogether? Our defenses were designed to look ramshackle, but a discerning eye would be able to tell how solid they really are. They would know that they require better equipment to launch a successful assault, but if my ambushers returned today the ambush had to have happened at least two weeks ago. It's unlikely that they're still waiting on their caravan. So what ARE they waiting for?

I stared at the map, trying to glean a clue as to what the enemy is up to. No matter how hard I stared, though, nothing came to mind. I scoffed and turned to my bed. I had just fed, so I wasn't feeling particularly tired, but it's important to remain on a schedule when one can. I removed my boots and armor, then slid under my covers.

As I lay there, I couldn't help but feel like the orcs were up to something and I was missing a key piece of information. I tossed and turned, my mind fighting over whether to think or to sleep. After what seemed like hours, I finally grew tired and fell into slumber.

'Well... you tried,' a hauntingly familiar voice forced its way into my mind. 'It was a valiant attempt to subvert the will of the divine, if nothing else.'

My eyes snapped open and caught a glimpse of the

dawn's early light shining through my curtain before my ears had a chance to register what had awakened me. Once they caught up, I heard screams, crashes, and the clanging of metal striking metal. The sounds of a battle taking place nearby.

I leapt from the bed and quickly donned my armor, nearly forgetting my boots in the process. Once I was dressed, I grabbed my sword and flung open the door and promptly froze in shock. There were orcs within my barricades, but I had already realized that was the case.

There was a hole in my barricade which had allowed the orcs access to my camp. The creation of this hole had to have been extremely violent, judging by the distance in which the logs had been thrown. The reason for my shock, though, was because my mind was trying to figure out how this happened while my eyes were simultaneously providing the explanation.

Orcs and drow were fighting tooth and claw while mages rode by them on hnarses, flinging the occasional spell to horrid effect. My soldiers had been taken by surprise, and hadn't yet recovered or formed up. In the middle of all of this was a great and terrible beast. Its red and yellow hide was covered in arrows and its massive, fang filled mouth was ripping my soldiers apart like they were made of paper. A Nahalim, and it was fighting alongside the orcs. How? Where did they get it? Did they tame it? HOW?

Once the Nahalim finished decimating a group of my soldiers it rose up to its full height, standing at least twice as high as the tallest orcs. Then the beast roared, a deafening and blood-curdling sound even from my distance. Its bellow made me wince, and this finally struck me from my stupor. I began to run toward the battle, determined to rally my men and push these bastards back. We would figure out what to do about the Nahalim once we'd killed a few orcs.

"FORM UP!" I shouted, trying to be heard over the clamor of battle.

I raised my sword and shouted again. A few of my soldiers heard me, and began to form their lines. A mounted mage rode past them, narrowly avoiding a swipe from a sword. An arrow narrowly missed his head, but that didn't stop him from locking eyes with me. I knew for certain what his target was.

I began to ready my blade to try to cut him down, but his staff was already pointed at me. The spell that slipped his lips formed at the tip of the staff and rushed toward me at blinding speed. Just before it hit me, I realized that this was wind spear. I sighed at the triviality of the magic being used, and then the spell hit me.

I flew backward and felt a crunch as I was forced through the wall behind me, then another as I continued through the next wall. I slammed into the ground alongside a load of rubble and tried to get up, but flopped back to the ground. My eyes weren't able to focus and I could no longer breathe properly. I felt my chest and checked my hand, barely registering that the blood covering it was my own. Then the abyss took me.

'We do not have a lot of time,' the familiar voice once again rasped in my mind. 'You remember our agreement?'

I tried to speak, but no air left my mouth. I vaguely recalled our previous conversation and nodded.

'Good. You are smart enough to know that there is

nothing further you can do, and the orcs will take your camp. Once they do, it will not take them long to figure out that you are the commander, and that you are also a half-breed vampire. This will result in a rather unfortunate demise for you.'

'Then what do you want me to do?' I asked.

'Flee to the west.'

'Not home?'

'No. After you flee, the orcs will find your sister and she will tell them all about you. Once the orcs learn of your heritage, they will gleefully inform King Lofin. Your home and family will be destroyed before the end of this week, despite your contingencies. If you are with them, you will also perish.'

A slew of emotions played through my mind. At first, I doubted this being's words, but quickly realized those doubts were likely wishful thinking. Even if the orcs didn't manage to capture Esmira alive, there are the slaves that have been converted. With some clever magic, the will that Alurgas imbued into them would dissolve, leaving them to their own devices. It would be foolish to believe that they would keep my secrets.

The contingencies that I put in place to prevent Lofin from targeting my family in my absence would also fail once my vampirism became public knowledge. No one would be stupid enough to be caught helping a vampire. Moorn and my trusted servants will die. My grief nearly overwhelmed me. Everything that I had built, everything that I have loved, gone. And there's nothing I can do.

'You will flee, then,' the voice rasped. 'You must go west. You will be pursued, but if you keep fleeing to the west they will eventually give up. You mustn't stop until you're certain they aren't following you.'

'Where am I going? What awaits me?'

'I would like to tell you, but...'

I awoke, gasping for air. I instinctively grabbed my chest, feeling a hole in my armor and the cloth beneath it. The bare skin that I felt assured me that the wound had healed. I stood and looked for my sword, but it was nowhere to be found. Swearing under my breath, I looked to the sky to get my bearings. The sun was still rising, so my destination was in the opposite direction.

I paused for a moment, gazing at the hole in the wall I had left. Esmira was in there, and I couldn't help but think about killing her. While it would better my mood to feel what meager life she has left leave her body, it would cost me precious time. I decided against it and began to run. If I'm lucky, King Lofin will find a way to kill her for me.

Before I could get far, a hnarse stopped in front of me. Atop the hnarse was an orc spell-caster with a very familiar face. He looked at me with surprise, not expecting me to be standing. His shock caused a moment of hesitation that when combined with his proximity to me spelled his doom.

Before he could raise his staff I leapt, landing behind him on the hnarse. I grabbed his skull and pulled his head to the side hard enough to hear a crack, and tore into his throat with my fangs. He began to seize as a sweet, coppery taste filled my mouth. I gulped it down greedily, but I couldn't have my fill. I had to get moving.

I threw him from the saddle and grabbed the reins, urging the hnarse to the west. It began to gallop as I heard shouting from behind me. A wind spear flew past my head, taking a small portion of my ear with it. I pressed the hnarse faster and lowered myself to avoid more close calls.

The gate had been left open, indicating that a portion of my forces had abandoned their posts and fled. Typical of King Lofin's finest. An explosion hit the gate as I cleared it, sending splinters in all directions. A large one took residence in my left arm, but I quickly removed it. The wound began to heal as I continued into the trees as fast as the hnarse could take me.

I continued to dodge both foliage and spells for most of the day, and eventually my hnarse tired. It was well-trained, though, and it kept going until it finally collapsed. I leapt from its back and continued running, nearly as fast as the hnarse had. A few minutes later, my pursuer's hnarses also tired and I finally lost them.

I kept running until the sun was in front of me, and finally slowed my pace. My heart was pulsing in my ears, and my breath was heavy. I wiped sweat from my brow as I continued to walk toward wherever my goal happened to be.

As the sun began to set, I found a small cave. After determining that it was empty, I decided to take a rest. I grabbed some nearby branches from a bush to mask its entrance, then crawled inside. After adjusting the camouflage a little, I made myself as comfortable as possible. Then, I was finally left alone with my thoughts.

I've lost everything. My family, my friends, my home, my career, and even my dreams. All I have left is my body and the clothes on my back. Which have a conspicuous hole in the chest. I felt my anger build up within me, but it was the cold sort of anger. What do people normally do to cope with loss and grief? Cry?

Crying would waste water, though, and I am in a survival situation. No, the best way to cope with my grief is to analyze what went wrong and learn from it. Unfortunately, I have no idea how I can learn from whatever mistake it is that I made.

A beast of the wastes had laid low my plans for conquest. Did they capture it in the wastes and bring it here? No, that would have taken them far too long. Could they have already had it tamed and ready to fight? If that's the case, why wasn't it used against my forces to begin with? Could it be that they stumbled upon the Nahalim, managed to capture it without killing it, and one of them knew how to tame it?

While it sounded ridiculous, that hypothesis resonated within me. The separate and unlikely coincidences happening all at once, culminating in my defeat. It absolutely reeks of divine interference. The question is, which divine? The one claiming to help me, or one of the other ones? Which of the little bodiless worms had decided to meddle with reality and force my failure?

'It was a group effort, actually. And I had no hand in it.'

I was so exhausted that I hadn't even realized I'd fallen asleep. I glanced around the abyss, trying to locate the god that had spared my life.

'Why me?' I demanded. 'Why would I be targeted like this?'

'They do not see it as you do. To them, you are

nothing. They didn't see a half-breed vampire trying to conquer the Night Kingdom and become king. Instead, they saw the vampires about to make a return to power. Obviously, they decided to prevent that from happening.'

'But why?'

'Their motives are as unknown to me as they are to you. They likely acted upon a whim,' it said with a cruel laugh. 'Yet, this is precisely what I wanted to demonstrate to you. As a mortal acting on your own volition, you are powerless against the meddling of the beings known as gods. If they care enough about your plans to dislike them, your plans will fail. Regardless of the thought or effort you put into them. All it took this time was a whisper to a beast and an orc.'

'Like you are whispering to me now?'

'No, I am speaking to you. A whisper is much more subtle. Your hearing suddenly becoming clear enough to make out what someone is saying in a busy marketplace. A sudden craving for a specific dish at a specific restaurant that a certain someone happens to be at. Even something as simple as fatigue can be used to guide you to where we want you to be, as you'll recall.'

And recall I did. I remembered the first time I had heard this being's voice. I'd become so tired so quickly that I thought I'd been poisoned. That was a whisper, then.

'As you can infer from our current conversation, we're capable of more direct interference. If you had managed to somehow disrupt their scheme with the Nahalim, one of the other gods may have spoken to the enemy commander and told him about the escape tunnel your orc slaves were digging. If the enemy commander failed, then a lightning storm may have formed and stricken your barricades, causing them to explode.'

'So why didn't you stop them? I thought you are trying to help me?'

I knew the answer to this question and felt foolish for asking it, but my anger and indignation forced it out of me.

'I am helping you in such a way that allows us both to achieve our goals, as was agreed. It should be obvious that I have no interest in your petty ambitions outside of what they can do to achieve my goals. And that's the point. If you listen to me and do as I bid you, I will help you achieve your goal. You will gain power and purpose, and no being will be able to look down on you again. If you do not, I will leave you at the mercy of the other gods to do with as they please. It is very unlikely that they will aid you.'

I allowed myself to calm once more, and thought about my situation. This being is promising to help me gain power, but not help me do anything except gain power. So what's stopping other gods from eliminating me once our bargain is completed?

'They will try, but not because they want you dead. They have another goal in mind, and you will be an obstacle to that goal. However, we can only interfere when we are allowed to. There is a greater being at work here that will make certain the coming contest will be fair. And if you survive, you will be allowed to do as you please, free from the meddling of beings like me.'

'Then what would you have me do?'

Chapter 50

Master General Kirain Yith
Adventurer Level: N/A
Half-Breed Drow - Balushenian

'You will awaken and continue traveling west,' The hoarse voice pierced my mind. 'By midday you will reach a well-traveled road. Go left and follow the road. You will meet a traveler who is not what he appears to be. Be wary of this traveler, but consume his blood. Take his clothing and dispose of his body and your armor out of view of the road. Continue on the road in the same direction until you see a smaller path, then follow that path.'

Expecting riddles and side-speak, I found myself somewhat stunned by how clear the directions were. Despite my shock, I endeavored to memorize them. Nothing will stop me from finding the power that this being is promising and annihilating whatever challenge awaits me.

'And what do I do when I reach the end of the path?' I asked.

'The path leads to a dungeon. Enter the dungeon and do what you feel is appropriate.'

The return to riddles and side-speak stunned me even more than its absence. It took more than a few moments for the confusion to leave my expression.

'You can't tell me more than that?'

'All I can say is that you're a vampire. Do what vampires do.'

'That's all? Why?'

'A being far grander than myself is preventing me from speaking directly of the events that may unfold within the dungeon,' it laughed. 'The very same being that will ensure fairness in the challenge to come. Go now, and find your purpose.'

I awoke before I could ask any further questions, not that I would have gleaned any answers. Do what vampires do? Likely a riddle that will become easier to solve within the dungeon itself. I arose from my temporary shelter and scanned my immediate environs. Birds were singing in the trees, which indicated that there weren't predators or monsters nearby, and there were no other signs of incursion. It seems I have truly lost my pursuers.

My muscles and bones ached from sleeping on the ground, and a quick stretch resulted in several satisfying pops and cracks. The stretch was able to provide enough relief to continue my journey. The desire to feed hit me as I verified the sun's position in the sky. I had used a lot of strength yesterday, and I would need to feed on blood again to restore it. Luckily, the entity had told me where to find my next meal.

I did my best not to think too hard about what caused me to undertake this quest, but failed miserably. My entire family is soon to be dead, my home razed to the ground, my dreams of world domination are all but dashed, and I am touched by a supposed god. These thoughts had just wandered to whether or not continuing my existence was even worth it when I finally came across the road.

It wasn't much of a road. The primary components of its construction were dirt and dust, unlike the roads that lined the countryside of the Night Kingdom. I dutifully turned toward my left and followed the glorified path. It wasn't long before my feet became tender and sore, and I found myself missing the carefully constructed stone roads of my homeland.

I followed the road for a few hours before I finally came across my objective. A dwarf wearing a high collared coat and large pack stopped and eyed me warily. I stopped as well, and regarded him head to toe. His coat and clothing appeared new and expensive, yet his pack and boots appeared well-worn. The dwarf was obviously trying to look like a merchant, but there were certain inconsistencies with his disguise.

"Who the fuck're you?" he asked.

"I could ask you the same," I replied. "You have the look of a merchant, but I've never met a merchant who travels alone."

"Well that's just cuz you've never met me," he grinned, showing a few missing teeth. "The name's Tarx. You?"

"Kirain."

"Well, Kirain, methinks it's a damn lucky day for you. I see you've got a hole in that armor of yours, and I just so happen to have somethin' that'll likely fit you just fine."

"Oh?" I asked, moving closer to him. "That would be quite the boon, if the price is right."

"I've got the cheapest fuckin' stuff you'll find in the middle of the road," he laughed as he pulled his pack from his back. "I'm more than willin' to cut you a deal."

He stuck his hand into his pack as I moved closer to him. As he began to remove his hand, I saw a glimmer and instinctively grabbed his wrist. My strength was beginning to wane, but it was more than enough to snap his wrist and sending the dagger flying. I wasted no time pulling him into his final embrace.

"The fuck?" he gasped as I bit into his throat.

He tried to resist, but I'd already taken a gulp and restored my strength. The warmth of the blood flowed through me, and I took more than my fill. After a few moments, the dwarf fell limp in my arms, completely drained of his vital essence.

I let him fall to the ground and studied him. I'd managed to avoid spilling blood on his clothing, but was faced with another problem entirely. Dwarfs are significantly shorter than drow, and his attire would not fit me.

My eyes darted toward his pack. On a hunch, I grabbed it and emptied it out. Several items fell to the ground, including another knife, some wrapped rations, about fifty feet of hempen rope, a water skin, several pieces of jewelry, a bulging coin pouch, and some rather well-made clothing. It would appear that Tarx was a quite a bit more entrepreneurial than a traveling merchant should be.

"Take his clothes, eh?" I chuckled, picking up the clothing.

I removed my garments and replaced them, finding them to be a perfect fit. I spent a little time packing the items back into the bag, with the exception of the large knife, and then disposed of Tarx and my former clothing out of sight of the road. Passing carnivores would find him and make sure he didn't go to waste.

Slinging the pack onto my back and securing the large knife to my waist, I continued my journey. Not a bad change of fortune. I was now far less conspicuous, and even armed. If I changed my mind about my destination, I would be able to survive for quite some time on the wealth that the dwarf had likely killed for.

I was still debating this choice when I came across the path. It was overgrown and rather uninviting, and if I hadn't known to look for it I would have missed it entirely. I stood at this fork in my journey and thought for a moment. Should I continue to whatever city this road leads to and seek my fortune with my own two hands, or should I accept the would-be god's challenge and seek power?

Voices in the distance brought me back to reality. Drow rarely leave the Night Kingdom, and I would have to justify my existence everywhere I went. I would also have to be wary of retribution from the scorned deity. I made my choice then and there, and began to make my way down the untended path.

The overgrowth made travel difficult, but before long I found my destination. A small building served as the dungeon's entrance. It appeared to be a type of mausoleum, with two smooth pillars lining either side of its arched entrance. The roof of the structure rested upon these four columns and depicted a skull being worshiped by reptilian beings.

I felt an immense dread enter my body as I took a step forward. Many people equate vampires with the dead, so I should feel at home in a crypt. However, my instincts screamed at me that something terrible lay within here. Taking a deep breath and snarling to myself, I drew my knife and entered the dungeon. One of the advantages to vampirism is the ability to see in almost complete darkness, but my eyes still took a moment to adjust. Once my blindness receded, I continued forward and I took in my surroundings.

The floors were tiled and the walls were unnaturally smooth. Neither showed any signs of tool marks, seams, or any other variety of imperfection. This indicated that they had been created magically. I recalled from my studies that the term dungeon isn't the most accurate description of these places. While they often serve to contain monsters and other threats to civilization, they've also been known to serve as lairs for powerful beings that would seek harm on others. The origins of most dungeons are a complete mystery, and how they came to contain monsters and traps is anyone's guess.

My footsteps reverberated through the hall as I continued on. It was a soft, steady melody that was almost soothing, until a sudden click interrupted my pace. The tile beneath my foot had depressed, and I barely reacted in time to catch the spiked grate that sought to impale and crush me. Even my vampiric strength struggled with the weight of the trap. I adjusted my footing and pushed with all of my might.

Just as I thought I was done for, the trap eased up and withdrew into the ceiling. I quickly moved forward before it could trigger again, being careful to avoid the tile I'd carelessly tread upon earlier. Before I could catch my breath, a screech announced the presence of several small reptiles.

The lizards were roughly the size of my boot. I readied my knife as they swarmed me, trying to pick off pieces of my flesh with their teeth and claws. I was much faster than they were, though, and began to exterminate the pests with my knife and free hand. They were easy to crush, and not very resistant to stabbing either. It didn't take long to finish them, and I watched as the few wounds I had received healed.

The bites were extraordinarily painful, and bled longer than they should have. Once they finally faded, I continued on. I was much more wary this time, trying to avoid any further traps by tapping my forward foot on the upcoming tiles. It slowed my pace, but quickly paid off as I encountered more traps.

After each trap, another group of lizards attacked and was defeated. Eventually, I put away my blade and began to use the little bastards as stress toys. This pattern repeated several more times before there was an abrupt change.

"FOR THE LORD!" a dwarf-sized lizard shouted, waving its spear in the air.

"FOR THE LORD!" its five comrades echoed.

I drew my knife again and charged at them. They hadn't expected this, and I managed to slit one's throat before they could recover. I grabbed its spear and flung it deep into the chest of another, then dodged back as the last four formed a formation of sorts. I grinned at them, baring my fangs.

"A sucker!" one of the reptiles gasped.

"Shit, what do we do?"

"We poke him 'till he stops movin', same as everythin' else!"

"FOR THE LORD!"

They charged forward, and I slid under their spear-tips. I used my claws to tear at the face of one and stabbed my blade into the heart of another. I dragged my knife out of its chest and through the throat of the one I had mauled. Disallowing any recovery time, I leapt over its falling corpse and bit into the shoulder another lizard before it could change the position of its spear, and threw my knife at the final one.

I grabbed the reptile's throat and lifted it into the air as its comrade hit the floor with my blade protruding from the space between its eyes. I spit its blood onto the floor and ripped the spear from its hands. The reptile looked down at me with absolute terror in its beady little eyes.

"Who is your lord?" I demanded.

"I ain't tellin' you nuttin'!" it shrieked.

"Then I shall find out myself," I said, crushing its windpipe and vertebrae.

As I dropped its body to the ground, it occurred to me that I might have used hypnosis on it. I sighed, disappointed at the missed opportunity to glean some intel. After retrieving my blade, I continued my journey into the depths of the dungeon. It wasn't long before I got another chance.

I tore into the creatures and tried to use hypnosis on the survivor, but I couldn't make a connection to its mind. At first I thought my hypnosis was being blocked, but then I came to the realization that the mind was too simple to be forced in such a way. It was like trying to hypnotize a pupper. I tore its head off in frustration.

Several more conflicts later, the hallway opened into a large room. Torches flickered to life as I entered, throwing shadows upon the smooth, gray walls. In the center of the room was a skeletal corpse sitting upon a golden throne. It looked lifeless, but I could feel massive amounts of magic emanating from it. Its eyes began to glow and it rose from its throne, levitating a few inches from the ground.

"Who dares to enter my domain?" it asked.

"Kirain Yith," I replied. "And who might you be, Lich?"

"What would my name matter to an insect that's about to be exterminated?"

"Why would you want to know the name of an insect that you're about to exterminate?"

I barely managed to dodge the ice spear it sent at me, and quickly tried to close the distance. Before I could, fire erupted from the floor and sent me reeling. The burns on my face began to heal, and I snarled at the creature before me.

"Ah, a vampire," it said. "I have no blood for you to suck, filth."

Once my nose healed, it caught a familiar scent in the air. I grinned at the lich, and threw my blade at its face. A magical barrier caught the blade and sent it back from whence it came, but I had already closed the distance with the lich. It drew back from me, but I grabbed its neck and squeezed, crushing the vertebrae in my grasp. Its body crumpled to the ground as I caught its skull with my other hand.

"You have bested me, it seems," it said. "Go on, finish me. I'll return again and again."

"You lied to me," I grinned.

"Pardon?"

I followed the scent and approached the throne. Hidden in the throne's finery was a rounded, crimson jewel. The invigorating scent was coming from this jewel. I struggled for a moment to remove the jewel from the throne, and once I was successful I found that I was holding a disguised vial of blood. I held it up for the skull to see.

"A phylactery. You DO have blood," I laughed.

"Perhaps we can make a deal," the skull said. "I can give you gold, gems, even teach you ancient and terrible magics. What do you require in exchange for the safety of my phylactery?"

"Why would I destroy it?"

"What? What else would you do with it?"

"You were once a mer, and I am a vampire," I grinned widely, baring my fangs. "I'm going to do what vampires do."

Milton Keynes UK
Ingram Content Group UK Ltd.
UKHW022359220724
445930UK00003B/50

9 798990 972483